Lovesong

A NOVEL OF COURTLY LOVE

Geraldine McCaughrean

Lovesong

A NOVEL OF COURTLY LOVE

Geraldine McCaughrean

ROMAUNCE
Cirencester

Romaunce Books

1A The Wool Market Dyer Street Cirencester Gloucestershire GL7 2PR
An imprint of Memoirs Publishing www.mereobooks.com

Lovesong: 978-1-86151-578-0
Lovesong © 1996 Geraldine McCaughrean

First published in Great Britain in 1996
by Richard Cohen Books.
Published in 2017 by Romaunce Books.

The address for Memoirs Publishing Group Limited can be found at
www.memoirspublishing.com

The Memoirs Publishing Group Ltd Reg. No. 7834348
The Memoirs Publishing Group supports both The Forest Stewardship Council®
(FSC®) and the PEFC® leading international forest-certification organisations. Our
books carrying both the FSC label and the PEFC® and are printed on FSC®-certified
paper. FSC® is the only forest-certification scheme supported by the leading
environmental organisations including Greenpeace. Our paper procurement policy
can be found at www.memoirspublishing.com/environment

Typeset in 10/14pt Century Schoolbook
by Wiltshire Associates Publisher Services Ltd. Printed and bound in Great Britain
by Printondemand-Worldwide, Peterborough PE2 6XD

For John with my love

Contents

PART ONE

Two Masters

PART TWO

The Liar's Daughter

PART ONE

Two Masters

I love because I live, I live in order to love.

Saint Bernard

CHAPTER ONE

Two Knights

Amaury of Herm arrived like the End of the World: a thing much talked of but, in the event, beyond all expectation. He and his entourage swept into the Castle of Lilies in a dazzle of chased armour. A dozen tourney lances standing in the stirrups of his squires flew white pennons - a bird, a cross, a lion couchant embroidered on them in wire. His troubadours came behind on foot, playing harp, trumpet, cymbals, bagpipes and rebeck. Gitterns and gigues, an organistrum and a Spanish penola, fiddles and viols, psaltery and rote were all borne on a litter by two pages, pillowed on cushions, like women, against the jarring.

'Are you sad? Are you sick in soul or body? Then make way for a *sobiran trobar* - doctor of the Gay Science! Make way for Sir Amaury of Herm, knight-troubadour and bringer of a cup of comfort! Drink deep, good people, and let your sorrows be salved! His elixir is music and his cup is song! Make way for Sir Amaury of Herm!'

'Out of a tedious landscape of unmoving trees and monotonous silence, this flourish of colour and noise and extravagance burst like sheet-lightning. It had gathered a following of astounded peasants. It set the dogs barking and the horses cantering in the fields. Everything was light - white metal reflecting white banners; white horses with oyster saddlecloths scallop-edged; white dustclouds trailing in the road way. Amaury also arrived at four o'clock, out of a low sun: a man capable of making stage scenery out of the cosmos.

Across the neglected gardens with their sea of blown flowers, the noise reached Oriole the jongleur. It reached his master, too, whispering, eyes closed, on his knees; Sir Jocelyn flinched like a sleeping dog.

For four months he and Oriole, the boy who sang his poetry, had knelt in the garden of the Castle of Lilies, praying and singing at the tomb of a lady. The lady was Jocelyn's lost love, his perfect, chaste, irreplaceable inspiration, his beloved. And the aim was to raise her to life again through sheer persistence of prayer.

A thrilling plan, but highly monotonous in practice. Prayer after *plahn*, day in, day out, come rain, come sun, come fatigue, come boredom, Sir Jocelyn and Oriole had prayed. Now, the noise from the roadway.

The newly arrived knight was conducted through the house by the dead girl's mother, to the garden where its resident knight troubadour knelt beside a painted wooden sepulchre. When he reached it, Amaury fell on his knees and kissed the effigy of the dead Lily. Jocelyn, who had just risen to his feet, was left to wait a minute, two minutes before the newcomer stood up and embraced him. Finally Amaury held his brother troubadour at arm's length and searched his face for signs of transfiguration. 'Dear saint,' he whispered, and clasped Jocelyn again to his metallic breast.

'These men have bigger souls than me,' thought Oriole.

'And was she very fair, your mistress?'

'Never one fairer,' said Jocelyn.

'And do you truly mean to raise her from the dead with a million prayers?'

'If God will grant them.' But Jocelyn looked jangled and uneasy. Amaury's jongleurs had spread out to encircle the grave, jostling him and his boy. One was a giant over six feet tall; one had no arm below his left elbow, another no eye to fill the right socket. One had a hare lip and one - most fearful of all - was a Spanish female as black as Unbelief Beside them, naturally, Sir Amaury looked handsome.

'Friend, I beg you,' said Amaury, 'let me hear you sing a plaint to your dear, dead *domna*!'

A childlike happiness lit Jocelyn's face and he thanked Amaury repeatedly and allowed himself to be led indoors.

The house had been a present from Jocelyn to Lily and her family a token of his love. But since the girl's death, Lily's mother had rather sickened of Sir Jocelyn maundering on in the back garden. She had used up her own stores of grief weeks before, and found the dismal tableau around the girl's grave slightly embarrassing and excessive. One only had to look at the splendid Sir Amaury to see that the once immaculate Sir Jocelyn had let himself go. He had grown shabby during his graveside vigil. There were stains on his clothing, and laces and fastenings which hung by a thread. His knees were muddy and his hair needed cutting. Amaury, by contrast, was without speck. His coppery hair sprang from two distinct crowns so that it swirled about his big skull like not one Caesar's crown but two, and he had thrown his cloak back over his shoulder to hang like couched wings down behind.

The boy Oriole was following both knights into the house, when one of Herm's men tripped him from behind. 'Was she worth it?' he asked. Two more closed in and jostled him between them. 'Well, was she?' demanded One Eye.

'Was she what?'

'You know! Giving! Did she grant him the Last Favour!'

It sounded civil enough. Oriole would like to have understood the question well enough to answer it. 'I don't *think* so,' he said helpfully. 'She didn't give him much happiness. Well, she couldn't she was dead so soon.'

'Didn't give out? Don't say much for your man, does it? ... Good to look at, was she?'

'As beautiful as the crescent moon full of stars,' said Oriole reflexly. It troubled him, in fact, that he could recall nothing beautiful at all about Lily, only a thin, brown, hollow eyed child with sloping collar bones and no breasts.

'He good, your man? Truly?' said the black girl.

Oriole closed his eyes and told the truth as he knew it. 'He's a saint. Like your master said'.

One eye looked him up and down. 'A saint, eh? That must be a stone in the plum'.

'He prays and fasts, and he can go about naked in the

snow and wear furs all summer! And he gives and gives and gives...!'

'Not to the likes of us, I'll bet,' said One eye.

'He gave me this coat and a horse and a rote just for singing!' They stared at him, incredulous. For a moment, they were silenced.

'So he'll do it then, will he? Raise her up? Bring her back to life?' They sneered as they said it.

'Of course he'll do it! My master can do anything!' And Oriole ran on ahead, giddy with pride, wanting to cut himself off from their jeering disbelief, wanting to recover the marvellous simplicity of his daily routine.

***

That evening the great hall of the Castle of Lilies was awash with jongleurs, cluttered with musical instruments and property chests. A pot of flowers had been placed on Lily's empty chair, and in the heat from the oil lamp nearby grew equally brown and round shouldered as the hours wore on. While the meal was in progress, Sir Amaury's jongleurs performed tricks balancing acts and juggling with plates, tumbling and conjuring. It was all a wonder to Oriole. He stared with wide, round eyes.

Given into the Church by devout, unsentimental parents, his child hood had belonged to God. Sir Jocelyn de Foicelles, hearing him sing one day in church, had stolen him out of his brown woollen fold and translated him to elysian fields of music, chivalry and Love. Even his name had been a present from Jocelyn: Oriole the Songbird. Their mutual lives since then had been so wholesome, so exemplary, that Oriole had never understood why jongleurs had such a bad name. Why were they considered such a scum on the world's waters? That night, watching Herm's crew of buffoons and drunks, he suddenly knew. Holy Bernard of Clairveaux called jongleurs sinners and harlots, lewd, desperate bawds, soulless curs sent from Hell to stink in the nostrils of Christian men. Herm's men lived up to the description.

It was the Moor who gripped Oriole's imagination tightest: a heathen burned black for her sins by a bigger, hotter sun than God had set over the heads of honest Frenchmen. There were those big white teeth, those pink soled feet. That evening the girl wore a garment like a nun's habit, but with her wild, woolly, luxuriant hair unfastened, and lips as swollen as bruises. It was not so much what she did but the way she made him feel which made Oriole so afraid of her.

Clearly there were two breeds of jongleur: those trained up, like him, by a virtuous, pious knight, and these others dogs held in check by a different manner of man altogether. Oriole began to taste the sin in the air, oily like the black smoke from the lamps and candles, and shut his lips tight against it so that he looked prim and womanish.

After dinner, Jocelyn began, white faced, to sing a *plahn* of his to the dead Lily. It was a great while since he had sung. He had been fasting to increase the efficacy of his prayers, and his mental acuity was blunted by the diet of water and crushed beans. He faltered once or twice, then found a pea still lurking in his mouth from dinner and in trying to be rid of it, set himself coughing.

So, like King David reaching for his harp, he reached for Oriole, his jongleur, his songbird. 'You know my *plahn*, don't you, boy?

'Yes, sir.'

'Sing it, then, to the glory of my lady.'

Oriole sang. He was proud to sing. A mixture of fright and pride tightened his vocal cords and piped out the music in creamy whorls of sensuous purity. He believed Foicelles' lament to be marvellous, a work of genius.

Amaury listened with one elbow resting on the arm of his chair and his face covered by his hand. At one point the boy looked across and saw that the fingers were parted and the eyes open, watching him, watching, watching, looking out. It made Oriole's stomach lurch. The room was so full of people that he felt his music soaked up and deadened by their bulk. By the time he finished, his throat ached with the strain.

Now Amaury got up and moved slowly down the room. His rich clothing swayed on him like the hay on a great wain-cart. His eyes were a soft, swelling green across which his lids never encroached, and his beard entirely hid his mouth. He came and lifted up Oriole bodily, as high as his arms would reach. He suspended him there, as a sheep farmer suspends a new born lamb to check its weight, its meat, its hips; then he set him down again without a word and knelt down on one knee in front of Sir Jocelyn.

'Sir. Today you have made a man fall in love, through sheer example, with a woman he has never seen.' Amaury had no difficulty in making his voice carry.

Sir Jocelyn made no attempt to hide his delight. 'My boy Oriole flatters a poor song,' he began self- effacingly.

I all the while distributing gold coins among every servant and jongleur in the room. 'But now you must give the assembly a taste of your poetry, sir. Far better than mine, I'm sure!

Amaury tossed his big head on its short, muscular neck, laughing, protesting. 'God forbid I insult the lady's memory with my humble efforts when God knows! She may walk through that door, raised to perfection at any moment ... Oh very well, since you insist ... A song, then! To your ladylove! To the divine Lily!' Amaury's crew took their places, as though they could sense what was required of them. Or had been rehearsed.

He's churning out some old thing he's used before, thought Oriole, feeling grownup in his cynicism. But Amaury's *plahn* was not some second hand, all-purpose funeral dirge.

It began in the dark - small and unpromising, like the seed of a mustard tree, then grew towards the light, doubling and redoubling, reaching out in questions, balancing the questions with answers. All the while images flocked to its branches as varied and colourful as the birds of the air. Then outdoor imagery gave way to a bed, and a dark place under blankets ... there were breasts and hands and tongues and knees all rising soft as smoke out of the angular skeleton of a bonfire. There was a crusade of lances rising in the cause of Love, troop upon troop, until God, moved to pity, raised not one but all the Dead to life. There were stars and planets, spangling with sweat the union of sky and earth, Living and Dead.

His voice was nothing - as rough and brown as unplanted timber - and he made little attempt at singing, merely spoke in time with the music. And while he spoke, his jongleurs performed a dumb show graceful, with movements akin to dancing accelerating at the same pace as the verse, into something strenuous, inciting, immodest. The anachronism of the voluptuous Moor with her big breasts and thick, glossy wealth of hair representing the thin, sickly Lily shocked and enthralled Oriole. He could not look away.

That a man could hold such pictures in his head! thought Oriole. That he should make his fellow knight look so small and talentless, and smile as he did it! It was astounding. It was monstrous.

But Sir Jocelyn displayed no resentment. Unthinkable that a man of honour should entertain such a mean emotion. Instead, he danced about Sir Amaury, thanking him. He vowed Lily would rise all the sooner thanks to Amaury's song. He enlisted the girl's mother to help heap praise on Sir Amaury. He said the debt was unrepayable. 'In fact you must let me make some paltry token of my admiration. You must have my castles at Pontdoux and that one at Toit-Tourtelle ... No, no, don't argue! Besides, what does a knight-errant like me need with more than one house? All I need is a roof to keep off the rain while I relearn my art. To think that the Gay Science has advanced so much while I've been at my devotions!'

And all the time he deflated, like a pricked bladder. What God would incline His ear to the chants of a Jocelyn de Foicelles when He could hear the like of Amaury of Herm? Oriole watched his master wilt like a spent daffodil: still gaudy in his yellow troubadour splendour, but shrivelled, shineless, dead.

'Your song was a feast to the senses,' said Amaury,

dismissing his own as something nothing, a bauble. 'And what a singer! Such a soprano! What an asset! What I'd give to have my songs sung by a voice like that!

'My Oriole, yes. He's a good boy. My Oriole. God's given him a good voice.' So plain. So stark. So functional. Foicelles laid the words down as if they were the last coins in his purse and small and worthless. 'You must have him too. Of course. It stands to reason.'

Have him? Like a coat, or a cat or a kindness?

Oriole heard the words, but he did not believe them. To be given away? To be thrown like a ball into that rabble of fearful strangers? Better to return to the cloister and the choir stall except that it was too late: he had become a jongleur, and the gates of Mother Church were shut against his kind.

'He won't take all those things you offered, will he, sir?' he said, holding a corner of Sir Jocelyn's half cloak as they both stood and stared at the painted booth in the garden. Oriole would have stood by such a man for ever, rote in hand and ribbons blowing. 'You only offered out of courtesy, didn't you? I mean, it was only offered in chivalry? Sir Amaury won't take any of it! Your castles. Me.'

'Jocelyn was powerless to stop looking at the tomb, turn away his eyes, powerless to tear away his life from this one spot. 'The substance is, you see, boy – I'm mad. Well, that's what happens, often. Plenty cases documented. A knight's lady dies and he runs mad. His wits can't hold together, you see.'

'But you're not mad, sir! I used to think so sometimes - when you did wild things. Took off your armour in the tourney. Rode around half naked in the snow. But now I understand better. And what about your lady? I mean, what will the Lady Lily say when she rises up again and you've got no soprano to sing for her? And who's going to bandage your hand?'

Foicelles looked at the fleur-de-lys of a hand left him by his grandest gesture of love. He had cut off three of his own fingers to throw in the grave. Now he was wondering, for the first time, what woman raised to perfection would welcome the caresses of a man with a crippled hand.

'I'll just sing a Paternoster, shall I?' asked Oriole, eager to ignore the events during supper. 'Or an Ave?'

'No, thank you, child. You can forget all that. Go and find your new master and learn your duties. You don't want to cross him on your first day. You don't want to be missing when he looks for you ... And listen, Oriole ... '

'Yes, master?

'Love him for me, there's a good child. I don't know why, but I find it doesn't come easy to me. To love him, I mean. Why's that, I wonder? You'll do better, I'm sure. You've a more generous nature. Yes. Truly. And you'd be doing me a service. By caring for him.'

Next day, Sir Jocelyn de Foicelles asked Sir Amaury's help to find some cave or ruin nearby. He declared it his intention to live as a hermit, forswearing all luxury, so that his prayers for Lily should prove acceptable to God, despite his lack of talent.

Fortunately, Sir Amaury of Herm recalled having spotted the ideal site just the day before. It was the vast bole of a hollow oak tree, one among six grouped on the summit of a prehistoric earthworks. It had been lived in but vacated by a hermit who had recently achieved his goal of an early entry to Heaven.

Whether Amaury intended Jocelyn to die or simply to quit the troubadour circuit, he never made clear. Nor did he trouble to return or find out what became of his rival. After all, he had two extra castles to include now in his summer circuit, if only so as to collect the rents.

In fact, Sir Jocelyn de Foicelles found he had no skill in his whole body which equipped him to live in a tree trunk. He did not know how to scavenge for food. He did not know how to keep woodlice out of his clothes. He did not know how to tie a bandage or even pull on his own boots. There had always been others to do it. And God did not come walking in the garden in the cool of the day. In fact Foicelles came to doubt whether God would ever toil up the earth works to smell the fungal damp, the infection, the unwashed sinner, or to look out across miles of tedious heathland.

So he took himself home to the smallest of his castles and shut himself away in a bleak cell of a room, allowing only two servants and a cook to attend on him. And he despised himself with a loathing which far outstretched any contempt Herm ever bothered to feel for him.

Thus Oriole the singer passed into the possession of Sir Amaury of Herm, knight troubadour. He was a Goliath of a man, built to with stand the arrows of disease, privation or violence. His creation must have called for twice the clay God expended on Jocelyn de Foicelles. If, indeed, God had had a hand in the making of Amaury.

CHAPTER TWO

Languedoc

'And is that the sum total of you? Song and rote?'

'My master had no call for conjuring or mumming,' said Oriole.

'No. I could see that. Where are you from?'

'From the brotherhood of the Cistercians,' said Oriole, unable to think back as far as birthplace or parents.

'Is that right? No excuse for being a drizzle of misery, though. Right?'

Despite his contempt for the priggish choirboy, Amaury found it hard to resist the boy's innocence, his openness, his ignorance. He swiftly observed that women were charmed by Oriole by his voice and by his looks and Amaury of Herm moved a great deal among women and valued their good opinion.

After collecting Jocelyn's rents, they travelled south, purposefully, like migrating birds. They slept each night in a tent, square framed, tasselled and pennanted. A single canvas arras divided the interior into two rooms. In one slept Amaury and the Moor, in the other slept his household, piled on top of one another like sweaty dogs. Their costumes hung fastidiously from the frame of the tent: fiddlers came two a penny, but a purple livery with pewter buttons was valuable.

Many nights Oriole lay awake, haunted by those dangling purple costumes. He feared the other boys, too, though he told himself that was foolish. One Eye or One Arm had taken from him his horse and cloak, so now they had no more reason to cut his throat while he slept.

He was more afraid of what they *said*: the irreverent comments they made about women, the unintelligible innuendo which set them all laughing. In the end they always turned their laughter on Oriole, because he did not understand what they were talking about. The monks who raised him had had that same aggressive contempt for women. He was glad that the Moorish girl slept on the other side of the curtain, alongside Sir Amaury. Even so, he slept with his rosary under his pillow and asked the Virgin Mary earnestly, in all his prayers, if she couldn't send an illness or accident to kill the girl called Kadija.

By day, Oriole learned to juggle cups, to balance on the giant's shoulders, to conjure a silk banner from inside his doublet, to disguise himself as a woman and play out in dumb show all the Arthurian legends. And, of course, he memorised Amaury's poetry.

Amaury's poetry. He composed loudly as he rode. Those following were required to pay close attention and learn both verse and refrain within a couple of hearings. Oriole, with his short legs, was forced to run every few paces to keep up, to weave his way between the drop pings from Amaury's horse. But his compensation was that magical shower of words.

'How do you do it? How do you think of it all?' he said in an unguarded moment of breathless admiration, when Amaury halted to drink from a leather bottle.

To Oriole's alarm, Amaury struck himself sharply on the forehead with the bottle. 'Look to your Bible. When Moses struck the rock in the desert out poured holy water, didn't it, a taste of the Divine. Well? I was banged on the head by the prophets, wasn't I, and out it pours. The stuff of the Divines running to waste on serfs and sinners.' And he poured rhennish from the bottle over Oriole's head so that his livery was stained and the peacock feather in his hat was plastered against the silk. By the time he had attempted to suck the damp, staining redness out of his clothing, Oriole was a little drunk. But he knew it was the poetry and not the wine which made him reel. He had developed a thirst for it, and listened open mouthed to the poetry that poured down from Amaury.

'This, Songbird, is the true Land of the Troubadours,' said Amaury, halting his train at the crest of a hill and surveying the view. 'D'you see it? D'you see the colour of the earth?'

Even under crop, even under vines, the landscape was red as a haemorrhage - a bright, rust red. If he had not been told Herm's realm was far, far away to the west, Oriole would have guessed this land had given birth to Amaury. The knight was of a colour with this hair and his curled beard.

D'you know how the earth came to be so red, boy?'

'Is it the wine, sir? The red grapes?'

'They're only the fruit of it and why the juice runs down red. No! This is the land where a troubadour came wooing and won the love of a lady. Her fool of a husband had a jealous turn of mind. By and by the lovers grew reckless, and the husband couldn't fail to see the state of things. So he stabbed the minstrel deep and often and hacked off his head and cut out his heart. Then he toasted it and peppered it and set it before his lady without a word of what it was, and she ate it down with a good appetite. And when it was eaten and the husband asked how she'd liked it, she was full of praise for it. "Lady, you've eaten the heart of your lover," said he, "and the rest of the offal lies in the yard."

'Well, when the power of sight and speech came back to her and she rose up from the rushes, she vowed the dish was the sweetest she'd ever eaten and the last she'd ever eat. Out came the sword in answer. But the lady meant to rob him of that pleasure as she robbed him of the other kind, and she threw herself off the castle wall on to the plain below. And her heart burst, and the heart's blood stained the earth from hither to yon, and ever after it's been red as gore.'

Amaury drove his heels into his horse and wrenched it off the beaten path on to a strip of cultivated land. Cabbages growing in ordered rows were set rolling by the horse's hooves as he pitched it, at a gallop, up and down, up and down, mulching the vegetables back into the red ground. When he had finished, the earth lay like a vivid, jagged wound open to the flies.

Oriole was burning to know: 'Who, sir? Who was the

troubadour? Did you know him? Is that the castle over there?'

Panting and sweating with agitation, Amaury stared at Oriole, his mouth open and hard rimmed, wiping the red wine from round it with the back of his hand. Then suddenly he grinned. 'Yes! Or that one,' he said pointing east. 'Or that one!' pointing west. 'Or that! Or that! Or that! Or one in Britanny or another in Spain!'

His jongleurs began to laugh, nervously. One Hand gave Oriole a push with his stump. 'Believe that old chestnut and you'd believe Mary was a virgin!'

'This,' said Amaury, leaning down and pulling the boy up into the crook of his arm to show him more of the view. 'This,' he declared, 'is the land called "Langue d'Oc". And do you know why?'

Oriole's ribs grated together; he could not get his wind. 'Because the people here say" oc" for "yes", sir. "Oc" not "Oil", sir!'

Amaury hoisted him halfway across the saddle, then let him fall headfirst on to the ground on the other side. 'No matter *how they say it. Enough that they say it.* This, Songbird, is the land where the women say "yes"!'

Oriole was not acquainted with mirrors; the monks had had no use for them. In the Castle Poussarou great sheets of glass gripped in gold painted claws showed him his face clearly for the first time: gingery hair, a pale, babyish complexion peppered with freckles as though a poppy head had exploded in his face; chevron creases to either side of his mouth to hold his songs in parenthesis. He had large ears which stuck out a little, and round blue eyes startled at the sight of themselves.

The mirrors held no novelty for the women of Castle Poussarou. They drifted there often to gaze at themselves for reassurance of the happiness they deserved.

The castle was shared by four knights. For this was a land where primogeniture did not apply, and each successive batch of sons shared out their inheritance into smaller and smaller lots. Now maybe forty families - nephews, parents in law, cousins, squires bachelor and hangers-on lived cramped inside the double walls. The overcrowding led to little flurried hostilities on the stairs, at the washing stoops and under the apple trees. And its isolation intensified its reaction to out siders. The fact that its men were all away fighting and its population reduced almost entirely to women and children made for an atmosphere like muggy summer before the sheet lightning breaks.

When Amaury of Herm arrived, he lifted the women's boredom like dust from the furniture.

He told them he was in mourning for a dead lady, and docked the ears and tail off his horse to prove the depth of his grief. They wept sentimental tears of pity for him but did not close their eyes to blink away the tears, for fear of losing sight of that red hair, that white armour. And when Amaury suggested an entertainment for them a battle of roses they instantly agreed: there was no one's permission to ask but their own.

They sent their little sons and pages running for canvas and paint. They fetched in the serfs off the fields to erect a mock castle. They stripped the gardens and the hedgerows of flowers, and filled barrel after barrel a magazine of blossoms for ammunition. Gradually, with the beat of drum and tabor and cymbal, Amaury raised the tempo of their dull, slow lives until he had them running urgently to and fro, with little raucous shrieks of laughter; to and fro, making ready for siege. What a spectacle they made that multitude of women.

The siege was laid by Amaury's jongleurs. But Amaury himself did not join in. He would only sit and watch from a bench in the shade of a tree.

As the beat of the tabors grew faster and faster, the castle's attackers rushed at the flimsy tower, taking the greatest care not to demolish it. They were greeted with a pelting of roses and ox-eye daisies, speared from above with foxgloves and purple flags, and showered with a glistening downpour of goldenrod.

Just as children frighten themselves with their own games, the women flushed red and white and bit their lips and threw their ammunition wildly, overarm, and skipped and leapt until the planks under their feet sagged. But all the while their eyes were on the troubadour sitting aloof from the game he had begun; little glances, shy smiles, the occasional encouraging tilt of a head to invite him into the game. His presence in the shade of the tree tantalised them.

What creatures they were! All the words that the monks had used at last made sense to Oriole. Women were indeed like snakes - those long clinging dresses dangling down behind in slithering, rattling trains. They were indeed painted, like the plaster sculptures in a church. They were indeed bestial, their extravagant hats distorting their heads into giant horns, like cows or unicorns. They were indeed abandoned, hair bursting from under its coverings, and dresses slipping to reveal a flurry of underskirt, an unfamiliar pinkness.

Unaccustomed to play, Oriole grew wildly overexcited, his feet dancing on the spot as showers of daisies rained down on his head.

A corner of canvas lifted and a foray of girls, their hats all awry, burst out on to the meadow-grass. Suddenly they were all around Oriole: their smells, their flounces, their boned hats and tissuey streamers, their long-nailed hands, their billows of skirting. They laid hold on him, and took him prisoner, back into the City of Women. Their laughter was so shrill and so close to his head that Oriole thought it would pierce his eardrums and let the women into his brain. Big shadows danced on the canvas wall. Their breath smelled of wine. Overhead, a plank bowed under the weight of too many women shuffling along the precarious ledge to view the hostage. He imminently expected the plank to break and to be crushed beneath a deluge of women.

When did his lover die?' was all they wanted to know. The wine made them more rough than they intended. When they pinched his cheek and thigh, their fingers left marks. 'You must know! He must sing about her! How *long*?' He could not fathom why the length of time was so important.

Just then, the shadow of a mounted horseman filled the panel of canvas from edge to edge. The women overhead scattered, shrieking. A sword tore a slash in the fortress wall and the grisly, mutilated head of Amaury's earless horse nosed its way through the vent.

'I've taken your castle!' declared Amaury of Herm. 'You forced me to take up arms, with your hostage taking. Give me back my squire or I'll be forced to lay your castle flat!' He was in full armour, his lower face masked by a mail aventail, his iron helmet plumed with the long black tail of his docked horse. The ladies' eyes gleamed with delight. Oriole crawled away, unnoticed.

Though one game was over, Amaury allowed no anticlimactic lull. Already one of his lads had begun juggling wooden skittles, and the blackamoor girl was whirling cloth streamers on the end of a cane. The women up high rested their elbows on the insubstantial battlements and watched the next entertainment. They also kept a shrewd eye on Sir Amaury.

'My principality?' said Amaury when they pressed him with questions. 'Just an island bounded by cliffs.' And when he described it, they saw Crete or Cyprus or the Azores.

There was no doubting his wealth, for he never spoke of it - of how he came by jasper clasps or a cloak lined with otter fur, a belt of Welsh gold wire and a saddle of red leather. His armour was dented but he never spoke of his adventures any more than he did of his dead *domna*.

That did not mean he was silent. His voice filled the great-hall every evening, as pervasive as the smoke from the hearth. Even the smoke seemed to wait about for the end of an anecdote or the last line of a poem before filtering out through the blackened louvres. Amaury recounted the great loves of his fellow knights. He told how his own father had discovered the Code of Love written on a parchment and hanging from the neck of a unicorn by a golden chain. He told of a tree whose fruit tasted of tears since a disappointed troubadour had hanged himself there. Amaury had travelled and could describe the dark sins practised on beds outside Christendom.

They listened with rapt faces: Maude who sat brushing the fleece of her pet lamb; her daughter, Eudoxia, scratching her bare feet against her chair; Béatrix, nodding sagely. Joanna sent her handmaid to and fro with little bouchées of food to refresh Amaury between songs. Guillaumette lifted a finger whenever she wished her clerk to note down something Amaury said.

Outside, the nightingales sang thrilling *fézélés* and bats flittered across a purple sky disorientated by the music.

The fishes in the distant sea were even now, said Amaury, putting on wings and flying to mate with the columba doves in towers of thistledown. In Spain the succubae were abroad whispering in the ears of knights, sliding between the covers of sleep to suck both love and blood from between their thighs. And lovers were meeting under sheets of moonlight, to caress.

Oriole listened too, gleaning wisdom like Ruth amid alien corn. Love, He did not understand what was being described, any more than he could picture the domes of Byzantium. And yet it was plain that every person in the room craved it above wealth or joy.

He fondly supposed that these tender-hearted women, all gazing so ardently at his master, must pity him his sad loss - the one he never spoke of - and care about his welfare. But to his horror, quite without warning, they suddenly one day arraigned him! They convened a Court and, frowning furiously, charged Herm to appear before it and defend himself!

Against what? 'What have you done, sir? What are you supposed to have done?' Oriole asked, but got no answer. Herm did not seem concerned, but his boy was terrified. As part of Herm's household, he was implicated in the crime. But what crime?

That evening the ladies' cheeks were redder than usual, spotted with a brick-red glow. Their eyes too were bright, and they ducked their heads often towards one another so that the horns of their headdresses jostled. Like cows unsettled by the thunder.

Sir Amaury took up his position, arrayed in full armour, on a low hammock stool whose leather creaked with every shift of his weight. His helmet stood at his feet with its horsetail plume swirling about his stool. His jongleurs mustered around him.

When Béatrix stood up, she was trembling; the bells decorating her coif tinkled. She fetched out from the deep cuff of her sleeve a scrolled document, raised it before her, and paused for dramatic effect.

'Read it, then!' yelped Eudoxia.

They had poured all afternoon over the wording of the document, but they wanted to hear it again.

'"The Court of the ladies of Poussarou is resolved to arraign Sir Amaury of Herm: - that he does wrong to desert the Fields of Love under the banner of mourning. This Court does assert that he should take up the knightly quest for joy again, as befits one of his calling. Or let him be thought a coward, fearful of Love's hardships."'

Amaury's face contorted with reproachful grief He looked at every lady in turn, lingering on each face an equal length of time so that not a one could say afterwards, 'he meant you', 'he meant me'. Then in an emotional outburst that sent Joanna's lamb skittering down the hall, he shouted at them, 'Before God, you'd have done better to arraign the Code of Love itself! It's that which has kept me from giving my heart again! There is one in this room that makes my soul chafe in its chains ... But no! My vow! I must be silent!' One hand went up to cover his face. 'I beg the Court's leave to retire for a moment. Or I fear you may see a man shamed by his own tears.'

The noise of him shutting the door behind him was not so loud as the uniform snapping shut of mouths that followed it.

Oriole followed him out of the room, expecting to find him prostrate with grief, rubbing ashes in his hair. Instead, he found Herm leaning against the stable door chewing on a straw, grinning so broadly that his teeth showed through his beard. 'Lewd whores,' he said. Oriole did not understand.

CHAPTER THREE

Juec d'Amour

It was a game - their game this time, but not of their inventing. It was a regular feature of a troubadour's circuit. The *juec d' amour*. The Court of Love, in which a troubadour is indicted for some offence against the chivalric Code of Love. Women pretending to have power over a man. The man pretending to submit. This trial would become enshrined in the history of the castle; something splendid and romantic, conducted with grandeur and panache. Their husbands must never know of it, but these ladies would know that once they had convened a Court of Love to try a knight-trobar. Herm defended himself, but no harder than the game demanded.

'And who was your lover, monsieur?'

'Ah, madam! I've sworn to keep it secret. You surely won't press me for the lady's name?'

'And you surely won't keep from us the date she died.'

Béatrix, his prosecutor, paced the slippery stone floor, up and down, up and down, wearing a channel in the rushes. She wore a scholar's robe whose high collar cut her under the ear and pulled her hair and cap to and fro with each step.

'Two years. My lady deserted me for Heaven two years ago,' said Herm.

A chock securing the trestle table dropped out with a loud bang as eleven pairs of feet fumbled and fretted at the footbar. The table swayed emotionally.

'Two years? But that's the span! According to the Rules of Love!'

'But don't you see, ladies?' he said appealing to them, 'If two years suffice in the common run, how much more than two years should I give to her - the lady above all ladies, the world's finest?'

For a moment it seemed as if the Court would not argue with him. Then Eudoxia jumped to her bare feet, sending her empty shoes clip-clopping off the front of the judges' dais. 'Oh no! That's not how it goes at all!' she protested. 'Two years is two years, no matter who. If it says in the Codes.' The other women were embarrassed by her lack of style, but in a hurry to agree with her.

'The Codes of Love, young man,' intoned Constance, 'were written as a guide to the most excellent of knights and ladies. You impugn those knights and ladies if you attempt to excel ... '

'Quite right,' Béatrix interrupted. 'One cannot be more perfect than perfection. '

Oh, surely you cannot expect me to agree with that,' said Amaury. 'I myself have seen ladies who excel perfection with their every breath. Why here alone ... '

A pause filled the room, so pregnant that every judge in the Court of Poussarou put her hand over her belly and panted a little faster. Amaury sank down once more and contemplated the floor. Maude stood her pet lamb on the table where it shivered and staggered and bleated. They all shushed the animal, fearful of missing a word.

'I am the bondsman of Love, and what Love instructs me to do, I cannot deny without being a traitor to my calling. And my God. Is God the source of all Love?'

'Naturally!'

'Of course!'

'No question.'

'Well, then, I must submit to God's will.'

They laughed. On and on they laughed, until they could none of them remember why they were laughing. He sobered them with a wave of his hand. He said, 'I've spoken my defence. I can say no more. If you find me guilty, I shall serve my sentence with a humble spirit. I vowed to mourn and already, in my wickedness ... as a man of flesh ... my heart *has* looked out through the bars of its prison and seen a lady afar off ...'

'How far?' yelped Eudoxia.

Amaury smiled to himself and sighed. 'Not so very far.'

'We must consider our verdict!' exclaimed Béatrix, and the judges of the Court of Poussarou squeezed closer together on their bench seat, their throne of justice.

As they conferred, Oriole studied each face in turn. Which had seized his master's affection? Maude's larded with fard? Joanna's, with strips of red on saffron cheeks, and with blue under her eyes? Eudoxia absently hitched high the hem of her gonnelle to show a pale calf mottled with fat. Béatrix caught sight of Oriole looking at her and threw one of her scrolls at him. It broke its seal and burst open at his feet; there was no writing on it.

When the Court reached its verdict, Sir Amaury stood within the swirl of his helmet's black plume, head bowed.

Constance cleared her throat. 'The ruling of this Court is that the plaintiff has ...'

'"Defendant", you goose. "The defendant",' hissed Béatrix.

' ... that the defendant has wronged the Code of Love by persisting obdurate in his mourning.' She looked at him, expecting a comment. The others urged her on to the sentence, like voyeurs at a gallows. 'The Court's sentence is that you be confined to a garden with the lady of your affections where you may practise and grow skilled again in the arts and sciences of Love which you have neglected these two long years.'

'Ladies,' said Sir Amaury, his voice broken with emotion, 'I bow before your judgement. I must submit to bliss. Show me the garden. I will raise my tent there and await my lover in a passion of grief and an agony of passion.'

'If it rains, you can come indoors,' said Maude as an afterthought.

The ladies of Poussarou were unjustifiably proud of their garden. The walled enclosure was green, but mostly with damp-mould. It failed to live up, in allegorical splendour, to the Gardens of Love described in literature. Its trees produced only crabbed little apples, the roses were going over. The soil was overworked, bleached and anaemic in comparison with the full-bloodied landscape outside.

Kale grew in one corner, for the kitchen, ugly and prosaic. There were vetches, too.

The tent reeked of incense - an evil, sweet headache of a smell which reminded Oriole of churches. 'Who's coming, sir? Which of the ladies? How will she know that she's the one?'

Amaury picked a blade of grass and, holding it between his thumbs, squawked through it: a ribald, brash sound. He took the stalk into his mouth, folding it in with his tongue. Then he spat it out. 'They'll all come.'

'But which do you love?' said Oriole, urgent to understand.

'I'll love them all. Love them as flat as flounders. I'm a chevalier, aren't I? When I leave here, they'll all think themselves the wick of my candle and the burden of my song. And if they don't - well, I'll've taught them a few things their husbands couldn't. It's what they've been waiting for, isn't it? Every morning. At their windows. Ever since they first heard of the breed of Man. A troubadour to fall in love with them and lift them up among the ranks of the Blessed. It's their vanity keeps me in fodder. It's their lechery feeds my horse - and you, so don't you forget it.' Now when he spoke, the knightly champion of Romance - doctor of the Science of Love - sounded just like one of his dirty mountebanks, speaking in a French full of glottal knots and tangles. 'Pay close attention, lad, and I'll teach you how castle walls are jumped these days. Draw that curtain across, will you?'

Oriole tried. He tried to draw across the ringed arras that had always divided the tent; jongleur from troubadour, varlet from knight. But the rings were rain-rusted, and the curtain would not pull.

'Will you have to give them all presents?' asked Oriole, clinging to the purely practical.

Amaury roared with laughter. 'You think everyone's as stupid as that knight of yours? God gave me hands to pick up not lay down ... Wait! Tune up, boy! I hear someone coming.'

The flap of the tent lifted. A lamb stood uneasily in the gap, wanting to retreat but being urged on from behind. Kicked in the rump, it tottered forwards, and a moment later, the Lady Maude flung the flap aside in a fever of apologies. Her naughty lamb had run astray. Where its desires had led it. Quite shamefully wilful. Drawn by the wishes of its heart.

'No, surely not. Drawn by wishes of mine, for did it not fetch after it the fairest of all shepherdesses?' said Amaury. Then he rose from the couch and embraced the lady, holding her to him with both arms and the curve of one leg. She wilted like a tired marigold.

At the sight of Oriole, Maude pushed Amaury hastily away and blustered and flustered and flapped a kerchief. But Amaury merely steered Oriole towards her by way of introduction. 'This is my Song bird. He longs to sing for you. Please don't send him away.'

'I'll go, sir. I don't mind,' said Oriole. Amaury's fist struck him in the kidneys and he folded himself, speechless, on to a cushion, staring at the strings of his instrument while they vibrated silently in front of his eyes.

'Oriole shall play for us and the angels, looking down from Heaven, shall keep time,' said Amaury, unpinning the clasp of her oversmock. Little by little, as Amaury raised the smock beneath, the dark veins in the backs of her legs were revealed, blue as rivulets on a map, with ovals of long hair at the mid-thigh.

'He has such eyes ...' said Maude, looking round at Oriole.

'He shall be as blind as Love itself!' And with only the smallest hint of irritation, Amaury took one of her hose and blindfolded his jongleur. Her misgivings were allayed. She gave herself over to the fantasy of Love in which she and her fellow women had agreed to conspire. Her shining knight had come.

Hooking his blindfold up with a thumb, Oriole gave himself one eye with which to play the rote. So he saw the vetches snap under the great heaving flank of True Love. He saw the sap spill white from their little broken stems. He witnessed secrets of the Gay Science by the dozen. He watched the fleas cling on like mariners clinging to a foundering ship. They kept their footing despite the wet decks and plunging shocks. They gorged incessantly. Oriole pulled his blindfold down again. A donkey was braying in the field beyond the wall: a ceaseless, monotonous noise.

So this was the mountaintop of perfection towards which the knight-poets aspired - the bliss which fired their art. Was this what Sir Jocelyn had prayed for as he sweated and froze, in hope of Lily requiting his love? Impossible.

Oriole found he was almost afraid for Amaury. It was a fearful thing to see a man devoured so, subsumed so. He was relieved when at last each woman was gored, subdued, defeated, split. It was just as fearful a thing as ever the monks had intimated. As steamy and rank as manure. It poisoned the garden.

They left behind them a litter of droppings - brooches, clasps, buckles, ribbons, laces, sweat and hair, and the smell of the hare's rennet which they used to keep from conceiving. They left behind promises, too; that Amaury should enjoy their faithfulness, body and soul, if he would just devote his songs to them alone, and noise their fame throughout the world. He promised as much to each successive lady: eleven whispered promises.

As Amaury pointed out to him on more than one occasion, 'I'm above every one of them in social rank - a duke. So they don't lose honour by it, do they?'

And he was right, of course. Within the ethics of Chivalry.

CHAPTER FOUR

The Conversion of the Heathen

The disruption that Amaury of Herm caused to the hearts of the ladies of Poussarou was paralleled in the kitchens by his jongleurs. Each night they ate themselves into a state of stupor or drank themselves into a state of war. There were brawls and breakages, assaults on the larders and on the serving women. The cackling laughter, the obscene language, the naked ugliness as wine-maimed fools peeled off their clothes - Oriole watched it all like God on Good Friday peeping into Hell. It was all around him. He could run back to the tasselled tent in the garden, but he knew that the demons would be there too, gusting and disgusting. Hell encompassed the Languedoc. Too far to travel to escape it.

And yet he was not stained, he told himself It was

revolting, but he was not a part of it. Oriole clutched his rosary so hard that its wooden beads made deep, purpling indents in the palm of his hand. He was not a part of it - the greasy mouths, the blacked eye, the orgasmic swearing, the pitchey breath, the broken vetches, the vaginas pasted with fard; the belching, the cudgelling, the cruelty. He saw it as a man sees in a dream - from a distance and raised up. He would be true to his own *domna* - to the Virgin Mary, Queen of Heaven, and write songs in praise of her.

One night he lifted down a rope halter hanging among the tack in the stables, and took it to the farthest end of the stable. With all the knights gone, the stables were largely empty. A nursing mare stamped as a foal drove its sharp nose into her belly. Oriole took off his short cloak, his absurd beak-toed shoes, his purple hose, his purple tunic.

He had taken from the kitchen hearth a stick of burnt wood. It looked like charcoal, but it was not. He was hard put to make a mark on the wall with it before, one after another, pieces snapped off with a smudge. But he managed, with spit and soot, to daub a kind of a figure, squat and thin-headed like a skittle, on the dung-stained wall. He pulled the halter over his head and stood in front of his icon of Mary. He would make his *domna* a gift of his lifelong chastity.

'Holy Mary, Mother of our Lord and our Defender in Heaven, here stand I, Peter Oriole, to worship and adore you. Take me for your serf to serve in obedient slavery. Here I give you my sworn troth that I shall never, never, never ...'

'What you doing?'

She reared up out of the manger, like a female anti-Christ. The pink tips to her fingers drew a long straw out of her clothing: his immediate impression was that she had won his soul in a straw-poll.

'I'm offering myself in serfdom to the Virgin Mary.'

'Is her?' Kadija half-climbed, half-rolled out of the manger and went and squatted down in the straw beside the sooty scribble on the wall. She traced the crude outline with one black index finger, while with the back of the other hand she wiped her cheeks as though she had been crying. 'Why you be horse? You look like horse. Or hanging man.' When she pointed at his halter, she found soot on her fingers, looked for somewhere to wipe it off. Her touch had polluted his altar, and yet she considered her black fingers to be dirtied.

'You have words. Lot of words. Like him,' she said. Again that finger pressed to the Virgin's outline. 'She like you? She give you thing when you want?'

'Of course. Yes! She's the mother of Jesus Christ.' Oriole prayed he was not intended to win her soul to the true Catholic faith. He did not want her in any religion of his. She might very probably slit the angels' throats once she was inside Heaven. He would much rather she clung to her false idols than show such an interest in his sooty madonna.

'She like babies so. You tell. You ask her for me. She take. She take away baby.'

'Baby? What baby?'

'My baby! My this!' She clutched her belly and thrust it towards him peevishly. She was (as the monks would have said in the house where Oriole was raised) ripe with the fruits of sin, dropsical with the rewards of lust. 'He find out, he kill me. He leave me behind. You tell your lady. She can have. Not me.'

***

Captured in an orange grove, Kadija had been picked from under an orange tree and carried north into a land full of white faces and godless ness. Even before her captor's baggage was unpacked, he had given her away - by way of a knightly flourish - to a passing troubadour, in return for a good song. Besides, his wife had found something repulsive about the thought of him ploughing a black before climbing into her bed.

And so Kadija had passed to Amaury of Herm who, irrespective of any *domna*, needed a woman each night if he were to sleep well. Her fear of him was absolute: she depended on him utterly for her next bite of bread. She could no more run away than the black sheep penned with five hundred white ones. She chose to sleep out each night at the foot of Amaury's bed, because rape awaited her a dozen more times on the other side of the tent's curtain.

She was fifteen and had learned to play the cither on the sunny roof of a white villa within scent of the sea. Now she tried to live within her cither's wires, confined her mind to the tiny prison of its sound-box, excluded all other sights, sounds, feelings. Above all she excluded the future as a thing of improbable proportions.

But the baby was kicking now: kicking her as every other cardsharp, beggar, whore, juggler and servant took delight in doing, demanding that the day-to-day routine of her hell should change, and change undoubtedly for the worse. She wanted to be dead, but feared the route.

Powerless and friendless, she found that sleep gathered round her like a cawl, stifling the portions of her brain which should be telling her what to do. She wanted to sleep. More than anything, she wanted to sleep - to climb into the manger and pull the straw over her and see nothing because she could not be seen. Lying there, in the rigid right angle of the wooden manger, she had almost decided to stay there and never come out again, to sleep out the whole of her life.

Then the boy came with his scratchy twig and his cave-painting and a horse's halter round his neck. He hated her more than all the rest, she knew that. He had always kept his eyes averted from her like someone with a horror of creeping things who knows there is a spider in the room. Now she saw that he was twice as frightened as before, because she was two instead of one.

In fact, that was not what frightened Oriole. Damaged and splitting already, like a wooden icon, his image of Amaury disintegrated now. Herm had betrayed the last illusion of Romance, the last possibility that he was driven by knightly, Christly, chaste ideals. Sir Amaury had let this black succuba into his bed.

And Oriole had sworn to love him. He had given his pledge to Sir Jocelyn to serve the knight faithfully. Listening to Amaury's poetry, Oriole had thought to be drawn up to a higher plain by his master's excellence. Now he found he was bound in service to the most abandoned of sinners. And if a knight went down to Hell, he would most assuredly take his household and jongleurs with him. This is how he reasoned, righteous Oriole, full of priggish disgust and divine logic.

There stood this girl he had always feared - a foot taller than him, telling him a life story so dreadful that it thumped in his head like a headache, and crying too desolately to be aware of her own tears. Something must be done. He was bound to Amaury, and Amaury was bound to this piece of Disbelief she held them all face-down in the black mire. Something must be done.

The solution came to him all of a sudden as he lay rigidly awake in the tent that night.

Fireflies were crawling across the skin of the tent - moving stars in a small-scale cosmos. The Moor was not on her side of the partitioning flap: he had lifted one corner to peep in and make sure. The great edgeless silence of night pressed down on the castle like a blanket used to extinguish a fire. It stifled the noise, it stifled the lit windows one by one. But the sound of a child crying somewhere high up, unattended, travelled with perfect clarity through the dense blackness.

Babies. His earliest recollection was of holding a newborn baby - a sister - a poor thing that had died not long after. He recalled singing to it, being watched and complimented on his singing by a priest in a rabbit-edged hood. That was the day, he supposed, that his parents had decided to give him away.

Babies and children: how little he had ever seen of them. They were a noise in the next room, a cry on a still night, an earliest memory, a swelling stomach.

These ladies of Poussarou hid their babies and the fact that they had children, in case it gave their age away: as if they were ashamed to be mothers. Babies. So small. So lost within the vast dark of limbo...

'She must be baptised!' he exclaimed all of a sudden to himself as he lay looking up at the fireflies.

The other jongleurs slept up in the mansion now, in the kitchen straw. But Amaury kept Oriole by him, sleeping on a paillasse on the other side of the curtain - in case he needed musical accompaniment for a lover's rendezvous. Generally, it suited Oriole very well to be isolated from that terrifying mob. But this evening Amaury returned to the tent drunk, hauling the Moor after him by the wrist. Kadija had tripped while wearing the stilts on which she danced. One of the ladies had asked distastefully if it were not 'the state of her belly that threw her off balance'. And Amaury had had to hide his surprise at the news she was pregnant.

Now he laid into her with his fists and his feet, calling her every beast in the Bestiary, asking what farmyard animal she had enjoyed in order to get with child. As he pushed "and threw her this way and that, her shape bulged through the partitioning canvas, lurching at Oriole: a hand, shoulder, knee; a face smudged flat by the tightly pegged cloth. She said nothing. She hardly even cried out. Her despair buckled the whole tent.

And Peter Oriole filled up with pity. He filled up with it till his heart was awash. It had a physical pain attached to it, and a bewilderment, especially since he could not put a name to what he was feeling: it simply crashed into him, just as Kadija and Amaury did through the cloth partition. The pole from which the partition hung thudded down with a rattle of curtain rings, and both girl and knight stumbled through on to Oriole, treading on his hands, splintering his rote. Amaury was startled to see Oriole. He stood staring at the boy, the sagging tent roof draping his head and shoulders.

'It's all right,' said Oriole. 'You can set it right. It doesn't matter.'

'You knew? You knew she was farrowing?' It only increased Amaury's drunken fury to find there were yet more people who had found out ahead of him.

'But it's all right!' said Oriole. 'Truly! I've thought of a way to put things right! She can be baptised! You can make her a Christian!'

The suggestion was so incongruous that it punctured Amaury's rage: it huffed out of him as laughter. 'So it's your doing, this baby, is it? You learn quicker than I guessed!'

'Oh no sir! Yours, sir, yours! She told me so herself,' Oriole was quick to assure him, thinking to please. 'And if she were baptised, your baby would be born a Christian!'

Kadija crouched between the knight's legs, as still as a dog on a church sepulchre.

'What is this? What's this about baptising? What's it to me what religion she whelps in?'

'No, sir, none, sir, but for your baby, sir. Your son, sir!' Oriole was angry with the wine for making Herm bleary. The matter seemed so wholly obvious, how could the man misunderstand?

'My *son*? My *son*? Come out of *this*?' He lifted up Kadija by her hair. 'Wash out your mouth, brat. What d'you take me for? Get a child on that? What d'you take me for?'

And in Amaury's maleable imagination, coddled by drink, he rejected all possibility of having fathered Kadija's baby. He had never slept with her, never made room in his tent for her. 'Here. *You* have her. You've plainly had her before!' The laughter unsettled the wine on his stomach and he began to retch. 'Blood and hair!' he panted. 'Isn't that a better gift than Foicelles ever gave you? Gave you a horse once, didn't he? Well, I've given you a whore! *And* she's in foal!'

He pushed Kadija with his foot so that she collided with Oriole. Then he threw himself down on to his couch and fell instantly asleep.

Kadija in the meantime pressed herself against Oriole, her protector. Appalled by her sobbing, the violence of her shivering, he stretched his arms around the whole crouched bulk of her. He found himself patting her as he would a horse, perhaps because she was so much bigger than he. Then the blood began to prickle in his bent knees. So he unbalanced her on to his bedroll where, still curled up, she fell asleep. Oriole sat rubbing the backs of his legs - partly to restore the circulation, partly to clean his hands of contamination. The baby in the castle was still crying.

Next morning, by the time he had brushed last night's vomit out of his beard and cleaned his teeth with a hazel twig, Amaury's good mood was restored. By noon, when the ladies rose from their beds, he had devised an entertainment for them that would keep them hilariously amused all day.

Sir Amaury's jongleurs were seated uneasily on a row of milking stools balanced on top of the great bench table. The Moor had perched herself on the extreme end of the row, and though Oriole had tried to secure the stool at the other end, he had been too slow. He found himself sitting next to her.

In the yard outside - Oriole could just glimpse it through the windows - stood the base of a wine vat carried from the press-house. Amaury had wanted it brought inside the hall but it had been too big to fit through the door.

The audience of ladies, bent on pleasing Sir Amaury, grinned already at the prospect of an entertainment. He jumped on to the table now, and wove his way between his jongleurs, declaiming.

'My jongleurs are, you'll admit, the finest pack of hounds ever to run with a hunting man over the world's green places!' Amaury was saying, in a sardonic, nasal whine. 'But I committed that crime so odious to the Church these days... I taught them *arithmetic.*'

The Lady Maude was so keyed up to laughter that she gave a little premature snicker.

'How right are the clergy to abjure it! For lo! Two of my jongleurs learned to *multiply!*' Amaury's weaving steps brought him between Oriole and Kadija. He laid a hand on the shoulder of each. 'Ah, see now, ladies, what danger I put you in! For have you not praised to me a thousand times the charming voice of young Oriole here, and the sweetness of his cherub face? What a wondrous deceit to keep a voice so high and be so precocious ... *lower down*. Look to yourselves, ladies! No lap dog *this* to be allowed into your laps!'

The ladies giggled hysterically but were still uncertain whether he meant to blast the jongleurs or simply to make sport of their sin.

'I don't understand, sir,' whispered Oriole, his shoulders slightly hunched against catastrophe.

'Ah, but there is some good - even in arithmeticians!

Here is a boy who has studied theology too - who was once bound for the cloister. Isn't that right, boy?' He swept on, giving Oriole no time to answer. 'This Songbird came to me last night to plead charity for his ladylove! To crave a boon of me. To cast his *petite amant* on the mercy of Chivalry!'

One or two of the women leaned forward and rested their faces on their hands. The joke was too long in coming: the smiles grew thread bare. '"Have her baptised" he said, "so that the child's born a Christian!"'

'Aah,' sighed Maude sentimentally, and would plainly still have taken Oriole into her lap and tugged at his ears and fed him bowls of milk.

'Well, I searched my heart and I looked deep into my conscience. And I said to myself, No! This decision's not mine. My hostesses must be asked! And so I convened this pied-poudre court here - this Court of Petits-Amours! What do you say, ladies? Proclaim your verdict! Shall the Moor be baptised? Shall she be washed clean in the waters of baptism?'

'Oh yes! Huzzah! Yes!' exclaimed Maude, but the other women, obedient to their role, pressed their heads together and debated the nice points of the case.

'Is she repentant?' enquired Béatrix.

'As sorry as any woman would be, to find herself in her present condition. '

'I think the boy ought to speak,' said Constance. 'Can he speak? On his own account?'

The legs of Oriole's stool jibbered; or was it his own legs as he stood up? I can speak, yes.' Amaury started towards him, fists clenched menacingly, but he could hardly hit the boy in front of the women. Oriole might

43

say anything. He drew in a shaking breath.

He could have denied the wicked lie, tried to make these women see that Herm was the father, see what Herm was. But Oriole knew they were deaf to any criticism of their communal lover. So instead he gabbled it out: '*Please* - let her be baptised. Don't let the baby fast in limbo.' Amaury relaxed his fists, well pleased.

Before Oriole could even sit down again, the women, shrill as hens, had fluttered up to the table. They settled on the Moor, tugged at her clothing, dislodged her shoes. They did not want to touch her, but they needed her down off the table, out in the yard. They called for a chaplain, called for chrism, but none of the stage properties had been left to chance by Amaury. Everything was waiting: the water and the words.

When the ladies of Poussarou undertook the redemption of the Moor, they tore her purple livery in shreds and delivered her up naked into the draughty yard. A goose had settled on the water in the vat, and it took brooms and flapping sleeves and an undignified commotion to displace the bird. Then, when it took off, its big feet showered them all with water so that they lost hold of the Moor and had to recapture her.

'Isn't she willing? Isn't she abject?' the chaplain wanted to know. But the women, absorbed in the sport their troubadour had organised for their afternoon, assured him, 'She's a savage. She thinks we mean to cook her and eat her.'

Eventually the groom from the stables grabbed hold of the naked, terrified girl and threw her headlong into the cold water of the wine vat. It slopped out over the ladies' shoes, wetted their dresses. 'You see how the soles of her feet are pink!' Maude remarked.

They could not fail to see, for it was all that protruded of Kadija. She had the greatest difficulty in turning turtle, and only managed to raise her head above water again after taking in water at nose and mouth. She emerged choking and shrieking, her arms over her head, like a child asking to be lifted up. But the water was too deep for her to stand on the barrel's base, so she had to cling to the rim, fetching her knees up as she searched for a foothold, fetching her hair up into the sunshine like a dipped black sheep.

Eudoxia sent a pot-boy back indoors to fetch one of the milking stools off the table: she was too short to see properly. The upper windows began to fill with faces - lewd boys pointing. Goose feathers swam in the water like white fish. Kadija's glossy, oak-brown skin turned a dull, shrivelled grey; strange, thought Oriole, that a white skin shone when it was wet and yet this looked rougher, drier. Her nipples were purple, as if, even in baptism, she must continue to wear the badge of Herm's livery.

Even in an overcrowded castle, even given the lack of privacy, it was an uncommon sight to see a woman naked. Most had not seen it since the tapster's wife had been forced through a hole in the frozen lake for the crime of coin-clipping. The crowd that gathered now wanted the same kind of pleasure from the day - a mixture of righteous delight and voyeuristic relish.

In a hectoring bleat, the chaplain demanded questions of Kadija's soul. He blasted insults at the demons within her. He began a peroration on the smallness of the eye of a needle and the Gate of Heaven, as if it should be plain to all present that Kadija's bulbous body would never squeeze through God's keyhole.

But the contours of the house created a chilly, swirling draught, and the ladies began to feel cold. Eudoxia's mother told her to give over her stool to the priest for him to stand on, and armed with a large wooden ladle, the chaplain ascended, wobbling and clutching his skirts to him. Shouting a little more abuse at Kadija's demons, and mispronouncing her name, he rapped at her knuckles with the ladle until she let go of the barrel and floundered in deep water. Only by sinking and pushing upwards again from the splintery base was she able to keep from drowning, and as she did so, the priest ladled the waters of redemption over her head shouting, 'Hands together! Hands together!'

The water ran into her eye sockets and the corners of her open mouth. 'Please!' she said. 'Please!'

Afterwards, no one knew how she was to be got out. Two ladders were sent for. They took a quarter of an hour to come. As she climbed up, with jibbering legs and heaving ribcage, just as she was straddling the rim, Amaury reminded everyone of the unborn child. The chaplain expressed the opinion that the unborn child could not be baptised, but was told to 'bless it, then', and teetered recklessly on his stool so as to lay a hand on the Moor's stomach. The boys in the windows whistled and jeered - it was not a part of the world where the clergy were held in high regard.

Peter Oriole took off his purple short-cloak and shoved it in a bundle towards Kadija. She only took it and held it in her rigid claw of a wet hand; it was far too small to cover anything of significance.

Now Amaury of Herm congratulated the ladies on having carried out everything in accordance with due form and ceremony. And they nodded at one another and felt a little cleaner, even though it was not they who had been left to steep for an hour in cold water.

'And now that the maid's a Christian,' declared Amaury, climbing halfway up the outer ladder and flourishing an arm in the direction of Kadija, 'let her also be a bride! A wedding, ladies! *That's* the entertainment I have planned for you this afternoon! Behold the bride and take hold of the groom!' Primed beforehand, the Giant grabbed Oriole from behind, his forearm across the boy's throat. 'Was there ever such a pretty pair?'

A dress was fetched for the bride: their extraordinary largesse towards the savage thrilled within the ladies' breasts. And they decked her like a maypole, with miscellaneous flowers. As they did so, Amaury began to extemporise: a hymn to Hymen.

Oriole put his hands over his ears and began to sway and rock in a misery of inarticulate horror. No words came to his aid. He stood bumbling and fumbling his way towards humiliation, as Amaury heaped verse on his head like burning coals. He could not stop the ladies of Poussarou sticking him with flowers like a suckling pig with cloves. He could not help but submit to their spiteful whims. He was to be lashed like a sailor to the pitchy keel of this big black boat and pushed out into deep water to drown. And there was nothing to be done about it, because he was nothing but a musical instrument, a stuffed purple livery.

Kadija clung to his elbow - a young woman clinging to a boy. Sir Amaury was mounting a play and although no one had told her about it in advance, still, while she had a role in it she was a jongleuse and not a castoff. She was prepared to do anything rather than be abandoned in the middle of a hostile foreign land. So she held her big lips between her white teeth and she tried with all her might to do what was expected of her. Last night she knew it had been Herm's intention to kill her. This morning she had thought to be drowned in public. Now there was talk of poetry and songs.

They went indoors again. The kitchen was alerted to the need for a celebratory meal of meat, and somewhere in an obscure yard a sheep or a goat was done to death in haste.

The chaplain did not approve of the idea of a wedding. He would have preferred stoning - as with wrens on Saint Stephen's day. They instructed him to lead the prayers of marriage, but in his heart he prayed for the return of sanity - for the return of the castle's menfolk from Spain, for an end to this Rule of Chaos by women and jackanape minstrels.

The ladies chivvied him through the preliminaries - 'Yes, yes! Come to the vows!' The Moor's grip grew tighter and tighter on Oriole's arm. Nobody noticed that he did not open his mouth: somewhere amid the chattering and giggling, the chaplain assumed the boy must have spoken his assent, and so turned to the girl. There was no mistaking Kadija's assent, shrill like the cry of a muezzin from a minaret. A ripple of applause and little shaken handbells drowned out the declaration that they were married.

'Let's have some dancing now!' exclaimed Eudoxia before the priest had even folded away his stole. All the ladies looked at their Master of the Revels, but Amaury did not speak till the whole room had fallen into a reverent silence.

'Shan't we see the bride and groom to bed first?' he asked.

Processions took no organising. Rank decided every position: it took only Amaury's choice of music to decide the pace at which the troupe of noblewomen, household officials and servants moved off through the castle's corridors. The happy momentum of their progress only faltered at the stairs, where the party-makers had to drop into single file to negotiate the narrow spiral and to keep from treading on the serpentine trains of the women in front.

Oriole and Kadija were goaded up the stairs with laurel branches ripped from the garden. And by the time the couple reached the first bedchamber, the covers of the bed were already turned down.

There was a hiatus. The Lady Constance whose room it was whispered, 'Not my bed, if you please.' She was scolded and reproached for making difficulties, but the procession reconvened and blundered on through the succession of bedrooms and ante-chapels, until Maude's chamber was reached.

Chiefly to spite the Lady Constance, she said she thought it would be sweet and charming if the couple were to consummate their love on her bed. She even tied the curtains tighter to their poles so as to grant everyone a better view. The jongleurs could be heard bursting with obscene jokes, like rosehips too full to contain their seed. The ladies confined themselves to giving dignified directions: 'Come along, then, boy. Undress your bride.'

'Come on, lady. Set your groom a fair example!'

'How can she set him a *fair* example?' Eudoxia piped up, and her mother slapped her forearm but laughed too. The half-circle of ladies closed in on the bed, so that bride and groom were forced to climb up on to it and kneel face-to-face. But they were as limp-armed and unresponsive to command as puppets with their strings cut through. Oriole, his eyes fixed on the pelmet of the bed, was saying between clenched teeth, 'I hate them. I hate them. I hate them. I hate them.'

Kadija, similarly looking over her groom's head and into the crowd of spectators, saw Sir Amaury casually draw his knife and stand with its blade in the pinch of finger and thumb. Her hands shot out and she grabbed the fastenings of Oriole's waistcoat and began undoing them with quick, certain fingers.

The outburst of laughter this brought unnerved the pet kids penned in Maude's armoire, and they burst suddenly into the room, scattering musicians and ladies and clerks. A lark fluttered so frenziedly against its bars that the whole cage was set swinging. Then One-eye and One-Arm and the Giant, unable to contain themselves another moment, began to chant: 'Marry her! Marry her! Marry her! Marry her!'

The rhythm incited Eudoxia to join in the chant, and the older women, not wanting to seem staid in the eyes of Sir Amaury, also picked it up: 'Marry her! Marry her! Marry her!'

Then, with a commotion which everyone mistook at first for the goats, a messenger entered the room and darted about it, seeking an attentive ear. He whispered his news to Lady Constance who swatted him away like a gnat. But as he backed off, nursing his nose and lip, she grasped the import of what he had said and snatched out at every dress within reach. 'The men are home!' she said, and soon everyone was saying it: 'The men are home!' 'They've come back!'

The wedding was forgotten. They were full off ears, full of questions. Had any died? Were any maimed? Were there trophies and spoils-presents or knighthoods? Why no warning letter in advance? Was it a test to surprise them in unwifeliness? Were there chickens enough in the yard and carp enough in the pond to make a fit homecoming? When they caught sight of Amaury, their eyes were those of children called away from a wonderful game with never a hope of returning to it; as if the first rains of autumn had put an end to summer haystacks. Finally they dragged him away with them - their last chance to touch his hand, press close against him.

Only the bride and groom were left, kneeling face-to-face on the bed, and the baby kids chewing on the hemp fringe of a mat.

The noise of panic drained down through the building. Voices came to them not up the stairs any longer but clambering up the outside walls, as servants hung banners and wall-hangings out of the windows like a Mediterranean washday. One was dropped and flapped down into the moat; there was a clatter of feet down a spiral stair.

Oriole only went on shaking his head, holding his doublet tight closed across his body with clenched fists. 'Married,' he said and the tears rolled down his cheeks at the never-ending horror of it all.

Kadija climbed off the bed and picked up the cleanest of the lambs - black, tight-curled and fetching - and brought it to him, almost like a peace-offering. He hugged it close, and its mouth found his finger and began to suck. In due course, she persuaded him to leave the room, for fear Maude's husband arrived and found them there.

CHAPTER FIVE

Empty-handed Jugglers

The knights of Poussarou re-entered their birthright in a quick, bellicose assault, like yet another of the towns they had attacked and plundered. Their mail vests swung around their hips and knees with a noise of dragon scales rippling, and they lashed out at servants and threw their mailed gloves or clouts of bread at anything acquired new in their absence. The oppressive littleness and discomfort of their shared patrimony closed in on them once more, and their resentment showed itself in a contempt for anything their wives might have achieved while they were gone.

They took those wives with a graceless, punitive haste and at the first opportunity. Lady Constance's husband imposed his conjugal rights at the top of the east-end stairs on the way to chapel. They took Communion, too, like a swill and a bite of bread crammed down during a lull in battle. And when they saw Amaury's tent pitched in the garden they were fully set to split its owner from crown to genius, despite their wives' cries of 'Sir Amaury is very rich, husband! Sir Amaury is very cultured!'

Herm assembled his jongleurs in what remained of 'the Rose Fortress and delivered a *sirventes* of welcome and acclaim that the heroes' achievements made the deeds of Charlemagne pale into nothingness. He said that the ladies had begged him to compose it - had pressed him to stay and sing it, even though he ought to be pursuing his circuit, singing in praise of his *domna*. The knights said nothing when it was over. They did not split him, but the surliness in their faces hardly abated.

'Oh, now you must hear the boy soprano sing!' exclaimed Joanna with a hasty flurry of skirts that set her train lashing. 'He has the voice of an angel, husband. Truly, the voice of a cherub!'

So Oriole was brought forward to perch precariously on the dilapidated wooden gantry and to sing an Ave Maria - 'The very latest in fashionable songs!' Joanna urged her husband.

Oriole's voice rose with the gentle gradient and translucent beauty of a rainbow.

Like a rainbow it failed to make the descent, disappearing in a tuneless growl. His face turned ashy white. After the fourth croaking line, he stopped trying to sing altogether.

God has taken away my voice, he thought, and could see the justice of it. The voice had been awarded to a boy destined for the Church, to sing to the glory of God. His marriage to the Moor had been the final offence too grave for God to overlook. He could even see the great calipers of light bending to either side of a cloud overhead, reaching down, excising the music from his throat, cleansing him of any talent. He put both hands to his neck. Down below him, the knights burst out laughing.

'Your oriole's turned crow!' jeered Joanna's husband.

'He shall be got rid of,' said Amaury pulling a long face. 'He does no service if he gives no pleasure.'

'And just who *is* this lady love of yours?' demanded Maude's husband, unassuaged.

'Well, who do you think, sir? Queen Eleanor, naturally.'

The women almost burst into applause. Such an ingenious lie on the spur of the moment!

Amaury struck his tent.

He had Oriole gather up all the empty phials of hare's rennet and bury them under a square of turf He had all the presents given him by the ladies concealed inside the instruments of his jongleurs, so that should anyone be found, it would be construed as theft by an expend able culprit. And he gave audience, as he packed, to a string of ladies, all flushed with the imminence of glory.

For though it brought a tear to their eye to admit it, everything else had been preparatory to this - the moment when Herm would set off upon his circuit of the world. He would carry the *idea* of them away with him, like God's name into the uttermost parts of the world. His presence they could spare, much as he had sweetened their lonely boredom. The true food that would sustain them through winter and summer alike was the knowledge that a troubadour-knight bore their fame round France and England, immortalising their beauty. He would sing of his love for them and raise them from their obscurity. He would describe them to courtiers in the palaces of Angers, Paris and even Italy. He would probably travel to the Holy Land and kiss the Holy Shrines with lips that had kissed theirs. After all, what good was a knight-errant who came to rest?

Thus they consoled themselves: Constance and Guillaumette, Eudoxia and Joanna, Maude, Beatrix and the rest, each holding to the truth, as sure as she clung to salvation, that she alone had fired passion within Amaury's heart.

They pressed on him gifts of jewellery, clothing, money, ribbons, a horse and saddle, wine and bedlinen. Such triumphs accounted for Herm's exceptional wealth.

They gave him strips of cloth, too, embroidered with their names or with touching verses. He left them strewn on the branches of silver-birch trees as he and his troupe of horse clambered out of the Défilé de l'llouvre, away from Poussarou, ascending in the direction of Saint Pons.

Oriole and Kadija kept very still, like frogs beside a pond. Perhaps if they did not move, they would not call to Amaury's mind their offensive existence: she six months pregnant and he with his voice breaking. They were of no conceivable use to him. Even so, neither of them dared believe that he would truly turn them off.

They were not without allies. The other jongleurs closed ranks round them. They too could recall losing their childhood voices. They too had lain awake at night wondering what life was like without the protection of a master. Whenever the troupe camped, Oriole and Kadija retreated into the darkness to squat out-of-sight, out-of-mind of Sir Amaury. One eye and One Arm would bring them morsels of food. They had crossed the Monts de Lacaune and were camping in the Bois de la Peyre-Blanque before the weeks of uncertainty ended.

In the centre of Lacaune, singing a ballad of Merlin stood a young boy. With bird-thin shanks and hose drooping, he looked as if he had been mobbed by starlings. His voice, though, was sound.

His little audience forgot him the moment Amaury's parade entered town. They broke away and ran to see the purple liveries, the pluming feathers, the red bridles decorated with bells, the human oddities, which made up Amaury's entourage. Christ on his colt would not have received so splendid a welcome. The waif followed the crowd.

At the inn, Sir Amaury, between mouthfuls of cheese and garlic, caught sight of him and called out: 'Play lute, do you?'

The child's eyes gleamed. 'And rebek and rote! And I sing, sir. I sing.'

'I heard you. I have need of a soprano.'

'Oh, but I .. .' Oriole began. He was invisible, inaudible.

'Mine has just married. So he has to give up the wandering life for domestic bliss. Jew-bread and butt-water. With this sloe-pie here for a wife. How d'you think they'll get along?'

'As well as I did, sir,' said the little beggar.

And so he was given Oriole's bed-roll, and scurried in under Herm's protection. The circle closed against Oriole and Kadija. Now that the interdict had fallen at last, there was no point in trying to shield the castoffs.

'If your voice mends,' said Amaury to Oriole, 'look for me among royalty. But don't bring any black cats with you.' He gave them each a golden ecu - but then there was an inn-yard audience watching him, ready to admire his philanthropy. The drinkers in the inn wondered at the waste of two golden ecus on discharged servants. It was like leaving money in the heels of an old, discarded pair of boots.

They were alone.

Left at the roadside like a couple of horses with their wind gone, they did not move off at once. They dropped their heads and cast about for blades of grass.

'No big matter,' said Kadija, drawing herself up tall as if to express a dignity never allowed her before. She had a little boy with her, and it was her responsibility to keep up his spirits. 'We minstrels now. We wander-about minstrels.'

'Yes. We are, aren't we?' said Oriole. The oppression of Herm had, after all, lifted and moved away like a thundercloud to a far distant horizon. And besides, he had a wife now and it was his responsibility to keep up her spirits. 'We can play music and juggle. And act. And I remember all the songs I ever sang. And we can teach the baby to tumble and make all manner of musics and dance with swords and turn magic and ... ' Kadija nodded. They were to be parents, after all, and it is the duty of parents to hope for the best.

But they were musicians without instruments to play. He was a singer without a voice. She was an acrobat without a sense of balance. They were actors without costumes, liveries without a master. They were emptyhanded jugglers.

'We'll find Sir Jocelyn de Foicelles!' cried Oriole, dazzled for a moment by the inspiration. 'He's maybe raised the Lady Lily to life again by now. He'll be so happy, he'll most likely give us a castle to live in!' But though they asked about for directions, the Castle of Lilies remained as distant as Heaven. Those they asked lived and died within an orbit of twenty miles. Those they asked looked at Kadija and crossed themselves and, more often than not, did not answer at all. Those they called out to, crossed the road to walk on the other side. Those they asked for shelter slammed doors on them, set dogs on them, threw pails of nightwater after them and abuse just as foul.

They left Lacaune. With the two golden ecu Oriole bought himself a flute and Kadija a timbrel and they played together at the roadside. Little children came and stared: they fetched their mothers to hear the pretty music. Crowds gathered and glared, grew intoxicated by the music and began to dance, were happy to be distracted from their work by a gaudy flicker of purple - as a man might pause on a bridge to watch a kingfisher.

Then they threw smiles. Or pebbles. And the clouds overhead threw down rain and drove the little children back indoors and their mothers, still humming, to warm firesides where they scolded their infants for standing so close to witches and sinners. The summer-baked road where Oriole and Kadija stood was spattered with coin-sized drops which melted into puddles. The cart-ruts filled up with welts of silver water. The welts mired down into slurry. And the travelling country side ceased to move for the duration of winter.

The purple liveries were summer silk. Kadija had to split hers at the sides to make room for the growing child. They sold the silk in return for hopsack shirts, and the drum for a week's lodging. The earth where they walked now was not blood-red. It was black, pitchy, without either passion or compassion.

They failed to find the Castle of Lilies or Foicelles' hermit cell in time for the birth. So Oriole took them instead to an older resort - to the refuge of his childhood where charity could not be refused. Not that the Cistercian monastery he found was the actual one where he had been raised, but it was hardly distinguishable from it: the same village of outbuildings and among them a hospital. He presented himself at the pauper's door, like Joseph burdened with Mary on Christmas Eve.

Oriole sat on the step beneath the swinging bell-pull and the echo of the bell, and explained the principle of alms to Kadija. It was a Christian duty, he said. She sat down beside him there and recognised in his words small glimpses of her own childhood religion. The iron bands that seemed to have bound her ribs, stomach and pelvis unaccountably relaxed - the manacle of hunger that had gripped her belly for weeks, the hoop of cold that had held her body so rigid that it ached.

'The baby is coming now,' she said.

The words tore away all the lies with which Oriole had tried to protect himself. It was the one small piece of Amaury of Herm that they must carry with them everywhere - a shackle which still bound them to the past.

A face appeared at the grille in the door. Only Oriole stood up. 'God keep you, sir. My wife's child is coming and she has nowhere to lay herself.' He was aware of his features adopting that boyish ingenuousness which had reliably melted the hearts of the ladies of Poussarou. He wondered if he had not become a hypocrite under the tuition of Henn. His voice did not break into a treble: the winter had aged him, too. The monk opened the door in order to show them the way to the hospital. When he saw Kadija he crossed himself and sprang away, for fear his habit brush against the woman on the steps.

'*What are you?*'

'Both Christians, sir, baptised and absolved and married!'

'Where are you from?'

'The Castle of Lilies, sir, in the north,' said Oriole. 'But pilgrims, sir. On pilgrimage.'

The monk's nerves were jangled. He pointed out the hospital the most distant of eight buildings linked by a cloister - then went inside again and shut the door.

They did not wait at the hospital door - went in as if they were under the instructions of the Pope himself. It was warm and camphorous inside. The old, the injured, the diseased mumbled the prayers they had been given by the apothecary, and pulled their blankets higher at the sight of Kadija.

The monk in attendance was not accustomed to thinking of birth as a sickness and not in favour of admitting women to his hospital at all, let alone a blackamoor. So he stood at a distance, arms folded. A pilgrim. Yes, it was just feasible. But he turned Oriole out into the rain and called to Kadija to cover herself with a blanket and to make less noise, and not to turn God's stomach with sights so unbecoming.

A handful of slummocking women, who had for the most part come to cook meals for sick husbands or children, and to nag them out of dying, gathered to stare at Kadija. They lifted the blanket to check that her feet were not cloven, touched her hair to be sure it was not lambs wool, retreated a few steps when she shouted out in Arabic Spanish.

And then somehow they could not keep their expertise to themselves; it overrode their misgivings, their superstitions, the injunctions of their husbands to 'keep well clear'. They began to shout encouragements, advice, proverbs and reminiscences of their own labours. The circle closed round the palliasse on the floor, and Oriole, watching from the door, lost sight of his wife.

'Is that your boy outside? Shall I show the child to your boy?' asked a woman, having forgotten completely that Kadija was black. And she brought Oriole a sight of the baby - a blotched, leprous-looking creature with luxuriant quantities of hair and indigent, reaching hands.

'He's not her *son*, you fool! He's the *father!*' said another woman laughing.

Oriole did not want to hold the child: he backed away, out into the cloister. But the women had been so catapulted into excitement by the triumph of a birth that they did not see his unwillingness. So they gave it into his arms, that scion of Amaury's, that offshore island of Herm. One shouted at him that it was fine and strong, while another whispered that he should 'get it blessed good and quick'. A third laughed and said it was 'like

Jacob's sheep - all brindled', while another noted, in an aside, how it was born too hungry to cry.

Then they abandoned him, eager to return to their comrade, to enlist Kadija to their guild of motherhood so that they could share its secrets with her. They moved away like a busy swarm of bees threading an intricate dance between one another as they milled about the bed.

The baby began to carp at him - not cry so much as croak like a spotted toad. The membranous lids parted over its bulging eyes and it looked at him with reproach for allowing it to be exhumed from a warm place to share his hunger and his cold. He sang to it because he remembered babies were sung to.

But as he sang, the eyes that looked at him were not Amaury's but hers, already dark and bewildered. His voice emerged pure and liquid. It filled his head like strong wine; it rose out of his breast like warmth off an open hearth. He was Zechariah whose voice was taken away until the angel's prophecy had been fulfilled in the birth of a child.

Oriole was filled with sudden gratitude towards the monks - for the shelter, for their tolerance, for building their house and hospice in the direct line of his life's walk. He ran with the baby to show them: that out of the Wronged came forth Sweetness. He wanted them to see that there was someone in the world even more helpless than he, especially now that his voice had been given back to him. It had been a test, and without knowing how or when, he had passed it, and God had rewarded him with a man's tenor voice as good as any that went before.

'Thank you. Thank you for taking us in!' he panted, without noticing that his voice wavered between high and low. 'We'll call her Mary because of the long journey and finding somewhere at the last moment. And Mary's my *domna*, besides, and now I can sing for her again ... Might I sing for you, sir? In token of my thanksgiving - and maybe a bite of something to eat for me and her?'

Out of this the monk extracted a kind of news. 'You're a minstrel,' he said, as a man might say who lifts a bite of meat to his mouth and sees the maggots there before him.

'Yes, sir, and I've learned some verses by heart in Latin, thanks to Sir Jocelyn de Foicelles, sir, who was a marvellous scholar, sir, and a wonderful master!'

'Filth,' said the monk. 'How dare you step over the threshold of an holy house! You who've not had the taste of salvation in your mouth! You piece of devil's-meat!'

Oriole was too taken aback to look penitent. 'I'll take Communion gladly, sir. I'd like to have done it oftener, but my last master...'

'Would you so? Would you so, you little servant of Lucifer? Well, get out, you and your black whore! Dung-cakes both of you! Dung cakes off the floor of Hell! Take Grace when the Pope's denied it? You would, too! I see it in you! Steal the wafer off the Holy Table, wouldn't you? Wretch. Degenerate. What does it take to fetch your kind to remorse?'

He barged at Oriole with his big stomach, as if to use his hands would contaminate them. And Oriole, his arms full of baby, dodged this way and that to keep from being rammed. The monk chased him back to the hospital, scattered the women like flies off a carcase, and began to rant and rage at the woman on the floor. She stared up at him with vacant, preoccupied eyes - and in response of his tirade, delivered up her afterbirth in a bloody and disrespectful evacuation.

His nausea was all that kept the monk from rolling her off the mattress and driving her out: this Eve who had besmirched his Eden by being a *jongleuse*. Not just a Moor, not just a woman, not just a fairground phenomenon with a boy for her keeper, but a *jongleuse* - one of that excommunicate rabble who dared to make a living in this Vale of Tears from song and dance and that other vile contagion: laughter.

CHAPTER SIX

A Married Man

They made a living by selling bogus medicines. Elixirs of all kinds. Philtres and potions. Once Oriole had set aside the notion of a man earning his keep honestly, he discovered starvation was not inevitable. He found himself an acceptable ledge above the abyss, on which to squat with wife and daughter and eke out a living.

The baby proved a compliant child. Her mother's lack of nourishment during pregnancy had bequeathed her a smiling vacuity. She rarely cried, rarely stirred in her crate.

And just as peasants sewed garments for a wooden madonna, Oriole wove a crude cape of lies around Kadija. Remembering how Herm had been chiefly loved for his lies, Oriole presented Kadija at markets as the daughter of a slave-girl who had worked for the English magician Merlin, grinding his compounds in mortars of gold beneath the floor of Camelot, in basements excavated by lions. He found he enjoyed the invention - then that it infected him, like the alchemist's obsession. There were words hoarded inside his head from his days with Foicelles and Berm. He wanted to spend and spend and spend them. There would have been no point in one of his social position to write *aubades*, *serenades* or *sirventes* ... And yet he could have done it. Sometimes at night he would lie awake imagining himself a knight-*trobar*. So he understood why the people did not see through his lies; why they wanted Merlin's magic to be clinging to the cheap muslin hem of Kadija's dress. They wanted to see, in their mind's eye, her mother swaying heathen hips between retorts and flasks, mortars and stoppered bottles. It made them believe they would be cured by her mixtures of soil, herbs and water.

His lies made them happy, happier.

Then spring came and, having survived winter, people seemed suddenly more amenable to music and to song. When Oriole stood beside a highway and played folk music, he felt less like a pillory, more like a wayside shrine. Carters entertained him to a swig of wine in exchange for doggerel. Brides and grooms offered him a role at their weddings. And goose-wives offered him more than they should, though he always turned them down and fled.

He bought again the instruments of his real trade, and cloth which Kadija dyed for him - a sunny orange with sunbursts of yellow where she had tied pebbles into the cloth before the dyeing. To its shoulders she sewed streamers, and down the breast rosettes of different coloured ribbon. No camouflage for him, then, like the men around him who blended into the green and brown of the land they worked. He emerged gaudy out of winter, like a butterfly out of a grubby grub.

The baby had a rattle now, and a fleece - even a barrow to push her in. The family owned a strip of cloth, a wood-whistle, a broken viol, a pair of shoes. He found the wood to make stilts, and bought Kadija an orange - an orange from Spain! He renewed his ability to juggle, then they ate the orange, pith and skin, like wolves swallowing the moon.

Winter scattered them; in the spring and summer, they regrouped: something out of nothing, goods out of bad. And all the time they were really searching for the Castle of Lilies.

It was at the hands of their own kind that they almost met destruction. They chanced upon the estates of a patron of the arts. Oriole said such a man must surely know of Jocelyn de Foicelles, the finest troubadour in France. So they called at the castle.

Unfortunately, the castle was rifer with talent than a hayrick with rats. And like rats under threat, the resident minstrels defended their territory. They were terrified of competition. They knew what life on the road was, and they never meant to return to it.

So Oriole did not even reach as far as the mansion doorway. He was cornered in a stable stall and his handbarrow kicked to pieces. All the soft bedding inside spilled out. Fortunately Kadija was holding the child at the time and only Oriole's instruments were smashed into matchwood and wire and the burst bladders of pigs. Even his voice, it seemed, was a thing to be kicked out of him.

Kadija fled with the baby; Oriole wormed out from between his attackers' legs and pelted after her, bringing them after him like clacks tied to a dog. 'Directions! To set us on our way! Just a word's direction!' he shouted over his shoulder. But their own noise deafened them.

Chased over the rim of the dry moat, sliding down through thistles and stones on the sides of their feet, Kadija and Oriole fell among the rest of the castle's litter - the meat bones, the excrement, the vegetable peelings - and were pelted from overhead with stones. They took shelter inside the great circle of a land drain driven through the castle's foundations, crawling to the far end of the drain's opening, pleading with the baby to keep silent. Their heads, hands and feet swept before them birds' nests, dead mice and cobwebs. The pursuers' shouting gradually faded into apathetic obscenities.

'Bastards. All of them,' said Kadija out of the dark.

'If I could have got to the real man ...' said Oriole. 'The gentleman. He would've heard of Sir Jocelyn.'

She put a hand on him no blacker than the filthy blackness. It was meant to restrain his noise. But she picked a moment when humiliation and outrage had got the better of him. He trapped Kadija's hand between his legs, and groped so violently at her that, startled, she let go of the baby.

Finding her limbs free, the child crawled out of her wrappings towards the lip of the drain and towards the possibility of her death a hundred feet below. They both made a lunge to catch hold of her, and lay face-to-face with the child pinned between them.

'You are my wife,' he whispered belligerently.

'Yes. Long time now,' she said amicably.

And when he threatened, 'Well, I could if I wanted then, couldn't I?' she simply agreed, 'Of course.'

And when his hand collided with hers in the darkness, she shook it as if she were encouraging a small child. 'Still. Bad place here. Very dirty here.'

'Yes. Yes. Filthy dirty. Yes. Very.' The gall suddenly sank to his stomach and gurgled there, uncomfortable, indigestible. The baby kicked him in the groin. He apologised under his breath to the Virgin and to his wife.

In the morning they discovered that the precipitous drop was a little farther off than the immediate end of the drain. There was in fact a reasonable plateau of flowers and grass outside the wall, on which to sit and warm themselves in the sun. Kadija sat cross-legged and deloused him - a pleasant, companionable pastime for a sunny morning. Nothing but birdsong disturbed the silence. Though the minstrels must still be growling and prowling, here on the outside of the town's fortifications there was nothing but redstarts, swallows and somewhere a blackbird singing himself sober.

She built a cairn of rocks to restrain the baby. Then she carefully made of herself a cairn - a byre, a baffle, a windbreak. A hand, a breast, a kiss - she coiled herself around him, taking the initiative she had daily feared he would take. There were, after all, far worse things than to be married to a pretty French boy. The older he grew, the less degrading it would be.

Oriole allowed the morning sunshine to pin him to the hillside, the bright light to redden his closed eyelids, the agreeable searching of her fingers after lice to digress to a bliss more acute. He did not open his eyes. She settled on top of him like the best, close-to-morning dreams, so that he knew he must keep his eyes shut or lose the pleasure.

He allowed her to take the initiative he had been daring himself to take every night for months. There were, after all, far worse things than to be married to the daughter of Merlin's slavegirl, to the Princess of the Amazons, to King Solomon's Sheba ... In they trooped, all the ladies he could invent - as many and varied as the ladies of Poussarou - into the tasselled tent of his imagination. He let Kadija play them all.

It might have been the beginning of a kind of happiness. But when they finally crawled back through the land drain into a moat infested with flies and cats, struggled up the thistly slope, and crept into the yard, they found the wreckage of his barrow. Even the broken pieces of his instruments had been picked over for their strings, reeds and pegs. His wealth was gone, as if it had been only a trick of the light, a little yellow sunshine resting on his palms. Even the thrilling, winging excitement of his newly discovered manhood deserted him. An hour before, he had thought to be happy for ever, his body more crammed with sensations than Solomon's treasurehouse. But somehow he could not keep hold of the delight. It trickled away through the holes in his clothes and left behind only the large, heavy pieces of sadness. It was with their inexplicable feeling in his stomach that he scraped the moat excrement off his shoes with a stick.

They gasped and flinched as a dark, hunched figure cast its shadow over them. But then it dropped down on to all-fours, they saw which of the castle entertainers it was. A bear came loping towards them, elderly, shag-eared, greying. Though they froze with instinctive fright, the creatures was harmless, a dancer rather than a pit-fighter - just another of the art-lover's jesters.

'Take the bear,' said Kadija, clutching Oriole's hand.

'What do I want with a bear?' he said scornfully, but was already edging towards it, his wife and baby shielded behind him. His hand reached for the rope that dangled from the bear's headstall. As he caught hold of it, the head swung towards him like a great bell on its bellrope. The beast looked at him with shineless eyes, one milky with cataract, and its flicking ears were grisled and notched. Oriole succeeded in looking almost as haughty as the bear. 'It's no more than they owe me,' he told the bear, arrogant in his first act of theft. 'Now we'll go and find Sir Jocelyn de Foicelles! All four of us.' He said it with an air of authority: head of a growing household.

And just as Kadija had given her dark and magical body into a little boy's keeping, the dancing bear entrusted itself to him too. It danced a few shambling steps on overlapping feet, then padded over the draw bridge behind its new owner, shaking the flies out of its antique ears. Yet another responsibility for Oriole the family man. He felt the burden settle on his back. Everywhere on his travels he had heard men groaning under the same burden: marriage, responsibility.

All of a sudden, however, there were no men to do the complaining. In more and more of the fields they passed by, the only workers were women. In the evening doorways only women stood watching the sun go down. Only women rested their aching backs to listen to a minstrel's song. But they had no money to spare for either songs or elixirs. Their menfolk were gone.

'Gone where?'

'To take the Cross, 'course.'

'Take it where? What cross?'

'Take the Cross, boy! Take the Cross! Everyone's gone. Everyone. The Holy War. The Crusade. King's vowed to pray at the place where Christ rose up from the dead. That's the kind of thing happens when a king makes vows.'

For two years King Louis had been declaring his intent to make war on the infidel enemies of Christ: Oriole had heard of the vow just like everyone else. And yet it had seemed like a fantasy, some mythical Arthurian quest. Now it could no longer be ignored. It was maiming his livelihood.

When the truth came to him, in the very moment of falling asleep, and catapulted him back to wakefulness, he could not understand what had kept it from him so long. Fatigue, routine, anxiety: they robbed a man of the simple faculty of reasoning.

'Kadija! He'll be there!' She too lurched back out of sleep, instantly, habitually afraid of loud voices. 'Sir Jocelyn will be there! Among the crusaders!'

'But he is hermit now, you said. Your old master.'

'Not if the King has summoned together all his knights! Don't you see? A Holy War! It'll make everything like it was before! Sir Jocelyn's bound to take up arms! He can't refuse, can he? Why should he want to? To pray at Christ's tomb! Imagine! Imagine it!'

'So he goes far off. Even more far off. We never find him.'

'No! Not at all! I mean, he'll be with the royal army! He'll join the King at Paris! All we have to do is find the army!' His revelation gathered momentum. 'I'll go with him! That's what I'll do. I'll go to the Crusades!'

'A war? Not a war, please God!' she cried.

He was instantly angry - had not been angry a moment ago but was raging now. 'So what? What's wrong with a war? Who cares what you think? Would you sooner we starve? Are we supposed to starve?'

He too hated the thought, now it came to him, of leaving her and the baby to go into filthy foreign parts full of barbarians who would do their best to kill him. She ought not to undermine him by making him think about it. Didn't she realise that when she had given him possession of her body she had also saddled him with the responsibility to feed and clothe it? When he looked up at the grey sky, there was no protection over his miserable minstrel's head: not law, not Guild, not even the blue habit of the Virgin Mary to whom he had now been unfaithful with a blackamoor.

But then again, a part of his imagination wanted to go - into sunlit territories - alone, unburdened, reunited with the hero of his youth, re-invested with promise and hope and infinite possibilities.

But how long the journey took. In every town and village along the way war levies had left nothing but hardship. The men had gone, as well as the money: six out of every seven men, so the women said who had been left behind: widows with husbands still living.

By the time he reached the muster at Metz, he was one among thousands of others, choking the roads, converging for the Second Crusade. On to every drab garment round about him white crosses had been stitched - some from strips torn from Holy Bernard's own white Cistercian mantle - but none with more care than Kadija had used in clustering Oriole's rosettes into an elaborate, raised design on his breast. Their crosses were white, his were of yellow ribbon. Was it really only three years since he had been a chorister, drab and anonymous, safe and sanctified, his life in pawn to God? It was as though he had blinked and three years had fallen away. Three lifetimes.

It never for a moment occurred to Oriole that his former master would *not* be among the mustered chivalry. No matter that he had last seen Foicelles bandaged and maimed, bent on living as a hermit. Holy Bernard and the King had commanded a crusade. Therefore every Christian knight would answer the call. Oriole willed it to be so, and no amount of cautionary, sensible warnings from his wife could dent his determination to find Sir Jocelyn.

Only at the sight of the assembled army was he daunted for the first time. 'How will I find him among all these?' he whispered under his breath.

Such a multitude of armour glinted in the sun that the ground was brazed blue with reflections of the sky. Such an acreage of chainmail hissed that it was possible to believe the sea just out of sight. Banners of every colour and cloth obliterated the horizons, each one a ripple in one torrential river of colour dividing sky from earth. And beyond, as far and farther than sight allowed, wagons broke up the landscape into a parterre of wood and canvas. The countless footsoldiers were earth brown and easily overlooked, but the chivalry and the vast shanty of wagons were unforgettable.

Obliged to bring Kadija and the baby much farther than he had meant, Oriole found she was not such a great rarity. Though the men of the land had left their women to dig for sustenance and keep the door bolted, the knights and counts and dukes and King had brought their wives with them for the sport: not just their wives either, but their handmaidens and maidservants and covered wagons full of women's indispensable little luxuries. Peasant women of enterprise had joined the Crusade too, their crosses sewn low down on the front of their smocks, like the marks made on treasure maps to incite men with the ambition to dig. There were tradesmen to service the great parade as well - ostlers and farriers and armourers, cobblers, chroniclers and wheelwrights. Barber-surgeons and priests. The bear, associating a crowd with the need to perform, stood up on its hind legs and danced.

'What if your knight isn't here?' asked Kadija yet again. But Oriole knew more surely than ever that he was. He must be! Everyone in France was there. The greatest army ever mustered by all the disparate little comtés and dukedoms of France had gathered under the scarlet oriflamme to extinguish the Infidel. Was there ever such an army? Was there ever such an elegant race of princes? Oriole's breast was stuffed with righteous pride. The pageantry elated him.

Someone must have given the signal to depart, but motion set in more like a thaw, the centre of the stream starting to flow and gradually aggregating a greater and greater body of movement. The pages and squires were delayed in pulling down apparelling pavilions, while their masters clip-clopped off in stately procession, unencumbered, free to nod their ugly helmets superciliously at men of equal rank.

Oriole took Kadija's hand and dragged her to the base of a tree. By climbing from her cupped hands on to her shoulders, he was able to reach the lowest branch and finally achieve a vantage point from which to see all the banners pass. Yellow. He had only to look for yellow ribbons, streamers, favours festooning the Foicelles heraldy. Below him the bear embraced the tree, lifting a hind foot enthusiastically as if it would climb up after him. But it settled for rubbing itself amorously against the bark, jarring the whole tree with its scratching. The baby laughed and pointed: she was fond of the bear.

Ladies' favours flew over the French army like bunting. Sleeves, gloves, ribbons, kerchiefs - even shoes and bedsheets were to be borne aloft as far as Outremer to ensure the lasting fame of a thousand mistresses. It gave the unfortunate impression that whole platoons had ridden under a wash line and snagged down all the washing. Only the fighting clergy had crucifixes in place of favours.

'Do you see him?' called Kadija up into the tree.

'Not yet.' Nicodemus squatting in his sycamore tree never gazed down with more wonder than Oriole on the workings of God.

There were women warriors; too! Not just wives and maidservants in litters and wagons, but ladies on horseback, riding astride, in armour and surcoats and swords. If it were not for the fact that the armour was ragged with scarves, the helmets carried underarm, the daggers only fit for peeling apples and the horses hemmed round with page boys, Oriole might never have guessed these Amazons were ladies of the realm.

Oriole mistook him, at first, for one of the ladies long golden hair, chevroned surcoat, rosy ribbons tumbling down over either ear. Then the ribboned head turned in the direction of the tree.

'Sir Jocelyn! Sir Jocelyn de Foicelles! Wait! Please wait, sir!' Oriole dropped from the tree like an apple and set off, pelting into the parade, ducking beneath the heads of horses, dodging the spiked bosses of shields, stimied by the slow passage of wagons, kicked at by irritable pack-mules. A dog attached itself to him, yelping along at his heels: perhaps Oriole smelled of bear. 'Sir Jocelyn, wait! It's Oriole! It's me! Don't go without me!'

Sir Jocelyn, as well as his new pink livery, had had gauntlets made for him specially. On the left one there were only three fingers, but these were embroidered with gilt wire and pink silk and the gloves extended as far as his elbows in great fluted cuffs. He drew in the reins of his grey mare with an exaggerated elegance which brought his cuffs up to his beardless chin. Behind him the column was thrown into confusion, splitting off to left and right like water round an eyot.

Oriole had been so preoccupied with catching up, that he had given no thought to what he might say. 'Sir! Sir! Take me back, sir! I'm a good jongleur, aren't I? I was always good, wasn't I? I'm better now than I was, even! I play plenty of instruments! Oh for God's sake, take me back, sir!'

Foicelles' company of jongleurs bridled visibly: new boys, young boys: they wore the same prim and sheeplike faces Oriole must have worn that day Amaury burst into his life. They stared with distaste at Oriole mud-stained to the thigh, open-seamed, fray-threaded and importunate with his, 'Take me back, sir! On my knees I beg you! In the name of the Lady Lily!'

'With all my heart, sir,' said the knight vaguely, deafened by the noise of the moving army. 'If you're game for the Great Adventure. I've taken a vow to lay my lady's favour on the altar of the Holy Nativity. Fall in, then. Fall in, if you want. Sing us a song, if that's what you do.' He kicked up his horse and Oriole had to spring forward and seize its bridle or be swept away from the spot.

'I have a wife now, sir! A wife and a baby daughter and nothing to keep them alive till the wars done - though she's a good jongleuse herself, and can use stilts and do dumbshow... She'll be useful to you when we come home, sir!' He pointed urgently in the direction of the tree. He, if not Foicelles, could see Kadija peering through the traffic, standing on tiptoe to keep sight of the group, and the bear, also on its toes, its big head sawing to and fro like an anxious mother-in-law.

The jongleurs in the pink livery opened their eyes wider than ever with dismay.

Like a conjuror, Foicelles produced from his saddle a purse of money. For whatever reason he had packed it, with whatever contingency or charity in mind, he tossed it to Oriole in a huge parabola and smiled indulgently to see the pleasure it bestowed. Though at present he could not call the lad to mind.

Back through the parade ran Oriole, looking behind

him time and time again to take bearings on the little ship of pink now being swept away on the river of crusaders. He dared not let it move too far without him, for fear it melt, disintegrate, a miraculous mirage born of his own wishful thinking. 'Here,' he said thrusting the money into Kadija's hand. 'Take lodgings in Vitry where we passed through. Don't trade. Nothing risky. Don't trade at all, I mean. You can live on this. There'll be more: I'll come back rich and we'll be household - Foicelles' household. Say, if you're asked, that you're of Foicelles' household. Under his protection, you hear? They won't dare lay a finger on you. Didn't I say he was a good man? Didn't I say he liked me? Didn't I say he'd take me back?' His fingers scratched agitatedly in the bear's chest-fur and his other hand he cupped around the baby's head. 'Don't let any bastard lie with you, nor draw you on to mumming or dancing. You're household now.' The baby began to cry at the stridence of his voice and the tightness of his grip on her head. The river of humanity snagged at his back; he let it tumble him away from wife and child.

She only said, by way of reply to his continuing babble of instructions: 'Live, please.'

And he forgot, what she did not, that Amaury of Herm would also answer the King's call and journey into Outremer.

CHAPTER SEVEN

Ida

And did she rise up from the dead? Did she?' Oriole asked, and instantly regretted it.

The soft-jawed, enthusiastic face steeled over a little. Then Sir Jocelyn drew up the drooping hair from his temples, and said, 'Yes! Yes! In a manner of speaking she did! God answers all prayers. Yes, of course she did. Yes!' He put out a paternally soothing hand. For a moment Oriole thought Jocelyn was going to lie to him. 'God bound up my broken heart and made love rise like Phoenix from the ashes. He sent me a new love.'

Oriole cursed his stupidity. He ought to have known from the pink. New livery, new love. So Lily was still lying lost in the long grass, under the rain dripping, painted angels who must have exchanged their bright livery by now for mildew and bird lime.

'She is the acme of all wonder,' Sir Jocelyn said.

'Of course. But what's her name?' asked Oriole, not

for the first time.

Foicelles lifted the thinning blondness of his forelock again and let it fall wistfully. 'I've not declared myself yet. I won't press myself forward till I've given her some grounds for a good opinion of me.'

'Yes, but does she have a name, at all?' asked Oriole.

'Ida. Her name is Ida.'

Oriole waited. 'But she has a title too, I'm sure.' He knew the names of various great ladies who had copied Queen Eleanor's example and joined the Crusade: Torqueri of Bouillon, Faydide of Toulouse. But Ida?

'Ida of Bamberg,' whispered Jocelyn all of a sudden, his eyes manically full of candlelight. 'She is the Lady Ida of Bamberg."

"I'm honoured you entrust me with the secret, sir,' Oriole whispered back. 'I will protect it.' But all he could think was, *She's German. Not even French. Bloody German.*

The French army was following on a fortnight behind the Germans - through the Balkans, towards the Danube. The vanguard led by Emperor Conrad had ravaged and pillaged their way through the countryside antagonising every peasant, burgher and farmyard dog, with the result that the French, following on behind, had to thread their way between a hostile population and starve for want of anything left to forage. One entire division of Germans had decided to go on a Crusade all their own, and turned aside to slaughter the Wends east of the Elbe. Oriole had a low opinion of Germans.

'You shan't rejoice in a sight of her till we catch up to the Emperor's forces, then, sir.'

'Not a glimpse. But you shall! You'll see her!'

'I'm sorry?'

'You shall have the joy of seeing her in my place! You shall go to and fro between us: to and fro with verse and song and gifts and ... '

'To and fro, sir?' Between the armies? Across enemy territory? Oriole's head cleared abruptly.

'To deliver my poetry, yes. And this.'

He drew from under his truckle cot a sparse wreath of laurel leaves, such as might be worn by a threadbare Caesar. 'Only it's not finished yet. I'll pass you the loose leaves and you can weave them in. I lack the fingers, you know. And while you do that, I'll teach you the words of my salutation ... '

Oriole thought he would go blind by morning. In the candlelight the lozenged dark was impossible to tell apart from the dark green bay leaves. Afterwards, whenever he practised Foicelles' song to get it by heart, he could smell the scent of crushed bay leaves, and the pupils of his eyes would contract and dilate involuntarily.

There were none of the big battle-horses to spare for Oriole's journey; he could not have ridden one if there were. Foicelles came by a post-horse, however, and armed with the laurel wreath and a single poem committed to memory, Oriole was sent on in advance of the French army to deliver his master's compliments to the Lady Ida.

'Is she truly making the journey all alone? Unprotected?' asked Oriole, impressed.

'Absolutely! A woman alone, pitting herself against a sea of Saracens, trusting only in her Saviour ... And her husband, of course.'

Oriole plunged in his heels and clung on, as his horse carved a path through cursing infantry, swaying litters and nodding knights dozing in the saddle.

It was a long time before he remembered how to breathe normally, for his heart was tucked up under his lungs, and the thud of the saddle jarred all his lights. He felt magnificent, an instrument of Chivalry, riding alone into unknown Byzantium, but it shook the bowels within him.

Many chevaliers had found the leisurely progress of the French army stupefying, hampering, and had pushed on ahead at their own speed. For several days, Oriole overtook clumps and companies of Frenchmen and was able to camp with them at night - even earn himself supper by singing and playing the flute.

He crossed the Danube at Branitchevo, however, the sole passenger in the ferryboat, and the days between there and Sofia were spent crossing a landscape peopled only by cedars and olive trees. Then all of a sudden, there were signs of damage - like the aftermath of an electrical storm in which lightning has struck here, struck there, with irrational accuracy. A field was charred black. A house was burned out but still smoking. Shortly afterwards he found a German earl lying unburied on the side of the road. He was still clutching a winesack, though the wine had all bled away. To judge by the man's expression, he had been too drunk to protest at the cutting of his own throat.

All at once Oriole felt vulnerable and isolated, watched by hidden eyes. He kicked his horse on to a trot, to a canter: it broke into a gallop of its own accord. Together they flogged on through the ruinous wake of twenty thousand Germans. And though an arrow once passed between his reins and saddle and left its fletches in his cloak, he was too weary to summon up the terror warranted. Later, he told himself He would be scared later, when there was leisure for such luxuries. He set his mind on Byzantium.

Byzantium! The word alone was onomatopoeic of mystery, beauty and myth. The Hellespont. The Thracian Plain.

But when Oriole reached the Thracian Plain, the sky over it was black with rain. A drenching drizzle scribbled out all trace of twenty thousand men and left only the shape of trees like blind lumbering giants shrouded in gabardine. The ground was slip-glazed with mud. Sometimes it even seemed to be moving, or his horse to be drifting sideways through it. Any remaining high spirits trickled down him in rivulets and gushed off the corners of his stirrups. But he could not turn back. He represented his master, and must imitate the behaviour of a knight.

He knew he ought to fix his mind on Ida of Bamberg or the Virgin Mary. And yet every time he curled up in his cloak to sleep, every time he woke up soaked to the skin, he thought of Kadija instead. He could not help it. He thought of creeping in under their mutual mound of clothes and blankets, of finding his way, like the cold, in under her various layers. The more he thought of her, the more he feared not seeing her again, feared dying.

Take this plain, for instance - a swirling morass of mud intent on undermining his horse and spilling him into a yellow drowning. It had already taken prisoner weeds, tussocks, twigs, rotten fruit, drowned rabbits, tent poles, canvas, cooking pots...

A soldier's helmet came spinning down the flood like a miniature coracle and behind it came the owner, more slowly, face down, showing the shaved back of his neck to the sky.

Oriole thought at first that a graveyard had been ploughed up by the rain and the dead been spilled into the open air. But then more and more of the corpses cried out to him - clambered to their feet, fell and picked themselves up again, yelling, *'Hilte! Hilte!'* through bursting bubbles of brown filth. One came down the incline on hands and knees, carried along like a craven frog on a lily pad of viscous brown slime. He made a snatch at Oriole's dangling reins, but the horse shied away out of reach and left him to fall flat again, spread-eagled in a mire of exhaustion and mud.

The flood had come down on them at night - a sudden inundation like God's requitement. Emperor Conrad, raised up on the higher ground of God's good opinion was untouched but had to look down helplessly while a torrent of mud swept Thrace clean of Germans like Hercules cleansing the Augean Stables. Pieces of armour were indistinguishable from cooking utensils, knights from their squires, infantry from their whores. Here and there a single hand reached out of the ground as if to beg for a last wage to spend in Hell.

In trying to help a fallen man to his feet, Oriole was pulled from the saddle, and when he tried to remount, found his feet too swollen with clogs of mud to fit the stirrup. So he wallowed under his horse's neck, half-dangling from the harness. Their faces blotted out by liquid clay, their hands too slippery to grip, they choked and snorted and retched the mud out of their noses, mouths, stomachs and lungs, blind men excavating for their own eyes. At every man Oriole shouted, 'Where's the Lady Ida of Bamberg? Have you seen the Lady Ida of Bamberg?' bellowing in their faces, shaking them like dead otters, gaining as much response as if they *were* dead otters.

'Oh please, blessed Mary! Don't let her be dead!' gasped Oriole, hooking his fingers into the cheek-straps of his horse to keep upright in the mire. He could feel the slurry swill down the inside of his clothing gathering in his crotch, cramming the legs of his hose, oozing wormy through the knitted stitches. 'Not like this, Mary! Not like this! For the sake of the songs I've sung you, Mother Mary, don't let the Lady Ida be drowned!'

A woman's double skirt flowered like the green leaves of giant dig weed rising out of the morass. He had begun to ladle slurry off her face with cupped hand before he remembered: he was not looking for skirts at all, but for armour and sword. This was no lady crusader - only a camp-follower with a linen cross sewn to her stomacher. In extricating himself, Oriole left his shoes in the mud and had to go on barefoot.

He did not find her, of course. By God's grace, but more particularly by right of birth, the Lady Ida had been camped on higher ground, close to the Emperor when the rains came.

He found her, at last, in Constantinople, a guest at the Blachernae Palace on the banks of the Hellespont. Gauzy curtains streamed out in the warm evening air. Domes gleamed with gold and the tints of a sunset sky. Even news of the mudslide could not diminish Ida's delight in the exotic glamour of her surroundings.

The Lady Ida's face was a long silver spoon oxidised by dark shadows around her forehead and jaw. Her bottom lip protruded marginally ahead of the top one, so that she looked slightly bellicose, and showed her bottom teeth when she spoke. They held Oriole mesmerised, those sharp little teeth masticating her words before she spoke them.

Devoted to fashion, she already wore the Byzantine clothes of Emperor Manuel's court - a man's bulbous turban and shoes with long malicious beaks that grated their gold-wire embroidery along the floor. After Oriole had sung to her, she asked him to sit beside her on a marble bench, and enjoy the view. She drew him close in a maternal way, bouncing her clenched knees up and down as though she were dangling a child on her lap.

'And when your master me saw?' she asked.

'Oh, I don't know. In France, certainly in France. Definitely in France.'

'Often in Germany I am not,' she said, apparently contemptuous of her own birthplace.

'Do you not recall meeting him? He carries one of your boots for a favour. I thought you must have ... '

'Ah! So this is thief! Very big nuisance that. To lose a boot. He must buy me new. Tell him.' Then she patted his chest encouragingly. 'How long? How long your master luff me?'

'Oh, I'm sorry. I don't know.'

'Or what friends we both know?'

'No. I'm sorry.'

'What a lot about your master you not know.'

'I regret ... He keeps his love as secret as possible, of course.'

'No matter. This you can me tell. A good face, his?'

'Oh yes, ma'am! As handsome as Chivalry and pale as Love!' She raised her eyebrows.

'How nice. You through many danger come to song me sing.'

'I' Oriole sheered away from the marble bench as someone else entered the cavernous atrium of the Blachernae Palace.

Uc of Bamberg, sumptuous in a robe of red and gold, bellowed from the far end of the promenade. He had been dressed by his host as a token of honour and was unaccustomed to flowing linens round his legs. Accordingly he minced towards them slowly. Oriole spent the time wondering how to explain why he was there. The Lady Ida solved his dilemma. She announced, 'Husband, this is jongleur of French troubadour who in luff with me is. Though I never him saw. Do you want boy his song again to sing? He is very good.'

Her husband's top lip was fat, its length exaggerated by a fierce moustache; it was impossible to judge its expression. Lord Uc drew from his sleeve one of the many curios he had 'collected' from around the Imperial Palace. Oriole could not quite make out its purpose, though it looked like a table knife, with prongs in place of a blade. Fortunately it was not well made, or was smithed out of some soft precious metal, for when Uc stabbed him in the arm with it, it immediately bent.

'He can sing what he likes,' Uc told his wife, 'so long as he sings it to some other man's wife. Otherwise, I'll split him to the balls.' He glanced down at the bent fork and threw it away over the parapet into the evening purple of the Hellespont. Then he left, trailing behind him a peculiarly effeminate smell of oriental perfume.

'Pay no heed!' the Lady Ida called out loudly when Uc had gone. 'I do as I please. Come.'

She gripped him by the biceps and he did not like to flinch or draw attention to the holes the fork had made. Then she kissed him with dry, rather scratchy lips, which closed over his mouth, touching first below then above. 'Your master, he come when he want.'

The Germans billeted in Phillopatium Palace stripped it so bare that afterwards it was unfit for habitation. Then they began to insult, rob and murder the local residents. So Emperor Manuel invited the German Crusade to go, to press on, with all speed, on its holy mission, and heaved a sigh of relief when they were gone. Oriole stayed behind to await Sir Jocelyn.

The knight listened eagerly to how well his poetry had been received, not so attentively to the mention of Sir Uc and his threats. (Oriole did not mention the fork: it seemed unheroic to do so.) Told of the kiss, Sir Jocelyn gasped, drew back his blond forelock, closed his eyes, and pushed forward his face. Confused for a moment, Oriole realised that he was intended to pass on the gift, just as he had passed on Ida's words.

Nervous, embarrassed, wondering if his breath was stale, he leaned forward and closed his lips over Foicelles', awkward, clumsy, trying to invest the kiss with some of the affection and admiration he felt the original ought to have contained. Years after, the rim of his lips could remember the taste and texture of Jocelyn's skin, salty with the sweat of exultation. As their mouths parted, Foicelles' blue eyes opened wide, sudden, staring, a hand's thickness from his own. The lover groaned his ecstasy.

'You shall go to her again! The verse is already hatching in my brain!'

> My love is for a distant, unseen bird
> And the sweet warbling of her voice
> Across the great greenness of a valley heard,
> Making my pure soul rejoice.
> My pulses rise, like a dreamer stirred,
> Or traveller at a crossroad's choice ... '

Ida was delighted with the song and even more with its delivery. She called Oriole over to her and gave him a drink of water from a little silver cup she had purloined in Constantinople. She was eating a sweet-roll which she dipped in the water and sucked, her eyes fixed on his.

Alongside her sat her husband.

The journey between armies this time had tasted of grit, curranty with flies. Dust and dung left behind by the great horses. Oriole was thirsty and aching from crossing a desert. The desert had been full of the temptation to turn back. He did not want to be here. But Foicelles' poetry must be delivered, no matter what: no matter that his legs shook with fright and his mouth was too dry to sing well.

Around Ida's tent was the cacophony of an army striking camp for a tenth day's ride through Turcoman territory. 'You should have gold,' she said. 'But these Greek rubbish - pah! Not value a tinker's shit.' And she threw a handful of coins in the air and swatted them like flies. She had not yet slipped her arms into her mail coat and it hung down round her waist so that her white wadding undercoat appeared to burst like a cotton boll from an armoured stem. Her big breasts pushed against the wadding, cradled in crescents of sweat. 'Sing to us all nights you can! Nobodies here can sing. Not a body.' She pressed the wet sweet-roll unexpectedly against Oriole's mouth and he bit into it awkwardly and closed his teeth round her finger. She withdrew the finger and sucked it, smiling, without complaint.

Unfortunately, Lord Uc of Bamberg was not a man sensitive to the nuances of a finely tuned poem. He only knew that Oriole had defied him. Throughout the song he had sat deep in a canvas field-stool, the canvas wrapped so close round his thighs that he looked suspended in a bo'sun's chair, and grunted like a dispeptic pig. Now he stood up and folded the seat flat with a deafening crack. 'Why didn't he come himself, your man?'

'He is a *distant admirer*, sir, with no impure ambitions!'

Uc kicked apart his camp cot and was left trailing a blanket round one leg.

'I'm just a voice, sir! Song and flute, that's all I am,' and Oriole held up his flute as if it denoted the slightness of his presence.

Uc snatched it and broke it in two, pushed Oriole over and set one foot on his stomach. He bent low over the boy, making great show of pretending to recognise him afresh. 'Didn't I tell you not to come near us a second time?'

'Ah, leave him,' said Ida, half-heartedly.

'I'm only the servant of my master's wishes. He didn't think, when you'd heard his song ...'

Uc kicked him in the ribs; a blow that emptied him of wind and words.

'You don't understand, sir! My master doesn't ...'

Uc kicked him in the stomach, a blow that emptied him of wind and water and sweet-roll. 'Still want to stay and sing to my wife?'

Oriole raised himself to his hands and knees and looked to the lady for her protection. She was holding the tips of her fingers between her teeth, but when he looked her way she gave him a bright, blithe smile. Her hopes had all been gratified. She had won.

'I know you come! Uc and me, we make wager, yes? He say you dare not. I say, "Boy will come! French are civilised. French are Romantic!" And here you come! Good boy. Luffly boy.' A servant came to pack away her chair. She hurriedly pushed her arms through her mail sleeves and shrugged the byrnys over her shoulders, tangling her hair in it. The walls of the tent collapsed round them and the sunlight came in, sharp as pain. A squire stood holding Uc's horse by the bridle, in readiness for the day's ride. A willow tree overhung the River Bathys. It was a pleasant place, a watering place.

Uc delivered a kick to Oriole's rump which sent him skidding on his face into the pile of tent poles. 'Now I'll show your master what I think of him.'

Oriole saw now how completely he represented the person of Sir Jocelyn, though the honour had pretty much broken his back. He lay on his side, curled up against the blows. And the ground shook with the movement of the army, eight thousand men stirring themselves: donkeys and horses and carts. He wanted to say, 'I'm not a knight, I'm a singer - just a go-between.' But he was not. While he had the man's words inside him, he was the embodiment of the man. Jocelyn's verses rattled inside his head like stones in a box.

Uc snatched up a length of rope and tied a noose into it which he looped over Oriole's two hands before mounting his huge destrier. 'When I'm done with you,' said Uc, 'there'll be a message writ large for your lecher of a poet to read. I write my lines in good red blood. Needn't think you can pull free. I tie a good knot.' And he jabbed his spurs into his horse's flanks so that blood showed through the hair.

The Lady Ida looked on with radiant eyes, not through simple love of cruelty, but because she had won her bet. Also, a French knight had been prepared to expend the life of his finest minstrel on her, by way of a compliment.

Oriole could see the ground over which he would be dragged - its yellow rocks, its cacti, its litter of weapons. And all at once he thought of the Languedoc and its blood-red earth and wanted to shed his blood there, not here. He thought of Amaury with sentimental affection - a knight who actually *wanted* the women he pursued, not simply to worship them from afar. He opened his mouth and he called on God for help.

But the Infidels came instead.

CHAPTER EIGHT

The Lie

All of a sudden, like a flowerhead closing in hail, the German army was contracting towards the river. The infantry came pressing round the cavalry with an unthinkable intimacy, their communal smell over whelming the sweet odour of horses. Knights looked around for their squires, for an explanation, and found only dirty faces and rank mouths shouting, 'They're on us! Quick! They're on us! Thousands of them!'

The Turks came mounted on little horses that made the destriers look elephantine, stuffed. They were gone before the archers had even unpacked their arrows. They were gone before the heralds could sound an alarm. And when they were gone there were archers and heralds lying dead on the ground, startled to death by the flash of sun on brightly fletched arrows.

Next time they came, there was time to comprehend

the strength of their numbers. How could so many mounted men have mustered unseen in the small cover of the desert? How could such low hills have hidden such huge numbers? How could such a wilderness have prospered these thousands of men and horses while the Germans panted and starved? Knights not yet mounted trampled the riverbank into mud then sank in it up to their knees. Meanwhile, the Turkish cavalry cut through the infantry like hedgers - first the nettles, then the hedge.

Uc, at least, was in his saddle, but his plate armour was off, his head bare, and he had no lance or sword. Still, he snatched a pike from a pikeman and the axe which hung from his saddle by a leather cuff. His spurs tore tussocks of hair out of his horse's flank.

'Uc! Uc, lift me up!' Ida called, scrambling nimbly up the bank. The great danger was to be caught on the ground: only a horse can outrun horses. But Uc could not hear her above the din of an army caught unaware: the discordant trumpets, the screaming horses, the orders no one knew how to follow or in which direction. Every time the Turks came on, the congregation on the river bank contracted like a pair of lungs. Less and less could it regain its breath.

Very quickly, the land over which he had meant to drag Oriole was dense with people; the jongleur was one figure among many, signifying nothing any longer. Uc forgot the excellent knots fastening the rope to the pommel of his saddle and was intent only on getting armour, getting arms.

But he was pushing on all the time, driving his horse on through crowds of fleeing footsoldiers, opposing the rush of men towards the river. In proper pitched battle this was never the way of it - the cavalry impeded by the infantry. Always the destriers were up in front, the rank and file loafing a mile behind. But here were pikes and standards and longbows and clubs all wagging in his face, and a sea of panic to wade through.

As for Oriole, he ran like a rabbit through a stand of corn, weaving between, swerving round, his arms at full stretch and his eyes fixed on the huge rump of the knight's horse. He was just managing to keep the rope from tangling. Like a ship's log thrown over the stern, he was towed along in the wake of Lord Uc, whose excellent knots still held. And he was amazed to see the blood reddening the rope around his wrists, for he could feel nothing but terror.

The entire Turkish army came down on Bathys, and gouged the German soul from its corporate German body with sharp-bladed excisions. The horseless knights stuck knee-deep in the river .mud somehow contrived to stay standing, but their heads lay at their feet and their souls were up among the starlings in the treetops.

Two horsemen closed on Uc from opposing sides, and though he piked one out of his saddle and went to split the other with the axe, he found his back swing impeded by a length of rope unaccountably stretching from his pommel. The knots were far too good to slip. While Uc cursed, the second rider loosed an arrow into him at point blank range. At last Uc disentangled the axe and dispatched the archer, but several iron mail-rings stitched to his shirt were by then embedded, along with the arrowhead, deep inside his ribcage.

When Uc fell from its back, his warhorse was both

lightened of his weight and panicked by its freedom. It found the energy to bolt, and Oriole, transfixed by the death he had just seen, was finally jerked off his feet and dragged behind the destrier.

Like a sea-anchor he was dragged, across a broken seabed strewn with wrecks and drowned souls. First scuffing along on his face, then whip-cracking on his back, he cannoned into the corpse of Lord Uc which in turn tripped a pikeman whose crashing bulk garnered in two and three more fallen men. And all the while, Uc's excellent knots held. The aggregate weight brought the bolting horse up on to its hind legs and turned it over backwards. The pommel broke off the saddle and recoiled with such force it would have killed Oriole had it hit him. But he was safely buried under a crushing accumulation of bodies and battlefield rubbish. By the time he had extricated himself and freed his hands, the horse had rolled from its side on to its belly and was scrabbling with all four legs at the shaly, treacherous ground.

He half-ran, half-threw himself at the ungainly animal, flung himself full length across the broken saddle and sank his fingers and teeth in the mane. So when the horse found its feet again, Oriole was astride it. It hardly seemed an advantage, but his only thought was to be up off the ground, up out of the dead and the caking earth. Now, not just green cactus heads were pushing up from the ground, but handfuls of fingers and facefuls of eyes. Hell's magma was welling up red through the soil.

The ground receded to an immense distance. The destrier stood twenty hands high - so tall that there was an illusion of being separate from events below him, superior to them. But with his legs stretched like a wishbone to breaking point by the huge girth and his brain jarred by the clumsy gait, he had no control. The horse took him back the way he had come, blundering through spinneys of unclaimed lances, cutting through Gordian knots of infantry, prancing sideways without the least regard for what was underfoot. Its head sawed up and down, up and down, so that the reins wrenched on Oriole's arms as the rope had done. Stupid for its safety, it plunged down into the river and raised a curtain of drenching spray, a bow-wave that set the corpses in the river rolling over and over.

No sooner was the horse out of its depth than it recollected its honour. For it seemed to want to turn back for the shore rather than drift aimlessly on the current. The light on the water was all knives, cutting Oriole's vision to shreds as he looked about him for a bolt hole. He could see the selfsame willow which had stood near Ida's tent. Or perhaps it was another, for only the trees remained stationary while the two armies heaved to and fro beneath them.

Archers began shooting at him. What? Did they suppose, because he was on horseback, that he warranted costly arrows fletched from coloured birds? They hummed through the air like rare breeds; they sped through the water like lampreys. He wanted to stand up on his saddle and show himself for what he was - not worth the expense of a rusty penknife. But he could not see the archers who had him in their sights: the river was too bright. All he could see was the green willow tree, hunched over the water, hunched perhaps over the Lady Ida.

He ought to return to her. *In loco Foicelles*, he ought

to go to her aid. But it was the notion of hiding among those dense green leaves that in fact made him desert his horse and flounder neck-deep towards the shore, spitting and gasping and sobbing for breath, just touching bottom with his toes, just staying upright by snatching at desperate handfuls of water. He tiptoed across the slimy river. What things were in the water? What unholy leeches, contagions or monsters? What venomous snakes or tentacled plants hungry for Christian blood? By the time he reached the shallows, even the willow leaves were green fingers in the water congealing onto his skin. He would have scrabbled up on to the bank and shaken himself like a dog if the bank had not been busy with the traffic of war. Instead he crouched in waist-deep water, the fingering willow dangling round his shoulders and his head entirely still.

The Lady Ida stood a short way off, against the trunk of the tree. She too had crawled there, hoping that its tent of shadow and leaves would hide her from the Turks. But as each paroxysm of battle sent men running by, then horses in pursuit of them, they brushed off leaves. A glint of sun on metal and a seldjuk turned aside to make the kill. Oriole saw it all.

She stood so close to the willow, her long wet hair stuck to its bark, her forearms and calves dark brown with mud, that she looked like a nymph half-translated into tree. The rider paused to adjust his eyes to the shade, his mind to the novelty. He was not in mail or armour, simply baggy, dirty clothing and sandals, his head bound up in a turban, a square or two of hide strapped on for protection.

'*Ich bin ein frau!*' she screamed at him. And she drew her sword - her silly imitation of a sword, with hollow tin blade - and threw it aside into the river. Though the splash entered his eyes, Oriole did not move. '*Ich bin ein frau!*' she shrieked and ripped open her wadding to show her breasts.

The seldjuk reached back and drew from his saddle a stout little throwing spear. He drove it in, underarm, just below her sternum, urging his horse forward until its wagging nose was nudging Ida's face. Until then, her wet hair clinging to the bark held her head upright. But now it lolled forward, as if to inspect the wound in her stomach.

The Turk was unable to withdraw his spear: it had sunk too deep into the willow's trunk. He dismounted rather than give it up. Besides, a mail byrnys was too valuable a prize to forego. He grunted slightly as he struggled to peel it down over the dead woman's hips.

'*She was a woman! She told you she was a woman!*' yelled Oriole, bringing the tin sword down repeatedly on the back of the seldjuk's neck. First it bent, finally it snapped in two, but he went on driving the broken end in, between hide and turban, until he had no more breath. The river water in his clothes ran down, trickled down, soaked down his body from head to foot, and made his boots too heavy to lift. He knew that he was as brown as an Infidel, silt-blackened and smelling of slime.

After the tide of battle had swept by, drowned half the German army, and shifted ground, Oriole climbed down from his hiding place in the topmost branches of the willow. He took the boots off the seldjuk he had killed and set them down beside the Lady Ida. He could not think of any other tribute. He might have sung one of Jocelyn's lovesongs, but the words, when he looked, had entirely gone from his head.

Plague or camp fever could have achieved the same as the Turks. There was no outrage of grief, no puzzlement at the slaughter. There was maybe just the smallest surprise that God, having bothered to summon so many men to take up the Cross, should not have even let them get as far as the Holy Lands. First the landslide, then the massacre. And they were barely into Outremer. Perhaps God, like the French, hated Germans.

The two armies rejoined back at Nicaea and set off again taking the more cautious coastal route. The remnants of the Germans (nine-tenths were dead) fell in behind and were jeered and denied rations by the Franks and Alsatians who wagged obscene gestures and shouted, 'Fuck the Germans,' all the way to Ephesus.

So the French knight, driving his horse against the flow of traffic, through the limping German ranks, was cursed and grabbed at, and his boots spat on. But Sir Jocelyn was oblivious to all but his panic. He asked after the Lord Uc but no one could give him a civil answer. He asked after his jongleur, but what was one jongleur among seven thousand dead? Jocelyn's unshaven head, his pink livery, his unbloodied sword all invited derision, but he only pushed on through them, his grey taking reprisals with its big, shag-hocked hooves.

Oriole saw him coming long before he was himself seen. He saw the grey bumping and boring its way towards him. But Oriole did not immediately wave his livery over his head and shout.

What news had he got that Jocelyn could possibly want to hear? Ida's death and the manner of it? Oriole was a go-between now from beyond the grave, and he knew just what gratitude he would get for delivering such news.

'And what did you do? What was your part in my lady's death?'

'I stood in the water up to my neck and watched her stuck like a pig.'

It would not do. It would not do at all. After making up his mind to that, Oriole pulled off his liveried tabard and raised it aloft on a borrowed spear. The dirty Foicelles escutcheon was barely recognisable, flagging down its owner.

Sir Jocelyn de Foicelles kicked off his stirrups, leapt off his horse and caught up his jongleur in his arms. Onlookers assumed it was father and child, but had they had the interest to look closer they would have seen barely six years between the two. 'Tell me! Tell me, boy! Tell me! Is she here? Is she safe? Have you seen her? Did she come through?'

'No, sir.'

'You mean you haven't seen her! Did she split off with the pilgrims, then? Did she go the safe route with Freisingen?'

What a temptation there was in that! To say that she might be safe, and postpone the sorrow.

'No, sir. She didn't go with the pilgrims.'

They stood in the lee of the mare, the moving stream of survivors parting and passing by to either side. They were not barged or buffeted. There was a strange stillness in that slack water behind the horse.

'What then? Is she gone? Have I lost her? Has God taken her?' The hard rim of his open mouth trembled as he lifted his wilting forelock of hair over and over and over again. He lifted his face towards the sky as though he were below water, a drowning man without hope of swimming up to gasp another breath. The tears poured down his cheeks: a phenomenon of tears so sudden and free-flowing as to rouse thoughts of miraculous springs. With unprecedented presumption, Oriole took hold of Jocelyn's face between two hands and looked him in the eye.

'Yes, master. She's gone. She's lost to you ... But in such a way! The angels will stoop like eagles to scavenge for tokens of her.' He had decided on the nature of his lie.

'The last time I saw her she was unhorsed, twelve lances all broken and her mare's heart burst with the vigour of the fight. But she'd found herself a high place - a rock - a kind of bluff. And with none behind and her buckler in front, nor archer nor horseman could find a mark. Still, there was no escape. Around her was a sea of sabres slicing through the sunbeams till the place was black as night. And only she the moon. All white. Her sword made of some stuff - I never saw the like - for though it must have carved through fifty heads of hair and pierced a half-hundred hearts, there wasn't a shred of gore to show for it. They thought they were seeing a knight, or the ghost of a knight.

'Over the heads of the cavalry she saw one rider, taller than the rest, and all in black. We all saw him. Afterwards I heard his kingdom was a thousand miles of desert sand in Egypt. I heard the title - "sheik" - but as for the name, well, I was at such a distance ... '

'Go on,' said Sir Jocelyn. He was sitting cross-legged on the floor of his Ephesian billet, while his jongleur stood balanced precariously on the sill of the window to illustrate the last plight of the Lady of Bamberg. Here was no private lie; no lie made in confidence between consenting friends. The knights of King Louis were crammed into some long, dormitory cavern: the kind of place Saint Paul might well have used to harangue unbelievers. The large audience both terrified and incited Oriole to greater extravagancies.

'When they saw him, this sheik, a kind of quiet settled - like when a king enters court. And when she saw him, it was as though a dart of lightning passed from her eye and rocked him in his saddle. She threw her sword high in the air and I swear every eye was fixed on it! She whirled it by its hilt till she was nothing but a blaze of light, like Catherine on her fiery wheel! Then she cast it aside, saying no man should take it from her ... No! Didn't hear. I saw her lips move. But I swear my soul was in such thrall to her that I read the words in her face.'

Sir Jocelyn nodded. He too was able to read the words on the lips of the lady besieged, even though the distance between them was ever so far. The other knights, sitting on their cloaks, their faces occasionally turning away, might not have quite such vision, but they were listening, none the less.

'When he saw her show-of-arms, I swear the sheik was so filled with the passion of envy that he swore no one but he should despatch the knight on the bluff. And the ranks parted for him - like Moses through the Red Sea - and he levelled a lance and he kicked up his horse to a charge!'

Sir Jocelyn threw himself full length on the floor, his forehead on the tiles.

'That was when she did it. Unmanned a thousand men. For she opened her doublet and showed them her breasts - white as the milk within, with nipples as pink as her livery. A thousand men caught their breath and cried out - they had not realised it before - *This is a woman!*'

Oriole sank down on the edge of the sill, crouching with his knees round his ears and his hands outstretched. Foicelles' face emerged from the rushes. The rest of the room held utterly still.

'Then the black lance shattered against the rock at her feet and splintered into a thousand pieces. And the sheik said, "This woman's death would be burning of Baby Ion's gardens! The fall of the Alhambra! This woman I must have, to breed me a race of heroes and to seer my body like the sands at noon. These breasts shall be my pillows and I shall give my sword into her keeping!" Then he pulled her down and had her covered with a veil, and swore an oath that none but he and the eunuchs of his harem should ever glimpse her again.'

Oriole counted to ten. Then he counted to ten again. He was a musician, after all, and instinct told him how many bars of rest should separate crescendo from coda.

'So. The lady is gone into the harem of the Black Sheik. Naked forever, and forever forced to yield the secrets of her body to a blood soaked infidel,' said Oriole.

Foicelles began to retch, quietly and restrainedly at first so that a boy was able to run for a basin - then with greater and greater momentum, ignoring the boy and the basin because he was unwilling to take his eye off Oriole.

'Ah, but the secret of her heart - that's different. There are grilles raised up around that which the sheik will never break down - not though he live to be as old as Abraham and father whole tribes on her!'

The boy brought a hot wet cloth, and Foicelles buried his face in it and wiped and wiped until it seemed he would wash away all his features. When he looked up at last there was a rosy redness to his cheeks and he looked healthier than he had for years. His voice was level, too, and calm. 'What were the secrets in her heart, Oriole? Did she trust them to you? Was I there among them? Or did I come too late?'

Oriole counted to ten, to twenty, this time to thirty, taking the tempo from his own heartbeat. 'Oh, you were there, sir. Between her honour and her Lord. Like Christ on the mountainside. Transfigured by Love.' He slipped down off the sill and received Foicelles' embrace like Thomas embracing the risen Christ after all shreds of doubt had been dispelled. The unbearable was made bearable. She who had been dead was alive again. Oriole had bound up the broken-hearted.

And how was the Lady Ida any the worse off for that?

Then, at the rear of the room, a pair of hands began to clap - such explosive, resounding cracks that Oriole flinched from the noise before he flinched from the implication: sardonic, mocking, derisive applause, like axe blows to the foundations of his story.

Heads turned in the direction of the noise. Oriole searched for it, scanned and scoured the sea of faces. By the time he actually picked out the red hair, the bristling beard, the green eyes, Oriole had already guessed that it was Amaury of Herm. Amaury winked at him, grinned broadly and called out, 'A tale well told. Bravo. Bravissimo! I wish I'd kept you with me now, to tell me stories on a winter's night.'

Oriole looked between the two knights - Jocelyn weeping into his shirtsleeves, propped against the wall; Amaury, smug, complacent, pitiless. There was a faint hope that Foicelles would be too grief-stricken to hear the implication of lying.

'Seems I lost myself a talented raconteur when I let you go, Songbird. Any chance I can buy him back, Foicelles? I know I'd be forcing my luck to hope you'd give me the same gift twice over - or do all your gifts home like pigeons?'

'You cast me off, sir!' protested Oriole, though it felt futile: to defend the truth having just perverted it.

'What are you saying, sir?' Jocelyn emerged slowly from his cocoon. 'That you have claims on my minstrel?'

'Don't listen to him, sir! Don't listen. He's joking. He's always joking!'

Amaury seemed to toy with the idea of staking a claim to the jongleur, then to toss it aside in a surfeit of ennui. 'No, no. Oriole and I parted good friends, didn't we, Songbird? Well, I even found him a jolly little black wife out of my household to keep him ... company. How is she these days? Karima. Kardoma.'

'Kadija, sir. A good Christian, sir and a varied talent. Thrifty, too.'

Amaury broke off from what he had been going to say and looked at Peter Oriole with genuine astonishment. He had never for a moment imagined it persisting - that pantomime marriage mounted for the sake of an afternoon's laughter. It seemed to inspire a kind of admiration ... and thus to remind him and bring him full circle to the reason for his applause. 'Well, Songbird, if you ever tire of that flamingo livery, I've always got room for a man who can tell a fine fiction. You put a shine on that piece of tin, you truly did.'

Jocelyn's mailed fist shot out and rapped him on the breastplate. Amaury looked down and let his eyes connect the blow incredulously with the three-pronged hand. 'Come in?' he said, condescending.

'Have a care, sir. You're on dangerous ground.'

'Am I?' said Amaury ingenuously. 'Oh, then I must find myself a lady crusader to frighten off my foe by baring her breasts.'

'I warn you, sir!' Jocelyn's was the reflex fury of a man already on the edge of hysteria. But Oriole felt only a howling, uncomprehending bewilderment: that anyone could be so wicked, so devoid of pity, so lacking in brotherhood towards a stricken knight! That anyone could demolish such a harmless, necessary lie. How he hated those wide opened green eyes, that ear turned with such affected attention to hear how he had offended.

'What? Are you telling me it was *true* - that excellent piece of prose?'

Amaury asked in tones of amazement. 'An eye-witness account? No! God strike me! That history should so oblige the cause of poetry! These are truly wonderful times we live in, aren't they?'

Jocelyn drew his sword, and the overcrowded billet erupted with knights making room, getting clear. 'Are you calling my boy a liar? Are you saying it happened somehow different? Were you *there?*'

Amaury held up two innocent palms, taking the opportunity to waggle the ten-ness of his fingers. 'Can't a man pay a compliment to a masterly storyteller? A dextrous painter of pictures? Is our science not that of painting with words? The jongleur has real talent; that's all I'm saying.'

Oriole found himself praying to evaporate, to dissolve, to shatter like the preposterous confection of his story. They must not fight. Over the truth of his story? Over the courage and fate of the Lady Ida? On no account must they fight! For God sided with the Truth, no matter how banal. God allowed no margin for embroidery, embellishment, for the well-constructed lie, for the well-meaning liar. If they fought, the victory would go to Herm, who knew a lie when he heard it because he was such a liar himself

'Do you dispute the manner of my lady's capture?' demanded Foicelles with hysterical pomposity. 'Are you calling my boy a liar?'

Oriole wanted to crouch down, to wrap his arms over his head, to swat away the swarms of words. 'Don't, sir! Not on my account!'

It made Foicelles turn on him. 'Well? Are you ready to see it mocked? What happened? There? At Bathys?'

Oriole shut his eyes and saw it all again, as he saw it each time he shut his eyes. The Bathys massacre. 'No, sir. Never ....'

'Draw, then, knight - if you have a name ...'

'Amaury of Herm, sir. Is it your eyesight or your memory that helps you forget it?'

'Draw or I'll kill you where you stand. Find comedy in a lady's death? Forgive me, but since when was grief good fodder for a joke?'

For the first time, the twitching, complacent grin left Herm's face. His mouth disappeared behind its bevor of beard, and he seemed in perfect earnest when he said. 'Ah now, grief. That's different. Rarely grounds for laughter, I agree. Nor for poetical narratives.' He too drew his sword.

'Please, sir!' Oriole broke in, stepping between them, turning his back on Herm. 'All this way, sir! Did you come all this way, sir, on a Holy Crusade, sir, just to end fighting another Frenchman?'

And Herm was there again, agreeing with him. 'The Songbird's right. This is no time for private quarrels. Let's see some sights before we cross swords, Foicelles. No hurry, eh? I'm going nowhere different. We're all together on the same journey. Some of us may even reach home again. Isn't that right, Oriole?'

There were tears in Amaury's eyes.

The assembled company of knights began to harangue Foicelles, telling him, yes; he must wait; the war superseded personal disputes. He stormed out of the room.

But Oriole did not immediately go after him. He stood transfixed to the spot. He did not intend disloyalty. And yet he did not go.

'Your master likes a good fairy tale, I see.'

'Needed, sir. Needed,' he found himself saying.

'And you gave it to him. Well done indeed. Quite masterly.'

Why did Oriole not go? Why did he not spit on Amaury's boots and go? And why were there tears in Amaury's eyes?

'Prefer it myself, sometimes. A good stirring story alongside the truth. Now 'take today. Jaufré Rudel died today, I hear. Rudel? The troubadour? No great story to it. Just an arrow in the gut and septicaemia. You're right. Where's the glory in that? Needs something more. Is that why wars always sound so different in the retelling than they looked at the time? Rudel dead. Nothing more to come out of him but maggots. Yes, I should think up something better next time I tell that one, shouldn't I? Maybe I should leave the job with you? Rudel dead and silent ... '

Oriole felt as if his boots had cleaved to the floor, his tongue to the roof of his mouth. 'He was a great poet,' was all he managed to say. He meant to find some insult, something on behalf of his master. 'A better poet than you,' he ought to have said. And yet when he opened his mouth again, only the truth came out, sounding like a second-rate lie. 'Almost as good as you, sir. I'm very sorry he's dead.'

CHAPTER NINE

Jerusalem

Sir Jocelyn went on believing in the lie. He did not reflect on Amaury's jibes and wonder if perhaps his go-between had exaggerated a little, improved on the Truth out of kindness. No, Oriole escaped all doubt, all cross-examination, all chance to withdraw the lie. For Jocelyn cleaved to it, preserved it word for word.

If that could have been the sum of it, Oriole would not have regretted lying. He might even have congratulated himself on leaving everyone so much happier than the truth would have made them. But it clung to him, that lie.

It was soon after reaching Ephesus that the whole Turkish army mobilised against them. Sir Jocelyn rejoiced in the news. For he said it would give him an opportunity to trample Turkish heads like grapes at harvest time.

When military discipline began to break down in the French army, Sir Jocelyn was the first to help his King re-establish order. Following Louis' example, he cut the hands off looters, the feet off laggards, the heads off deserters, while exhorting the rest to fresh endeavour, swearing that every Christian martyr would be avenged with the death of a thousand Saracens.

When enemy harassment escalated to a full-pitched battle, it was Jocelyn de Foicelles who regarded the billows of Turkish robes, undaunted. There was a sneer of contempt on his face, and his faith surpassed Moses', for he rode directly towards the horizon without waiting for a miracle to clear his path. He scattered all obstacles through the sheer momentum of his charge, by brute force. The weight of hatred inside him impelled him into the thick of battle like a boulder from a trebuchet catapulted clean through fortress walls. The only time his jongleurs and pages caught sight of him was when he came raging out of the press, demanding another lance, another buckler. His horse's mane was hogged short by Turkish short-swords; his own pink ribbons stuck to his armour with sweat or blood, for all the world like strips of skin flayed from the enemy. The nasal of his helmet was bent so out of shape that it rendered his face grotesque, buckled.

Whereas most of the knights fought with a professional indifference to their own safety, not holding anything back for tomorrow, still they could not be said to hate the enemy. There was probably more ill-will between Frank and German, between crusader and Byzantine than between the cavalrymen of opposing sides. But Foicelles was different. He had a score to settle. He was God's flail pounding on the chaff. He used his horse like a battering ram to fell whole stables of Arab ponies, whole tribes of men. He carried his life in his teeth; he cursed and insulted each man he killed, so great was his righteous indignation. Because of the lie Oriole had told him.

It was Jocelyn who forced a firebreak through the forest of Turks and began the reversal which should have seen the Turk crushed against the walls of Pisideon Antioch. And when - by some bizarre diplomatic coup - the enemy disappeared inside the citadel, it was Foicelles who sat astride his winded mare, head thrown back and both fists shaking as he brayed up at Heaven, *'Fire and brimstone! Send fire and brimstone!'* Thus great was his hatred of the Infidel. Because of the lie Oriole had told him.

Well? Would the Truth have led to anything different? Oriole asked himself at first. The enemy had killed the mistress of Jocelyn's heart. Would that not have given rise to just as much wrath and vengeance?

No. For then the Lady Ida would have been in Paradise, walking like Xenocrates on the walls of Heaven. She would have been overhead, watching with pride and trepidation her champion's shows-of-arms. Safe. Where no one could lay a finger on her. Then he could have continued to carry her stolen boot over him in battle, its magic fit to kick the Unbeliever out of all Outremer. As it was, Jocelyn no longer carried her token. Because Oriole had miscalculated in the lie he had told.

Sleeping in the same tent at night, Oriole could not help but know this. When the other exhausted knights were snoring their way through peaceful, dreamless nights, Foicelles was awake and pacing. Foicelles wanted music from his jongleur - something that might soothe him to sleep but never did. Foicelles wanted Oriole to recite every sirventes he had ever memorised - something that might occupy a knightly mind, while he paced up and down, up and down his tent, biting his fingernails and dragging that crest of blond hair up and back, up and back.

For Foicelles had an imagination every whit as sexual as Amaury of Herm. The woman whose chastity had been so crucial to his worship of her lay bound there each night in the harem of his mind. Had she been dead, no rival could have sullied her, disturbed one strand of her golden curls. Now, thanks to Oriole, Jocelyn nightly imagined her debauched, deflowered, forced against her will to submit to the well-chronicled perversions of an oiled body black as sin.

And he, like a harem eunuch looking on, had been rendered impotent any longer to love her.

So Foicelles did not sleep. And he threw himself against the enemy like a wave at a cliff, without the magic of any *domna* over him for protection.

He will die because I lied to him, thought Oriole every waking night between that Christmas and New Year. And no matter how much he inwardly argued his good intentions, Oriole found himself weighed down with guilt.

He did not want to stay and see Sir Jocelyn cut down in battle - a man so appallingly alone, a lover without a mistress to love. Yet never once did it occur to him to recant - to retract his lie. Somewhere, at some moment during the Cheravas mudslide or the massacre at the Bathys River, seeds of wickedness had lodged in Oriole's heart. Perhaps it had happened as he crouched in that river, fumbled by the tree roots and unseen plant-tendrils. He harboured vague hopes of purging himself in Jerusalem, at the altar of the Virgin, but only the feeblest of hopes - like a man who means to gouge out a splinter when he has a free moment, but knows that all the while the skin is healing over it.

Besides, he wanted to live. Come war, come pestilence, come famine, come-what-may; Oriole wanted to return to his wife and child and bear, and to take home more than he had brought; to show a profit on the war. To do that, he must stay in the service of his knight.

With every one of Foicelles' suicidal onslaughts on the enemy, he was acquiring new pensions, accolades, tokens of King Louis' esteem and appreciation. Why should Oriole not share in them, who had almost died on his behalf? Retract his story of how Ida had been taken? Foicelles would have cast him off quicker than he had discarded Ida's boot. Try to describe the true circumstances? Foicelles would never choose to believe them. So while Oriole's guilty conscience shouted in one ear that he had robbed his master of all happiness and peace-of-mind, his newly acquired wickedness shouted in the other, *'He risked your life. He owes you a living. You have responsibilities ...* '

Besides, it was a good lie, an excellent lie. Even Amaury of Herm had admired it - had seen it for what it was - a great journeyman's masterpiece of a lie. As an artist, Oriole cherished it.

The road to Attalia on the Caramanian coast was littered with dead pilgrims. It dragged itself over high, wintry mountains cantankerous with storms. Crusaders who had sweated inside their mail and taken it off at night to find the iron ring-pattern scorched into their flesh, now found red rust stains on their bodies instead, and they cursed the cold. The Lady of the Golden Boot (as Louis' Queen Eleanor was dubbed by an admirer) had abandoned mounted grandeur, along with the other women crusaders, and opted for the marginal comfort of a draughty litter. In place of vowing to visit this shrine and that altar, the ladies vowed simply that they would never go crusading again.

But though it cost such pains to get there, Attalia was hardly the answer to a pilgrim's prayers when they arrived. It was a little port surrounded by unproductive countryside and already short of pro visions because of Turkish raiders. Of course the local merchants charged what they could get for what little they had to sell. Of course there were not ships enough moored in this tiny, out-of-the-way place to carry all the surviving crusaders on towards the Holy Places. So when King Louis decided that the Crusade should continue on its way by sea, he of course meant only the officers. He said the infantry must continue along the pilgrim trail on foot, and that God would protect them from misfortune.

Drawn up in a crescent (not by any command, for there was no one left to command them, but according to the geography of the place) the terrified, abandoned infantry of the Second Crusade and the few hundred pilgrims travelling in their shelter, watched their officers and perfidious King sail out to sea and away over the horizon.

Oriole leaned on the ship's rail and watched till they

were out of sight. 'Is that how a father treats his *enfants?*' he said, off-guard, assuming that Foicelles would share his dismay at the King's behaviour. 'I think you could teach him a thing or two of Chivalry, master, for all he's a king.'

Foicelles looked askance at him for only a moment and said nothing. But ten minutes later he burst out into one of his rages (no longer so very rare) and, while Oriole stared at him open-mouthed, demanded to know how a jackanape minstrel dared to criticise the judgement of a king. 'By God, I should pitch you over the side to swim home. How dare you! How dare you! How *dare* you!'

The Queen dared. She questioned the King's judgement. She practically called into question his parentage and his sanity. In the end she said his entire *corpus regni* wasn't worth so much as a rotten pear. People clearly heard her say it.

It was not the evacuation of Attalia over which they quarrelled, but after the ships docked in Antioch. Her rebellious spirit, warmed through by the Syrian springtime, allowed her opinions on the war to blossom and increase. Her uncle, Prince Raymond of Antioch, escorted the royal company up from Saint Symeon harbour to his city and feted them with kids' meat and pomegranates. They drank sweet water from the aqueduct, and wore new, outlandish clothes as they listened to Raymond's renowned tactical logic. Eleanor had a high opinion of Raymond's tactical logic.

But Louis did not.

Prince Raymond recommended a strike against the seat of power of Nur ed-Din - against Aleppo. It was not so very far away. Raymond even took a contingent of knights up to its walls, like an estate merchant accompanying prospective buyers to view an empty house. Nur ed-Din had been picking off Christian fortresses one by one; but the seizure of Aleppo would hamstring the man. Queen Eleanor smiled on her uncle's plans; smiled with that serene blessing of a smile which said, 'Very well. You have convinced me. That is how it shall be.'

But King Louis said, damn Aleppo: he would go to Jerusalem, because that was what he had vowed to do. And the more his wife told him he was stupid, ungrateful, ignorant of local politics, deaf to sound advice, the more devoted he became to that vow. The King would go to Jerusalem, not Aleppo.

Sir Jocelyn de Foicelles and his household could hear the sound of raised voices ricochetting through the halls of Prince Raymond's palace. The whole Chivalry of France could hear it. Distance blurred the specific words, but there was no mistaking the venom.

That was the first time the word was whispered, the first time the unthinkable was voiced: divorce. Rumours rank as sewage blew abroad, fanned by sweaty mysogynists who liked to suggest Eleanor slept with her uncle. Some knights sprang gallantly to her defence. Some sided with the King. The facts of the case had little to do with who joined which faction.

Eleanor of Aquitaine was Queen of Hearts, a living patron saint of troubadours and artists. She drew poets to her like moths to a flame: by beauty, by largesse, by the brightness of the new, by sexual charm, by favourable comparison with her monkish husband. Louis was an ascetic with less and less interest in the cult of High Romance. He also appeared singlehandedly capable of losing the war. And so the seam began to strain within the French Court, the threads to pull, the fabric to give, the royal raiment to show itself for what it was: a union of two very different cloths. The farsighted began to question where they would choose to stand if a rift came.

Not Jocelyn. He saw no rift, perceived no friction. He was sunk too deep in writing *sirventes*, hunched over close-clenched knees, scratching with a quill like a surgeon dissecting a brain.

Not the King, either. Louis did not agonise over Eleanor's lack of wifely obedience. He simply sent armed men to her room one night and forced her aboard ship - out of Antioch - away from the influence of her uncle and those who shouted down the small clear voice of God in the name of 'tactical logic' .

Jerusalem was aswarm with thousands of crusaders. So Oriole found it extraordinary – significant - strange beyond coincidence that he should chance upon the very billet of Sir Amaury and his retinue within a week of his arrival. It did not occur to him that he had walked the streets of the city for hours on end, half-looking for that red head of hair, that lavish, swaggering livery. Did he happen to mention the name, too, to an ordnance officer? Was that how he first found, among the narrow roads and souks, the little white house with its striped awnings and vine-hung pergola? Surely not. He remembered only coincidence, astonishment, as he stood outside on the street. So this was where his tormentor Amaury of Herm resided. Oriole stood for a while and looked, then turned back for the pilgrim hospital where Sir Jocelyn had chosen to billet.

Foicelles had chosen it in the spirit of humility, and Oriole could plainly see how his master would prefer the shadowy austerity of the long, low building. Apart from the hot sun lifting the skin off his fair scalp like flaked fish-flesh, there were sights outside of such extraordinarily seductive beauty that men had been known to throw up Christianity and live like Moslems, never going home, trapped inside a sensual maze. Foicelles only ventured out of his cloister to visit the Holy Sights. En route to them, his eyes fastidiously avoided the fountains at the crossroads, the white doves tumbling like plump fruit through the branches of cedars and great bay trees. There were turbans moving like a thousand Gordion knots between the woolly hair of black African slaves who walked naked through the lanes. There were olive-faced Arabs on the street corners. The lady crusaders had put away their armour. Now they went veiled like Moslem women, and painted their eyelids, and minced about flicking their beamy Frankish buttocks like horses pestered by horseflies. They were powerless to fire any admiration in Sir Jocelyn. Even the prostitutes of Outremer could not turn his head, and they were fabulous.

The one reclining on the divan in Sir Amaury's house, when Oriole next strolled by, was adorned in all her worldly wealth. Coins wound about her forehead like thoughts of avarice. Gemstones and mirrors sewn into her garments glanced out through slits. Bracelets manacled her arms and ankles like a galley slave, but there were no callouses on her hands, no sunburn on her shoulders. Her shoulders were pale: that much Oriole could see. Her legs were pale too: Oriole could see that through the tissuey stuff of her skirt. She was eating preserved fruit out of an ivory box carved to look like lace. As a negro came in off the terrace, his wicker tray emptied of lemonade, she complained wordlessly that she was hot and he fanned her with the tray, making her henna'd hair lift along with the fringing of a Persian rug on the wall behind her. Above her the ceiling was painted, and beyond her the big window looked eastwards over green gardens to a green orchard.

Oriole had left his master writing a eulogy in verse concerning the Great Assembly at Acre (which had just decided to storm Damascus, despite it being a potential ally). The jongleur had set off to fulfil his ambition to stand on the geographical Centre of the World ... but his feet had brought him here instead.

Amaury sat in the little courtyard, surrounded by admirers, beneath its canopy of red Tyre-cloth. Beside him a brazier burned incense and aromatic herbs to keep away disease and flies, and the scent mingled with that of hot cooking oil, sandalwood and musk, sheep and goats. Nothing else attested to the sheep and goats - no dirt to be walked in on to the pretty mosaics of the floors indoors. Only the regular white streaks of bird lime calibrated the vine-leafy wall where milky doves came now and then to peck on the naissant grapes. Amaury was eating almond paste out of a wrought copper bowl, using little mops of white bread. Oriole had not meant to enter at all, and yet somehow there he stood, there at the foot of the sun-white steps leading to the roof Amaury broke off when he saw him.

'So. Foicelles' storyteller.'

You had no further need of me, sir. I went back to my first master. I hope it won't come to a fight between you. Not on my account. I hope you won't let it. I only told him the truth as it should've been.'

'Always wanted to see things as they aren't, that one,' Herm said to the men at his feet. 'Idealism he called it. Half-witted, I say.' Amaury was sitting in an armchair of inlaid cedarwood. 'Is he in love again yet? Some new *amor de logn?*'

'He has the war, sir, to impassion him. He's writing a chronicle of the war in verse,' said Oriole primly and felt he deserved their laughter. God knew what impulse had brought him here to stand with one foot in the enemy camp, like a child defying its parents' disapproval. Now he would be obliged to defend his master against Jibes and insults.

'Very apt. Very apposite,' Amaury sneered.' A fool to write the chronicle of a folly. I wonder what rhyme he'll find for Attalia.

"Failure?" Fiasco would be truer ... This, gentlemen, is a onetime jongleur of mine. Left me to marry a black wife, didn't you, Songbird?'

Oriole blanched when the squires stared at him. But the stares were not disgusted, only intrigued, almost envious. A knot loosened in Oriole's stomach which had been tied tight for a long, long time. 'She can make do nicely out of nothing at all when she has to. And I taught her a deal more instruments. She works a bear well - we have a bear. And she is a good. Christian.' He added impertinently, 'I said she would be.' In thinking of Kadija, he could not help his eyes straying indoors towards the woman on the divan.

'She's not. A good Christian, I mean,' said Herm, seeing the glance, then, to his admirers, 'Oriole has a taste for sunburned women, but he likes them Christian. Ouzais there's an infidel, I'm afraid, Songbird. Pays a toll to ply her trade here among good Christian customers. Isn't that right, Ouzais?' The whore acknowledged her name with the lift of a hand heavy with rings. 'Well, Songbird? What brings you to perch on my garden gate? Or have you come to tell us another story in the grand style? A talented narrator, this one. Well, Songbird?' Still Oriole hesitated. 'Or will you give us something by that rosy flamingo of yours? What sort of thing does he do these days? Your master.'

'I said, sir. He's writing a chronicle of the Great Crusade.'

'Yes, but is it good stuff? Fit to stir the blood? Well written? Inspirational? Does it live in the brain? Does it linger in the heart? Is it witty? Does it do him credit?'

Oriole felt cornered, harangued. 'I'm no judge ...'

'You're not? You who've travelled through the world alone and sung for two masters (not to mention God)? As I recall, you had a passable feel for the Sciences yourself'

It was the first time in his life that Oriole had been remembered by more than his name. So many months of time. So many miles of space. And yet Herm remembered everything about him. It was flattering, no doubt about it. To be asked his judgement was even more unknown to him than flattery.

'He borrows too much.'

The squires yelped and howled like dogs in their delight at the insult. *'You mean he's a plagiar?'*

'No! Not at all! No! Never! Only ... I was only going to say how, lately, he borrows from himself too much ever to write a truly new thing.' Amaury was looking at him through half-closed eyes. 'And he doesn't look around enough any more ever to see a new thing to write about it.' A second knot untied in his stomach without his understanding why.

'In fact, you could do better yourself,' said Herm.

'Oh, I never said that, sir! I never meant ...'

The almond paste was almost all gone. Amaury lifted the bowl, his fingers wrapped round its stem as if he would throw it at Oriole's head. The squires ducked, click-clicking their tongues. But Amaury only tossed the dish gently into Oriole's hands. 'That's for telling the truth, as well as you tell a fiction - a lost art among Gay Scientists these days. And is that why you're here? To ally yourself to talent? Do you want to come back to me?'

'Of course not. I didn't come here ... I mean, I was only passing by ... I only came here to ... I should be getting back now.' He twisted the bowl between tortured fingers.

'Well, you'd best decide soon,' Amaury persisted. 'There'll be a royal divorce soon, and I mean to stay close to Eleanor. She'll be the only rallying point for men of soul. Your man'll stick to the King. A twosome. Thick and Thin.'

'The King and Queen divorce? No. I don't believe you. The Church won't let them. I mean, how could they? Divorce? It's against religion!' The squires resumed their expressions of sneering condescension: they had been debating the divorce ever since they arrived in Jerusalem. To them it was a *fait accomplis*. So they laughed at him.

'Oh, but it's the Church *wants* it, Songbird! On grounds of consanguinity. Suddenly, they're too closely related, Eleanor and Louis ... Wonderful times, eh?' Oriole was flustered and incoherent, Foicelles' little jongleur again, shocked by blasphemy. Herm went on, 'Saint Bernard wants a divorce. So there'll be one. That's that. And where's the place for a knight-*trouvère* in a Court ruled by bloody clerics?'

Who wants ... ?'

'Saint Bernard. You know. That bastard politicking killjoy with a soul you could fit inside a pod and still leave room for the peas. Didn't you know? He's the raven sitting on the King's shoulder these days, shouting in his ear: *"Divorce! Divorce!"* One fool advising another. Archbishop Suger was reasonable - Suger I could stomach. But not Bernard. So I'm tucking my feet under Eleanor's table and I'd advise you to do the same, Songbird. I'll take you back, if you can still sing ... I'll give you a livery. Who knows, I'll maybe even let you write a line or two. What d'you say?'

Oriole stared down at the bowl in his hands. Flies were flocking to the sweet-stuff inside, feeding and multiplying. Like the blasphemies. This sworn knight felt no loyalty to his King whatsoever. And to heap such slanders on Holy Bernard who had been like mother and father to Oriole in his cloistered days! Bernard want to undo the marriage vows? Never. This Herm - with his shiny gifts, his offer of a livery must be the Devil's Tempter-on-Earth. It was a wonder any jongleur stayed with him, hearing his blasphemies day after day.

Oriole turned and set off to run, pursued by derisive laughter. He ran all the way up the Street of Judas Arch, repeating to himself Amaury's crimes over and over again. As he passed the Church of Saint Mary, he recalled his own neglected *domna*. He also realised that he was still holding the silver cup. Didn't he owe Mother Mary a tribute for having brought him safely through danger and temptation?

Stepping into the gloom and cool of the church, he placed the cup, alongside various coins and little votive carvings, among a thicket of tallow candles all buckled by each other's heat. He looked up at the wooden madonna and asked for a long life sealed with honour, within the service of Sir Jocelyn de Foicelles.

The madonna was not moved to reply.

CHAPTER TEN

Treachery

The Moslem crescent had been removed from the Templum Domini, and, as Oriole passed by, a giant golden cross was being raised on a pulley and winch to replace it. It banged and jarred, banged and jarred its way between rough wood scaffolding. Huge crowds had mustered to see this spectacular feat - to see whether the beautiful gilded thing would successfully reach the crown of its Moslem Golgotha. The sun glinting on it pricked the eye like thorns. Oriole wandered inside the Templum, but the place was crowded with crusaders chipping at the Holy Rock for relics. His prayers were not for victory in battle. He nursed a more personal ambition: today he would stand on the Centre of the World, and make his mark in the Church of the Holy Sepulchre. He ran all the way across the city.

Pelting through the Great Souk, through the vegetable markets, he wove a path between stallholders who reached out to tempt him with open pomegranates and weeping oranges, or dipped their hands into great baskets of millet, like misers gloating over gold. The smell was sweet and earthy, half-rotten, half-enticing.

The Street of Drapers were ruched with swags of silk, lawn and silvery stuff. Hangings were danced in front of Oriole with intricate mazes of velvety pile in colours as rich as golden pheasants. Water glistened in the Patriarch's Pool.

Inside the Church of the Holy Sepulchre, in one of the patches of dark among the archways, grilles and alcoves, Oriole laboured with his knife to notch the stone floor, turning and turning over his work like a bee dancing within the darkness of the hive. The blade chipped, blunted, sparked, but he went on and on gouging, as though to fail would leave him out of God's Book of Gold.

He had to leave his mark. He had to prove to the world that he had existed: prove it to the world, prove it to himself.

He went and stood on the Centre of the World, sharing it only with one of the dozen stray cats patrolling the holy shadows. The cat looked up at him with demonic green eyes, and he psst it away, his spittle landing blasphemously on holy ground. Just beyond the world's centre lay the candlelit Chapel of the Angel, antechamber to a small dark cave the size of a kennel, where Christ lay down and rose up again from death, saying 'I am the Truth'.

Amaury *had* told the truth. King Louis was a bully and a fool. He was no model of Chivalry at all in his dealing with his wife, with his *enfants*. Amaury could judge between the truth and a lie - even admire a good lie for its craftsmanship without feeling the need to believe it, to be deceived.

The Centre of the World. Oriole looked down at his feet. What was it, then, the centre of his world? Love was central to Life: Jocelyn had taught him that. On this very spot, in love, Christ had plunged into Hell and, in love, God had raised Him up again to glory. So from this spot bubbled up all Love's rivers - love of parent for child, friend for friend, servant for master, gentleman for lady.

But Jocelyn had lost his Love. Jocelyn had laid aside love poetry in favour of war songs. Jocelyn had caught an infection from the war: hatred.

Knights of the Order of the Holy Sepulchre moved about the church unaccoutred and therefore silent, like ghostly warriors.

He wishes he were dead. That's why he throws himself into battle the way he does. Why did it have to be Jaufré Rudel who died? A man who lived to love living women, a man who celebrated life and love in his poetry. Why could it not have been Jocelyn who died, since he had such a contempt for Life? Sometimes it seemed as if only Foicelles' doggerel would churn on and on for ever while the real *trobars* died, one by one. Unless at Damascus ...

Oriole glanced over both shoulders, held his breath to listen for signs of anyone standing nearby. He felt as if he had spoken the wish out loud in the whispering gallery of the world, and that it was reverberating in broader and broader concentric rings to the very rim of the earth. A potent wish, surely, uttered in the very ear of God. He had meant to save his most devout prayers for this spot, and he felt like the man in the folk tale: I wish I'd not wished that.

'God knows I love Sir Jocelyn!' he assured the cats in the corner, the angels in their dingy kennel. 'I'm lucky to be in the service of a pure man. And if God wishes me ever to write poems of my own, He will make straight the way.'

Still, if Jocelyn were to die at the siege of Damascus...

Shielding his head from the low arches, Oriole ducked his way out-of-doors. It would never happen. Foicelles' purity must make God cherish him, protect him.

Unless, of course, the Lord loved talent more than purity.

'Where have you been?' asked Foicelles, flying into a rage at the sight of Oriole. 'Inspiration came and I had no one to take dictation!'

'I'll get vellum, sir.'

'It's no good now. It's no good now. The thing's gone now. Where've you been?'

'To the Holy Sepulchre, sir, to pray,' said Oriole. He felt, when those blue eyes looked at him, that they must see through to the substance of his prayers, to the treachery of the thoughts beyond the prayers. 'I heard a wicked rumour, sir. About a divorce between the King and Queen. I went to pray for the blessed union, sir. And for God to protect the sweet Lady from unchivalrous lies, sir. You always told me to pray for a lady abused by rumourmongers.'

He had to explain himself two or three times before he could break through the cocoon of concentration. Then the knight looked at him with eyes so pale blue that they seemed, overwashed by tears, to be losing their dye. Jocelyn invited Oriole to come closer, with the curve of an arm.

'Take this,' he said, passing him the tiny quill pen. He seemed to misjudge the distance for he actually broke the quill against the back of Oriole's hand. 'Write for me.'

Oriole pulled a stool between his legs and perched awkwardly to write while Jocelyn dictated:

> The King is God's anointed minister.
> The King is my master's master.
> The King's word is the word of the Law.
> The King is my ransom in war,
> my Father in peacetime.

This doesn't scan, thought Oriole. Nor rhyme. More like a psalm than a song. 'Is that a new line, sir? "My Father in peacetime?"'

'As you like,' said Sir Jocelyn and went on dictating:

> The King speaks and I listen.
> The King's enemies speak and I retch up my bowels...

'Now eat it.'

'... now eat ... I beg your pardon, sir?'

'So you may, when your mouth's clean enough. Eat it.' He crushed the work inside his incomplete left hand and pushed it between Oriole's teeth.

His saliva at once dried up. He gaped like a suckling pig, as much with astonishment as the unriddable ball in his mouth. He took it out to tear it up finer, his hands shaking and his fingers failing to shred it. 'But, sir...!'

'Drink,' said Foicelles, putting the pestle-shaped dish of ink up to Oriole's lips.

'But, sir! The Queen!' He tried to think of all the epithets he had ever heard knights-*trobar* heap on Eleanor. 'I thought that in Chivalry ...!'

'*What do you know about Chivalry?* What do you know about anything but whores and washerwomen, you kennelfly? Pray for that whore? Pray for that Devil's woman? Sent to tempt the King's eyes aside from Jerusalem - and you'd commend her to God, would you? What are you, a pimp to commend a whore?'

'I only said ... ' Between the protestations of ignorance, the ink filled his mouth with all the filthy words in the world, with heresies and obscenities, with abhorrences and aberrations, with all the blots ever written. *'I didn't know!'*

'You have a black wife, don't you? I heard that foul-mouth Herm say it. He gave you a black wife. You used to couple with a Moor, didn't you? Black sticks. Black cleaves. Black climbs in at the mouth ... and the eyes ... and the ears and all the openings of a man!' (Oriole closed his eyes tight against the ink till the veins in his eyeballs blazed inky black and he thought he was blinded.) 'Doesn't it, boy? Doesn't it! That's why you can't see the filth in others. That's why you're stupid to it!'

Oriole's stomach revolted against the black emetic: he tried to pull away from Foicelles and run outside, but the knight kept hold of his arm, twisting it till Oriole was bent double and retching. Foicelles had learned real cruelty from the war.

Every man had. It had swept through the crusader army surer than dysentery, that malicious desire to inflict pain. He wanted some culvert now for the overspill of his violence, and Oriole had come to hand.

'What happened to Chivalry?' Oriole shouted, but only inside his head. The blasphemy that spilled out of his mouth was bad enough. It splattered Sir Jocelyn, spattered the verse-chronicle and the breast of his pink livery: inarticulate vomiting.

It was Jocelyn who finally pulled away and rushed out of the room as though its walls were pressing him to death. He pulled at his collar as he went, cursing the lack of air.

While the door-hanging still flapped, another of Foicelles' little pages entered, backwards, staring after his frantic master. He looked about him at the wreckage of the room, the gules of ink gleaming like fresh blood on Oriole's livery. 'What did you do to cross him?'

Oriole knocked the page down with all the violence that came to hand, but said nothing. Not a word. Not one word. Even though his belly was full of them. A million inky, unwritten, inarticulate words.

Instead, he went back to the Church of Saint Mary to retrieve the little silver cup. A warden saw him do it, and kicked him to the ground and wrested the thing away from him, using a foreign language to call him a thief Oriole had to let the gift lie. He hoped the Virgin would not send him bad luck as a result - the bad luck of a long life bonded indissolubly to Sir Jocelyn de Foicelles.

Damascus supplied Foicelles with fresh enemies to kill. He volunteered readily to go in among the orchards skirting the city walls and to eliminate the sniping archers who hid in the branches of the fruit trees. He rode through acre upon acre through the mesmerising dapple of leaves and maze of tree-trunks. He carried an axe in his two hands, hacking down oranges with juice as red as blood. Fruit and offenders - the limbs of ambushers, the quivers of archers, the heads of hiding banditry: they rained down on him in a glorious shower of sweet red juice. Or so it looked through the one small window of his helmet, the one small window of his brain left unobscured by his raging lust for destruction. The chroniclers who recorded his bravery had more sense than to go into such places. They relied on hearsay.

By night, more Damascenes infiltrated the orchards to squat among the leafy branches, right over the heads of the crusaders who camped there. Foicelles said that the fruit trees should be all burned down. But in the end (the chroniclers said) a filthy conspiracy of lies and bad advice made the King move his army out on to open ground where it was hacked to pieces by two armies approaching from behind. Cynics such as Amaury of Herm said that King Louis' own stupidity had betrayed his troops to slaughter.

Jocelyn, Conte de Foicelles was shot through the thigh by a wooden arrow a metre long and tipped with silvery metal. The shaft was painted with a spiral of red and blue. Such trouble to expend on so expendable an object as an arrow.

The wound was nothing. Slowed by grazing the edge of the fauld, it hit the skirt of his chainmail and only unforged a couple of iron links into the flesh of his thigh. But blood-poisoning set in, and he was hurried back to

Jerusalem and entrusted to the care of the Hospitallers of Saint John. The grateful King had such a special care for his health, it was said.

By the time Oriole arrived there, however, typhus was loose inside the long hospital building within the precincts of Solomon's Temple. The smoke of fumatories wreaked so pungently that it stung his eyes to tears even in the street outside. The nine sergeants allocated to each ward patrolled with whisks of bunched herbs, chanting religious formulae for the relief of sickness, and the brazier burning in one corner smeared out all detail, so that once inside Oriole tripped over mattress ends, trod into bowls of half-eaten food, peered about him without seeing or wanting to see.

There were both men and women. A child was being born somewhere, in another of the long, vaulted rooms.

'What are you doing here? You're not allowed in here! Get out of here. Do you want to spread the contagion?' One of the sergeants swatted at him with his herbal bouquet.

'Sir Jocelyn de Foicelles. He's a patient here. Wounded at Damascus. A pink livery. I'm his jongleur.'

'French? Pink? I've got thirty Franks just in this ward,' said the sergeant. 'There is a knight, though ... Wounded, yes. Typhus after. There.' He pointed towards an alcove curtained off from the rest of the ward, and Oriole ran towards it. His head knocked a fumitory which hung from the ceiling by a chain. Its smoke wrapped itself around his head, blindfolding him.

Behind the curtain, a sergeant was just covering the body of a dead man. Oriole was too late to see the face:

he did not choose to lift the blanket off again. Whether the livery had been a true pink was hard to tell, for the clothes were burning in the brazier and had turned all to black or grey. Just as when Foicelles became a hermit.

Oriole knew, though, that they were Jocelyn's clothes in the brazier, that it was Jocelyn's body stinking beneath the blanket. For Oriole had stood on the Centre of the World and wished him dead. Of course he had died.

No further word came from Saint John's - no deathbed instructions for his household. They disbanded by slow entropy, falling away from their employment like the planets gradually distancing themselves from the sun. The jongleur Oriole was not the last to go looking for a new livery.

'Have you come to sing to me, Songbird?' Amaury greeted him, lying on a mattress on the flat roof, sheltered from the sun by the red Tyre-cloth awning.

'In a manner of speaking,' said Oriole.

'And can one sing "in a manner of speaking"? I'd call it recitation.'

The awning cast a wrath-redness over the man, which frightened Oriole, made him lose all confidence in his success, made him small and supplicant. 'Well? Do you want something of me?'

'Only your livery, sir.'

Amaury raised himself up on one elbow. 'What's this? A change of heart? Did you finally tire of copying *sirventes?*'

'My master's dead, sir. After Damascus.'

'No!' The blush of the sun through the awning obliterated any loss of pallor. 'Then God's a man of taste, after all! Wouldn't see the world flooded a second time with second-rate doggerel. I knew we could rely on Him. I'll offer up a *Non nobis.*'

There was nothing to be gained this time by shocked prudishness, by running away from this devilish-red man. Oriole held his ground. 'Your livery, sir ...'

'It's yours.'

'And my bear? And my wife?'

Amaury shrugged. 'By all means. Though I'd've thought ... ' Oriole waited. 'There's many are taking the opportunity to go home from here bachelors. Where did you leave the thrifty, versatile and Christian lady?'

'In Vitry, sir. On the way out of France.

''Mmm. Pleasant enough place to be widowed. Now supposing you'd died - as you might well have done in the service of that pink zealot ... Mightn't a man come home from this place ... newborn, almost - redeemed into newness of life by his pilgrimage? A young man? No clogs hanging down behind him?'

After a man weighed down by a tremendous pack sets it down, he feels as if he is floating, weightless, airborne. Oriole experienced a strange light-headedness as he took Amaury's meaning. Let Kadija think him dead? Become a single man again? Taste what life might have been if Kadija had never come along?

Amaury had married him to the Moor. It seemed therefore perfectly within his power to unmarry them. The sun was hot on the top of Oriole's head. Or was it the eye of God scorching down?

'I'll consider it,' said Oriole. But inwardly he saw them: cast off along with the pink livery, all the misfortunes of his youth, all the responsibilities which had come to him too young. 'And you'd let me write a song from time to time, and sing it?'

'If you have the art.'

Oriole nodded. He knew he had the art. His stomach was, after all, full of ink. He had swallowed so much at Jocelyn's hand that he had only to open his mouth and the words would write themselves in the air, black and cursive. The gift that separated knight from common jongleur had once seemed an insuperable barrier. But somehow of late that gulf had narrowed. He had had a bellyful of one master poet; now his belly was full of poetry for another, no worse than many and better than some.

CHAPTER ELEVEN

The Queen of Hearts

Suddenly everything was easy. There were no decisions to be made. When at last-finally-King Louis admitted to the failure of his Crusade, and took ship for home, his Queen sailed in a different vessel. It was a standard precaution against shipwreck. Or it was a taste of things to come.

Sir Amaury and his entourage sailed with the Queen - in the selfsame ship as the Queen, furnishing her with music to lessen her sadness at leaving Palestine. Oriole passed his time writing poetry, persuading himself that he did indeed adore the Queen Eleanor. Was she not, after all, the archetype of beauty – blonde-haired, blue-eyed, tall and talented in every way? She had accumulated round her a congregation of worshippers, though she did not keep troubadours simply to flatter her, to bolster up her self-esteem. She admired talent and she prized originality and she rewarded wit, however blasphemous, subversive or bawdy.

She also liked good-looking men. As other princes plant trees in a landscape to enhance their outlook, Eleanor peopled her prospects with poets and musicians bent over their instruments like classical statuary. Amaury of Herm was among them. And crouching in his shadow, was Oriole.

He was an attachment of Herm's and Herm was now an attachment of the Queen's. Life was easy. Oriole did not have to wonder whether divorce between King and Queen was wicked or unavoidable. He simply clung close and let the political maelstrom boil round him. Holy Bernard was by now vouching that Louis and Eleanor were so consanguinious as to be virtually brother and sister. The Pope was pretending to deliberate. The King made show of grief. Oriole knew better. They were all pretending. Their only concern was how to keep Aquitaine after the marriage was annulled. Aquitaine belonged with Eleanor, and if she left the marriage, Aquitaine went with her.

Oriole did not send for his own wife. He would wait (he told himself) to see how the political situation resolved itself before sending for her. And there were women enough to be had about Court by a personable and talented young man. So he passed his days writing poetry to Eleanor and playing ardent, inconclusive games in the gardens of the royal palace. Women found him attractive and underestimated his age: he saw no reason to neglect these advantages.

The fashion in minstrelsy was for two voices, parted by barely more than a two-notes. Oriole and Amaury paired well, attacking the note from slightly below in a way that could undermine the heart. Eleanor herself said so. They wore her livery now, in the rich materials of Greece and Outremer. Her own preposterously long-toed slippers, the silk turbans, even her Arabian djellaba defied the Normandy climate, and she painted her eyes and sometimes even went veiled. The poetry they unfurled before her (like haberdashers unrolling bolts of cloth) were woven out of exotic images of Araby. Day by day, Amaury and Oriole carved a deeper niche in the Queen's affections.

When the annulment happened at last, Eleanor fled the King's juris diction before he could make a strategic remarriage for her and so keep a hold of Aquitaine. It was treachery to abet her flight, but such words no longer had meaning for Oriole: he and Amaury fled with her, northwards. Wherever Eleanor came to rest, Oriole told himself, he might send for Kadija and the baby and the bear. He might.

And there again he might not. One day soon, Amaury had promised to let him sing a composition of his own before the Queen (or rather Duchess of Aquitaine as she now was). That one promise stirred more adrenalin in Oriole than all the dangers of Outremer. He knew it was childish. Everything that made for strong feeling was childish. Amaury had taught him that. No feeling penetrated the grownup Amaury any deeper than a louse under his shirt. So Oriole too cultivated ennui - an air of sleepy indifference - and was greatly admired for' it by his fellow jongleurs. But he still burned in secret to write an *aubade* and sing it to Sweet Eleanor.

Meanwhile, he made it his business to watch and imitate the bored, the calm, the collected Amaury.

'Damn! Hell! Shit! Curse the bloody woman!' The sides of the tent shook, then Herm burst out of it, raised his arms high in temper and shook from head to foot. Oaths and curses dropped from him like fruit from a tree, and struck everyone standing nearby. 'Now I see what she's about!'

'What's the matter, sir?' asked his white-faced page.

Herm clawed at his fiery, bristling hair. 'She's going to marry him!'

'What's the matter, sir?'

'Means to have England and France both! God blight her.' His shouting set all the tethered horses pitching and tossing. The other jongleurs ran to Oriole and hung on his arm. 'What's the matter with him?' they begged, certain that Oriole would know. Oriole spread his hands in bewilderment but they pressed him: 'Find out! Find out!' In the meantime, Amaury had gone back inside the tent.

'Sir?' ventured Oriole, like a hunter cautiously prodding at a shot bear. 'Sir?' The knight had flung himself face down on his travelling couch. 'Sir?'

'You see where she's running, Oriole?'

'The Queen, sir? The Duchess, I mean. Out of France, sir?'

'To Normandy, you imbecile!'

Oriole looked back through the tent flap at the open northern countryside. 'Yes, sir. Normandy. It's not France but ...'

'Normandy, you fool! To Henry of Normandy! She

means to marry Normandy! And he'll soon have England!'

'He's very young for her,' was all Oriole could think to say. The man was practically sobbing. Oriole went down on one knee beside the field-couch. His hand hovered nervously over Amaury's shoulder. Could it be that Amaury's love for Eleanor was real? Could it be that, for all his outward cynicism, the poor fool had harboured hopes of winning the first woman of France?

Amaury cursed and swore and beat his fists on the frame of the couch so that his whole body shook. At last Oriole's hand could no longer refrain from pitying Amaury's trembling back. 'She may give him Aquitaine, sir, without giving away her heart.'

Amaury reared up like a whale beneath a harpoon. 'Stuff and skewer her heart!' he bawled. 'They'll end in England, that's where! She'll take her bloody Troubadours' Court to *England*!'

There was no denying the words' power to alarm. England. It was a country of barbaric anarchy, ruled by robber barons - torture and extortion, dungeons hung with skeletons, men pressed to death in boxes of rocks. Currently it was being squabbled over by a dozen disputatious heirs; the wonder was that anyone *wanted* it. But why should Amaury so despair at the thought of England? Did his realm not lie offshore of its western coast? There must be a reason why he never returned home there. Banished. That was the reason that sprang most readily to mind.

'And may we not follow her into England?' asked Oriole from a safe distance. Here was a man whose schemes to climb the starry firmament had met with a broken flight of rungs.

'I've got enemies there,' was all he would say. 'Everyone there has enemies.'

Then surely she won't choose to go there, sir. Maybe she won't marry this Normandy. Maybe she won't marry at all.'

Amaury turned over on his couch, turning his face to the wall and his back to Oriole. It was an extraordinary display of childish pique, thought Oriole. The voice emerged muffled by the tent canvas. 'Why didn't I see it coming? That's what galls me to the guts.'

On Whit Sunday, eight weeks after the annulment of her marriage to Louis, Eleanor of Aquitaine married Henry Duke of Normandy, heir apparent to the English throne. While awaiting his inheritance, they made their court at Poitiers.

From that date onward, Sir Amaury of Herm was looking for an alternative route to the stars. He displayed the bitterness of a man who has met with undeserved illness, unrewarded service, unrequited love.

A strange atmosphere prevailed at Poitiers, that first year of her marriage, an atmosphere charged like the sky before thunder. Ardent admirers still sat perfecting their rhymes, jongleurs tuning their instruments, outside Eleanor's door. But now, on the other side of the door, she and her husband gorged on one another like lions. The noise of their passion reached the antechamber daily. It was clearly audible. Hearing the noises, some gaped at the ceiling, their tongues wavering a little in their mouths. Some sat totally engrossed in composition, counting syllables on their fingers. Some absentmindedly derived the cadences of their music from the pattern of panting in the next room. None, as far as Oriole could see, burned with erotic envy. Their love for Eleanor was entirely esoteric.

More embarrassed by far were the visitors and supplicants waiting in the anteroom for an audience with Duke Henry. They often coloured as red as the earthenware floor tiles, and would loosen their collars and strike up loud conversations with whosoever stood alongside, in a feeble attempt to drown out the lovemaking in the next-door room.

'My wife's a great beauty,' said a florrid man to Oriole. With his shaven head and bull neck and cloak hemmed with fur, he looked like a standing stone accumulating moss from the base upwards. His mouth was full of subsidiary stones-half-circles of teeth, none quite touching; his tongue pushed up against them between sentences. Beneath the cloak was a pilgrim smock, proving the man had interrupted his pilgrimage to petition Henry on some pressing matter. Iron penance crosses swung and clashed to either side of his great belly. 'She's a lovely woman. Lovely woman. My wife.'

'I'm happy for you, sir.' It jarred Oriole's nerves. He had just that moment been thinking of Kadija.

'Reads. Sews like a spider; A wonder at cat's cradle, too!'

'She must thank you for spreading her fame,' said Oriole absently. He was actually wondering whether he should send money to Kadija. She must be in desperate want of it by now. She probably supposed him dead. And the gift - even if he sent it anonymously - might convince her he was not. Well? Why unsettle her? He could hardly send for her, could he? She would hardly be a suitable accessory to a musician in the inner circle of a duke and duchess. What? A Saracen and a bear and a half-caste child? Bad taste.

'Her blood's noble from three different quarters, you know,' said the bumpkin, still rambling about his wife. 'Stands to get half the Camargue in time ... '

Of course Kadija might have died, thought Oriole. Such a long time. Besides, she hated Amaury - would not want a place in his household again - sooner be a widow. Probably she would apply to Jocelyn de Foicelles for succour and discover he was lost, and think her husband gone too.

'All you men hankering after the same one lady!' said the bumpkin. 'What wouldn't you think, if you saw my Alazais!'

'What indeed,' said Oriole. He could imagine her, the female equivalent of her husband (except that she could read) with a rump like the Massif Central and a bosom like Viking earthworks, her hair coiled round her ears and her lap cradling cats.

'*You* could write a song to her, I'll warrant.'

'Oh, me? Oh, I'm only a jongleur, sir.' He had said it before thinking. The man's rage was wonderful to see. He filled up with it, like a vat filling with rhenish. 'Jongleur? Why didn't you say?' He pulled the slate out of Oriole's hand and smashed it against the wall. He had mistaken Oriole for a knight-troubadour. 'I don't waste my time on underlings! I want the best! I only deal with the best! Who's the best around here?'

He was a merchant, Oriole decided, here to try to secure a charter or an order for woollen hose. 'Him,' said

Oriole, pointing towards Amaury. 'He's the best there is.' He only said it out of spite, hoping that the fat bully would try his hand with Amaury and get the short shrift he deserved.

Just then, however, the Duke Henry's bodyguard opened the doors of the bedroom and everyone in the antechamber stood up and separated. Those with a suit to the Duke pushed forward in an unseemly brawl, while the troubadours waited, patient, for a glimpse of the Duchess Eleanor. They drew in their feet from under the trampling stampede of landlords, respondents, aggrieved heirs, disputations burghers.

None had the speed or volume of the man in the pilgrim smock. He hurled himself face down on the floor and skidded up against the legs of the Duke in the very doorway of the bedroom. 'Sir! Sir! Your forgiveness on a miserable sinner!'

'Oh Barral. What is it now? Do get up.'

No one could fail to hear Barral's business with the Duke, for he roared it at the top of his voice. 'Don't judge me, sir! Don't judge me till you've heard me speak! You recall I went on pilgrimage - to purge my soul of the ... the other thing. And I did! I went on my knees. With this cross look, this weight of iron round my neck, and I walked on my knees right the way up the Via Dolorosie! Lent my sword here and there - to the Templars and the Hopsitallers and such. Wherever it was needed. Anyway, home I come. Humbled in body and soul, by Christ my Saviour, yes! Dressed like this. And what do I find?' Barral was climbing up the Duke now, hand over hand.

'What did you find, Barral?' asked Henry.

'Ay! You might ask! You might ask! I find that

bastard, piss swallowing, termite of a duck-fucking brother of mine has laid claim to sixty furlong of vines and beanfields and harvested the crop and sold it for a half-sou more than buggerance and spent the money building himself a castle - a bloody citadel to judge by the foundations - keep! Motte! Chapel! - To keep me off my own land, by Christ! Keep me off my own ...'

'Was the land in dispute, Barral?' Henry was clearly acquainted with the man and the subplots omitted from his stories.

'Disputed? Never! I've always known it was mine, no matter what he said!'

'So you don't wish me to settle the argument?' said Henry.

'God's grief, no, sir! I'd not waste your time ... No, sir! If you'd just hear with an understanding ear, that's all, and not believe slanderers and coveters and villains. Or brothers.'

'Oh lord, Barral. What've you done this time?' And yet there was no real reproach implied: Henry understood; he too was subject to filthy and uncontrollable tempers.

'I nailed the bastard to his front door.'

Even the troubadours and minstrels were moved. The room at large sucked in its breath. 'Oh Barral! You've not killed your brother! Your own kin!'

'Not killed. Just nailed him there. Well, what else can you do with a man that steals your land behind your back, eh?'

'By his clothes? By his hair? How "nailed" him?'

Barral knew he had the attention of the room. He turned his head to right and left, and there was a nervous grin on his face. 'By his hands and feet, that's all. Just while I burned down that filthy fortress of his.'

There was some laughter; some clenching of fists and shifting of shoes, but mostly laughter. The Duke himself told Barral he was incorrigible, but laughed as he said it. "I ought to fine you for breaching the peace.'

'Oh, fine me! Fine me!' Barral pleaded earnestly. 'My own angel wife told me. "Don't do it, Barral," she said.'

'And you should've believed her,' said Henry with the peremptory glibness of a busy man. He was anxious to get on with other affairs of state. 'But I take it this wasn't on any of your Normandy estates? Down on your Barbary coast, I suppose. It's really no concern of mine what you get up to on your bought land. Really. No concern. Ten thousand ecus.' The other petitioners began to press forward with their scrolls and documents and hang-dog faces.

'I never saw a man ask to be fined before,' said Oriole.

'That, my man, was a negotiated settlement,' Amaury observed, and watched through the window Sir Barral walking on his knees across the courtyard towards the Royal Chapel to pray, a page at each armpit to keep him from weighing too heavy on his kneecaps. Another ran ahead to kick pebbles out of the way. 'It put money in Henry's purse and pre-empted a lawsuit from the brother. Money's a thing Barral Nerra can afford better than a falling out with his Duke. Besides, Henry doesn't give a tinker's curse what happens in the Camargue.'

'The man's an animal,' Oriole ventured to suggest.

'Barral? Barral has the brains and manners of a sow. He feels his way by animal instinct. Last year he branded his bishop like a cow for taking in his tythes before Barral took in his. Took the abbey plate and melted it down.

Hence the pilgrimage and the penance. Metes out justice on himself before any other kind catches up with him. If he weren't a bean-brain, I'd call him clever - a man who can keep his hide intact like that.'

'Not this time, though,' said Oriole. 'Ten thousand ecus?'

'Wha'? Pocket money. Couldn't count the fortune he's got if he used all the fingers in France,' said Amaury and spat. 'What did he want of you?'

'Who?'

'Sir Barral. Just now. You crossed him.'

'He mistook me for a knight-*trobar*. Wanted one to write about his fat new wife,' whispered Oriole jeeringly. Unconsciously, he imitated the way Herm was standing: arms folded, one boot crossed over the other.

'He wanted a song written?' Any more relaxed, any more indifferent to the answer and Amaury might slither down the wall, surfeited on ennui.

'I told him. Everyone's affections here are given to the Lady Eleanor. Told him you were the best here, but quite given over to ...'

'Write me something.' In his ennui, Oriole overbalanced and fell up against the window as Amaury tossed him his entire purse. 'Well? You're always begging to show your skill. Write me a *serenade*.'

'To the Duchess Eleanor?!'

'To Barral's wife, you fool. He's going to be our new patron.'

Oriole swallowed his disappointment. 'By all means, sir. But I've never seen her. What does she look like?'

'How should I know? You only just told me he married her! What does it matter what she looks like, for God's sake?' But Amaury thought better of losing his temper and caught hold of his jongleur with a conciliatory fist. 'Think. Barral Nerra's as rich as money can make a man. What manner of a woman would *you* buy if you had that kind of money? There's your theme: the best that money can buy.'

***

But Oriole was a perfectionist. He wanted to see the subject he was to write about. A scholar's research. Discovering that she went each day to hear Mass in the Mary Church, Oriole went there too, armed with slate and chalk for making scholarly notes.

But the slate lay blank by his feet, and his chin rested on his hands as he knelt, pretending to pray, in the choir stalls of the Mary Church.

Alazais, it proved, had skin the colour of honeyed milk and hair like porter pouring from the keg. She wore it in the old Frankish way, loose under lawn. Her eyes were blue like the buddleias that draw butterflies. The movement of her lips in prayer made the lobes of her ears move infinitesimally, and her fingers intertwined as long and deli cate as hops on the pole. Her body inhabited its clothes like a butterfly its chrysalis: she dressed in blues, like the Virgin, but one colour's name is not enough to encompass all the different lovelinesses of Alazais.

After so many professional excursions into the mazes of Love, here was one passageway he had never trodden before. Remarkable. Oriole's head spun. The blood rang in his ears. Remarkable, he told himself in the flat voice of ennui, but the voice broke into a soaring, piping treble.

Remarkable! That a man could make so many forays into the fields of Love without feeling the dart hit home before. He felt it quite distinctly, somewhere between the skull and the base of his neck.

Kneeling so still for so long, he ought to have recognised the warning signs, the distortion of sound, the explosions of colour in front of his eyes. But never having been in love before, Oriole succumbed to the faint without even an attempt to save his nose from hitting the reredos when he fell.

CHAPTER TWELVE

Ascesis

Though Sir Amaury had attached himself to the household of Barral Nerra, he was forever looking back at the Court of Normandy as a lost opportunity. He was embittered and resentful - always hungry for news of the Duchess, yet always incensed if it came. 'I'd've overtaken them all by now,' he would say sourly. When Bernart de Ventadour prospered, Herm would spit at the mention of his name and say, 'That should've been me.'

'Why leave, then?' asked Oriole, but got no satisfactory answer. What he really wanted to do was to put his shoulders against Herm's back and yell, *'Go there, for Christ's sake, why don't you? Leave me here with her!'* But he kept silent, kept his place. At least now he was permitted to write.

On the journey south to Barral Nerra's ash-coloured territories Herm seemed to have left behind his taste for writing poetry. He was quite content to present his jongleur's poetry as if it were his own, confident that Nerra would never notice the difference. 'Anything'll serve for him,' he said, with surly contempt.

It was perfectly true that Barral Nerra had no discrimination in artistic matters, but he had a strong craving for people to think he had. The status of having a noble troubadour paying court to his lovely wife was one he wanted at all costs. The King's wife had followers. All the great knights were *trobars* or had *trobars* among their households. And since Barral was richer than most, it followed that his wife must have the best, the most admiration: must be seen to have the best. It had been part of his reason for travelling all the way to Poitiers - to attach a troubadour to his wife, just as he attached ingots of gold to the massive talisman round his neck.

Barral bore all his wealth ostentatiously. He had been known to roast an ox using a thousand candles, burning away the costly tallow in a magnificent incineration of money. The beef tasted of wax and soot, but the cooking of it lived in the mind. So did the time he had dug a trench, filled it with straw, pitch and fifty fine horses, then set light to their tails. Barral's wealth was a miraculous obscenity, a braggardly proof of God's approval.

His enemies, of which there were many, watched closely for signs of Barral out-trying God's patience. For he was prone to such dire sins as must surely one day cause his downfall. Perhaps he would remain childless, they cheered themselves, but with the arrival of the lovely Alazais their hopes receded.

He was of the House of Nerra and therefore a relation of the Counts of Anjou - a very distant relation, true, but related nonetheless to Fulk Nerra. *'From the Devil they came and to the Devil shall they go,'* Saint Bernard had said of the house. For Fulk Nerra was reputed to have married Melusine, a demon from Hell, and fathered on her the Plantagenet line to which Henry of Norm any himself belonged. Having given birth to her sons, Melusine had promptly flown back to Hell.

An alternative version said that Fulk Nerra had burned his wife to death on the cathedral steps: razed her to the ground, as he did castles, villages and monasteries. Such was the heritage in which Barral Nerra gloried, however far he was removed from the 'royal' strain of the family.

His own fortune was actually made from the rank étangs of the Camargue, boiling salt out of the seawater. His kingdom was one of grey salt dunes - a monochrome landscape stretching for acre upon acre, killing the ground beneath, poisoning the rivers running by. But since his fortune was founded on the salt of the ocean, it was just as bottomless as the sea. God had given into his hands the salt mill of the Frankish world, and so far did not appear to have thought better of the gift. Barral might be a sinner - he made no effort to deny it - but did he not always repent and make reparation to God? Did he not always spill tears of remorse and do penance? Even though Barral had repudiated his first wife for the crime of infertility and growing old, had he not squared his account with God by placing his brother's eldest son in Holy Orders? Once, when his horse cast a shoe, he had burned an entire village of his to the ground for the offence of having no forge. But had he not sent four golden horseshoes to the Pope along with a flask of penitential tears?

Barral was a man who wept very easily - wept and raged and swore oaths. He did not resort often to thought, accounting himself a man of deeds. His wealth brought him everything he ever wished for - divorce, forgiveness, roast beef, the lovely Alazais; he would never have understood if Herm had refused his offer of hospitality and patronage.

Fortunately Herm complied. He mustered his household and made the immense and tedious journey from corner to corner of France, to a romanesque barbican surrounded by a landscape of salt, to adore another man's wife.

Oriole could not credit, at first, that Herm could see Alazais and not genuinely love her. But to his great relief, Herm's private ennui persisted, undisturbed by Barral's beautiful wife.

Oh, he made a grand enough show when he first saw the lady, staring and staring, falling on his knees, pressing the cloth of her skirts to his face, begging to know from what treasurehouse of beauty Barral had stolen her. But to Oriole the insincerity seemed so glaring, so ill-disguised that he thought Barral must see through it.

On the contrary, credulity and childlike gratification daubed Barral's face. He had applied for a second opinion on the worth of a recent purchase, and an expert had confirmed its value. For all his power and wealth, Barral Nerra lacked brainpower. He felt his way through the world, doing what he saw others do, believing what he had heard was true.

'Might I sing to your wife in private?'

'How d'you mean? Between mealtimes, d'you mean? Of course! Of course! How, "private"? - Alazais, are you listening?' (It worried Barral that Alazais did not pay sufficient attention to her knight-*trobar*.)

'Just myself and my jongleur - in the garden where she walks, or in the chamber where she sews. I must be brought close to the flame if I'm to be tempered by the fire.'

Barral gazed at him, his mouth a little ajar. Inside the mouth his tongue moistened itself in fresh saliva. Nerra was not a man who could resist temptation; that was what impressed him about these poetical types: they did it for a hobby.

Apparently, they liked to tempt themselves to the limits of endurance so as to strengthen their characters - their *pretz*. He had made enquiries; Nerra never undertook a thing but he did it wholeheartedly. .You hear that, wife? Are you listening? The excellent Duke of Herm wants to sing to you in private. What d'you say?'

In the corner of the room, Oriole clutched his rote so tight he could feel it bruising his ribs. He tried to tell himself that she was only a woman - like all the rest - and would succumb to flattery just as soon. But he did not believe it, did not want to believe it.

Suddenly the woman spoke. 'I hope I'm not so selfish as to want the Duke's excellent songs all to myself, shut away in private. I'm quite content he should sing in front of the whole household. As he does now. At dinnertimes.'

'Horse piss! Pig shit! You heard the man! We have to nourish the flame, eh? Nourish the flame!'

'For myself,' said Alazais, her eyes on her lap, her fingers pinching her dress into a seascape of folds, 'I am quite content with the love of my husband and I have no ambition to raise hopes in any other man, which I can't satisfy.'

The words entered into Oriole like strong drink: first a heat on his stomach and then a dizziness. She was chaste! She was good! He had known it all along!

Unfortunately, her husband was already drunk. His temper flared. Why was she not more pleased with the toy he had brought her? She saw his annoyance and tried to fend it off. 'You know how shy I am of strangers, Barral. I've so few words in my head, I need you beside me when he plays, to praise his music.'

'Well, I'll *be* there! Of course I'll *be* there.' Nerra blustered. 'I'll be *watching*, naturally!' Barral clearly did not like putting it into words. It sounded footling and really rather bizarre: to watch one's wife complimented in secret. But then fashion commonly is footling and bizarre. 'Go for a walk with the Duke tomorrow in the morning, and I'll be there watching,' he told his wife, and she inclined her head obediently.

Oriole turned his attention to Herm. He had clearly *not* been expecting Barral to be present at all: at least he had found out in time, Now he leapt to his feet and bowed to the lady with a great many flourishes of his free hand, avowing his delight. He did not fool Oriole. Oriole knew him, inside-out.

After the novel set-back of finding Alazais a genuinely chaste wife, Amaury concentrated all his efforts on the husband. 'After all, he's the man that feeds me,' he told

Oriole. 'He's the one showering gifts. He's the one who wants a troubadour at his hearth!' He made no mention of the fact that Alazais did not care for him.

'I do believe the lady's afraid of you, sir,' Oriole said, breezy, casual, his voice quite sing-song high with indifference.

'Yes. Mmmm.' They were just entering the castle's troubadour chamber and Amaury crossed at once to his row of panniers lined up on a spare bed. He pulled out mirror and comb and began absently to examine and preen his face and beard. Apparently the reflection reassured him, for he said after a moment, 'She'll soon soothe down.'

'Maybe she just loves her husband,' said another of the jongleurs. But the idea was so absurd, so preposterous, so grotesque that Amaury did not respond, and Oriole gave the boy a jeering push that knocked his head against the wall.

Oriole turned his back on the salt-encrusted landscape beyond the window and crossed to put away Herm's mirror and comb. When he caught sight of his own face in the glass it was grey and bloodless, like the salty Camargue outside. His heart inside him had drawn in all the blood from his veins. She would, of course soothe down. They all did. They always did. It would be almost a relief: to find fault in her. In the meantime, Oriole went and bought himself a purgative from the apothecary, to ease the ache in his bowels.

'You are shy, lady,' whispered Amaury. 'There's no need. We are Eve and Adam restored to the Garden. I for one am in Paradise.'

'God grant, then, that we learn by earlier mistakes.'

'Amen, Amen,' said Amaury. 'The great thing is to remember that Love is Innocence and that nothing evil can spring from it. Even a kiss ...'

'A kiss? In a garden, monsieur? I remember the story. One of betrayal, as I recollect.'

They were both aware of her husband standing badly hidden amid the boughs of a lilac. He looked like a beast transported to the wrong habitat. Oriole's music prevented him hearing anything which passed between his wife and the troubadour.

'Do you fear betrayal, madam? Then someone has broken your heart! Tell me his name, and I shall avenge your unhappiness!'

She dropped her voice to an angry whisper. 'No one has broken my heart, sir, though you may well snap my patience.' She was for a moment distracted by a sudden discord on the organistrum. Oriole looked from one to the other, biting his lip in apology.

Suddenly she seemed to think better of the outburst. 'Forgive me, sir. I feel you may not be aware that my husband enlisted you without consulting me. I am a newly married woman, and feel no need of the attentions of a troubadour. Indeed, I don't know or understand why a man like you should persist in such a suit when there is nothing - absolutely *nothing* to be had by it. I admit, your jongleur has a very pleasant voice and makes very pretty music, but I wish you would spare me any more protestations of love. I am a wall newly pointed. Your suit runs off me like rain. I have nowhere about me for your compliments to lodge.'

'Oh, there is one spot,' said Herm darting his hand into the folds of her overmantle.

She put out a hand to fend off the lunge, and inadvertently caught him in the eye with a finger. He recoiled abruptly.

'Oh, I'm so sorry. I hurt you, sir?'

'Your heart, my lady. I meant that my compliments might lodge in your heart.'

'I don't doubt you did, monsieur.'

Just then, Barral came blundering out of the lilac. A butterfly had attached itself to his ear and he mistook it for a wasp and tossed his head. But his far greater anxiety was for Amaury. 'What's the matter? What's happening?'

Herm got to his feet, his hand still over his eye. He started to protest his innocence: 'Nothing! Absolutely ... ' Then seeing that he was not under suspicion, 'I'm afraid I looked at the sun and I was momentarily blinded by its brightness.'

'My finger accidentally caught the gentleman's eye,' said Alazais crisply. 'I was not expecting him to move so close. Not expecting it and not wishing it.'

'Then I'd best remove myself to a greater distance!' Amaury declaimed. 'The anguish of separation will make me a better man and a finer poet!' And he set off for the gate of the garden. The hand that laid hold on Oriole's upper arm was fierce with repressed annoyance.

'Well, it was a right pretty song!' insisted Barral, hurrying after them. 'Was it new? Did you write it specially for my Alazais?'

How would he know? thought Oriole peevishly. He had sat up half the night composing it. But Herm took the credit. Of course he did.

Amaury's grip slackened on his jongleurs arm and he left the garden arm in arm with Barral. Oriole stayed behind, perfectly immobile, so as to escape their attention. He noticed that Alazais too stood stock-still. Only the breeze moved the blue cloak of her dress around her like the water falling from a fountain. She was waiting for him to go too. Or perhaps she wanted to speak to him. She looked as if she wished to speak to him. He persuaded himself of that.

'Madam ....'

'Young man?'. 'Did you like the song?'

'What? Oh. Yes. Thank you, jongleur.' She felt for her purse and unlaced it from inside her mantle. 'I didn't realise.' She held out money towards him.

'I didn't want anything. I only meant ... I wrote the song myself' She looked through him to some more distant anxiety. '*He* didn't write it, I mean. Did you like it?'

'I'm sorry. I wasn't listening very closely.'

First she mistook him as asking for a tip, then, on top of all that, she had not been listening. A great upheaval shook Oriole through and through, but all he said was, 'Christ!'

'What! Must I apologise to you too now? For not listening to foolish ness in my own garden? You at least I can order to go, surely? You at least have to go when I tell you. Go on! Go! Go away! Get out!'

Oriole pulled in his head as though starlings were mobbing him. He ran to pick up his lute, steering a huge circle around her and, finding the garden fence too high to jump over, edged his way back round her towards the gate. Apologies were falling from his lips like broken teeth after a blow. He felt as if he had left his heart impaled on the fence.

'Wait!' She called him back just as he was about to close the gate.

'Wait.'

He had to slide the lute round again to behind his back, so as to fit through the foolish little wicket gate. And then, by the time he reached her, she claimed to have forgotten what she meant to say. He fell on his knees in the grass. 'Could I speak?' he asked.

'If you must. _ What? Something from him?'

'No! No! Not at all! ... Don't trust him, that's all. You're right not to trust him. That's all I wanted to say. Don't believe what he says! ... I mean, they're not even his own songs!' He was inarticulate; he was gabbling.

'You are very kind,' she said, resting one hand on his hair. 'My home is a great distance from here, you know. Sometimes I miss my brother's good advice very much.'

'Amor purus ...' said Amaury of Herm drawing a heart on the tabletop with a finger wetted in wine, 'Pure Love. Amor purus is the sweet discipline of the soul. It inhabits the mind and the heart, and while it is there it purifies them.'

Barral strummed his lips. Amaury was educating him in the Gay Science and had just recounted the story of the Eaten Heart. Barral was still extricating himself from its horrid fascination. 'Thinking about women, eh? Well, it's a cheering kind of pastime, I'll give you that. Thinking about women. It's purifying, you reckon?'

'As fasting is to the soul. To want without having. To

see without enjoying ... The scholars say there are three things arise from female beauty: the desire to kiss it, the desire to embrace it, and the desire to mount it.'

'They had to study to find out that?'

' ... And since the first two are permissible, a tension is created - a tension, you'd agree?'

Barral shifted his big thighs in his seat. He was a man full of appetites and the mention of bedding women - even of not bedding them - was enough to make his breeches bind uncomfortably. Not in a barracks, perhaps, or by a campfire, or among men as uncouth as himself But coming from this exemplar of courtesy, the smell of royalty still clinging to his plush red hair, talk of sex was oddly exciting, inciting. What did Barral know of 'tensions'? If a seam pulled, he opened it up with a knife. But he nodded and said, 'Tensions, yes,' as if he understood.

'The Ordeal of Ascesis is the anguish which strengthens a man. His pleasure is the very pain of pleasure withheld. The eunuch in the harem. The monk in the brothel. That exquisite agony of restraint. That's the heightened state of mind to strive after. It germinates the seed of poetry. It tutors a man for suffering in the world at large. It *assays his soul.*'

Oh, Amaury had researched his man. He chose his words carefully: 'pleasure', 'pain', 'watching'. He saw the great bulk of Nerra rock on its leather-clad thighs, on the edge of the seat. The woman may have proved difficult, an unexpected - almost unprecedented setback. But her obduracy in the garden had only confirmed Herm's decision to cultivate the husband rather than the wife.

'And this kiss ...' Barral reflected.

'The First Desire, yes?' said Herm. 'What of it?'

'D'you want to kiss her, then?'

'With all my heart, sir! Naturally! I'm a moth drawn to the flame of her lips! ... But why tell you? Surely you've tasted them? Aren't they lips fit to make a man ...'

'All right.'

'Sir?'

'I say you shall!'

Amaury rose to his feet, fingers spread on the tabletop to steady himself. 'Sir. Please don't joke. I'm a man of flesh and blood, after all, like you.'

'And I say you shall have a kiss. Good God, man! You've had a long enough journey coming here! And if it helps you write your poetry ... Isn't that how it works?'

'Precisely,' said Amaury. Barral shook the large deal box containing his chessmen: its rattle brought servants in at every door of the room. 'Tell my wife I want her.'

While they waited for her to come, Amaury protested his unworthiness. He said he would have preferred a week's anticipation, to feel the moment swell like ripening grain, etc. But Nerra (who had acted on impulse and was already suffering doubts) only shut his eyes and shook the box continuously to drown out both words and misgivings. On and on the sharp noise echoed until his wife, standing in front of him, took the box out of his hand. He opened his eyes and his colour deepened with pleasure at the sight of her. 'Sir Amaury wants to kiss you,' he said.

Her face, by contrast, turned a stark white. 'Then I hope he can bear with his disappointment, my lord.'

'And I say he shall ... Never mind all that. Protests. Bashfulness. I've given my permission. Kiss the man.

Says he needs it for his poetry ... What are you waiting for? It's all right. He's a troubadour. They do that kind of thing. Don't mean a thing by it.'

'I wish, then, that he had asked me. I would have refused him as kindly as I know how.'

'Asked you? How's that? *Asked* you? If I'd wanted Duke Amaury to borrow my horse, I s'pose you'd've had him ask the horse! Give him a kiss, woman, and don't be difficult. Always making difficulties. They do that, Herm. Take it from me.'

'But surely, Barral, it wouldn't be lawful! I'm a married woman!'

'Not lawful? Not lawful? If kissing was a crime, the prisons would be fit to split, eh, Amaury? The prisons would be ...'

'In the eyes of the Church, husband! Surely. I know it would be a sin.'

'Where? Where's it say in the Bible? Don't quote Holy Law at me, woman! I know my Bible, me! I've been to Jerusalem, me, remember? Don't you try and tell me the Bible troubles itself with kisses. Where? "*Thou shalt not kiss?*" Where?' Her recalcitrance, especially in front of a guest whose good opinion he valued, fuelled in Barral a greater and greater obstinacy. The sea's salt might turn to soot now before he allowed himself to be gainsaid, in public.

After the great ranting of his tantrum, her slight, sweet voice was plaintive. 'I never thought to give my kisses to anyone but you, my dear.'

'Enough! Not interested! Do as you're told, woman! Why does no one ever do as they're told anymore?' He flailed his arms, and Amaury, in pure obedience to the gesture, stepped up and took the kiss.

He stood with his feet set wide apart, and taking hold of her two hands, folded Alazais in an embrace which pinned both arms behind her back and bent her backwards. His open mouth covered hers. Like a lion gorging on something dead, the folds of his cheeks were pushed back, and they could all hear the wind whistle in his nostrils as well as the protracted sexual moan he made.

Barral Nerra half-rose out of his chair, his mouth open, the high colour shrunk to two spots of red in his hog-like cheeks. Then he sank back down, but on to the leading edge of his chair where he rocked forward and back, forward and back, like a man on horseback.

Even when Amaury finally gave Alazais back the use of her mouth, he did not immediately let her go, but held her against him. His eyes were screwed shut to imply both ecstasy and the agony of abstention, the little death of bliss. Barral studied that face. He watched it as he had watched the face of a witch he once had drowned in an icy lake, held under with forked branches. Amaury had tasted his wife like a connoisseur and confirmed her priceless value. But Amaury could take nothing more, whereas Barral had total possession: she was his today and every day. Barral Nerra was a happy man, grateful to the knight-*trobar* for showing him his happiness afresh.

Alazais' face was hidden from sight, of course. Her chin rested perforce on Amaury's shoulder, away from her husband. A pinprick rash encircled her mouth where Amaury's beard had pressed. Her eyes were not shut. They looked straight ahead, so could not help but meet with Amaury's jongleur. The tongue-tied young man. The one who wrote songs. She might as well have been looking in a mirror, for she could see her revulsion reflected in Oriole's face. He stood on the balls of his feet with his hands clenched and elbows bent, as if he were about to run towards her or fling himself flat on the floor.

'Well? D'you think you might get something out of that, Herm?' Barral blurted out, brash and banal.

'A lifetime's inspiration,' Amaury replied, retracting his face and weaving his head about in front of hers, trying to get mastery of her eyes. '

'Good. Good. Excellent. Must see if we can't help some more. Yes. Good. You. Alazais - Are you listening, woman? Come with me. I've got something ... matters to discuss with you. Come on. Come on.' He took her hand, gripping it tightly - a little punitively perhaps - and led her out of the bleak audience chamber with its one table and litter of standing visitors. Man and wife went upstairs to their bedchamber.

'And will she smooth down?' said Oriole, knowing that his voice would emerge expressionless. The jeer was all inside, tamped down, hidden away.

Amaury wiped his beard as if he had just been eating meat off the bone. 'What if she won't?' he grinned. 'Why trouble smoothing down the wife when the husband can be pricked up? The end'll be the same, by the broad road or the narrow. I'll have her anyway.'

'But the broad road leads to destruction,' thought Oriole. And that was the first moment in which he contemplated killing Sir Amaury of Herm.

CHAPTER THIRTEEN

The Embrace

So well did Amaury's new patronage suit him that even the news from England - that Henry and Eleanor were installed King and Queen there - had no power to move him.

'She might increase your estates. If you were there,' Oriole ventured to say.

Amaury responded, smug with self-congratulation. 'There's more to be got here.' And he settled back in his embroidered chair, feet stretched out on the embroidered footstool, luxuriant, arrogant, vain. The indolent, indulgent life he had secured in becoming Barral Nerra's lapdog had made him paunchy and unfit. When Barral staged tournaments, he left the arrangements entirely to his troubadour, with the result that Sir Amaury made showy passages-of-arms in front of the lovely Alazais. But he seldom rode in the lists himself. Inspired by news of the English Queen's magnificent Courts at Bermondsey and Nonesuch, he mounted water jousts or horse baiting or Arabian polo. Harmless stuff. But he did not take part himself. It confirmed Oriole's opinion of him as a coward.

Even Amaury could not fail to see his jongleur's infatuation. 'Infected by the disease of your betters,' was how he put it when he made fun of him. 'Comes of rubbing yourself up against their legs asking for cream.'

'I don't know what you mean, sir,' said Oriole clinging to secrecy. Vanity however blinded Amaury to the actual, small friendship which had grown up between Oriole and the Lady Alazais. He knew, of course, that she lived in terror of his own sexual advances, but omitted to notice where she ran for reassurance, who she tolerated in her flower garden, whose arm she rested on when the smell from the étangs laid its suffocating hold on the castle and gave the ladies migraines and nausea.

When Amaury suggested his next torment of ascesis to Barral, he sowed the seed gently, patiently, and allowed it time to germinate in Barral's deepest, darkest places. Amaury wished, he said, to see the object of his love unfettered, unadorned, unseraphed and in her purest essence, free of the injustice of clothes. He wished to see her undress.

It was not unprecedented or, of course, Barral would never have considered it. The cult of the troubadour was growing steadily. Nothing was so *de rigeur* at an affluent castle as the maintenance and entertainment of a knight-*trobar*. If he could not be fighting, declared Nerra, with greater and greater conviction, he would as soon be listening to a good poet singing in praise of his wife. But to have the poet see her unclothed?

Day by day, Sir Amaury showed him his wife afresh. It was fortunate, really. It counteracted some newly emerging faults in the sublime Alazais - like her melancholia. Amaury also counteracted boredom, that most fearful corrosive in any marriage. It was Amaury who had suggested she dress as a shepherdess and had even arranged a cast of sheep. Amaury had shown him his wife in armour; had commissioned a costume made wholly of flowers and addressed her in verse as the goddess Flora. He had even caused her to be dressed as a nun. Amaury could think up a different sport for every day of the month. But to see her undress? That was something to stir the imagination. That was Amaury's best notion yet.

'You must refuse! No one in the world could blame you for refusing!' Oriole told Alazais.

'And do you really think my voice will stand against Sir Amaury's? On the strength of past experiences?' In her distress she had pulled her hair loose and it splashed against Oriole like scalding water. What a malicious sense of humour God had that He made goodness draw like a magnet but sear like molten lead. 'It's a little thing,' she said, trying to make light of the prospective ordeal. 'My serving women have no privacy to undress at night. Why should I prize my modesty above theirs? It's a kind of vanity.'

'So you'll let Amaury have his own way in everything?'

She smiled her sad, stranded smile. 'Oh, there's a great many privations I'd wish on Sir Amaury. I'm afraid I dislike the man very much.'

'Most women don't deny him a thing.'

She nodded. 'I see it. I see it in his face. He's found the sweet things too easy to come by. He's stopped wondering if he'll succeed. So the wonder's gone out of him altogether. That's why his eyes are dull. They don't look. They just don't look.' She straightened her body like a candleflame when the draught is stopped up. 'I shall fix my mind on those eyes of his. Then I shan't mind. Not at all. Very little.'

She exasperated Oriole. 'You must love your husband very much never to refuse him anything,' he said bitterly. When she did not reply, he was just a little heartened. 'You don't, do you? Do you? Can you? Do you love him?'

'Love. All this talk of love,' she said irritably. 'My mother says it's a phase. A fashion. It'll pass, she says. Marrying won't pass. Marriage was God's making, she says. To draw the line where sin begins. I don't want to sin, Oriole. I've got no taste for it. Maybe I'm unnatural – l know women who make it sound like quicksand pulling them under. But I don't even feel drawn to go close. There's not a thing your Amaury of Herm has ever offered me that I want. I'm Barral's wife. That should be all that needs saying. Why do I have to go looking for modern reasons for an ancient practice? A hundred years ago there was nothing else, and a hundred years from now it'll still stand. Will this "Love"? All these "troubadours"?'

Her voice was even and soft. It rose and fell in shallow modulations, as though she had the firmest control over her emotions. And yet her hands were all the time entwined, rubbing and chafing as if she were washing. And tears appeared miraculously on her cheek: no contortions of the mouth, no screwing up of the lids, no running nose or sobs, but miraculous tears like those he had seen in Jerusalem wept by cold stone columns grieving over the death of the Saviour.

She fleetingly pressed her cheek to his, in gratitude for his sympathy. After she had gone, Oriole stood touching his cheek. He wondered if she were aware of the little rewards she paid him for his devotion. He supposed not. And yet at night, such little gestures of affection as her cheek against his, her squeeze of his arm, gave him grounds for fantasy, and Oriole's fantasies were the closest he had ever come to bliss.

Sir Barral and his lady did not sleep in the same bedroom. In a time when carnal love, even in marriage, was something the Church could barely bring itself to condone, conjugal visits were fleeting, not compounded by allowing flesh to touch flesh all night long. Husband and wife were encouraged to sleep in separate rooms.

That may have helped, in a way. For it would have been quite absurd for Barral to hide in his *own* bedroom to spy on his own wife while she undressed, whereas to hide in his wife's was relatively novel. Herm would undergo his Ordeal of Ascesis, and Barral could share the man's excitement vicariously without having to share his abstinence. Amaury sent for one of the oversized banners which hung from the battlements of his castle on feast days and had it fastened, in Alazais' room, across the alcove which narrowed into a window slit. This was to be their hiding place. In winter the slit was stuffed with oiled paper to keep out the draughts. But it was summer, and the slit was open to let in a little light; better the draughts than the dark. The banner made the room dark, so Barral had a dozen oil-lamps installed on every ledge and sill in the room to compensate for loss of daylight. Then he and Sir Amaury took up position in their hide.

Beside him, the knight-*trobar*, the supplicant lover, trembled like a greyhound. He recited prayers under his breath, experimented with rhymes, described his symptoms of agonising anticipation.

Unfortunately, an hour later Alazais had still not retired to bed, and Barral, restricted to standing up or resting his great bottom against the sloping windowsill, had cramps in his legs. He flapped his way out from behind the curtain and shouted at someone in the next room to fetch him a chair. He came back rubbing his thighs and complaining that his knees ached like the very devil.

'Listen! I hear her!' cried Amaury in a strangled whisper, holding one hand to his ear and one against his heart. 'She's coming!' Barral squeezed himself back behind the curtain, still showing signs of disenchantment.

Amaury complained, 'Where's the music? Why doesn't my wretch of a jongleur start playing? I told him to serenade her to her door.'

'I sent him to fetch me a chair,' muttered Barral. He was not acquainted with whispering.

The door opened and Alazais entered the room carrying a candle whose light was overwhelmed by the blaze of oil-lamps. An oily smell had begun to permeate the room, but the combustion sucked cold air in through the window and drew the banner out into the bedroom. Alazais stood staring at it, her face full of sadness. She blew out her candle and took off her headband and veil.

She folded the veil slowly, disconsolately, and laid it on the pillows like the angel folding Christ's headcloth separate from the other graveclothes. Then she unfastened her overdress. As she did so, she turned her back on the banner bearing her husband's heraldry.

Barral had just forgotten the pains in his legs when there was a knock at the door.

'Who is it?' Alazais asked in genuine astonishment.

'Oriole the minstrel, madam. With a chair.' She opened the door to him and he blundered in behind a high-backed oak carver, taking several attempts to fit the chair between the doorposts. 'Where shall I put it, sir?'

A growl like a flatulent bear's came from behind the curtain, and the chair, on its side, was pulled in behind the arras. When Barral sat down on it, his knees made two bulges in the hanging, and his feet protruded underneath. Both Alazais and Oriole found themselves looking at the great leather toecaps and studded welts. She even smiled and shook her head wistfully. 'Won't you play me some music, jongleur, to help me sleep?'

'I have orders to,' he replied brazenly. 'My lute's in the next room,' and he moved backwards towards the door, keeping his eyes on the lumpy banner as if, by looking, he could increase the absurdity of the charade.

'No. Don't play out there,' she said. 'I can't hear you from there. Bring your instrument in here.'

'Certainly, madam. If you wish.'

It was her retaliation: if you let that man watch, then I shall let this one, she was saying to her husband. The mutual pretence of the hiding place meant that Barral could do nothing about it.

There was either no time to consider how Oriole

would feel about it, or else she considered it a kindness, a reward of sorts. On the other side of the banner, Barral Nerra was wholly unmoved. He simply did not think in terms of Oriole as a man: only an instrument in Amaury's orchestra. Now he looked sidelong at Sir Amaury and, in imagining the man's sexual torment, his pleasure in the evening really began.

She could have climbed into the bed fully dressed and drawn its curtains round her. She could have rushed to bed in seconds, and pulled the covers over her head. But Barral would only have beaten her for spoiling his entertainment, and Amaury would have persuaded him to restage the travesty. So she moved slowly about the room, loosening her hair. She removed her shoes and set them neatly side by side at the foot of the bed. She removed her sleeves and placed them in the press, her belt and hung it behind the door. Her dress had no fastenings. She lifted her hems, leaned forwards, her arms over her head, and the biased gores of the skirt turned inside out like the flute of an umbelliferous lily, her hair the stamens.

Ascesis. Peter Oriole watched what he could never have, and his trunk filled up with molten liquor. Every nerve in his thighs felt the wool pile of his hose as though it were horsehair. And worse than the ache in his loins was the ache in his chest - the void bigger than an open mouth screaming. *'Stop! Stop! Stop!'* it screamed. *'Don't make me see what I can't have!'* He was Dives condemned to eternity in a lake of fire, cool water forever out of reach; his fingers scrabbled over the lute strings. How could this make a man 'better', this kind of torment? When a man was taken off the rack, he was only ever a broken man afterwards; invalid, crippled in body and mind.

Alazais had worked herself to a pitch of resentment - angered more by her husband's stupidity than Amaury's cupidity. She took hold of her shift at the knees and her fingers began to gather it upwards, fold by fold, from the floor, showing her ankles, calves, knees ... She saw her friend the minstrel look quickly to and fro between her and the banner, waiting for Barral to call a halt. She knew better than to wait for Barral to draw the line. He was a man without moderation. Pulling off her shift in one swift, defiant stretch of her arms over her head, she shook her head so that her hair remustered in a single flowing column.

A falling cadence of hair, a cacophony of beauty so loud that it made Oriole shield his ears, folding both arms around his head.

An exceptional gust of wind swirled in at the window and blew the banner out into the room - lifted it horizontally so that those on either side of it could plainly see one another. Barral had one hand between his knees, gripping the chair so tightly that his knuckles were white. The other arm encircled Amaury's waist, hugging him with gratitude or sympathy or both. His mouth was slightly ajar, and his bottom lip wet. His delighted face was that of a man in a cockpit watching his bird claw the eyes out of its rival.

In the crook of his arm, Amaury of Herm stood impassively grinning, almost too engrossed in his success with Barral to derive any sexual pleasure from the sight of the naked Alazais. The billowing curtain subsided, leaving only the eyes of the men showing through the slits they had cut.

Amaury tightened his gorge. 'Might I embrace my *domna?*' he asked in an awed whisper. 'Now? Now!'

The saliva had formed a reservoir in the back of Barral's mouth; he choked when he tried to speak. Not waiting for permission, Amaury stepped from behind the banner, wrapped Alazais in his arms and kissed her breasts, her stomach, her thighs.

'Oh yes!' came the orgasmic bellow from behind the curtain. 'Oh *yes!*'

Barral lumbered back into his possession, rending down his banner and inadvertently trampling his own heraldry. 'Out! You, him - out!' he shrieked through brays and snorts of his own laughter. 'Oh, isn't this Romance grand stuff! Grand stuff! Isn't it? Isn't it the grandest stuff in the world?'

Amaury took leave of his *domna* with an empassioned kiss to her throat, taking the opportunity to whisper in her ear, 'Whenever I choose, madam.' The woman's persistence in resisting his suit had begun to annoy him. In fact he had taken quite a strong dislike to Alazais; it was evident in the menace in his voice: 'Whenever I choose, madam.'

Then he pulled Oriole to his feet and hustled him out of the room with a parting wail of preposterous theatricality: *'I have lived and died inside a single minute!'*

CHAPTER FOURTEEN

Adultery

'Say the word, lady, and I'll cut his throat,' said Oriole.

'That would damn your soul and mine deeper than his,' said Alazais.

'You'd do better praying for me. That my husband should see through that transparent man.'

'But surely! When you told him what I told you! About the women at Poussarou. About the way he cuckolded ... '

'I didn't tell him.'

'You didn't?'

'Oh Oriole. Where's the proof? The ladies would deny it to their last breath.'

'I could tell a man where to dig! Where to find the empty bottles! The rennet bottles!'

There was another witness he could have offered, of

course. But Kadija's suffering at the hands of Herm was one crime he did not wish to lay before Alazais. Kadija was like someone he had known in a different lifetime - a childhood mistake.

'And anyway, how would I know about the ladies at Poussarou without your having told me?' she said. 'If you were to blacken him with Barral, I think Amaury might kill you, my dear.' She spoke as if she were soothing a child, and it began, just a little to jar with Oriole's picture of himself as her confidant and strong defender.

'You must get away, then. I'll help you get away from here. To some convent, and you can claim sanctuary till your husband comes to his senses.'

The idea had been in her mind too, a shaft of light, an escape route. 'Could I? Would you help me? Secretly, I mean? There's a Cistercian house at Floret-des-Etangs. I know Barral would come round in the end. He loves me better than you'd think.'

'The man's a beast and a lecher,' said Oriole, confidently dismissive, surprised only that she did not immediately agree.

Instead she said, rather coldly, 'Sir Amaury is the only source of my unhappiness and danger, Oriole. I couldn't endure another taste of him.'

Oriole spat. 'I swear if he lays one hand on you ....'

'Oh, don't swear, Oriole. Please don't swear. I've heard oaths enough to blow a large ship to Africa. Nothing said ever lasted.'

It was too much for Oriole. He fell on his knees at her feet. 'Oh, but that's not true, Alazais! I've made plenty of oaths in secret, at night, with no one to hear but God. And those will bind me till the day I die! I love you,

Alazais! I swear you're the blood within me, the air outside me, the sun over me and the ground under me!'

She stared at him for a long, long time, her astonishment complete. 'Does Sir Amaury know this?' she asked at last.

'Of course not! Do you think he'd let me near you if he did? It's past Amaury's imagining. He wouldn't know real love if it slept in his bed. He's blind to it.'

'I certainly was,' she said with a wry, anxious smile. 'Do please get up, Monsieur Oriole.'

'Haven't my songs said it? Now you know I wrote them? Don't they make everything plain to you? I'm your *drut*. What was ever surer than ... '

'What's a *drut*?' she said.

'You've been all tenderness to me. I know you care for me. You've said as much. You don't want to see me come to harm.'

'I don't wish anyone to come to harm through me,' she said. 'And what's a *drut*?' She stood as still as Lot's wife, her eyes resting on the window and the kaleidoscope of clouds turning and reforming within the rectangle of stone.

'I am! Say I'm your *drut* and I'll keep Amaury from you, by all I hold dear. By my life! I'll never let him near you! Never, I swear it. By the Virgin Mary, I swear it!'

'So *many* oaths,' said Alazais, and then repeated, 'What's a *drut*?' though in truth she knew already. When she looked back at particular instances, tried to remember where Oriole had been sitting, what he had been doing, thought of his expressions as she undressed a yard from his face, she realised that the problem had been there all along

'Forgive me. I'm not very familiar with your "Gay Science". So many terms and phrases.' She had taken a step or two backwards and in following her, on his knees, his hose had become baggy at the calf and were stretching to the limit their attachment to his belt. 'Lover. Is that what it means? *Drut* means a lover.'

'Yes!' He sprang to his feet, his ears red-rimmed, his freckles holding her attention, keeping their eyes from meeting. At last she said very flatly, with a weariness that brought her down to below his height, 'Must I sleep with you too, then? Is there nothing left in this whole world that goes by the name of friend?'

Oriole fled. He fled the disparagement in her eyes and the indictment in her voice. And as he ran, the phial of rennet in his purse banged in his groin giving the lie to all his grandiloquence. Yes, he had meant to sleep with her, but only to vent a love too huge to contain a moment longer. Yes, he had thought the honour would be granted in gratitude for his rescue of her. But that had not sounded like blackmail when he contemplated it! Not the way she made it sound! More like a white harbour, seen from a homecoming ship, growing more clear with every passing minute. Their coming together.

'Oriole, you have visitors.'

Like a thief running from the scene of a crime, Oriole stopped running, turned slowly, and gave Amaury one of his most ingenuous smiles. 'The Lady Alazais asked for music. I was just going to fetch music, sir.'

'Then I'll go for you,' said Amaury with a smile equally wide. 'I mustn't keep you from your visitors. Hurry!'

He should have known. A smile like that. It promised a knife between the ribs. He should have known. Lately he had made the mistake of thinking himself superior in intellect to his master - more cunning, silently outwitting his rival. How absurd.

It was Kadija. Herm had sent for Kadija.

She looked just as she had when he left her - not just unchanged by age but dressed in the same dress, her hair tied round with the same scarf, the sleeping child carried on the same arm, the same dazzle of teeth as her face broke into a smile at the sight of him. She was the same, but shabbier, the colour washed out of her: out of the dress, out of the scarf, out of the child's dress too. Shabby and creased. Her clothes had always been creased, of course, but now her face was creased too, as if left unspread to dry. So very black, as well. She seemed to Oriole blacker than he remembered.

The smile faded. They were looking at each other like old acquaintances too embarrassed to admit to having forgotten names.

'Your master wrote. Said you were missing me,' she said. 'He sent money, too. To fetch me here.'

He tried to remember when he had let slip to Amaury the name of the town where he had left his wife and daughter. What a mind the man must have, all the time to be storing away such trivia for future use; all the time collecting the pebbles to sink a man. 'Where's the bear?' was all he could think to ask, staying by the kitchen door, not stepping any closer. She swayed a little towards him, but her large, broad feet held to the one spot: big feet with protruberant bones, like fardles of wood bound round by the sandal straps, overspilling the sole. They were white with dust to the ankle.

'He died,' she said, 'He was very old.' And then after a long while, 'I thought you must have died too.' Her French had changed, of course. She spoke it as though it were her own language now. A little presumptuous that, thought Oriole, to make free with a language that doesn't belong to you.

'I almost did. We were no sooner back than the King and Queen split, and we followed Eleanor rather than the King.' He could hear his voice rising and falling, singsong and intense, like a child making up fibs. 'Then in Poitiers. No sooner settled that we were up and off here. We won't be here long, I daresay.'

She had hardly noticed the hardships of the journey down France - as difficult a route as any eel squirming overland to reach its birthplace. Now the weariness caught up with her. The joy she had felt at seeing him again after so very long was extinguished by the draught from the door: he was still holding open the door with one hand, as though for quickness of flight. 'You don't ask about the girl,' she said.

He shrugged. His mind was full of more important things. Amaury had sent for Kadija and the baby, to blacken Oriole in Alazais' eyes. There were steps to be taken, plans to be made. Where could these two be hidden from Alazais? 'She seems as she was,' he said and went and tousled the girl's curly black hair in dutiful affection. But his fingers caught in the child's tangled curls and she woke up momentarily and blinked at him with sleepy eyes before remoulding herself to the con tours of her mother's body. He was the one to gasp.

'Well? Did you not think she might have grown a little

in four years?' said Kadija bitterly.

'I recalled her the size she was.'

'But didn't recall her very often, seemingly.' She thumped herself down on the bench where the servants sat to eat. All the rigours of the journey overtook her and her eyes seemed to sink away then and there into deepening sockets. 'The other's dead. Same time as the bear almost. Just after. I left her with neighbours. Fell down some stairs into a cellar.'

He was disgusted, horrified. 'What were you doing leaving her? Where were you? They probably pushed her. Took the chance to push her down the stairs. You probably gave them the chance they'd been waiting for.'

'Maybe,' she said impassively. 'It was hard. Being Spanish in a French town. All alone. I wouldn't have left her but for the labour coming on me.' She looked at the child in her arms: a detached, faraway look, as though she had never been asked before to compare the worth of her children: the one she had got in exchange for the one she had lost. 'This one's not simple,' she offered as an afterthought. 'I had plenty to eat while she was coming. You left me with plenty to last me for the first year. I called her Jerusalem, because you were there. They told me it wasn't a fit name for a girl, but she was already christened. What could I do?'

She said more, but he could not follow it. His mind was too swamped by the revelation. He lifted the child out of her arms and held her up at arm's length. She woke and was frightened, but he did not notice that either. He was too busy seeing his likeness in the round brown face, his seed in the strangely exotic flowerhead trumpeting in his face. 'She's mine. This one's mine. Yours and mine. I can see it. She's mine. My daughter. My child. Jerusalem! What's wrong with it? It's a fine name!' He whirled the child around and she swallowed her cries like unchewed bread. She tried to reach out to her mother, but was only held the tighter by this stranger with the white face and gingery hair and gleeful, noisy mouth. 'There's none of him in this one. Nothing of him at all. His one died, didn't it? His is dead. This one's mine, aren't you? Aren't you? Aren't you!'

'God gives and God takes away. That's what your people said.' Since the death of her first child, a certain distance had opened up again between Kadija and the Catholic Church. The priests in Vitry had not been charitable towards her, though she told them that her husband was one of God's soldiers fighting to regain the Holy Places. They had refused to bury her dead child in Christian ground, or to church her after the birth. And when the money had run out that Oriole left for her, and she had had to earn money in the best way she could, they had excommunicated her, calling her a black whore, the rag on which Satan wiped himself.

Oriole, delighted as he was, still had to hide his marriage from Alazais. He took Kadija and Jerusalem into Arles and lodged them there. But by the time he returned, there were messages at every door - 'Your master's looking for you!' - at every window and wicket. 'You were missed at dinner. Lord Barral asked for a song and Sir Amaury had to sing without you. He'll skin you for sure.'

Not a bit of it. A few blows with the reins of his horse and Amaury's wrath was used up. He was far too well pleased with the way dinner had passed off.

'My Lady Alazais missed you at dinnertime,' he said moving his horse sideways across the bailey yard so that Oriole was forced back and back and back. 'But I put her mind at rest. I told her your good news. Wherever you were, you were sure to be bedding down your wife and child, I told her. These Moorish women need to be kept warm in the cooler climates.' And just as the space closed between horse and stable wail, with Oriole trapped between, Amaury dug in his stirrups and the beast lunged away through the low postern gate. Lord Barral was waiting outside. The two left at a gallop, racing the twilight to reach their weekly appointment at the brothel in ArIes.

He tried to explain to Alazais. He told her how the marriage had not been of his making - how he had never loved the black woman - no, not for a moment - never thought of even mentioning her, since the tie was so loose. He quoted ruling precedents from the Courts of Love: that true love can only exist between the unmarried. He summoned to his command all the best of his verses, throwing them at her like streamers of ribbon intended to catch in her hair. He vowed vows and swore oaths and declared himself her only true friend.

Then she looked at him with lilac eyes and said, 'Jongleur. Earlier, before I understood ... '

' ... You took me for an opportunist! You thought I was trying to copy Herm! Trying my hand at seduction!'

'Earlier,' she repeated, 'this afternoon - before you *declared* yourself, almost all I could refuse you was love. Because I never felt any for you. But now, now you've stated your case ...'

'Now? Yes?'

'Now I can gladly refuse your company, your music, your presence and everything you like to call friendship. I find I don't like you, sir. Like or value you. Do you think I haven't suffered Sir Amaury quoting me Pythagoras and Champagne? Do you not think I've read my Bible that I don't recognise the voice of the Serpent selling apples? I'm very, very glad that my husband is summoned into England. Maybe this is God's answer to my prayers. I pray Barral won't find room in his baggage for garbage like you and your master.' Her voice rose from a whisper to a shout, like an incoming wave that overwhelmed Oriole in icy coldness and, as it withdrew, washed away all the treasure out of his pockets, all the wealth out of his hands. The only thing it could not wash out of him was the great iron mass of his obsession, the burning phosphorous of his desire. That alone remained inside him, as large as pain.

CHAPTER FIFTEEN

Trial of Love

'I've written nothing today,' said Oriole. 'I lacked the inspiration.' Amaury laughed out loud. 'What's this? A sulk? And I thought you'd be so grateful to me for fetching home your kin. Yes, and why have you billeted her so far out, the delicious Karima?'

'Kadija.'

'I'm sure no one here would think less of you for having such a wife. It's a nice point that - an interesting topic for debate - whether anyone could think less of a man who began his existence so far down the scale of general consideration.'

'The man's my equal who takes the trouble to insult me,' said Oriole.

In fact they were, at that particular time, about as

equally balanced in interdependence as they had ever been or ever would be again: Oriole supplying the verses, Amaury supplying the rank. The only difference was that Amaury had planned the route ahead, whereas Oriole was stuck so fast on the sandbar of his obsession that every tidal day threatened to rip him in pieces. It had worked a peculiar sea-change on him.

'So you're not going to write me a song for the water joust, eh?' Amaury beamed with amusement. 'And you think that's going to tax me to the quick, do you? That I can't still cobble together a pair of verses without your help. Well, *there's* a sleight. Enough to make for a challenge, I'd say. What about it? A trial in the Courts of Love. A contest in the Lists of Poesie. You against me. A song in praise of the inestimable Alazais? And written down, too! For posterity to judge us.'

Oriole pretended to give it his consideration, but his heart had leapt at the idea. The gentry of the entire Camargue and half the Languedoc would be at the water joust. Oriole resolved to shine so brightly that Amaury would be cast into the shadows. Barral would find his prized status symbol had been nothing more than a tame monkey jabbering the words his jongleur had written for him. And most important of all (he told himself) Alazais would be obliged to hear the difference between Amaury's tinny insincerity and a song inspired by true love. Patron, esteem and *domna*: he would win them all with his song.

'I'll compete with you, Lord Amaury,' he said with a sleepy ennui. 'A song written down in praise of the Lady Alazais. A trial in the Courts of Love.' He went at once to the desk in the troubadour chamber where he customarily wrote, pretended to be writing as Herm left the room. 'One thing, my lord!' Oriole called while the door hanging was still jerking on its rings. 'One thing I forgot to mention. Did you hear that the Lord Barral's summoned to *England* by the King?' There came a noise outside of someone kicking a log-pile to pieces.

Next day, the castle emptied, dozens of wagons transporting the last minute chandlery of a waterborne joust down to the river: the gilded oars, the lateen sails stitched with heraldic beasts, the pointed bowsprits carved into spirals as if to gore the hulls of rival boats. The Lord and Lady Nerra required music to accompany them as far as the river, and every minstrel, every jongleur, every herald with a bugle, was pressed into the procession. Down on the coast the encrusted cauldrons were cold; the day was declared a holiday and the unaccustomed lack of steam in the air brought the mosquitoes off the étangs with holiday appetites.

To be on foot amid other troubadours' jongleurs did not much demean Oriole. It was only a temporary abasement. When Amaury came by on horseback, overseeing his grand pageant, Oriole called out, brash as a cockerel, 'Your song finished, is it, my lord?' as he flourished his own over his head. The jongleurs round about him looked him over with cynical, disparaging eyes, thinking him a simpleton.

The river above Arles was barely visible for the multi-coloured bulwarks of the fleet of barges moored like pontoons, from bank to bank. They banged and bored each other, restive on the current.

The oarsmen eased and squeezed past one another, endlessly swapping places. The knights enlisted to joust were balanced on foredecks at the prow of each barge. They rolled on wide-apart feet, with varying degrees of confidence.

The ladies were stacked in a gantry whose cloth fascia was painted to represent a ship. And tied alongside, so as not to mar their view of the sport, another galleon-in-miniature had been constructed of scaffolding timber over a landing-stage. A crow's-nest, with pretty golden balustrade was raised no more than twelve feet off the ground, but encompassed space enough for a gallery of minstrels as well as a high-backed bardic throne of a chair. Everything rolled a little on the current.

The jouster coming downstream had the distinct advantage; the barge fighting its way upstream was jolted more by the pull of the oars and the knight on the prow would peck and stagger, his lance dipping and wagging. The return run evened the odds. And besides, the dosing speed was what chiefly mattered, the collisions and woundings of such violence that the losers were thrown bodily into the river. Little butty boats clustered about every prow, like sea lice on the jaws of salmon, ready to rescue fallers from the water. But early on, the weight of their armour carried two men under so quickly that even divers could not find them. Recovery of the bodies was postponed until a time when dragging the river would make fewer inroads on the festivities.

For once, Amaury was competing in his own joust.

It was glorious, gilded pageantry. It was picturesque in the extreme, the barges far brighter than any real, full-size ship, a creamy bow-wave added to every prow in white paint, to exaggerate the speeds. But Oriole had no heart for it. His eyes wandered again and again to the figure of Alazais, in a blue gown that made the river look foetid and green.

Amaury's boat steered a course almost nose-on to its opponent. It came careering downstream, while a poltroon of a bachelor flailed at it with a wagging lance. But he held his ground, that bachelor, and his lancepoint caught in the strake of the oncoming barge and was snatched out of his hands, smashed between the two boats as they collided.

They jarred together. Crewmen fell this way and that, comical in their pratfalls, tumbling out of sight. The butty boats were shunted this way and that. The spectators on the gantry laughed and pointed and screwed their eyes against the light to see better. (Except that Alazais did not smile: Oriole noticed that. She did not smile. Lately she never smiled.) Both knights were gone from their foredecks. Sweet indignity! Amaury eliminated from the lists! This was Amaury's day to lose and lose and lose, thought Oriole. He would come out of the river covered in duckweed.

The oarsmen grimaced and sweated. The strain was killing. They cursed whoever had concocted such a day's sport. They were ostlers and farriers and grooms and armourers - men accustomed to horses and dry ground. After a while, they began to miss their tempo, clatter their oars, barely keep pace with the current when they turned upstream. They were heartily grateful for a pause in the proceedings.

'A pause for music and refreshment!' declared Sir Barral staggering ashore and kicking at the ground for not lying still beneath him. He was a survivor in the jousting. His great ballast had made the prow of his barge bite deep into the water. Solid as a turk's-head knot, he had deflected the wavering lances of lesser men and knocked them into the bilges. He was well pleased with the day. Otherwise he might have been more aggrieved with his knight-*trobar* (where was the man?) for making such a poor show. He went and placed himself beneath the golden crow's-nest, where Oriole sat marooned, a little nauseous at the motion of the landing stage.

Barral addressed his guests, bellowing. 'My troubadour - you've heard me speak of him before - has a protégé!' he declared. Oriole gripped the crow's-nest's golden battlements. 'They entered into a challenge, so it seems: the troubadour and his jongleur - to do best justice to the subject of my wife - the treasure of my house - the exquisite Alazais. While the oarsmen rest and the maids bring to you rosewater and wine, let the Trial of Love commence: between Amaury of Herm and his jongleur ... ' He snapped his fingers above his head. Oriole was astounded that the man should even know where to find him. 'What's your name, boy? I forgot.' Astounded, dumbfounded. Where was Amaury to deflect all those staring eyes? *'What's your name, I said?'*

'Oriole, sir. Oriole.'

'Gloriole! So. Yourselves the judges, my lords and ladies. First of all the jongleur, Gloriole. Gloriole of Herm ... Where's your words, lad?'

'I have them by heart, my lord.'

'I have Herm's here,' Barral muttered, more to himself 'Where is the man?' He was holding a roll of vellum, sealed with wax: even from his mast-top Oriole could recognise Herm's seal, an island ringed with crenellations. It frightened him, that seal. It drew attention to the difference between them, master and jongleur. He recalled that day at the Castle of Lilies when Amaury had submerged Jocelyn de Foicelles like honeysuckle smothering a wall. Was he about to do the same thing to Oriole? And where was he? Whichever way Oriole looked, from his crow's nest, he could see Barral's stewards searching for the troubadour. They craned their necks, scouring the busy crowds. They hailed the rowers coming resting by the bank - hailed them with exaggerated gestures and not shouts, for fear of interrupting the recital.

Maybe his careless contempt of Barral made him think he need not actually be present to read his own poem. Or maybe he knew his verse was so bad that he feared to show his face. Yes, that was it!

Thus Oriole resurrected his courage. Summoning up his *serenade*, he read it off the air, winding out the predictable tune like wool off a distaff. Directing his words at Alazais, he saw her sitting sorting her fingers in her lap, not hunched with shame - more straight-backed in martyrdom, pinioned as she was by the gawping spectators. The crowd's heads turned to and fro between poet and subject, comparing the aptness of his similes. The noise of the river muffled everything. He had almost to shout to make himself heard - as if commending her for sale.

What is this exquisite light that over yonder

Burns like the sea of Troy so fiery bright?

It is sweet Alazais who fires such wonder
As pales Helen's glory as day over night.
She arms the mounted year with lances twelve;
She decks the branching year all o'er with May;
She wounds the heart with spears of joy that delve
Full deep the secret chambers of ...

What drivel. The words grated between his teeth like black cloves stuck in a rotten apple. A trashy tiny artifice of a song. He had laboured so hard to outdo Herm that he had forgotten how to say a thing straightforwardly, how to make a poem say, 'I love you'.

The last line was greeted with paroxysms of applause. Even the other minstrels stationed below the crow's-nest clapped him. The crowd threw smiles across to him in his gilded crow's-nest like oranges to a tethered bear.

Even Barral wore the look of a customer well pleased. After all he had bought a mare and found it was in foal: his knight-troubadour had brought him a second talent to parade in front of his friends. 'Well done, Gloriole! Well done, indeed!' But where in all Creation is Amaury?'

There was animation farther down the river. The stewards had gone aboard one of the barges and were remonstrating with the exhausted rowers, demanding that they put out again into midstream. They got nothing back but abuse and divots of river water slashed off the watertop with oar blades. The rowers did not want to go looking for drowned men.

'Must've meant his jongleur to sing his song?' queried Barral. 'Mmm? Yes. Here, then. Take it. But mind you do it justice!'

They were pulling away from the shore now, the stewards up at the bow, peering into the water, poking and prodding at mare's-tail weed with lances and boathooks and oars.

Oriole broke the seal. The words stood there on the paper like so many reeds sticking out of a running river. Preoccupied as he was with the search going on down-river, he could not at first make the letters form words, make the words form sense. Then he saw what they said.

Best that Amaury should be dead: if not drowned then pushed back into the river as he crawled ashore, trampled face-down into the mud of the bank, cut through with the keel of a boat or beaten to slurry with a rower's oar. 'I can't read this, sir,' he said aloud. But Barral had gone from the landing-stage - gone to take his seat beside Alazais. He had already determined that Amaury should not be insulted with a win by his jongleur. A laurel wreath lay in his lap which he fully intended Amaury to wear.

The minstrels below the crow's-nest poked at Oriole's feet, their awe giving way to derision. 'I can't read this,' he told them, and they thought he was just jealous.

He was not jealous. He was bereft, bereaved, desolate. The river hissed him.

'*Oh, do get on!*' bellowed Barral.

'*I can't, my lord. I can't find a tune ...* '

'I can!' An eager jongleur - boy of no more than eleven, glimpsed an opportunity to rise in the world. He shot up his hand. 'I could find one, my lord!'

'*Do it, then. Good lad.*' The boy climbed up and snatched the paper out of Oriole's hand.

'Oh, it's very short,' said the boy.

Rejoice with me all you who ever loved or kissed
For I have entered in upon my bliss.
Last night when raised, it met no scorn, my hunter's
horn
She simply silenced it with kisses three and four
And gave me more than I had dared implore.

Oriole watched the words pelt Alazais like so many rotten eggs as she stood in her gantry like a pilloried whore. The gasps of the crowd diminished suddenly as Barral got to his feet - a volcano of a man whose tremors shook the entire stand and whose eruption might swamp them all. A few, on the row-ends, actually broke away and ran, trying to dissociate themselves from the public cuckolding of Barral Nerra.

But he did not begin to break things then and there. He strode down the chairbacks of the gantry as though they were stairs. He walked on to the landing-stage with its imitation mast and silly crow's-nest. 'Give me that,' he demanded of the minstrel holding the songsheet with its broken seal. When he had it in his hand he ran his eyes over the inky erotica then wagged it overhead. The letter shook but the man did not. He even tried to laugh. 'Is this your doing, Gloriole?' he asked. 'A prank? Come on now, Gloriole. No harm in a prank.'

'No, sir. On my oath. It's Sir Amaury's hand. See for yourself ...

But it's not true, sir. A poetic invention. The Lady Alazais never ...'

'And where is he to tell me that?'

Powerless to answer, Oriole looked impotently towards the river. The stewards came running with their own catastrophe.

'...He was dislodged when the boats collided, seemingly...' they reported with giant gestures of bewilderment. '... not been seen since . . . whether he was picked up or not by the small boats ... 'They tried to deflect the blame for Amaury's disappearance by exaggerating the strangeness of his disappearance.

If Amaury could have been found, Barral might even have let him laugh away the crime. He was a showman, after all - Master of Revels. He might have convinced the chevaliers, the petty gentry, the clergy and the wives that his song was a saucy make-believe, a boast, a crow, a joke, a dream.

But Amaury had disappeared. Amaury was nowhere to be found. All that remained was the song sheet with its pretty seal as irreparably broken as a virgin's ring; the sheet of paper and the author's pretty jongleur and a crowd shaken by sporadic hysterical giggles. There was also Barral's wife, standing white-faced amid whispering faces half-covered by hands.

Barral wrapped his arms around the mock ship's mast and hugged it to him like a bear scratching itself against a tree. Great grunts of rage and exertion burst from him as he raised it out of its socket in the landing-stage and spilled it - crow's-nest, minstrels and all - into the river. Then he turned and screamed at the women and clergy and children and elderly gentlemen to 'get out and be damned'.

'All except *you*.' And he plucked up one of the burning torches demarking the stage and brandished it at his wife.

They abandoned the gantry as they would a ship at sea already alight, but even before the last matron, the last arthritic baron or bishop had climbed down, Barral was jabbing the torch in between the chairs, commanding them to burn, demanding that they catch alight.

Still standing erect and aghast in the centre of the seating, Alazais realised that she was to be given no right of defence against the imputations of the song. Barral believed them.

He who had given his friend her mouth to kiss, had given his friend a sight of her naked, had suffered his friend to touch the Holy of Holies - had been betrayed. The ingratitude offended as much as the crime itself. But that Alazais should give away her husband's possessions into the hands of a usurper: that was a crime so perfidious, that the very river should coil out of its slime and swallow her out of the sight of decent men.

'Barral, I hate the man!' she shouted down at him. But he only went on poking the burning torch again and again between the benches, setting the ladies' embroidered cushions alight until plumes of blackening goose feather burst into the air with irregular thumps of ignition.

Alazais fled to the end of the gantry and gathered her skirts close. Lascivious flames were groping at her underclothing. Barral stood below her. 'So! You had to taste, did you? Where's that prim face now? Where's those protests of yours now? Where's that mouth that wouldn't kiss? Eh? Eh?'

After his fall from the crow's-nest, Oriole came up under the staging. There was barely any clearance between water and planks. Only by turning his head sideways could he bring his mouth up to breathe, and every wave slapped him in the face and choked him.

But he had stood in a river and watched a woman killed once before. The awful familiarity of the sucking silt transported him back to the Bathys river, back to the massacre of the Germans. He handed himself, hand over hand, out from under the planking and reached up over the staging for a handhold to pull himself out. The young boy who had sung Amaury's song was panicking nearby in the water, his grip sliding on the felled mast and his head disappearing repeatedly below water.

The ladies were screaming and dragging against their husbands' determination to walk off along the towpath. Either they wanted their menfolk to intervene or did not want to miss seeing the outcome of the excitement. But only Oriole bobbed at the riverbank, trying to pull himself out of the water so as to deny the song, to deny the calumnies and slurs of the song, to deny his own association with Amaury and the song. After all, the man was gone, lost, washed down river, tangled in his own inexplicably evil motives, and there seemed no one left alive in the world but Oriole who knew the truth about Alazais' virtue.

Barral was divesting himself of the huge gold crucifix with its pilgrim medals, as though it would free him of Christian restraint - mercy, tolerance, forgiveness. But in fact he only meant to use it for a weapon. As the gantry of burning seats began to decay at the centre and fall in like a honeycomb spilling its yellow honey of fire, Alazais jumped. She landed at her husband's feet, stumbled on her dress and fell up against his legs. And he swiped at her with the crucifix, its heavy chain knotted in his fists, its clutter of amulets jingling. He flourished it like a flail, with a systematic, even rhythm, his heels lifting off the ground with the force of each blow, gratified only when he could see the sin winnowed out of her in flying red seeds which stained his corduroy.

'*Stop! Stop! Stop! Stop! Stop!*'

The sun on the gold was so sharp it cut the eyes. Momentarily Oriole hesitated just beyond the scope of its arc, like a child waiting to run in under a skipping rope. But Barral could not see or hear him. His ears were full of his wife's Screams and his eyes were full of tears. More than his pride had been sawn through by the ripsaw of Amaury's verse. Its teeth had gone deep. After all, hadn't the knight-*trobar* invested great time and industry in teaching Barral to love Alazais?

'*It's not true! It's not true! Herm never touched her!* He's a liar. He was always a liar! He lies and lies!' Oriole caught hold of the crucifix as it sliced past his face, and wrenched it down hard behind Barral, so that the chain was pulled tight across the massive shoulder and the great stoop of the man's back. 'He's the Devil himself,' Oriole panted, suspended from the chain.

But there was madness in the man, a giant, hereditary madness that could destroy and destroy without seeing what it destroyed, through the sheer energy of anger. He felt Oriole pulled close up against his back, cold, slight and wet; and he heard the word 'Devil', and experienced it as a chilly burden between the shoulderblades. He shook himself with revulsion and shook the Devil off.

He was drunk. The rage inside him actually impaired

his co-ordination, his balance, his speech, his reasoning. 'So you love her too, do you? You've had her too, have you?' When he finally unfastened Oriole and sent him somersaulting in the grass, he stamped at him as he would a beetle, raising one foot and wavering on the other before stomping down again and again. A troll, an ogre, inflated to giant proportions by his fury, the little world shrank to insignificant repellence: an ant's nest.

All Oriole could do was to cover Alazais with his own body, knowing that she would otherwise die, unsure whether she was not already dead. He could not help it that the act of protecting her looked so very like the sexual act itself, man and woman face against face, trunk against trunk, the woman still curled up against the blows.

Barral peered through the smoke of the fire and he saw in the flesh what Amaury had only described in words - his wife covered by a man, and he a spectator, excluded, made cuckold in open view. He gave such a roar of grief as God must have made at the sight of First Man and First Woman coupling.

'*I repudiate you!* I repudiate you! In the eyes of God and before these my neighbours, I repudiate you, Alazais of Florriac. I repudiate you for a whore and I put you off. I call upon God and my neighbours *never to call you wife hereafter!*'

His neighbours had melted away. There was no one to witness the repudiation but Oriole and a few minstrel boys bobbing in the water like Halloween apples.

'I witness it, sir,' said Oriole very quietly. He whispered it like an endearment, in at the ear of his beloved. Then he waited for Barral's sword to run him through, him and Alazais both, as they lay on the ground entirely vulnerable.

But Barral had no weapon with him. Even the crucifix had disintegrated at last and lay, chain here, medallion there, glinting in the sun. He did not trouble to gather them up, but reeled away, still drunk on rage and disappointment, still insensible to having destroyed his own happiness.

CHAPTER SIXTEEN

To Hold and To Have

'Fontevrault,' said Oriole lifting himself on his elbows. He spoke it into her face as though he were renaming her now that she was his. 'Fontevrault. I shall take you to Fontevrault Abbey. The Duchess - I mean Queen Eleanor - she meant it for women like you -'

'Women like me? Whores, you mean?'

'For wives abused like you. To keep them safe from their husbands.'

The face beneath him was cut open like a windfall apple attacked by birds. The gashes swelled and coloured as he looked at her, to purple and black. They exaggerated the unnatural pallor of her skin and made her look already dead. The eyes, though open now, had a lifeless glaze. 'But I'm not a wife, am I?' she said. 'You heard him. He's put me off.'

He wanted to say, 'So much the better for you. What's lost?' But he knew what it was to be put off. He knew what it signified to be cast out, defunct, relegated to the world Outside. Instead he said, 'Oh, but he'll undo all that. When he knows the truth.'

She closed her eyes against his stupidity, though she wanted, wanted to believe him.

'Come with me. Can you get up? I'll take you to my house. Kadija will look after you. She's very good. Balms. Potions.' For a moment he was accidentally swallowed up by his own fictions: his wife, the healing mystic. But then anything was possible today. Magic was at work. Amaury was drowned and Oriole's beloved was to sleep under his own roof. When Alazais did not move, he picked her up in his arms and carried her to the cart which had brought the scaffolding poles. The driver complained every yard of the journey about his loss, about the burning of all his timber. 'Will he pay for what's burned, that's what I want to know.' Oriole did not listen, only whispered reassurances to Alazais that it was worthwhile to stay alive.

She did indeed look close to death. The burns to the back of her legs were slight, and no one, however lovely, dies of facial cuts and contusions. But the great internal vessels of the body, of which he knew nothing, might have been fractured by the kicks and be leaking even now, as they clattered by the amphitheatre. As he approached his own house, he bellowed for Kadija to 'Come and help, can't you?', to 'Be careful! Go gently! Show some tenderness for once in your life.' Once Alazais was installed in the one bed, upstairs, her presence filled the house with a mixture of reverence and fear, like a holy object stolen from the high altar and hidden overhead. Downstairs they waited for repercussions.

Operating in total ignorance, Kadija sensed that something momentous had taken place which would change life irreversibly. She also sensed she should not ask questions; her husband was wound up to the point of hysteria - alternately exultant and aggressive, looking up to the ceiling with the eyes of a devotee, finding fault with Kadija for her noise, the squalor of her house, the anarchy of her daughter.

'Can you spare all this time to be with us?' she ventured to ask only once. 'Aren't you needed back at the castle?'

'Who by? By who?' he crowed in a high-pitched voice she did not recognise. 'Amaury's gone and Nerra's possessed by demons. Who wants to be in a place like that?' And she was left to wonder what dire occurrence had brought her to what predicament.

She went and asked about among her neighbours. The whores at the brothel were able to recount the events at the river joust, between sobs and groans and loud lamentations for Amaury, drowned Amaury, their best customer. Kadija, dry-eyed, returned to her house and sat down by the doorway, and pulled sewing into her lap and looked at it, thread by fraying thread.

The journey to Fontevrault could not begin at once. The injuries Barral had inflicted on his wife demanded rest. More debilitating still was her state of mind, shocked off-true like a building after an earth tremor.

Oriole had also to discover whether Barral's repudiation had been passing pique or a thing carried through: Church formalities, papal legalities. He tried to find out if Barral had taken any measures to secure the Truth about the wife he had accused. But he only came up against foolish, overheated rumour: Amaury's boots had been found in Alazais' bedroom-semen stains on her sheets, trinkets hidden among her clothing. It was preposterous.

When Jerusalem pulled over a stool on top of herself and bumped her head and cried, Oriole's rage erupted with the whispered hiss of steam escaping compression. 'Can't you teach that child any civilised behaviour? Does she have to wreck the place like a savage always?'

He went upstairs, ostensibly to apologise to Alazais for the disturbance. But he was gone a long time.

Kadija, riding out the storm in the pretence that it was a passing thing, asked him cheerily when he returned, 'And how is the lady?'

'She was asleep,' he said remotely. His frown implied she had shouted her question into the ear of a man with a blinding headache.

'You stayed a long time, then, if she was asleep,' said Kadija, exerting herself hugely to sound cheerful.

The frown dissolved. He was in need of a confidante. The comradeship in her voice undermined him. She had no right to question what he did, what he was thinking, but he did so lack for a friend to confide in. 'Yes. I was looking. Just watching her sleep. She is so beautiful, isn't she? Even now. Even battered about. She's so ... well ... '

'Beautiful. Yes, she's very lovely,' said Kadija, inexpressive. Her face registered nothing but impartiality. Only the child, whom she pulled close to her in a rigid, protective embrace, began to cry with intuitive fright.

After that, Oriole spent a great deal of time upstairs, watching the Lady Alazais sleep. He would stand at the foot of the bed, watching the soft rise and fall of the bedclothes as she breathed, watching her hands open and close as she dreamed, watching the eyeballs flickering beneath their purple-rimmed lids.

After a few days, it did not seem any great progression to squeeze between the bed and the wattle barrier separating his section of the roof void from next-door and to arrange her matted hair more agreeably on the bolster, to defend her from troublesome flies, to lift back the covers a shade to see how the bruises to her breast were turning from yellow to purple.

He did not question why she never disturbed out of sleep in all the times he stood looking at her. He never noticed that her eyes were sometimes so tightly shut as to trap the lashes at a different angle, and that her lids trembled. He was sunk so far into fantasy that he envisaged her sleep as something magical - a hundred-year suspension of suffering granted her by fairies for her marvellous goodness. Sometimes in the evening, when Kadija took her lentil broth, there was a murmur of voices like doves in the chimney. But he himself never saw Alazais awake.

Then at last, when his wife prepared a basin of warm water made disinfectant with wine, Oriole suddenly snatched the bowl from her and ran up the rungs of the ladder and drew the curtain closed across the entrance to the upper room. Kadija retreated down the ladder and stood at the bottom, her fingers clenched in her hair as she might clench the mane of a runaway horse. But she knew that no amount of tugging would restrain Oriole.

Any reins she had ever held were broken. He had been set loose in Paradise. His obsession had taken possession of him.

Oriole set by the bowl and drew back the covers, a priest uncovering the Holy Sacrament on Easter morning. Alazais, lying on her side, did not stir but the tendons in her back appeared to contract. He put his head close to her; she smelled of sweat and camphor, but beyond was a savour he had known all along would be there. It struck him as miraculous that he should have known her scent ahead of time. He even remarked on the wonder of it to Kadija, emerging from the bedroom in a trancelike stupor, wearing a foolish grin, easing the front of his shirt to allow his heart more scope.

She was a picture of domestic calm, sewing in the doorway for the sake of the light. A bobbin of thread lay spinning on the earthen floor, but he could not trouble to wonder what had set it spinning. The little girl was asleep, stretched out on a straw sack in the abandon of deep sleep, her head tipped back so that the lids stood half-open without her being awake. The whole scene was reassuring. It shored him up within his happiness. He needed to confide.

'I love her *so much*,' he said, sitting down opposite, bright-eyed like a child at its mother's knee. He smiled remotely, his head tilted on one side. 'Oh! Have you any idea how much I love her? She's like a dragon inside me. I don't know, though, no: it's as if she can *summon up* a dragon from somewhere inside me - deep inside.'

'Dragons do wicked things,' said Kadija without looking up from her sewing.

'No, no, no. Nothing that's not in their nature! The

birds and the beasts - they follow Nature's way.' An obliging skein of ducks flew over soon after, though, to Kadija, their honking sounded derisory. 'See! Following the paths of instinct, that's what they're doing. If we could be high up like them and look down and see the natural path printed out ... '

'But instead we only have God,' said Kadija deliberately. 'Looking down.'

But Oriole was deaf to criticism. He had rescued a maiden from violence and calumny. He loved her with a love too magnificent to encompass anything unworthy; a love so white hot that it must scorch away any smut on the great shining disc of his heart's escutcheon. He contemplated what he had seen in the upper room. The damage done to her face was no more than to a papier-mâché mask which, in this heightened, visionary state, he could lift off to see the unblemished perfection beneath. The bruises to the body he could not even see as he stared now, and stared and stared with the eyes of a seer, at the Grail of his quest.

'What are you going to do?' asked Kadija, though she knew already. Better than he did.

'I shall look after her,' said Oriole standing up reflexly. 'I'll take her to Fontevrault. She'll be safe there. I shall dedicate myself to clearing her name. I shall lay my songs and skills at her disposal - for her to send me where she wants when she wants. I'll ... '

'But first you'll rape her.'

She did not appear even to have said it. Her head was still bent low over her sewing. Her needle still stabbed in and out, in and out. With an incandescent crackle of straw, the child woke and sprang up on to her knees, laughing:

'What do you know about Love?' blared Oriole, and crossed to the ladder and went up it so fast that its feet jumped in their worn sockets of earth. The child called after him, 'Where did Papa go?'

In the upstairs room Alazais was awake too, raised up on her elbows, clutching all the bedding to her breast.

'What does she know?' said Oriole, declamatory as a Roman. Alazais said nothing. 'I give my life into your service, lady!'

'That's more than I asked and more than I ever wanted,' she said at last. 'Perhaps a little help to reach Fontevrault ... ' He had begun to take off his clothes and to lay them on the foot of the bed like tributes. She pulled the cover over her head and began to rock to and fro, saying, 'Oh Christ Jesu, but I don't love you! Not you. Not him. Not any of you!' He did not seem to hear her. 'What is this word?' roared the voice beneath the covers. 'You think you have only to say it and everything's allowed. "Love!" Oh Christ! Oh Christ! Oh Christ! Do it, then! Do it, do it, do it and be damned to you. Then just let me go to Fontevrault!'

Inside Oriole, the dragon's flame guttered. It was a conspiracy. Both women wanted to undermine him, wilfully misunderstanding him. Perhaps their female brains were too narrow to comprehend the full grandeur of Love. For a few moments, Oriole harboured thoroughly misogynistic feelings towards them both - a low-water of affection - before the tides of passion swept back and submerged Alazais' unkind ness. A bitter outrage would always separate him now from his stupid, insensitive wife, he knew that, but no misunderstanding would be left standing between him and Alazais once he had broken down the barriers of flesh between their two souls. He sprang on to the bed and, holding her head between his two hands, kissed her.

She hardened her lips over her teeth and spat him out of her mouth. She turned her head aside and looked at the floor, her lilac eyes full of tears. She was not even willing to entrust him with her eyes.

The dragon fire within Oriole fizzled out and left rum stumbling about in clouds of black, choking smoke. He retreated, crammed to the jaw with self-pity, on the verge of tears himself, went outside and sat on the rungs of the ladder, halfway up, or rather halfway down from Paradise. It was cold, but although he gathered his clothes round him, a refugee's baggage, he did not put them back on but sat still, staring into the lower room's darkness.

It was a thick, material blackness. The daylight wedged in the door way and sifting through the damaged wattle walls was only a leak in the pitchy hull of darkness, a localised lack of darkness. Nothing at all impinged on the darkness within him, where his dragon-fire had burned.

But a man's silhouette - no, several silhouettes - did impinge on the sunlight in the doorway. A priest stepped indoors with a presumption only priests can show towards privacy. Behind him, a head of fiery red hair glowed in the backlighting, incandescent: a corona round the black sun of an unlit face. In his surprise, Oriole stood up and his scalp grazed the joists of the floor above.

Behind Amaury came a whore from the brothel next door, with a mare's nest of henna'd, purpling hair. Also two professional knights, ducking their heads under the door lintel, feet still planted in the sunshine.

'Is she here?' said Amaury.

Afterwards, Oriole could not think that he had said anything, uttered a single word, while Amaury chattered on. He thought it the greatest of jokes to go on and on thanking and thanking and thanking Oriole in tones of heartfelt bonhommie, making him ridiculous, turning him back into a tool.

'We thought you were dead,' said Kadija in stark surprise.

'Quite right that you should. I went to great pains and a deal of outlay to have people think so. I even had to take a wetting and leave some of my armour on the river bed. And thanks to your husband's excellent endeavours, I succeeded very nicely, thank you, ma'am ... Who won the contest, by the way, Oriole? Or did the proceedings break up early? I hate that. I hate to see an entertainment spoiled, business half-finished. That's why I went back to the castle from Arles. After I climbed out of the river.'

'Is everyone ready to proceed?' the priest interrupted, tense, impatient and uneasy. 'Is this the lady?'

'No!' Kadija had no notion what the priest wanted, but his manner was all aggression, accusation - as if they might have come to flourish at her bell, book and candle. She kept asking Oriole what was happening - the day was quite dreadful enough already. But he had been struck dumb by the sudden resurrection of his master. He just stood bare legged on the ladder rung, gaping.

'Is she up there?' Amaury asked. 'Have you kept her safe and sound for me? There's a good fellow.' He invented Oriole's replies. 'Still recovering from Barral's temper, eh! That man really should curb his temper. Too ill to appreciate visitors, would you say? Well, no matter.

The Moor here will serve as proxy. You'll do that, won't you, woman? Not a very onerous task, I promise. Oh, and I can vouch this woman's a Christian, Father, I was at the baptism myself'

The priest was plainly a conspirator, an accomplice whipped in at high speed by a combination of bullying and bribery. But he bridled at a proxy, said, 'No! I must see the true woman. She might be dead for all I know! Or gone away.'

Amaury gave no more than a swerve of his eyes and the two men in the doorway blundered into the overcrowded room and plucked Oriole down off his perch. One went up the ladder, pushed his head through the door hanging and grunted with satisfaction. The priest's robe was an impediment to him climbing the ladder, so the second of the professionals lifted him and posted him up the stairwell, to see for himself that the woman in the upstairs bed was alive.

'I'm content,' said the religious, and waving away the knights, he gathered up his gown effeminately and climbed down again, showing a pair of white, wire-haired legs, a fine linen undergown and a pair of expensive shoes. He began the wedding service even before he had reached the ground.

'You mean to marry her?' said Oriole, his voice huge and full of horror. The prelate paused, then droned on, speaking the required words while his eyes shifted anxiously about. It was nothing new for him to have his words ignored, talked down. After all, they generally concerned sin and prohibition. 'You're going to marry her?' said Oriole.

'Well, of course, little friend. I wonder you didn't do it

yourself while you had the chance. She's worth twenty thousand ecus and fifteen hundred acres again, now her husband's put her away. She's fair game to be seized on now ...'

'But he hasn't put me off! He won't!' Alazais stood at the top of the stairs in her shift, her blonde hair dark with sweat, the circles round her eyes exaggerating the depth of the sockets. Hers was a face that had fasted a month. But she had managed to convince herself 'He won't. Not without proof. What's one poem?' Her shift filled with air in the updraught from the open door.

Amaury opened his hands helplessly. 'Ah, but the stains on the bedsheets, lady! All those little tokens so badly hidden in your chamber. I'm afraid we made a poor fist of concealing our love.'

'He went back,' Oriole told her in a flat, desolate bellow. 'He went back. While I sang. While Barral was beating you half to death. He went back. To the castle. He went back. He fouled your bed. He left tokens.'

'Won't you join us, lady? Beloved?' asked Amaury. 'My dear, you must have known the extent of my determination. Just as you must know how pointless it is to protest.' And he waved his hand about the assembled company to demonstrate the impossibility of escape. Alazais retreated two steps and pulled the door-hanging in front of her. Oriole could hear her breathing, crying just a little on every outward breath. Like a dog whimpering in its sleep.

'Do you, Sir Amaury of Herm, take this woman, Alazais of Florriac, for wife?' the priest was saying, doggedly.

'Oh, no question there,' said Amaury. 'I do, I do, I do.'

'And does this proxy Alazais of Florriac take this Amaury for husband,' the priest asked Kadija.

She was crouched down by the open door, her daughter clinging to her in fright at such a bombardment of faces and noise. Kadija's face was a scowl of confusion, of resentment at the intrusion; of bewilderment and resentment at the grief Alazais had already brought into her house, her marriage. When she hesitated, one of the professionals pulled her to her feet so that she dropped the child. He twisted her arm behind her back.

'Yes! Yes! All right!' she cried, the words startled out of her. And then, seeing that her words would marry her husband's obsession to another man, 'Yes, I do. I do take him.'

There was a single cry from the upper room. It halted the proceedings only as long as the cry of a barn owl might halt the burning down of a barn.

'Now, it must be consummated,' said the priest, anxious to be gone.

Amaury went up the ladder without use of his hands. He drew back the hanging and left it drawn back. But no eyes tried to follow him beyond the flapping blanket and its clattering rings. The priest regretted the need to stay. Kadija regretted her collaboration now that she saw what it meant for Alazais. After all, she had nursed the woman, fed the woman, found her pleasant, likeable, almost pitiable despite her wealth; felt now a comradeship with her. The professionals, restraining Oriole now, lobbed obscene, monosyllabic jokes across the top of his head, snorting uproariously.

As for Oriole, he stood between them, bound like Samson to the pillars of the Philistines. And if he had been Samson and not a slight man, built like a ginger tomcat, whom people mistook for a boy, he *would* have pushed down the pillars, demolished the house, brought down the wattle and joists and planks and roofbeams. He would have brought down the clouds and the sky beyond it, the spheres and all the windows of Heaven with all the reservoirs of water above them. He would have shaken the earth till the planets fell like fruit. But since 'he was a slight man, built like a tomcat, he merely stood between his guards, and wept.

He could have seized on her. He or any man in France could have seized on her - upon her twenty thousand ecus and her fifteen hundred acres, upon her perfect body and her maleable name. She was a ball Barral Nerra had thrown in the air with all the force and inaccuracy of blind wrath: she might have fallen to any man who cared to open his hands and catch her. And instead, Oriole had helped her, cherished her, admired her, assisted in her ravishment by the man both she and he chiefly loathed.

She made no sound. No noise at all came from the upper room but the thud, thud of the bed; the wood frame encircling the straw sacks had never stood level on the floor. *Thud, thud, thud.* Between the planks of the ceiling, strands of straw and little gouts of dust fell on to the occupants of the room below. Oriole watched those winnowings of straw, watched the spiders dislodged by the thud of the bed's fourth corner.

Ever since Poitiers, Amaury had been closing on this moment. Like a hyena which wears down its prey by sheer endurance, sheer persistence of cruelty, he had waited his time, closing closer in with every nightfall. Every step had been one patient step nearer to Alazais' repudiation and the chance to rush in under Barra's arm and seize from him the prey.

When Amaury reappeared at the head of the stairs, he was gasping like a man who has been too long underwater. The grin was clewed to his face with rusty staples of drying blood, but the scratches clearly caused him no pain. He beckoned the priest to witness that all the requirements of marriage had taken place, but the priest only mumbled that he was satisfied and waited out of doors in the sunshine for the furtive exchange of money. The professionals too were paid to spread the news: that Amaury of Herm was married into the estates of Florriac.

At the door of Oriole's house, Amaury stood and laughed with sheer delight in himself It set Jerusalem laughing, too. He swung the little girl round by her hands. Two earthenware pots were knocked from the table by her feet and smashed. But she went on laughing, in imitation and delight. Oriole tried to snatch Jerusalem away, but Amaury simply tucked her under his arm, where she dangled like a piglet won at a fair. So Oriole said, with all the malice in the world, *'That's not your one. Your* bastard died, you know. Fell down some steps and died.'

Amaury looked down with some distaste at the child under his arm and dropped her unceremoniously on the floor. When he was gone, Oriole picked up his daughter and held her to him, barely knowing who or what he was hugging so close, only aware of the need to empty out affection, shed it, be rid of it for good.

CHAPTER SEVENTEEN

Bridegrooms

He stayed with Amaury, of course.

He told himself that it was the only means of keeping close to Alazais. He told himself that he could at least supply comfort and friendship to a woman beset by wickedness. He even told himself that he might one day kill Amaury and take back what he had stolen.

It was none of it true. Amaury, having seized on her land and inheritance, and feeling nothing but a vague dislike of the woman herself, committed her to a convent. An austere, joyless prison it was, chiefly patronised by fighting men, pilgrim knights and merchants who travelled long distances and did not care to leave their wives unattended.

The women moved in a grey limbo, neither given over

to the holy life (and therefore avoided by the nuns), nor living the life of married women except in their conversation which revolved eternally round the subject of their husbands. Having no life of their own, they lived vicariously through their husbands, so that each newcomer underwent a rigorous interrogation exactly to place her on the ladder of social rank.

Alazais of Herm and Florriac was relegated to the lowest status, for she refused to tell anyone anything about her husband. She concealed from them his island realm in the west bounded with cliffs, left untold any of his noble exploits in Outremer, and failed to mention the vast sums of money she alone had brought to the union.

Some of the women (having established their husbands' importance and influence) complained nostalgically to one another of abuses, violence, deviances, mental cruelties. But Alazais said nothing of those either. The women concluded that she was not a wife at all, but a mistress, or had been cloistered away not for the great danger of her beauty (as they liked to account for their own incarceration) but for some shameful, unmentionable failure. As soon as they glimpsed her husband, none could believe any fault lay with him.

Amaury visited her once a month. He begged the *mère ancille* to send a messenger informing him each time the moon exerted its influence over his wife's tidal flow, then visited Alazais within the fortnight. But since Oriole trained the messenger to bring *him* the news, he contrived to distort the moon's influence a little. He laid a tide rip between Alazais and the chance of her conceiving. That was all the protection he amounted to:

a time buffer. Of course she might always have appreciated the solace and companionship of a child - even Amaury's child - but such a thought was beyond the range of Oriole's imagination. He was, after all, a man.

So while he accumulated a string of children - all daughters - his master got none, something which confirmed Amaury in his dislike of Alazais. When, after a year, she had still not conceived, he grew bored with observing so strict a calendar and allowed his travels to take him farther and farther afield.

He picked up the chivalric lifestyle of a wandering knight as if a mere season of inclement weather had kept him from it. He went in search of a *domna* in whom to sink his adoration.

Like a ship sinking its anchor through the soft spine of an unsuspecting skate.

He had shifted ground, of course. Leaving behind the salt-grey landscape and smell of rotting vegetation, he shifted inland, north of Marseilles, so as to orbit his newly acquired estates. It was not the blood-red Languedoc, but that was to his advantage, somewhat, since there was no chance of encountering any of the ladies of Poussarou or his other, earlier conquests.

He was greeted by Alazais' relations as her saviour: the chevalier who had rescued her out of the teeth of that savage beast Nerra: the man who nailed his relatives to church doors and was probably descended from the Devil. When she did not re-appear in person to confirm their good opinion, they had ample compensation in Amaury, the charming and talented acme of the Age of Talent and Charm.

Poetry was in the ascendant. Poets were the darlings of the hour. Amaury of Herm and Florriac planted his feet beneath the tables of Alazais' forebears and grew in wealth and repute. He thrived. And since Oriole grew like a mistletoe, parasitically, from the boughs of the great man, he did not shrivel and die either. Not outwardly at least.

There were other river jousts, other tournaments held in gardens tropical with Mediterranean flowers. At first, seeing the lances blessed before every tournament, Oriole looked for the justice of God to strike Amaury out of the saddle with a sanctified wooden point. But it soon became plain that God admired enterprise, rashness, the man with initiative, just as He had cherished Barral Nerra. Unless, of course, He thought more slowly than Man, operated on a more ponderous time scale.

It was to Amaury, socially and politically esteemed Amaury, that the legate in Paris sent consuls to request his help.

A castle, in the chain between Amman and Aqaba had lost its Frankish ruler: dead of dysentery. Being a money-fief, the King could not reclaim it: it now belonged to his widow, a sturdy but headstrong woman of twenty-two.

'But widows can remarry,' the diplomats told Amaury. 'That woman - she's a vacuum waiting to be filled.' The citadel encompassed the Springs of Giguel and dominated several lucrative caravan routes; its peninsula of sand, separating Transjordan from Sinai as it did, must on no account slip out of Frankish hands. Cyprus and Jerusalem were already commending to the widow various strategic suitors: strategic, that is, to Cyprus and Jerusalem. It was vital that Princess Ingrid, as she chose to be called, should marry someone sympathetic to Frankish interests.

Amaury thought at first that they were suggesting he marry the woman, and pointed out that, though his wife chose a retired, solitary life, he was in fact a married man. But they were not in need of a bridegroom - simply of Amaury's expertise. A volunteer to marry Princess Ingrid had been found - one Comte Raymon Tirrel. But since the Comte was fifty-five, his success was not guaranteed.

'So what we suggest,' said one of the consuls, 'is that you employ your very great knowledge of the Arts of Love in the sentimental education of Comte Raymon. The better to further his suit.'

'Woo the lady for him, you mean,' said Amaury, and they squirmed in their chairs and nodded. 'You were recommended very highly to us.

Incur the gratitude of both King and Church with one favour? It was too tempting an opportunity for Amaury to decline. He had thought never to go east again, to eat sand again, to go where he could not control the degree to which he sweated. But the mission appealed to him. The vicarious wooing had to be kept a close secret. (The Comte was sensitive over his shortcomings as a lover.) So the party was to be kept to a minimum. Amaury said that he would take just one jongleur: it would suffice.

Oriole was crossing the yard, just then, leading a pair of dogs. When Amaury called his name, he shielded his eyes against the sun and looked in their direction. A scowl. A studied recalcitrance. Nowadays, he cultivated a surly shabbiness, a shag of ginger moustache, a disregard for buttons and whether or not he combed his hair; a certain lack of personal hygiene, though once he had been fastidious. The diplomats found the sight of him alarming. But they were unable to dissuade Herm from taking this particular jongleur to Krak Kerak.

Amaury had long since lost the taste for finding different ways of repeating himself on the limited subject of Love. He had become reliant on his servant for the writing of songs and did not feel easy about leaving him behind. Oriole was in every respect like a dog - the kind subdued by blows rather than affection; utterly reliable - would never stray. But leave him unattended for too long and Amaury suspected one might return to find the furniture and fittings chewed and soiled, the library shredded. No, he preferred to keep Oriole on a short leash.

Oriole was horrified at the news of the trip to Kerak. It struck panic into him. To leave the convent unattended, its treasure protected by nothing but high walls and metal grilles. He felt premonitions of disaster. Though he never saw, never visited, never communicated with Alazais, Oriole believed himself to be her guardian, deluded himself, as the years passed, that in some way he kept her flame from extinction by the holy ritual of his worship. He would have pleaded not to go, if pleading made any difference.

'The worst risk is from the Templars,' said Comte Raymon. 'They're a law to themselves. They think they can do as they like and not answer to anyone.' The Comte had teeth the shape and colour of pistachio nuts crowded all to the front of his mouth as if, when he grew too excited, they would spill out along with his words. The passing of generations had eroded his jawline which was now no more than an overhang crumbling directly from lower lip to Adam's apple, and the tip of his nose drew back in terror from the overhang. But this last great adventure in his life had captured his imagination and he served up his plan of campaign to Amaury as though the dish were hot and he had run with it all the way from the kitchen.

'There are the Greeks, of course, but what nice girl would marry a Greek? Or a Cypriot! She'd have to be unnatural to take a Cypriot, wouldn't she? No, it's the Templars we have to worry about. They have a candidate, make no mistake. There they sit throned in their fortresses, lording it over the country from Jerusalem to Aqaba like ... like ... like ... '

'The gods on Olympus.'

'Just so! Excellent! Very good! Like the gods on Olympia, and they cast about for ways to swell their influence and sway events. There's no restraining them, you know? No sense of fealty. None at all. No national pride. Like a new breed of ... like some new nation of ... like a race of. . .'

'Titans.'

'Mmm. Them too. But don't set me talking about the Templars: since they've started to treat with the Byzants and God knows who else, they're my absolute antipathy. Not to worry! I have you to second me, don't I? I have you to ease my path into the lady's ah...' He thrust his hand through the sleeve of his coat and hunched it on to his shoulders. His exuberance for good sport was undiminished by the years, but he was fifty-five and needed helping to his feet, thanks to arthritis in his knees.

There was no disguising his disappointment on seeing Oriole. 'And you say women like him?' he murmured anxiously. But having heard the jongleur sing, both alone and in harmony with Herm, his confidence returned in double measure and he told the grooms to wake them up before dawn so that the journey to Krak Kerak could be accomplished as quickly as possible.

'I hear she's no rotten apple, you know. Shouldn't tax you to the limit.' (Tirrel knew nothing of poetry himself - had never found time to indulge. But he had every confidence in Amaury.) 'What shall we do? Will you coach me in what to say and how to behave? Do you want to see my wardrobe? Advise me on what to wear? And eat? I hear it matters what I eat. Or is it *whether* I eat?'

Amaury waited until he had his protégé's full attention, then instructed him in tones of earnest solemnity. 'You'll pitch you a tent with your banner over it, half a mile from the fortress. In plain view of the battlements. And you'll stay there and not put head or hand outside till I send word.'

'What, not come in, even, you mean? Not hear all this singing and so forth?'

'Not come in.'

Raymon was bewildered. 'You mean you'll do everything? Shan't I do anything at all?'

'Fast and pray,' said Amaury decisively, and the Comte was visibly cheered.

'Oh, I can do that, yes!' but he repeated the words to himself, in case he should forget. 'Fast and pray. Fast and pray ... You must remember to tell her how I can cut the head off a camel with a single swordstroke, don't forget to tell her that!'

'Extraordinary,' Oriole was moved to say, and the Comte beamed at him.

'Not extraordinary to me, man! I practised on horses in France, and when I came out here I practised on camels - oh, from my boyhood days I could do it. It's all a matter of finding the gap in the vertebrus. And strength, of course, brute strength.'

'And you can do it still?' asked Peter Oriole, fascinated.

'Show me the camel and I'll show you its windpipe!' Raymon exclaimed threatening to draw his sword.

'I'll hold it in reserve for a fitting moment,' said Amaury.

Whether or not Amaury would have liked to make note of the camels, his block of wax had softened within its frame and would no longer hold words intact. They were under desert skies now, not French ones. Flies were the only punctuation on the silent trail to Krak Kerak. Amaury discarded the tablet face up in the sand, his horse's hooves scuffed sand over the white square, and a small skink of some kind scuttled across it and sank mired in the liquifying wax. It strained, open-jawed, as if shouting, but no sound came out of its gaping mouth.

Comte Raymon pitched his tent and decorated it with every bauble and piece of glitter he had brought with him in his baggage. Like a bower bird he laid out his statement of intent. Then he ducked inside and sat, with one flap raised, sweating on a straw-stuffed cushion, awaiting the flash of a mirror on the battlements to summon him in to his wedding.

At night, the cold was such a torment to his arthritic knees that he could not sleep. So he passed the time contemplating the delights of being married to a young widowed princess. He decided he would adopt the title of 'prince': everyone else did in this part of the world.

'And does he have a person to match this sweetness of soul?' asked the Princess Ingrid. She had moved, by slow degrees, from pressing her erect spine to the carved chairback, face full of mistrust, to perching on the seat's edge. Now, like a canary on its perch, she swung forward and back in time to Oriole's music. Her fists, carbuncled with jewellery, were gripping the arms of the chair, an excitement Amaury was well accustomed to seeing. Her eyes ran delightedly over his mane of red hair and studied the falling folds of his clothes, as though he were the suitor, not just the messenger.

The Princess Ingrid had adopted Arab-style clothing - a short taffeta coat over a long underrobe encrusted with golden wire and semi-precious jewels. And she wore a muslin veil 'to keep her skin from darkening', she said, though it seemed unlikely that the strongest sun light would find its way through the dense glass in the windows.

'Is he a very great friend of yours, that you praise him so highly to me?' asked Princess Ingrid.

'Dear as a brother.'

'So that you couldn't easily spare his company for a great length of time.' She gaped her eyes at him over the gold rim of the veil: they were painted so startlingly black that her sockets resembled the twin impacts of sling shots - holes deep and ragged. 'I mean to say, you might visit him often.'

'Oh, then I fear I should lose his friendship,' said Amaury, 'for an envy would grow up between us. Even so ... ' He left the conditional hanging in the air - a piece of bait hanging in front of the tempted fish.

The Princess got up and minced, prowled, swayed like a cat along a high wall. Her hips wagged from side to side and she crossed each slippered step over the step before, while one hand couched on her hip and the other rested on her breastbone. The walk gave more an impression of incontinence than sensuality, but then she had been widowed a relatively few weeks and had only recently thought to practise. 'I suppose you must hurry back to your wife.'

'Indeed. Her health is frail and she pines for my company.'

She uttered a sigh full of might-have-beens, then said, 'You may tell Monsieur le Comte that I cannot think badly of a man with such a friend as you ... Oh no! Don't go! I didn't mean you should tell him now! Tomorrow. Tell him tomorrow.' She wilted a little against him and almost lost her balance when surprised by a sudden burst of shawm music from the minstrel in the corner, brassy and ribald honking, like an alarm of Roman geese.

The Princess retreated to her chair, but its bolsters - tasselled oblongs of brown brocade - had rolled into a heap and there was no recess left for her haunches. She lifted one of the bolsters and held it clasped to her vertically, sat down with it between her knees, her face peeping round at Amaury. Perhaps she was being coy.

Perhaps she was simply nervous of saying what she was about to say. 'I suppose I must wait and hear what this other gentleman has to say.'

'Other gentleman?'

She ducked behind the bolster. 'My advisors recommend it. It seems I am a very political person of a sudden, though it's not quite what a lady wishes to hear from her wooer.' She left her mouth ajar, waiting to hear that the strategic position of Kerak meant nothing to the Comte de Tirrel.

But Amaury, furious with himself for arriving late, had jumped to his feet, crossed the room, and was flicking at his minstrel's chest with the back of his fingers. 'I thought you said we were first on the scene,' he hissed.

'We were! We are! There were no other horses in the stable when I looked!'

Amaury was alarmed. 'Stay here. Give her another song while I go out to Tirrel. I must get some money to buy off these "advisors" of hers.' He called from the doorway, 'I'll take my friend what few encouragements I can, then, Princess! How long shall I tell the Comte he must allow to this "other gentleman"?'

'Oh, not long at all!' said the bolster, clenching its jewelled fists and lifting its feet a little way off the floor. 'Only just to hear what this Templar has to say for himself. Seemingly he's come just now from Krak des Chevaliers. To commend himself to me.' The bolster laughed nervously. 'Haha! A Templar! Isn't that commonly what *old* men do, join the Templars?'

Amaury's moment of panic passed. Even Comte Raymon would look more attractive to a young widow than some dour professional killer with the manners of a bedouin. He hurried away to bribe the Princess's advisors. Oriole broke out into song. The Princess talked incessantly through it - asked Oriole questions about Tirrel, questions about Amaury, kept up a nervous gabbling to herself and to the minstrel.

Suddenly a sharp draught caught Oriole in the back as a door hanging was drawn aside. Extraordinary. The weather outside so stifling, yet the draught so sharp, as if the Knight Templar who entered himself emanated cold.

But then ghosts are reputed to chill the air. And this was certainly a ghost. Oriole, as he crossed himself over and over again, had no doubt of it. For he had wished Jocelyn de Foicelles dead, and here was the dead man himself, in Krak Kerak.

Not far down the road, the risen Jesus had similarly walked in on his treacherous disciples, and made them feel their guilt.

CHAPTER EIGHTEEN

Trial of Strength

'Is that all you have to say?' asked the Princess, sitting erect within her throne of cushions, confidently displaying the jewels on both hands. 'That the Krak Kerak is of strategic importance?'

'In the protection of pilgrims and the defence of the region,' said Jocelyn. 'Honour enough for one Christian woman, surely? To secure the region for the defenders of Our Faith?' He had grown cadaverously thin and the sun had carved into his face lines as deep and symmetrical as the emblem pilgrims carve in the walls of their home churches in thanksgiving for a safe return.

Jocelyn had safely returned from the brink of death, thanks to the ministrations of the Knights Hospitaller. He had thought at first to join the Hospitallers, but they had insulted him by convening at prayer and discussing his acceptability. So he had opted instead for the Knights Templar - often the resort of seasoned warriors who have used up their passions for all but God and politics and death. The Order was full of widowers, malcontents, second sons and professional knights proud of their intelligence and their knowledge of the Holy Lands. They shared a common contempt of the enemy, but despised the pilgrims even more who came burdened with as many misconceptions as sins and took both home undented. They despised the crusaders who dashed like ferrets into a warren and sank their teeth into Outremer's goods and blessings then dashed back home within their forty-day amnesty from sins. Out of mutual respect (and hatred) the Saracen never took a Templar prisoner, but killed without exception - unless he was the one to die.

'And what's to say the Comte de Tirrel wouldn't defend the region just as well as you?' said the Princess, her heart more firmly set on Amaury's friend every time the Templar spoke.

'I am open to direction from the powers which know best.'

'Even to the point of marrying simply to secure a valuable trade route,' said Amaury cockily as he returned from satisfactory negotiation with Ingrid's master-at-arms. Jocelyn turned on him a look of monumental distaste. But Amaury did not see Jocelyn de Foicelles: he saw only a Knight Templar, an Arab-style kefieh over his helmet, the face no more than an extension of the armour.

'And yet you expect me to marry you when I might marry a man who loves me?' asked the Princess, speaking down her nose.

'My means and wealth equal his.' Jocelyn did not say it wheedlingly, as though to tempt. There was just the stark truth. Even if the Princess had been susceptible to the temptation of lucre, he offered her no flattering euphemism to hide her greed behind.

This man's heart isn't in his work, thought Amaury smugly.

'Do you think your virtues entitle you to buy a wife, then?' asked Ingrid haughtily. She allowed herself an exchange of smiles with Amaury. Though she would rather have secured the knight-*trobar*, it would give her pleasure to marry his friend. 'I hear no talk of Love from you, sir knight. And I see no tenderness in this person who wishes to *take mastery if my castle*. Am I not worth your consideration in that respect, or is your heart already given elsewhere and only your hand left available for marriage?'

'The Convention of Templars thought the matter too pressing to consider your tastes in men, madam. I, on the other hand, left no anxiety in their hearts as to the safety of the Krak. As for love ...'

It was at this inopportune moment that Raymon, sweltering in his tent and keyed up to further apoplexies by Amaury's sudden request for money, could not hold off for another moment. He burst into the room, red as a radish, his hair plastered flat by sweat and his cap flapping by the clip which fastened it to his only remaining hair. Even his teeth seemed to be sweating, for as he caught sight of Ingrid and hailed her - 'Princess! At last!' - little drops of moisture burst from his lips.

The look Amaury flung at him curbed him like a

lasso, and the whole room fell into a stillness in which Raymon's panting synchronised with the little shallow breaths of the Princess wrestling with her disappointment. The pause seemed endless.

'As for Love,' said the Knight Templar, looking his rival up and down, 'I see you have been allowing this *libertine-trobar* to summon up the demons of his trade. Love. Singing. Poetry. Desire. *Carnality*. Song is the corrupter of chastity. Love is the septicaemia of the soul. Your confessor will advise you to close all orifices of the body against it.'

'Oh!' The Princess jumped to her feet, her knees clenched tight together, her hands rising as if she would cover her ears. The orifices of her body were far more outraged by Jocelyn than they ever had been by Amaury. Amaury kicked Raymon's legs from under him so that he sank into an attitude of abject devotion. Peeping out of the corner of his eye for stage direction, he ducked his head and clasped his hands over his heart.

Through the red mists of pique and embarrassment, Ingrid regarded her kneeling suitor, trying her hardest to superimpose upon him the qualities of his debonair second. Even in his own, unappealing form, Raymon compared very well with an arrogant and offensive Templar who could talk only of septicaemia and *orifices*. She turned on Foicelles: 'Sir Jocelyn, I *would* say you come too late, except that I don't believe you could ever come too late for my liking. You see I have already decided to marry the Comte de Tirrel. Your journey was wasted, I'm afraid.'

Raymon gave a great whoop of triumph and, still on his knees, wrapped Amaury in his arms so that they appeared to be dancing, two dancers up to their knees in stone.

The Knight Templar stood rooted to the spot, his face so pale he looked like something disinterred from a rock tomb, his eyes sunk so deep that the yellow arch to each socket was not eyebrow at all but the skull pushing through. The deepest creases in his face ran vertically down the cheeks - as if his smile had been circumcised in some dreadful desert initiation.

But to Oriole he was indeed someone raised to life from a rock tomb. For here was God in person. God come for justice. The Lord had not been blind or absent during the desolation of Oriole's life: His timescale was simply bigger. He moved slowly. Slow and inexorable. Here was the knight whom God had kept chaste so as to make him the scourge of inchastity. Here was the knight God had preserved in the dry air of the desert, so that Amaury might be delivered up to him for justice. Oriole pressed his back and neck against the cool of the wall and smiled the complacent smile of the avenger biding his time.

He would tell Jocelyn what Herm had done: to Alazais, to the Gay Science, to God. And Jocelyn would draw his sword and slay the dragon Evil. He should have known that God would stage the final confrontation in this crucible of desert cliff and plain. For the territory of the Krak Kerak was the red of dried blood speckled with fat-flecks of yellow rock. Cliffs of blood towered over plains strewn with boulders like the chunks of flesh cut from a knight's body during holy combat.

'A show of arms, madam!' cried Raymon getting to his feet. Though his arthritic knees yelped their protest, Raymon of Tirrel declared that his betrothal must be marked with a show of arms.

Amaury did not forbid it. He might have done, if his
attention had not been given at last to the Knight
Templar: something familiar ... He had just put a name
to Jocelyn de Foicelles when he heard Raymon standing
on the threshhold bellowing for a camel.

'A camel, I said! Bring me a camel! Is everybody dead
or what? Fetch me a camel!'

The camel stood, oblivious of its role, in the central
courtyard of the castle. The Krak Kerak was of Arabian
origin and in the depths of its body were lungs - cloistered
yards open to the sky, aspirated by fountains. The camel
was not especially large - on the contrary, Amaury had
looked for the smallest he could find. But inside the
confines of the little yard, between the two fountains, it
looked very big indeed. The playing of the water incited
it to loose a fountain of its own and a jet of urine hit the
paved ground and splashed up again to the height of its
knees. The soft, sensitive frogs of its huge feet pawed at
the unfamiliar surface uneasily.

A saddle-cloth of red and gold had been thrown across
the slightly grotesque slump of the hump-like an old
woman's dug - but there had been too little warning to
groom the beast or starve it. It brought its flies and
fermenting cud into the castle with it, like the Horse of
Troy full of unwelcome secrets.

But the Comte de Tirrel, on familiar ground now,
demonstrated a new vigour, a lightness of step which
belied his age. He took up a position in front of the camel,
his sword drawn, checking that the constraints of the
yard would not restrict his swing or follow-through. He
wore a white linen coif which concealed his lack of hair

and chin. And with the scabbard of his great sword hanging down between his knees, studded with silver like Orion's belt, there was a certain theatrical grandeur to the man which held the eye.

'... paid het his unwelcome attentions while he sponged off Nerra,' Oriole was saying. 'Then, when he couldn't have her the usual way, he blackened her in public with a lie!' He swarmed over Jocelyn like a squirrel storing its winter larder in a tree. He loosed all his hard, vile secrets out of the pouches of his jaw and hid them in Jocelyn's ear. The Knight Templar stood in the courtyard's upper gallery, a good vantage point for watching the show-of-arms.

'... disappeared, pretended he was dead,' Oriole was saying. 'Then when Nerra put her off, back he came to get what he wanted. She was at my house! Under my protection, master! He came and he forced her! Married her - took her lands - took everything. He raped her, sir! He raped her! So you'll challenge him, won't you? You'll call him to combat, sir? You'll be God's executioner, won't you? It's all true! No word of a lie! And there's no sin in you, is there? I can see that. Everyone can see that. You only have to look at you to see it. No sin at all. He couldn't last above a minute! I'd've told Barral Nerra but he's a black pig himself - only a merchant! But you're a true knight. You can offer a challenge to another knight, can't you, master?'

Oriole dodged and darted to front, to back, to either side of Foicelles, ducking down behind the balustrade in an attempt to keep out of sight of Amaury below in the yard. The Knight Templar had passed no comment on the Princess's choice of bridegroom. His frosty face had simply set more rigid, his eyes sunk deeper. He had put back on his gloves: each glove had five fingers as if Foicelles had grown to physical as well as spiritual perfection within the Krak des Chevaliers.

The Comte Raymon began to make practice strokes, whirling his sword. Oriole broke off from his tale-telling to watch the famous feat accomplished. The camel flinched from the sudden whoop of the practice sword-strokes, pushing its big, rug-roll lips forward and gargling in its throat. Even from up in the gallery its big vat of a stomach could be heard bubbling like a still.

'For the Princess of this land! For the queen of my friend's heart! For the Lady Ingrid of Kerak!' Amaury was declaiming from the opposite end of the gallery, 'A *feat of strength! A flourish of manhood! The decapitation of a camel with a single blow! That the lady may know what strong arms will defend her always from danger and disappointment: a show of arms by Raymon, Comte de Tirrel!'*

Raymon grinned sheepishly. He liked the fanfare; he admired Amaury's way with words. He felt a deep gratitude for this renewal of virility, this glory he had barely expected to see again. He lifted the sword till its hilt rested on his shoulder, its blade drooping down behind. He was heard to say, rather banally, 'I hope I can still do this,' then, with the grunt of a wrestler, he launched such a blow that its impact filled the courtyard with a wetly explosive bang.

The camel's head flew through the air and hit a wall with the sound of a melon bursting. The adhesive compound of blood and marrowbone held it momentarily to the ceramic tiles, ears trembling, before it dropped down at Amaury's feet blurting out its tongue. The rest of the camel remained standing, its splayed legs locked at the knees, its bowels emptying in two pats that fell like hand claps in the silence. The claps were taken up by eager hands overhead, and a wild outburst of applause ricocheted round the gallery. Jocelyn de Foicelles was alone in withholding his admiration.

Several gallons of blood were liberated by the sword blow - a third fountain, red between the two of white water. It made the ground at Raymon's feet slippery. Missing his footing he sat down abruptly: they heard him curse at the indignity. Then he started to get to his feet again.

The camel, however, had a larger, more inevitable need to fall. It capsized like a ship, and though Raymon had risen as far as his hands and knees, it dropped on him, engulfed him, crushed him beneath the hairy sternum so that only his head was left showing. 'Oh damn,' said the head, but only in the manner of a posthumous spasm, like the two pats of dung falling on to the pavement.

The many witnesses stood immobile, their applauding hands glued together now, silent, in front of their breastbones. Speaking from the head of the gallery, Sir Jocelyn de Foicelles intoned, *'Vanity! Vanity, saith the preacher. All is vanity* ... Perhaps this casts a new light on our marriage, Princess.'

The Princess deemed it better protocol to cry salt tears over the balcony's edge than to answer.

'We dislike spurious words. Prattle. So duplicitous. So listen,' said Jocelyn. 'We took the precaution, of securing the Krak Kerak, irrespective of today's *comedia*. A detachment of Knights Templar is even now entering the castle, Princess. I would strongly advise you to accept my offer of marriage without further delay. We will take the place with or without you.'

The Templars - Turcopoles for the most part - emerged from every doorway, weapons drawn, and herded the household, its guests and its slaves, into the large water cistern beside the Springs of Giguel.

In the winter season, a rise in the water table filled the cisterns nearly to the brim. At this time of year, however, the detainees found themselves standing no more than ankle-deep in a stagnant residue of blood-warm water full of dead flies, locusts and unidentifiable leaves. There were no trees nearby to account for the leaves.

They looked like the Damned consigned to cauldrons to make everlasting bouillon.

'I thought you were dead, master. I was sick with grief!'

'So you attached yourself to Amaury of Herm,' said Jocelyn.

'Writing words for him, yes! The man lost all his art! Too idle to compose - too jaded. I wanted to perfect my trade, you see? I had great hopes of breaking away - in my own right, you see, sir?'

'So you lent your black art to the Devil to help him practise seduction the better. Made Satan more plausible, yes?' Oriole's mouth fell open. He could not believe what he was hearing.

Sir Jocelyn had shut himself away in the Princess's *retraite*, cracking his cloak behind him like the thunder, plunging into sudden silence. It was like seeing the hinder parts of God leaving the Holy Mountain: Oriole wanted to take off his shoes in reverential awe. But chasing after him, slipping between the hands of the Turcopole guards, denying absolutely that he had any real association with Raymon Tirrel's entourage, he burst through the raffia hanging into the little room at the head of the stairs, thinking to find the knight at prayers or writing a dispatch to his Prior.

Jocelyn was doing neither. The room had windows to it - not the stained glass of the churches Oriole had seen in Paris or Jerusalem, but thick, blue-green glass faulted with bubbles. So the office-room was as cold and dark as deep water - Oriole was plunged underwater and could see his own pent breath escaping in strings of bubbles up the sea-green lancets but never reaching surface. The knight had taken off his kefieh, helmet and gloves. His white tabard, with its big red cross, was folded in a separate place. And he was smoking opium.

His yellow curls had been devoutly cropped away too much to conceal the stark geology of his cranium. His flesh was stretched so tight that the strange piebalding of pink with white might have been the skull protruding through translucent tissue. There was no red left to his sucking lips, and his teeth were discoloured behind them, so that his mouth appeared ragged, damaged, worn out by speaking too many words over the years.

'If I'd known you were a rival for the Princess, naturally I'd've found a way to tell her about you. I had no idea that you ...'

Foicelles cut him short. 'To me personally, it is offensive that matters of military and political strategy should depend at all upon a woman's inclinations towards copulation. But I follow orders. Naturally. We Templars are obedient to discipline - more so than any other body of fighting men. Fortunately she decided as she did. It permits me to follow our alternative course of policy and to take possession of Kerak by force: a more straightforward and satisfactory route.' His eyes were as opaque as the thick glass in the deep recesses of the windows. They did not fix on Oriole but wandered, all the time seeking to rise as something hollow does when constrained underwater. Now and then they disappeared into the top of their sockets and the bottom lid rose, and the closed eyes trembled, marbled by dark purple veins. 'My prayers were answered. I had no personal wish to marry the woman.'

'But you will still challenge Herm to combat, won't you master? For the dishonour he's done to Knighthood! For the hurt he's done to the Gay Science! For all the things he's done that I told you!'

The water pot at Foicelles' feet bubbled with its narcotic fumes - a noise like the camel's stomach rumbling before its head was off. Jocelyn was silent for so long that Oriole thought stupefaction must have robbed the man of sight and hearing. He breathed in to speak louder and his head filled with smells and sensations which made him nauseous and dizzy. But just then, the bottom lid rolled down and behind it the eyeball, and Jocelyn, when he spoke, did not slur the words. His constitution was well used to the effects of opium. 'Necromancy,' he said. 'The *Gay Science?* Give it its true name and call it the Devil's Science. Used by lechers. Praised by whores. Poetry. Chants to raise demons and tempt virgins. Song is the exhalation of Hell.'

'But master ... '

'Minstrels. Jongleurs. All bawds and monkeys.' Oriole froze.

Jocelyn's limbs twitched with some involuntary spasm. One foot knocked the cooling jar of his opium pipe and he reached out, reflexes unimpaired, and righted all the copper apparatus. Parts of it must have been scalding hot, but he righted it even so, with a hand dappled the same as his face. Jocelyn was turning to snow. Not only had he lost the feelings of his heart - for Love, for Beauty, for Art - but the loss had permeated through his inadequate coverage of skin so that he felt no bodily pain either. No pain in body. None in spirit. Oriole, on the contrary, could feel such a quantity of fear inside him that it was spilling out through the palms of his hands.

Jocelyn saw how his eyes rested on the mottled hands. 'Oh yes. You're quite right. I have it. They say it's a judgement from God. Leprosy. For the sins of my youth.'

'But you never did any - '

'Oh many. Many. Please don't attempt flattery. It vexes me more than any other form of lying. I know my sin. The abomination of Verse, for one. And this, of course. This.' He flourished the stem of the opium pipe. 'After Damascus, the Hospitallers used opium for the pain. It came to me as a mercy, you see, and I kept it for a vice. My life has been full of vices. Words. Thoughts. There was a time when my mind was quite taken up with filthy contemplations. Quite taken over.' His voice had at last lapsed into the singsong exaggeration of a man intoxicated. Suddenly he shouted, *'But I repented!* I repented and I gave myself to the Templars. To God's body-guards - Oh, quite literally. We guard the places where Jehovah took on flesh and dwelt. *Ergo,* God's body-guards. They have shaped me to their needs. I let them. Let God shape me. It was so plain after Damascus. My life had been spared for a purpose. And so I bend. I am shaped.' He sat there and said it, as inflexible as the rock wall behind him, and said it: 'I bend. I am shaped. And now God has sent me leprosy that I may feel no pain when I fight. Not a judgement. A gift. D'you see? Not a judgement. A *gift.'*

'I see. I see.'

'So if I were to fight *"Amaury of Herm",* I should be wearing the armour of God.' He was emerging, through some climactic release, on to a level of quiet, deliberate, transcendent pomposity - a height from which he looked down on Oriole as something infinitely small. 'But why would I stoop to spitting a chicken? "Amaury of Herm", pht! "Amaury of Worm."' He drew energetically on the opium pipe and said, 'You recall, Oriole'

It was the first time he had used the name. It astounded Oriole that his name was still there, within that mangled reconstruction of Foicelles' past. It chilled his blood.

'You recall, Oriole, how the man pitted himself against me in Ephesus? Well, after that I made inquiry into "Sir Amaury of Herm". It took a great time. Documentation of his realm was hard to find. Small. Very small, you see. Do you know, Oriole, what the place Herm is?' Jocelyn laid a limply heavy hand on the minstrel as he asked the question.

'An island, sir. A great island. To the southwest of England.'

'Mmm. Well perhaps not quite an *island*. More of a rock. Well, perhaps not quite a rock. More of a pebble. A speck in the sea. A hazard to shipping and a roost for seabirds and a den for seals. Do you suppose the man's a seal himself that he rules over a realm of seals? A comte of puffins. The Duke of Gulls. Oh, a king over all gulls, no question of it. You see, there is no souzerainty of Herm, Oriole. No fief. No castle. You have bound yourself in service all these years to a dungboy - a carrier of buckets, a scraper up of strewings. A gypsy for all I know, born under a hedge. He's a passer - off. A liar. A charlatan. An impersonator. A fraud. An impostor. A mouth. And that's where you choose to put your words, is it? Well, very apposite. Very fair, as I see it. Cess into a cess pit. Piss into a kennel. Challenge it? *I wouldn't tread in it!*'

'That's why he could never go into England,' said Oriole, but said it only to himself. For the few moments it took for the news to settle home, Oriole was unaware of his surroundings.

Amaury was nothing. His livery was a mummer's costume. His heraldry was painted scenery. His whole life was a scam. His household, his staff, his entourage, his minstrels had attached themselves to a fair ground quack. Perhaps only Oriole, who had pedalled quackery himself, could measure the size of such a sin. As for Oriole, his life had just been devalued: alchemist's gold translated into lead. Everything was gone.

Everything was gone - not least his protection in a vicious, vengeful world.

'When you found this out,' he said quietly, as if trying to question a madman without provoking violence, 'why didn't you send word back? Defame him? Tell the King? Have him taken up?'

'Ah, no, no, no, no, no,' said Jocelyn, holding the pipe at arm's length and examining it with one eye closed. 'He preys on the weak, and the weak need purging. The weak, the vain, the lecherous. Whores and painted women. Women like this Nerra strumpet you were telling me about. Men like her husband. Scum like you. The likes of Herm are put on Earth to winnow out the damnable. Draw them to him like iron to the lodestone. He serves his purpose. To destroy the vainglorious.'

'So you'll leave him, then? To God?' whispered Oriole, and was all of a sudden relieved, heartily relieved.

Jocelyn turned on him a face of mystical amazement, the opium fraying out the hard edges of his reality. He forgot that he had actually sent a letter to the legate in Paris to bring all this about. He forgot recommending to them that one Sir Amaury of Herm 'might aid the suit of any Frankish suitor with his fetching verse and charming disposition'. Though he had manipulated events to his own precise end, he now saw only God's hand at work - Divine coincidence fetching his enemy within reach.

'I simply allowed God's justice to work itself out. And lo, God has brought him to me - delivered him up to me for the administration of His holy judgement. Fetch him. Fetch your master here.'

Oriole bowed and left the room. A moment or two later, two sergeants Templar fell in beside him to make quite certain that God's will was done, that Amaury was fetched. God, as Oriole was learning, left nothing whatsoever to chance.

To right and left of Oriole the walls of the Krak Kerak seemed to be melting in the heat of the sun. The heavy seas of sand had holed its hull and sunlight was bursting in in torrents of yellow, in clouds of spray. The floor was insubstantial under his feet. He was Judas sent by the Sadducees to kiss Christ.

What if Judas had shouted at the last moment, in the Garden, '*Run!* For God's sake, run!' Suppose he had.

What hatred, what years of envious rivalry and imagined maltreatment Judas must have suffered at Christ's hands that he could make that long walk to Gethsemane without slowing to a standstill. One of the sergeants pushed Oriole in the back, asking why he had stopped.

He walked on across the yards, the ground burned out from under his feet by the brightness of sunlight. And then the moss-green shadows cast by the giant water cistern swallowed him up. 'Sir Jocelyn wants you!' he called upwards. Paddling in water, Amaury looked like a figure set in a derelict fountain, reduced by distance to rather smaller than life-size.

Amaury was born the son of a vavassour, penniless and without prospects, but with ambitions big as Byzantium. After considering all the marketable products in the world, he had concluded neither saffron nor pepper would bring him as choice a reward as Love. So it was Love he had made his commodity. Securing a post as minstrel at the Court of Baux, he had managed to win the patronage of a lady there: she would give him livery and horse and equipage if he would just carry word of his love for her hither and yon, near and far. This first piece of vanity had enabled him not so much to sing his lady's praises abroad as to attract the eye of a dozen other ladies. They all paid him to be their champion in the world and to love them *solus*.

To be a knight-troubadour required immense wealth - lands, the wherewithal for endless gifts and profligate extravagancies. But a knight-troubadour on his seasonal pilgrimage of Love can only carry just so much. So once afforded, Amaury's entourage of musicians, his white livery, his purple livery, his pennoned and tassled tent spoke convincingly of his 'far-off' lands, his rank, his favourable repute at Court. He learned to talk fluently of the lives and possessions of the rich. After all, he had envied them for so long that he knew every coil of their intestines, every fold of their clothing, every weakness in their armour. The more he travelled, the more he saw of his own kind - that is to say, the kind which he had chosen to adopt, to cultivate, to milk.

But many, many years before reaching Krak Kerak, Amaury of Herm had ceased to feel like a mountebank. For he had grown into his role. If he felt any difference in rank now between himself and his hosts, it was a superiority of intellect on his part. Amaury's imagination, like his invented realm, was an island principality bounded by cliffs - cliffs no longer penetrable by reality. He had come to believe himself to be what he said.

'Sir Jocelyn wants you!' called the voice of his jongleur from the moss-green shadows lapping the base of the water-tower, and it never once occurred to him that he was a lesser man than that damnable, cheating Templar who had just lost the game but kept the winnings.

'And I want him! On my lance's point. Tell him I'll meet him face-to-face when there's a horse under me and a sword in my hand!'

What a foolish piece of over-acting, thought Oriole. What a pale imitation of a chevalier. He could not fathom why he had been taken in for so long. He should have seen through the flummery years before - seen that Amaury was no more of a knight than he. A man just like him. An imitator of his betters. 'He wants to speak with you,' said Judas, and the sergeants to either side of him nodded and beckoned with their quarterstaves.

Amaury vaulted down over the cistern's edge - a huge jump to the ground below which bruised his heels: he did not say so or evince pain, but walked to the castle gingerly on the balls of his feet, muttering under his breath. He still claimed to be outraged at Jocelyn's seizure of the castle and treatment of his peers.

Stupid bravado, thought Oriole, from a craven peasant. A man no better than me. A man just like me.

Near the door of the *retraite*, Oriole blurted out the truth, with vengeful gratification, 'Foicelles made inquiries. He knows what you are.

Amaury turned on him a look of such shock that his heart thumped with misgiving - one sharp look such as Christ must have cast on Judas. But there was no time for Amaury to ask what it meant - 'knows what you are'. The Turcopoles pushed him on through the curtained entrance and a little of the smoke penned up in the ill-ventilated booth escaped into the passageway, as sulphur fumes might with each new consignment for Hell.

Oriole was left outside, the property of a convict, confiscated from his pockets on arrest. There was the sound of a scuffle but no shouting. Oriole could hear Jocelyn pontificating about 'mouths' and 'unclean lips'. He heard Foicelles enjoin his prisoner to *'keep your tongue from evil and your lips from speaking deceit'*; heard him endict Amaury with the sins of the Israelites: *'They flattered with their lips; they lied with their tongues.'* But though the Templar's voice rose and rose in volume, it won no reply whatsoever. Perhaps he had thought to embark upon a holy argument: saint versus sinner. But Amaury said nothing. Nothing. Nothing.

Of course he says nothing, thought Oriole, listening behind the curtain like a silent bird in its shrouded cage. I am his furnisher of words. It was as if Amaury had never strung a sentence, never composed a song, never spoken a word but Oriole had been the originator, inventing Amaury's thoughts out of his own disprized genius. Now Oriole thought he could see the truth: that he was more troubadour than Amaury of Herm had ever been. He drew the curtain a little and attracted the attention of Sir Jocelyn, now rampant with opium and holy wrath, who summoned him in. Amaury was being forced down into a squat by the two sergeants, his legs folded awkwardly under him. 'Hold his head for me,' Sir Jocelyn told Oriole.

The red hair was soft plush to the touch. The long ears were still a little gritty with sand blown into them on the journey. The neck was bull strong, with white in the creases where the sun had never penetrated, and patches of sunburn and freckles where it had. No, it did not tan, skin like that. Oriole knew. His own skin was the same.

With his hand resting on the man's throat, he felt the vibration of Amaury's voice just as he had felt the strings of a lute quiver in the sound-box. 'What, will you slit my throat?' Herm said, but he was unrepentant. There was no acknowledgement that Jocelyn, by right of birth, had the power of judgement over him.

'Say after me, "My lips will not speak falsehood and my tongue will not utter deceit."'

Not going to kill him, thought Oriole; not going to kill this man so like me! Words, not blood! He only wants words. Nothing but a few words. Amaury's lips did not move, but Oriole could hear himself sobbing out the vow on his behalf - on behalf of this man so like him that their hair was the selfsame red. *'My lips will not speak falsehood and my tongue will not utter deceit!'*

Then Jocelyn forced open Amaury's clenched teeth with the tip of his dagger and with the deftness of a man who has punished many a petty criminal, sliced out the troubadour's tongue.

He gave it to Oriole as though it were something he had requested. A treat from a grown-up to a little boy. A sweetmeat. He spared Amaury's life and only cut out his tongue.

CHAPTER NINETEEN

Master of the Man

Ejected from the *retraite* like a drunk from a tavern, Amaury howled and screamed, demonic, running on buckling legs around the gallery, down the stairs and out into the sunshine, searching for the way out of his nightmare. He offered to slave and steward and pilgrim alike cupped hands full of blood as if it might purchase their assurance that it was none of it true. He left his mouth agape as he hunted high and low for a mirror, a shiny surface to prove what his senses told him - that his tongue still lay in the bottom of his mouth. He tried to stop the spray of the fountain from breaking up the shiny surface of the water around it. But he obliterated what reflection there was with his own bloody spittal. Then, all of a sudden, he fell on his knees and cracked his crown against the Moorish ceramics of the fountain's base and lay senseless beside the defunct camel.

But he came to no lasting harm. Oriole saw to that.

Oriole brought Amaury salt-water mouthwash and tinctures of exotic astringent to stop the bleeding, and emetic to eject the blood he had swallowed. The pilgrims wondered at his loyalty to a mere convict.

At first, Amaury would try to speak - automatically begin to say something without remembering the impediment. At the first subhuman grunt he would silence himself and his face would redden and distend as if a torrent of words had been turned back by a dam and piled up behind it. His hands were always in front of his mouth.

Then he learned to be silent; to sit and stare at a wall, a saddle, a rug and to impersonate dignity. It was not necessary to ask for anything. Oriole anticipated his every need.

The first time he tried to communicate - to experiment with what remained of the power of speech, they were several days' ride out of Krak Kerak, camped on the Jericho road in that strange pit of a desert lower than the sea. Amaury snapped his fingers to fetch Oriole: he had realised that he could summon, with some clarity, 'Paper.'

Oriole fetched a square of expensive vellum and fastened it flat on the ground with four large stones. Amaury wrote on it, ' am Amaury of Florriac still. Make for Florriac.' Oriole squinted at the words, reading upside-down. 'But surely, sir ...' he said, his voice puzzled and soft. 'You're no more Florriac than Herm, are you? Married under a false name? What kind of marriage is that? Sir! There was no Amaury of Herm when the vows were made. No more than there's an Amaury of Florriac now.'

Amaury bared his top teeth in a snarl of impatience. 'Ooo u oh?' he grunted.

'Who's to know, sir?' asked Oriole, removing the four stones with all the precision of a chess player. 'Well, I am, of course. I shall write to the Lady Alazais today to tell her she can petition for annulment. Tell her she's free of you. Tell her what you're brought down to.' He crumpled the vellum into a ball, crushed it between a clap of hands, right in front of Amaury's face. Then he pushed Amaury back against the tent centre-post, stunning him. 'What? Nothing to say for yourself? No, well you wouldn't, would you? You made me your word-man, didn't you? Whispered *my* words to all those ladies. Spent my poems like notes of credit. Sponged off my genius after yours dried up. Kept me dumb as a hedgepig, while you sang your way into all the pockets and plackets in France using my songs. Let me accompany my own lines with my own music while you took the applause and all the pretty presents.' He pushed Amaury to the ground and stood astride him, his feet on the man's wrists, dropping the stones on to his face one by one. 'Well, now I'm all the mouth you've got. Now I'm the troubadour and you're my mumming-man - my dumbshow - my dancing bear. I'll lead you on a halter round all the courts of France and you can learn to jig and roll your eyes and mime wenches and blackamoors, and fall on your bum to get a laugh ... Must master an instrument or two, mind! And tumbling, and how to balance a chair on your head. And learn to cringe, of course. First and foremost you must know how to creep to heel, *in keeping with your rank.*' He bellowed the words into Amaury's face, mouthing each consonant and vowel with such precision as to show how the tongue was employed in the construction of every syllable.

He would go back to Florriac and take receipt of Alazais' gratitude for her freedom from Amaury, from the convent life. And he would show her what it was to be seized upon in the name of Love by a troubadour, rather than in coldblooded greed by an impostor.

'Oriole of Florriac.' She owed him that much. His devotion had earned him that much.

And he dressed in Amaury's clothes, and he rode on Amaury's horse, while Amaury was allowed a pack mare amid a retinue of donkeys. The donkeys were as valuable as Amaury now, for they carried Raymon's intended marriage gifts for the Princess Ingrid and represented their only remaining portable wealth. But because the donkeys slowed their return journey into France, Oriole did write ahead, as he had said he would, to Alazais, setting down in cogent detail the truth about Amaury, the illegality of her marriage, the justice that had overtaken her persecutor, the depth of his undying love.

All property is considered communal within a community. So of course the conventual wives seized eagerly on Oriole's letter. Denied information by Alazais herself, they had become quite shameless in their curiosity. So when a communication arrived out of far-distant places, they tore it open and read avidly. It ran to several pages. Long before Alazais even knew of it, they had chewed its contents to shreds between their sharp, squawking beaks.

Lady Alazais, the Sabine of a strolling minstrel? Lady Alazais coupled to a peasant charlatan without so much as a tongue to wag in his head? Lady Alazais, the concubine of a penniless busker who had carved out his career between the sheets of gullible housewives? Each gossip recoiled in delicious revulsion from the letter's news - then passed it on to the next eager, reaching hand.

Alazais was the last to learn of her husband's fate, of her no-husband, of her 'freedom'. They shrieked the news at her. They howled it into her cell. They scrawled it on the wall beside her crib. They spat out their disgust in her face. They divided her dresses among themselves, saying she had no claim to the trappings of a lady. The *mère ancille* confiscated her crucifix and little carved madonna, unnerved by the outbreak of hysteria into believing it must have some justification.

'My title I was born to,' Alazais began to explain when called upon to apologise for her pollution of the convent. 'It comes from neither one of my husbands, though I consider myself, in the eyes of God, still married to Barral Nerra des Etangs. Nerra is my first and only husband.'

'But you are possessed by a second and encourage a third,' said the *mère ancille*.

'Possessed, yes, possessed,' said the Lady Alazais, though she was barely audible across the great carpetless expanse of stone floor separating the two women. 'As the mad are possessed by devils.'

The news contained in Oriole's letter naturally reached Florriac only hours after it reached the convent. It burst like mud from a spinning cartwheel and spattered the entire conté. It blotted Amaury's escutcheon and obliterated all Oriole's chances of prosperity. For his letter achieved what Jocelyn the Templar had never troubled to do - it defamed Amaury in his own country.

If it had not been for that letter, Amaury might have come home accounting for his lost tongue with stories of Moslem torture heroically resisted, of heathen atrocities. Even the legates who had employed Amaury would be unlikely to ride as far as Kerak to discover the truth.

And Oriole might have been sole mouthpiece of the maimed knight. What tricks and what changes might he not have worked, if only he had not sent that letter? As it was, the conté petitioned the King himself and begged him to give the feu into the hands of some knight of merit, so that Florriac might recover its honour and wash off the shame of being ruled by a housecarl.

Amaury's spurious knighthood, the fictitious fiefdom of Herm, the fictions perpetrated on women of rank were the talk of the troubadours, the comic scandal of the moment, the traffic of Languedoc gossip. There was even a song written of the Troubadour-Langue-Docked, which took great delight in all the phallic associations to be made with the smooth and insinuating tongue.

The old Amaury might have brazened it out. But the Amaury of former days no longer existed, except inasmuch as he did not die. Oriole saw to that.

There was nothing to return to. But not knowing this, Oriole made a fierce and foolish haste to reach it. Even Amaury, for all his surly, uncooperative resentment, was also in a hurry to reach the comforts of home, the aid of a surgeon, an escape from the flies that made perpetual attempts to storm his bloody mouth.

Meanwhile, as Alazais metamorphosed, in the eyes of her companions, from lady to dung-beetle, she was kept better informed. She knew there was nothing for her to return to: no castle home, no parental sympathy, no source of daily bread.

'No one could sleep with a man and not know his true rank,' declared the conventual wives behind their hands. Alazais must have conspired with the Busker to cuckold poor Barral and deceive the countryside at large. 'No one could sleep with a sinner and rise up without sins. And he visited her here! She did it here! Under a holy roof!'

The *mère ancille*, dismayed by this turbulence in her quiet, reputable retreat, feared loss of patronage. The knights who placed their wives in her care might query her hygiene, her husbandry in letting diseased and crossbred stock consort with their thoroughbreds. She sent for Alazais to tell her she must leave. But Alazais did not answer the summons.

'A very wilful and intractable woman. I'm beginning to see that,' said the old nun, pulling herself painfully to her feet. Now she would have to deliver the eviction in person.

Amaury looked out from under lowered lids and plotted the reprisals he would take on Oriole now that they had re-entered his own territory. The brat might fool himself that he had the upper hand, but lords have ruled before now with disabilities greater than muteness. Why, the King of Jerusalem himself was a leper.

Once Amaury got back to Florriac, he would place blocks of paper on every level surface, wherever his hand might come to rest. And he would wear a hat full of quill feathers and write down his commands.

And Oriole's reward would be a dungeon at Florriac, some oubliette, sunless, below ground.

For a time, Amaury harboured thoughts of awarding the treacherous creature his own affliction - of cutting out his tongue. But in the cooling light of reflection he decided that Oriole's voice represented his only material worth. So Amaury resolved to put out his eyes instead. That way the wretch would be able still to sing and to play. Amaury wanted to maim the whole world - to geld it - to hear it scream.

In the meantime he washed - as often as water was available, he washed. Keeping up the appearance and practices of a gentleman, he told himself, though he had never been so very particular before about his personal hygiene. He washed and washed and washed.

Their route into Florriac took them past the derelict clutter of cottages, sties and barns at the foot of the fortifications - the overspill housing of castle families and dependants. Next door to the forge, Oriole had lodged Kadija and his children.

Kadija was part of another life. During the surreal homeward journey, Oriole had moved on to the anticipation of a higher life, a plain of existence raised up by love and wealth. Kadija had been only an enforced necessity; Alazais was the centre of his world now. Even so, Kadija and the girls must be provided for. Besides ... they could furnish him with a welcome bite of dinner.

He even relished the opportunity to show himself off in his borrowed feathers, to tell them he was a made man: He rather wanted to make the children gape. As he dismounted, he saw the neighbours come to their doors but keep their distance, talking behind their hands. He put it down to jealousy of his fine clothing.

At first sight, he thought that Kadija had vacated the house, for it seemed to be stripped bare and the windows crossed out with planks. Then his eyes accustomed themselves to the gloom, and he saw her sitting on a roped travelling chest, the girls perched to either side of her, nibbling raisins and waiting, waiting, like Israelites on the night the Angel of Death passed over. She greeted him ferociously.

'Where've you been? At last. At last. I'd only've waited another day. I thought they'd bum us out. Find a cart. You must find a cart. Now. This minute. It's not safe for us here no more.'

Months of travel, its fatigues and mindless routines had slowed down Oriole's thinking. He blundered about the room, trying to re-orient himself. All the way back he had taunted and hectored Amaury with their changed status. But there had been no replies to make sense of. Now he found it difficult even to assimilate Kadija's words. 'Get me a bite, woman. I've got news for you. I've got great news for you. Where's my little girlies? I've got things in store for you you'll never "... I'm hungry. Get me a drink.'

'No time for that. You can eat and drink in the next place. Did you get any pay from that bastard? Do we have any money?'

Her agitation took her as far as the door and she looked out and saw Amaury. Neither his jongleur's livery nor his sackcloth hood, nor his emaciation from lack of eating gave her a moment's difficulty in recognising him. 'What's *he* doing here? Why've you brought him here?

Why didn't you cut his throat on the way?'

'Cut his throat?' Oriole bleared out again into the sunshine. Amaury, catching the drift of what was being said, began to laugh - a function unaffected, as he discovered, by the loss of his tongue. That made him laugh all the more, long after the humour was dead and gone out of him.

'Well? What is he?' Kadija ranted. 'Anyone's allowed to kill one of his sort. Give me the knife and I'll do it. What is he? Only a minstrel, isn't he? No law against it. Look what he's brought us to.'

When the truth finally broke through to Oriole - that Amaury's disgrace was known everywhere, that the castle, the conté, everything had gone, there was no cold galvanising splash to wake his wits. He floundered on through a mire of sleepy nightmares.

He pulled Amaury off his mule and pushed him indoors. 'Get in there. Hide in there. Don't show yourself. Don't stir.' He herded the pack animals into the house as well, where they turned and turned about, upsetting furniture, looking for a manger in the half-light, lightened of their saddlebags. Oriole transferred the bags to his own horse.

He would leave them all there, he decided, all in the one place: all the complications and mistakes and impediments of his life so far. All his sins. With his only realisable wealth piled in front and behind his thighs, he galloped to the convent, beating on the door, swinging on the bell.

Here was the centre of the world - more surely than ever the one he had shared with a cat in Jerusalem. Here was the end of his pilgrimage. What pain it had cost him was minimal in comparison with the Heaven that lay ahead: his reward of bliss.

Alazais would have jewels. She must have friends. She would know of quiet haunts secret from the common herd. *And the Truth shall make you free. And the Truth shall make you free ...* The Gospel Latin moved his lips like a wizard's magic incantation. Though all else was lost to him, nothing was lost, nothing, if through his efforts he had won the love of Alazais - if the truth had made Alazais free. Now even he would be free from the lies, he told himself He might one day even feel magnanimous towards Amaury who had caused him to meet Alazais in the first place.

A few livres would do. Some little house, some span of happiness. The foundations at the foot of the world had been pulled away and everything was tumbling down, but Oriole would bury his face in Alazais' lap and not see it. His faithful love, carried through desert and briar, months and years, was about to claim its reward. Not a shred of doubt.

'Messenger for the Lady Alazais of Florriac!' he told the face beyond the grille. 'I must speak to her in person. Let me in.'

'There's no one of that name here.'

Yes, yes, there is. Lady Alazais. Wife of...Alazais! I know she's here. Go and tell her, please. It's very important.'

The nun was flustered. Her only resort was to tell him she would 'go and see' and then to disappear. When she did not come back, Oriole circled the walls calling Alazais' name. He would have declared snatches of the poetry he had written her but, oddly, every one that came to mind was the work of Amaury - brilliant lines from the old days of the young Herm. As if, with the clothes, Oriole had put on the man's memory too.

Above his head, in barred apertures, the silhouettes of women gathered – the grass-widows of the place, dragging their boredom behind them on ling, dark, dusty trains, looking down at him. They enjoyed too much disdain to call down, too much curiosity to depart. Alazais was not among them.

'Alazais! Alazais! Is she there? I must speak to her!'

'What's he? A customer?' said one woman loudly to the next.

I thought it was *him*. It looks like him.' She seemed almost disappointed. 'The hair. The clothes.'

'No, it can't be him. It speaks.'

'Someone had better tell him, whoever he is.'

'Alazais! Fetch the Lady Alazais to me, won't you?'

The *mère ancille* offended at having to evict Alazais in person, was still more offended to be kept waiting at her door. She rattled the latch irritably. She fooled herself that she heard a surly groan of acknowledgement and bustled in, sharp and scolding. But there had been no groan. Only the creak of rope against timber as Alazais swung in the breeze from the window. She had hanged herself from the rafter of her cell the day before, but no one had noticed until now.

'Someone had best tell him she hanged herself,' said a voice loudly and deliberately from beyond the window grille, though none of the silhouettes chose to be seen saying it. None were any longer on view. Only as Oriole rode away did the horns and spikes and crescent moons of their hats lip into sight again around the lighted window, like cab-ballistic symbols written around the edge of yellow parchment.

Transition

Their childhood was full of hardships. The sisters would vie with one another, saying, 'It was harder for me, than you.' But early recollections are notoriously unreliable. And for the most part, they had all shared the same grinding, wicked misery.

Jerusalem was closest to her mother, having lived through those days of the Second Crusade when fathers were as remote and unimaginable as God. The money her father left had been their daily bread, his purse kept like the Sacrament in a shrouded box approached only with awe and gratitude. But the money had dwindled to nothing, and Oriole did not return from his adventure. Other men came back; Jerusalem saw them. After the money was gone altogether, men used to visit her mother and leave offertory money where the purse had once been. But their kindness seemed to overwhelm Kadija, for it always left her in tears. Jerusalem remembered. She almost remembered her sister - the one who had fallen down steps and died. After the accident, to keep her away from the cellar steps, her mother had told her there were monsters and wild animals at the bottom. So she formed the impression that her dead sister had been eaten by the beasts in the cellar.

Jerusalem certainly remembered the journey south into the salty Camargue. Someone had sent money; someone her mother feared more than the monsters in the cellar. Even so, they had hurried south.

After that money came, there was a sudden wealth of food stretching a stomach accustomed to hunger; her mother sitting anxious beside her, clutching a shawl on her lap. The shawl was stuffed with worthless possessions including a hank of the Dead One's hair (presumably retrieved from the cellar). Her mother tried to bed her down on the journey, her head on the shawl, but knowing of that hank of hair, Jerusalem had refused.

Jerusalem, of course, remembered far more than her sisters of life at Nerra's castle in the Camargue - that age of plenty talked of with such massive regret afterwards: that Paradise lost.

Not she nor any of her sisters born later recognised their lodger from those early childhood days. He was of a later time - something Father had brought home from the deserts of the East, along with ruin and homelessness. Being mere children they were frightened more by him than by the great abstract terrors that overhung their parents: starvation, old age and the like. Only Ouallada was unafraid of that tongueless grin, that man who talked in his sleep in words with no consonants.

Ouallada - the youngest - was born when Jerusalem was eight, on the back of a flat cart, in a storm of hail.

The stones fell suddenly, out of a sunny sky, and the girls huddled under the cart, listening to the rattle on the wooden boards, thinking their mother was being pelted to death above by a white God with a white wrath. And when the rattling stopped, Ouallada's crying began. For a long time her sisters believed she had fallen from the sky along with the hail.

She benefited most from the mixing of races. She was beautiful from the outset, with a northern mouth enlarged to the brink of southern sensuality; with skin the colour of the elixirs her mother sold at market fairs; with hair like a thundercloud fringing into rain. And clever, too.

The girls' father - that melancholy bully who cursed them daily for being hungry and thirsty - was transformed by Ouallada's birth. He doted on her. He would take the baby away from her mother, cradled in his arms, and turn his back and whisper things to her, so quiet, so furtive, that Kadija would go and slap at his shoulders and demand the child back. His attitude did not change towards the others; had they been owls he would only have fetched voles and mice to cram down the throat of Ouallada, and let the rest fend for themselves. He had plans, he said, for Ouallada. 'Ouallada will save us all from perdition.' At which their mother laughed - a sharp bark of a noise jolted out of a body unaccustomed to laughter. It startled even Oriole.

Once Ouallada reached the age of three and four, her sisters stopped envying her. For their father started to educate her, with a ruthless disregard for whether she wanted to learn. Left to her own devices, Ouallada would have toddled about in the long grass watching how snails weighed down the dewy stalks. But he taught her to read. She would have chosen to climb up and balance on dry-stone walls - a fearless child - and watch the foals suckling and the geese gleaning grain. But he taught her to write. He did not need to teach her to sing. Before she could control her bladder she could sing a tune heard. She had perfect pitch. It confirmed Oriole in the wisdom of his secret plans. 'Ouallada will save us all from perdition,' he would say, and slap his wife for laughing.

His investment in her was not wasted. She learned anything and everything he could teach her, ignorant only of its purpose. By five she could recite poems by Marcabrun and spell 'amorous dalliance' (though the words made no more sense to her than Egyptian hieroglyphs).

Not that Oriole neglected his other daughters entirely. He had Kadija teach them to dance, to juggle, to tumble and to make mouth music. A travelling minstrel needs a good cast. They loved his singing. When he sang in some innyard or market place, they hovered nearby to listen. They also knew that if they dropped an apple or tripped in the dance, they would be rewarded afterwards with a punch or a whipping.

Oh yes, and he taught them, too, that the world was a wicked, pernicious place where the rich and powerful have all sold their souls to the Devil, where churchmen sit in their great stone hides watching for minstrels to maim; where other minstrels are all talentless gallows-meat; where whores hang wide-legged as spiders, to trap men; where young men lurk behind every town wall, waiting for maidens to deflower; where man's natural state is to hate his neighbour, and where merit goes unrewarded. If, during his songs, they ever heard mention of Love or hearts or troths or happiness, they had only to look at their parents to see how poetry differed from real life.

After the death of Alazais, Oriole hated his wife. He associated her with his Great Disappointment, his ruin. He associated her with the need to go on living and working and grubbing together an existence when he had no wish to go on living at all. He blamed her for saddling him, like a pack-ass, with an insupportable weight of daughters. He associated her blackness with the drainage pipe below a castle wall, with roofless nights, with the leafless, lightless winters of his greatest poverty, with dirty lodgings and impending thunderstorms. Most of all he hated her for not being Alazais, a fault which she had no means of rectifying.

She tried her hardest, understanding that Love was the occupational sickness of a minstrel; her husband had simply succumbed to it as a quarryman succumbs to the stone-cutter's cough. But her own natural affection did not survive, and it grew hard even to like him after the trip to Krak Kerak. She thought that a scorpion must have crept in at his ear during his desert journey and laid its eggs in his brain. After his return, after the ruin of Amaury's reputation, after the suicide at the convent, the nest of scorpions had hatched. Though the man looked the same, he was altered inwardly - his thoughts too full of venom, his soul corroded all away. She had to sleep with her head away from his at night. It was hard, despite the tattered Christian faith she clung to, not to loathe such a man as the years wore on. When he beat her children, called them black scum, heathen little demons, leeches sapping the blood out of him, when he taught them to juggle with long-bladed knives, some of those scorpions migrated across the straw from his head to hers, and she found herself on the verge of hating Oriole. That was why ... But well, even that petty revenge had its ironies.

Ouallada, too, found grounds to dislike her father. For all she was the darling of his days, she was an independent, observant child and saw the world through her own pair of dark, black-fringed eyes. She did not resent the rigours of her education, for the long hours he kept her from her bed, for the pain of practising with soft fingers on stringed instruments while candle after candle burned to death. On the contrary, his horde of instruments was her menagerie: the lute with its tortoise carapace, the pipe with its snake-fang flicker of reed, the birdwing cithera. As a very little girl she would talk to them, and sure enough they rewarded her gentleness in time. The strings bit into her fingertips less and less. No, Ouallada did not reproach her father with any cruelty towards her, only with his barbarity towards dumb beasts with less means to defend themselves. When Oriole drank away a day's earnings and came home flailing his fists, she had only to sing a song, play the rote, for him to crumple into mawkish delight: 'Ouallada will be our salvation! You see if she isn't!' But her mother had no such means of deflecting his violence. Nor did the fish he ripped open for its swim bladder to make a drumskin, nor the sheep whose guts he strung into wires.

Nor did the poor creature in the corner.

He called Amaury his 'dancing bear' and used him for mummings. In spring he would dress him up in green streamers, covering him from the crown of his red hair to his soleless boots, to lurch about in time to rustic doggerel. When Oriole treated the tavern crowds to a story of the Crusades, Amaury would be stationed within a pentangle of benches, like some Satanic sacrifice. On each bench lay a hat or a wig of hair. And he would run from one indignity to the next, impersonating the grimacing Saracen, the captive maiden, the cowardly Turcoman, the faithful warhorse, while Oriole alone represented the crusader knight.

Amaury balanced chairs on his head, even though he was capable of playing a lute. When drunken louts banded together, incited by a Sunday sermon to drive the minstrels out of town, Oriole would send Amaury to soak up the abuse until the cart was safe away. He made a good scape-goat, a man without a tongue. Oriole considered him useless for much else. Oriole often said that if he could sell him to a bearpit for a good price, the dogs might have him and welcome.

Ouallada had always assumed Amaury to be simple, until one day she found him writing poetry with a stub of charcoal on the side of a split fish-crate. She moved up quietly behind him, and read over his shoulder. It was poetry better than any her father had taught her, or so it seemed, riven by splits in the wood, struggling around the rim of knotholes themselves as round and dark as tongueless mouths. It was a simple and poignant poem, about a salmon dying on the shallow redds where it was born.

When he caught sight of her, he split the wood across his knee and threw it on the fire. It burned with a smell of fish so acrid that it pricked tears from her eyes. His face showed alarm, and he seemed to want to keep secret what she had seen. She promised to say nothing. And he smiled, as though for all his mumming and miming, his face was out of practice, and wrote a gallant kiss on the back of her hand. His was not a mouth for kissing.

After that, she sought out his company, preferring it to her father's.

'Why do you stay?' she asked him. Amaury halted the mess of bean paste balanced on three fingers on its way to his mouth and showed it to her as all the explanation necessary: food.

'Why does Father treat him so vilely?' she asked her mother. Out of her husband's hearing, Kadija would usually side with her girls, and Ouallada rather expected the reply, 'Oh, you know what he is. You know what he's like.'

But Kadija turned on her a face disfigured by emotion. *'We feed him, don't we?* It's more than others would do.'

Her sisters were accustomed to thinking of him as 'the dancing bear and were afraid of being tom to pieces. So Ouallada was Amaury's only friend. It was she who suggested they make an alphabet out of the sol-fa, and talk to each other in music. They plucked their laborious way through so many words that when she next came to play a proper tune, it spoke to her in jibberish.

After that he could have told her anything about himself - his life, his crime, how he came to have no tongue. But when she asked, he spoke to her only in stories and poetry, as though a great store of invention had built up inside him during his years of enforced silence. He spoke of knights-*trobar* and Courts of Love, of supplicant lovers and chaste *domnas*, of island dukedoms bound about with cliffs, of royal courts, river jousts and tournaments. He picked out, in plucked notes of music, pictures of lives as far removed from her own as the starry beasts in the sky. She asked him how he knew it all. He said he had been there, watching. But after she had been with him for a while, she could almost believe that she had been there, too, watching, and so she was unsure whether to take him literally.

Hearing Ouallada laugh one day in the company of Amaury, Oriole took up a sword in each hand - (How should a family of their sort own *two* swords, she had often asked herself) - and came at them. Amaury placed himself in front of the girl to shield her. But Oriole only rammed him in the stomach with the hilt of one sword and said, 'Teach her to fight, then, if you must use up her time.'

Why should Amaury know how to handle a sword? And yet he did. And he seemed to see a value in her learning, too, though the real swords were far beyond her strength to swing and he had to make her lighter, wooden ones to practise with. It was after the weaponry lessons that she began to fantasise about Amaury's background, to picture him in plate and helm, to pretend he was really a knight in disguise as a beggar.

In the winter of 1171 - 2, great gales ripped up the landscapes of Europe like carpets taken up for beating. Fortunately, Oriole had found employment lasting between Christmas and Twelfth Night and been given the use of a barn for shelter.

Given the daily pursuit of food and shelter, the world's affairs were of little interest to an itinerant brood of beggars. But now and then Oriole and his family heard snatches of gossip concerning the world at large. They learned, for instance, while employed over the whole of Christmas tide, that England's prime archbishop had been murdered, reputedly on King Henry's orders, and that miracles were already happening near the scene of the killing. They learned that, in the East, the villainous Nur ed-Din was dead and some Egyptian general was the up-and-coming power in the land. And they learned of fearful wonders, such as earthquakes that had shaken down whole cities that year throughout Outremer. Even the impregnable Krak de Chevalier, bastion of the Knights Templar in the valley of Jericho, had been shaken like an old man till his teeth fell out. Many of the Templars had been killed.

The news made mute Amaury gasp and clutch his arms across his chest.

The mysteries of Nature were at the forefront of everyone's mind just then. Gales coming in from the east were leaning against the manor house, hammering on the doors, kicking down the cow byres and sheep folds in the fields. It was a restive and inattentive audience which Oriole tried to cajole with carols and a Christmas mumming. His crew of daughters, thanks to the weather, were rigid with fright and cold. His dancing bear, on the other hand, stamped and rolled and wagged his head in an impromptu dance to the Christmas cannon, shaken by spasms of laughter that unnerved the ladies and had their children burying their faces. The host was not pleased at the way his feast progressed.

Later, Oriole and Kadija were asleep in the barn's loft, the girls nestled here and there in piles of ricked corn. The wind groaning in under the walls set the planks vibrating, and the loose stalks on the ground swirling round and round - a great whirlpool of corn, hissing.

Ouallada had never seen weather like it, but found something thrilling in the welter of noises that sent her sisters burrowing into their straw. When she saw Amaury get up and go outside, she followed him, a hessian sack pulled round her smock.

The gale was at its height. Their cart was lurching, leaping, dancing on its axles as the wind eddied underneath it. A rabbit coop bowled down the road leaping from corner to corner, the spotted animals inside being flung about like die in a shaker. The whole barn was distorting, leaning, bowing out of shape. The water on the pond threw up grainy spray, like a threshing floor.

Amaury was standing in the middle of the cart track, his feet tilted over by the ruts, his shirt full of wind and lifting now and then to uncover his nakedness. His red hair blew upwards from his head. Arms and hands were conducting the music of the storm, exhorting it to greater and greater exertions, imploring a crescendo which would pare the countryside off the very rock of its bones. *'More! More! More!'* he shrieked with the hard rims of his empty mouth. A tree was torn out of the ground and carried as far as a neighbouring spinney which it felled like a warhorse crashing into cavalry. Ouallada stood still, but the wind jostled and barged her so that she had to take little running steps just to keep her balance. The wind toppled her into Amaury's scope of vision. He stared at her, exultant, staggering himself against the wind. 'Ah bib vif!' he bellowed through the noise of loose shingling clap- clap- clapping.

It was the first time he had ever tried to speak aloud to her.

You did this?' said the nine-year-old, ready to believe him.

'Ma! Ah bib vif! Ma wim! Ma ray!'

'Your wind. Your rain,' she said.

'Ma hay!'

'Your what?' A gust of wind set about them both like footpads, and stripped them of all words. She ran into his lee to catch her breath, and he bawled into her ear, 'Ma hay!'

It was snowing moss stripped from the roof. One by one, slate tiles began to crash down like crockery. The roof they came from was not even visible for the onset of rain, but they pitched into the ground here, there and beyond, shattering into grey shards, cutting wedges out of the ice-hard ground. He grabbed hold of her and pulled her close, folding his head and shoulders down on her to shield her from the hurtling slates. 'Ma ung! Ma for!' He whispered them, words as misshapen and hacked off as the stump in his mouth. But she was not put to a moment's thought. His hate. His anger. His fury. It was as if she had always understood them to be the source of the elements.

Jerusalem, looking out through a sudden tear in the skin of the barn, saw her sister held in the embrace of the dancing bear, its head bent down and its great mouth gaping. 'Father! Father! The bear is eating Ouallada!' she screamed.

Her father looking out through the tallet window saw

his daughter in the embrace of half-naked Amaury of Herm, the two of them rocked by paroxysms of wind and rain. He slid down the ladder, ran out into the yard, and picking up a piece of slate from the ground, struck Amaury repeatedly in the back of the neck until he fell to the ground with Ouallada beneath him.

He may even have thought, as he died, that he had been killed by the wind and had at least saved the child.

The wind suddenly abated, withdrew to mutter amid the drunken trees and to kick dead rooks along the lane. Oriole pulled the girl from under Amaury and slapped and kissed her with the ferocity of a father frightened half out of his wits. 'Has this happened before?' he kept asking, but she misunderstood him.

'No! No! He never spoke before!' And when he shook her with impatience, she admitted to the only secret she had ever withheld. 'I saw him write poetry once!'

She kept trying to turn back towards the dirty white heap in the corner of her eye, but both mother and father cooperated to force her back inside the barn. It was very cold, and the rain was falling faster now that the wind had slackened. Fortunately, she too was of the impression that the elements had struck Amaury down: his own fury, his own raging frustration at being a poet without a tongue inciting Nature to riot. He had stung himself to death. Like a scorpion.

Her sisters, though they had been watching, did not enlighten Ouallada. That their father should kill a member of the household put them in speechless terror for their own lives: Oriole made certain of that: 'Not a word. If anyone asks you, you saw nothing, you hear? The slates were flying all over. You saw nothing.'

'Nothing, Father.'

It was just as well that Ouallada did not discover the truth, or it might have altered her feelings towards her father from dislike to something worse. After all, she had been (as Kadija had often been at pains to point out to her husband) passing fond of the bear.

Whether the felling of the yew trees by the gales let in the evil spirits, or whether they were driven ashore off the open sea, by 1173 Europe was cursed with sickness. It was the year, they said, when people everywhere were coughing up their souls. The sickness picked off the family of Oriole. The minstrel himself escaped it, of course, for lung fever is the reward of kissing and sharing, and he was no longer acquainted with either. But one by one, his daughters died, and as each one coughed her soul, as a fine silver sputum, up into the face of the sister tending her, Oriole knelt and thanked God that it was not Ouallada.

Some days it seemed as if there was no money ever to be had again. The world had gone behind closed doors to die. But at least, in compensation, God eased Oriole's burden of responsibility and the drain on his purse. Soon he had only to feed and clothe a family of five, a family of four. With no taste left among the peasants for dancing, he spent his time writing poetry and pious hymns to Mary, teaching Ouallada the different forms of verse.

Once she said, 'I know that, Father. Amaury taught me. Amaury wrote wonderful verses.'

He struck her with a bridle - the last item that remained of Raymon de Tirrel's tack and the journey to Krak Kerak. After a while, remorse made him say sullenly, 'D'you think I couldn't do the same? Do you? Mine was every lick as good as his. Better. Mine was better. But where's the call for it, eh? Show me the call for it and I'll write you a song to match anything he could do.'

Then Kadija fell sick. It was astonishing that she survived as long as she did when each girl's death swamped her like a breaking wave. Finally the undertow was just too strong. She could not right herself, find her feet. Oriole never reached out a hand to help her and so she foundered on the grief.

Before she died, she signalled that Oriole must sit beside her, since she had words to say. He told the priest that it was unfair; that it was bad enough to lose her, without having to look Death in the face. But the priest was adamant: he had long since learned to avoid long bedside vigils with dying strangers.

'What do you want, then?' said Oriole awkwardly, twisting his rump on the three - legged stool beside the bed.

'I have to tell you a thing,' said Kadija.

'All this theatre. You never could bear to be left hid behind-scenes, could you? You don't even have the cough. Why did you have to go sending for a priest? You're a fool, woman. You're as fit as a horse.'

'Our horses are all gone now,' she pointed out. 'All dead or gone. I have a thing that needs saying. I want to say it. I told the priest, but I want to tell you. Now I don't have to live with you after. There'd be no living with you after. There's been no living with you a long while now.'

'Who asked you? Never asked you to stay, did I? Could've taken yourself off.'

'I'm your wife,' she said, though she could see in his face a whole host of alibis and excuses troop up to qualify such a stark, simplistic statement. So she qualified it herself 'I am your wife. But I lay down with Amaury and he got a child on me.'

Oriole slapped all the fleas on his arm irritably. 'I know that. Tell me something new. What of it?'

'Not the first,' she said, moving her fingers among the strands of a ribboned hank of cut hair. The souvenir contained several shades now, of brown and black. 'Not the first. The last. Did you never wonder why she was so pretty? Or so clever? Our Ouallada?' And when she said 'our', it excluded Oriole one last time in a lifetime of exclusions. 'I pitied him, you see,' said Kadija, shutting her eyes and rolling her head away from his. 'And besides, I was lonely. You'd grown so very ... *loveless*. Strange. In a man who thought he was a troubadour.

PART TWO

The Liar's Daughter

God let me penetrate through love
that which I taste through knowledge.

Saint Anselm

CHAPTER TWENTY

Princess of the Harem

It was hard to bear. But once he had made up his mind to disbelieve Kadija, her words had no power to harm him. And once he was left alone in the world with no one for company but Ouallada, there was no impediment to the lie. No one remained maliciously to undermine it. No one remained to deflect Ouallada from her perfecting of it. And it was to be the perfectest lie of all.

'You are the daughter of Ida of Bamberg and the Sheik Obeid ben Zefir of the Tuaregs. Your mother was taken captive at the Bathys River and held confined in the sheik's harem, and you were born under canvas at Sakra Wadi.'

She was twelve years old. Another child, when told she was a princess, would have gasped and giggled and patted her hair and tilted her nose and said, 'Am I really!'

But Ouallada looked back across a childhood landscaped by the grinding study of bizarre, unexplained subjects. She was crammed to the gills with literature, history, music, chivalric etiquette - everything her father could teach her of how the nobility lived and thought and took recreation. She had never been indulged in games of the imagination, never been congratulated on her beauty or her endeavour. She knew the heraldic motto that flew over her head: it read, 'Ouallada will be our salvation. You see if she isn't.'

So she looked back at her father with her sad, liquid eyes and said, 'That's why you gave me the name.'

'That's right. And from now on it shall be Princess Ouallada, orphaned of her mother, cast out from her father for defiance of his Moslem barbary - for clinging to the faith of your mother. Left to die in the desert."

Did the angels bring me water and figs? Like Elijah?' she asked derisively, and her father seized on a thing said in jest, and spliced it into his narrative.

For five more years he perfected her in her role, forbidding all reference to the true Past, denying her all reminiscences - as though they were the lies, and his version of events the only true gospel. Indeed, by the time she was seventeen, he had virtually come to believe his own invention. After all, no one remained alive to contradict him. 'I was a troubadour once,' he used to tell her, darkly insinuating that envious rivals had conspired in his downfall.

Ouallada said nothing, but plucked on the *gitarre*

Moorish tunes which her mother had sung her as lullabies. Her father, liking their Moorish authenticity, congratulated himself. This daughter of his would make the consummate liar, indistinguishable from the genuine article. She would succeed in the world.

Amaury had managed it, after all.

The day of the troubadour had reached its noon. The talents of Peire Vidal, Chretien de Troyes, Guirault de Bornelh and Raimbaut d'Orange were building, on crude foundations, fabulous castles of verse, great edifices of poetry so brightly painted with the colours of Chivalry and Romance that every man raised up off the muddy ground was dazzled. There were women, too: Marie de Ventadour and Béat rice de Die. For Eleanor of Aquitaine had wrought a miracle on the Frankish mind and raised womankind above the status of cattle and chattels.

Men everywhere were reconstructing the past, tracing back their bloodlines to the Courts of King Arthur, peopling prehistory with dragons and giants and the kind of ancestors capable of slaying them. They had even embellished Christ's history - with grails and lances, handkerchiefs and shrouds, fragments of the True Cross enough to build a second ark. Five churches claimed to own His foreskin. Itineraries mapped out more precisely every year the journeys accomplished by Mary and Joseph round Christendom.

So Oriole considered arming Ouallada with the sword of Saint John - the one drawn in the garden of Gethsemane - but his courage failed him. A lie like that might blight his luck. He lighted instead on a Code of

Love. No matter that one had already been found, written on a scroll and bound to the throat of a unicorn by a chain of gold. If one version existed, others might.

The answer came to him in a flash of inspiration. His Code of Love would come from *The Book of All that is to be Known.*

Everyone knew dimly the story of villainous Gerbert, who had begun his evil career by setting out to analyse the Bible logically (as if it were the work of Man). Everyone knew how he was really a necromancer in feu to the Devil. When the Devil came back for his due, Gerbert fled him into Moslem Spain and studied forbidden sciences. Seducing the daughter of his Saracen host, he then stole, with her help, *The Book of All that is to be Known.*

Fleeing south into the deserts of Africa with his great prize, he abandoned the Sultan's daughter with neither water nor Chivalry. But in the next valley the Devil, who had dogged him all the way through Spain and across the sea, finally brought Gerbert to account. Shaping his anger into a spiral funnel of dust, he flung it at Gerbert, and the grit flayed off his human body and left him mere skull and bones. It ripped out his soul and stuffed it into a scorpion hole, and his mind into a pit of snakes, and condemned him to walk the seering sand for eighty thousand days. That was the history everyone knew.

'And though he would feign have set down the book,' - ran the version Ouallada learned to tell - 'which was massive and bound in heaviest leather, he found 'could not and must carry it always, for his sins were listed in the book and ran to a hundred pages. Over and over he read them, asking the vultures why he had not kept to the road of salvation.'

Sometimes in Ouallada's dreams, it all became real, so that on waking she was caught suspended between two lives, the real and the invented. Sometimes in her nightmares, Gerbert's eyeless sockets would rise over a yellow pillow of sand and fasten on her a look of anguish that horrified her more than the maggots seething in his hollow nostrils.

'But his lechery was so great in life that, even after two hundred years, the sight of a maiden of royal birth wandering in the desert moved him to a great lust. And he chased her with all the speed that his great burden would allow.

'I fled him. At first I outran him easily. But his rattling feet were accustomed to wading in the soft sand, and mine were not. He was accustomed to thirst and the drumming of the sun's drumbeat on the white tambor of his hairless skull. I was not. He gained on me at last and overtook me and fell on me like the bones from a scaffold, and held me close.

'But he didn't have the flesh to press home his filthy ambition, and he broke away howling. And I was left with nothing but my terror and a page or two torn from the book while we struggled. Since then I have wandered the world up and down, up and down, seeking the country where men and women live their lives according to his "Code of Love", singing the songs of my heart's own making.' At this point, Ouallada would hold up the sheets of writing. The vellum had cost her father his last sou, the writing hours of painstaking recollection, thinking back to Poussarou, trying to recall his one glimpse of the Code of Love.

By this point, the lord and his guests would be rocking on the brinks of their chairs, envying Damned Gerbert his rape on this miraculous beauty, while the ladies fixed their eyes on the wagging vellum as though it contained the formula for the Elixir of Life.

Which, of course, it did.

For Love was everything. Over recent years it had swept the courts of Europe more surely than lung fever, altered the landscape more than the Great Storms. Love's rigorous codes were the bars of a pig-crate that bound men now and kept them from crushing the smaller, weaker creatures who lived in their shadow. Not only were women respected, they could hope to be worshipped, adored, treasured like African pearls - at least in their youth.

Oriole planted her in the Languedoc, of course - in the heart of troubadour country, in that blood-red soil so manured with the myths and legends of Love that she could not fail to flourish.

After making her speech of introduction to her host, Ouallada would take the knife out of the lord's own hand and pin the vellum to the door with it - high up (since she was taller than most) so that the ladies could only shabby it with a few more oily fingermarks. Vellum bruises, and her father had been at pains to bruise his with two hundred years of touching. It sometimes seemed that he had worn his fingers through to the bone priming that vellum, for they were white these days, and cold and wasted. Only callouses cushioned them against the wires of the rote.

While the ladies elbowed and jostled one another for a sight of the writing, Ouallada moved forward into the room, and stood to the windward of the hearth (so that the smoke would not catch her throat) and sang, unaccompanied. She withdrew her hands inside her cloak and closed it round her so that no movement of fingers or detail of clothing distracted from her face, singing. And she sang a song she said her mother had sung to her - a lament concerning her mother's love for a white knight of the west:

> ... Before I was captive here,
> He caught me in nets like a golden lion
> And were I still bound to him now, with hoops of iron,
> I should tell you all what it is to prowl
> Open-mouthed among the golden guinea fowl ...

They stared at her till their eyes stung with the drifting smoke, her black hair tumbling down the grey precipice of her cloak, her eyes liquid as black oil expressed by the earth's sighing. Such sad, large, desolate eyes, set on something so far distant that they would turn and look over their shoulders to see where she was looking.

Oriole had wanted to write the song. Indeed, he had written one. But Ouallada did not use it. He had given her her clothes (Conte Raymon's wedding gifts brought back from Krak Kerak in a mule's pannier). He had given her her past. He had given her her instructions and stage directions and told her to be sure to stand to the windward of the fire. He had even tried to give her the words of her song. Ouallada had nodded her head as if she concurred.

But she had preserved one private place within

herself. She had barred one door against the masterplan which ruled her life. She would not let him use her mouth to sing his words.

So when she sang, she sang her own words. And if Love sounded like a stranger to her, something she had still to meet face-to-face, then that was all well and good in the circumstances. It added credibility to her father's lie.

The deceit terrified her, of course; the prospect of being imminently found out. And yet it never once occurred to her to reject her father's plans for her. What was the alternative? Nothing that might happen to her held more horrors than starvation, illness untended, the begging life, the burden of her father's hatred and disappointment. Better for a horse to hurtle against a jump insuperably high, and to break its neck, than to starve between cart shafts and be flogged to death.

The men stared at her, their mouths ajar, their unchewed food visible, their hands cupping the flare of the candles out of their eyes. The women stopped babbling, looked back up the room and listened. If a glee-maiden or jongleuse had wandered in off the lanes, with a red jacket and red stockings, jigging feet and a head full of songs, she might have earned herself a purse of coins, a hot meal. But this girl, timing her arrival at sunset so that she was a thing of candle-flare, smoke and red back-lighting, was an exotic creature out of a foreign land - a story contained within lavish clothes and a cloak of hair. When she finished, she took down her pages of vellum and made as if to leave, so that, of course, she was pressed to stay. A glee-maiden with guitar and wolfhound would have been offered a bed in the kitchens. Ouallada the troubadour-princess, was shown to the troubadour chamber and a lit fire.

Outside, beyond the pale, Oriole crouched and shivered, his flesh seemingly porous to the cold which blew quite through him, whistling up and down the pipes of his hollow bones. He had visited enough castles like this to know the lie of it: a round, rotten tooth sticking out of a swollen gum of countryside. He knew where the troubadour chamber would lie, where to look for a glitter of firelight through the window-slit.

Tomorrow, when she was able to slip away unnoticed, she would come and tell him of her triumph - how his song had carried the evening, who had heard it, who had praised it and how many gifts it had brought. She had made her entrée into the courtly world of the Gay Science. She had broken into the troubadour circuit as a conjuror links the Indian rings, with one quick, sure, brazen blow. But Oriole was the magician. The achievement was his.

Unable to contain his exultation, he moved inside the curtain fence and walked towards the base of the round tower. His eyes fixed on the glimmering slit near its base, he walked through piles of ordure and dung directly towards the sparkle of his salvation. Of course the scale of the castle defeated him, for the closer he got, the greater the stone trunk spread in girth and the higher the vents rose above his head. There was no chance of peeping into the troubadour chamber. But then he could see it in his mind's eye clearly enough. His daughter would be sitting, in a lake of silk skirts, brushing her hair while the firelight exaggerated the geometry of her face. Beyond her hems, where the darkness encroached, sat all the Virtues at her command: Comfort, Wealth,

Admiration, Fame. She would marry noble blood, give birth to noble children, redeem his family name from squalor and obscurity.

Of course he hated his name, because it had been given him by Jocelyn de Foicelles. And he hated Ouallada, because she had been given him by Amaury of Herm. But then he had long since learned that hate was the only real driving force in the world. It simply went about - like Death in its red mask - dancing to music and disguised as Love.

CHAPTER TWENTY-ONE

La Belle Aude

As it was planned, so it came to be. Ouallada was assimilated into the world of troubadours and courtly entertainment. Did they believe her story? The women did, for the most part, having seen nothing of the outside world and knowing it to be full of wonders. The lords and squires saw no need to differentiate between fiction and fact, for they regularly used the one to lubricate the other.

In all probability, her fellow troubadours took her story for what it was - a pretty invention. But then their admiration for craftsmanship outweighed all considerations of truthfulness. A good invention, to them, had nothing to do with lying. And when she proved to be a fair poet and to have an excellent voice, to play either, rote, flute, rebec and viol, they expressed their respect and made room for her at table. They called her 'Princess', but a rank devolved on her no higher than the fourth sister of a count. At very best.

Oriole's notions of marriage were ridiculous, of course. Jongleurs and minstrels might tie themselves to anyone at all, but there are limits to what gentry can do. The lotus-eaters of Palestine might marry Christian foreigners, but Franks at home would never speak the words in the same breath: marriage and blackamoor.

Her beauty invited a great many other propositions, naturally. It was even assumed by some of her hosts that the door to the troubadour chamber would stand open to them at night. It was then that Ouallada discovered why her father had had Amaury teach her swordsmanship. Her visitors rarely came armed with more than a lust for the exotic. And though the sight of her, sword and dagger in hand, excited them even more than her loose, voluminous hair or the rise and fall of her breast, they quickly retreated. After that they appreciated her for what she was: a thing best used for their guests' pleasure, rather than as a quick, selfish pang in the dark.

It also increased a man's honour to treat generously any visiting troubadour. So Ouallada acquired the rewards of excellence: gowns and horses, linen and plate, ribbons for her hair and strings for her rote. It was just as her father had said: gifts given to aggrandise the giver. As for love-tokens, it was usually ecuries or clerks who left them outside her door, jongleurs who wrote apprentice-pieces and tacked them to her lintel.

At first she was a novelty among the Gay Scientists, then, after a year or two, an acknowledged landmark in the shifting seasonal scene - a face recognised by fellow Scientists with a smile and a nod and a making of room on the musicians' bench. Ouallada ben Zefir was accepted.

What she needed now was a patron. Ouallada knew what Love was: her father had told her. It was the obsession of the rich, one for another. What she required, therefore, was a patron in need of an eloquent voice; she must make herself a vessel for the plying to and fro of someone else's passion.

So she came into her own at last at the Court of Aude, unmarried souzerain of Haut-Beziers.

Aude held the shears of fate poised over a dozen ardent suitors, and had done so for a year without ever telling them which would triumph. Ouallada served to sharpen the blades of those shears.

Aude was the beauty of her age. Her skin was white as leprosy, her hair the kinked coppery coils that leap from the engraver's chisel. She removed her hairline back beyond the protruberant dome of her forehead, plucking out each strand with a wince. Like genuine lepers, it seemed La Belle Aude felt no pain. She certainly felt no one else's.

Ouallada was mesmerised by the beauty. It implied a life blessed by virtue, the promise of personal splendour. When, despite being adopted and befriended by Aude, she failed to find any great intellectual merit there, she put it down to her own jealousy. Aude must be perfect, for every male troubadour she met was categorical in his praise of La Belle Aude. (Except the Railing Bishop, of course.)

Aude's parents had named her not only after the nearby river which cut its way through the Roussillon countryside, but after the hero's betrothed in the *Chanson de Roland*. In fact, they had raised her on a diet of historical legends, from Charlemagne to Arthur. But whereas her namesake had fulfilled her role in legend simply by swooning and dying at the news of Roland's death, Aude d'Haut-Beziers enjoyed a robust constitution and more far-reaching ambitions.

Love ruled her life in every facet, but she had not yet made up her mind whom of her many suitors she should love. At first, Ouallada tried to guess at one lover favoured above all the rest. But she soon gave up, for there were too many misleading clues, too many feints and diversions. It was unlikely Aude would actually take a lover before she was married, and yet no one ever said as much. She conducted herself as if she were always on the brink of *la grande tryste*.

'What do you think to Gaston Mauriac?' she asked Ouallada, standing on the threshold of the girl's chamber. 'Don't you think he's as handsome as anyone can be with brown hair?'

'He's very charming,' Ouallada agreed impartially.

'I know what you're going to say. He's too young to be fully a man.'

Ouallada had been going to say nothing at all. Gaston Mauriac did not invite reproach, but then neither did he invite any spirited defence on her part. She felt no need to hold an opinion.

'Did you know Auxerre d'Impt once broke thirty lances in a single day? I think it would be very easy to love a man who can break thirty lances in a day, don't you think?'

'It would be a comfort if you had thirty enemies, I suppose,' said Ouallada diplomatically, 'but I doubt you have one.'

'Of course, I've always been a *little* in love with Simon Bobignol. We played together as children, you know? Just like brother and sister. I could tell you secrets about him that his own mother ... though some days I don't know why I should waste a thought on him. Such a *homely* boy. Not when there are titans in the world. I mean Bobignol could never tax one's heart to great aching ecstasies, could he? And I do think passion is the final quotient, don't you? I shall only ever go where Passion leads me.

'And will you judge that through the eye or the heart?' asked Ouallada. She fulfilled, she sometimes .thought, Aude's need for a jester, priming her with neutral comment to allow her the chance to continue a monologue which lasted all day.

'Oh, my bowels! With my bowels!' cried Aude, scampering squirrel like into the room and sitting down at the troubadour's feet. She nestled herself into the haven of Ouallada's skirts and took the cither out of her hands, to be sure of her undivided attention. 'When I find the perfect man, I shall give myself to him then and there! Right away! Wouldn't you? I've always known that. No silly coyness. Not a moment's bliss to go to waste ... Not that I could say so to him, but then there's the sweet paradox, isn't it?' She reached up and rested her hands on Ouallada's forearms, stroking them absentmindedly, lost in a delicious, familiar reverie. 'It's not wrong, you know? It's all here. It's all here in the *Bréviare* - well, you'd know that better than anyone. I suppose you've read it through and through. You've read everything through and through. You're far cleverer than me.' The book hung from her waist by a fine gold chain, L*e Bréviare d'Amour*, the essential guide to a fashionable conscience. 'A lady who sleeps with a true lover,' she read out, from an extremely dog-eared page, 'is purified of all sins, and the joy of love makes the act innocent, for it proceeds from a pure heart.' Equally absentminded, she drew Ouallada's hands down till they covered her breasts and held them in place, indulging the sexual arousal which contemplation of her favourite subject brought to her. None of the men she mentioned had the smallest hold on her affections. When the man arrived who did, then his name would be too potent to speak without swooning, too precious to share with mere woman friends such as Ouallada ben Zefir. In the meantime, the mere contemplation of him made her writhe luxuriantly.

Ouallada did not disturb her patron's smiling daydream, but put the time to profitable use trying to compose a few lines of verse. It was Aude's practice, since she had acquired a troubadour-sister, to hearten her suitors with small songs of encouragement - a kittenish invitation to play - songs addressed to an anonymous lover with hints and clues sprinkled throughout to convince each hopeful that he was the unrevealed choice of her heart. Typically Ouallada sang:

My sister, oh my sister
Has been taken in a hunter's net.

Her wings flutter and her eyes are wet;
Her feet are tangled, claw on claw, and yet
She feign would to kiss the golden fret –
The cage he has prepared for his pet.
My sister, oh my sister, flyaway!
Or he will pluck your plumes by break of day.

Not for the first time, she caught a glimpse of just what cords bound those dozen different men and held them in thrall. Sexuality rose off Aude as reekingly as camphor, paining the sinuses, confusing rational thought. An intimation came to Ouallada of something frightening and primordial, like seeing the earth buckled by magma moving beneath it. Where it belonged in this cosy domestic household was not at all clear to her, but she could sense it, even so. Best that Aude choose a lover soon, thought Ouallada, sensing that a breach was needed in the ground if the pressure of that magma were not to build up to a dangerous pitch.

'So would you like me to praise the breaking of lances in a song?' she asked. 'Or the virtues of youth? Or the faithfulness of childhood friends?'

'Yes, yes. All of them. All of those. And a little about landlessness, too, for I shan't ever love a man for his money and station. That's what husbands are for, after all.'

Consequently, the song that Ouallada next composed concerning her 'lovelorn sister', had something to please and encourage every aspirant in her retinue, and though it stretched her powers of obfuscation, she turned out a masterpiece of bewilderment. It concerned a butterfly tasting the liquor of a dozen flowers and finding a little delight on every dewy petal.

Aude was entranced. 'Even the Bishop's there! You even planted out old Foulque! I did spot him, didn't I? "The purple-headed thistle all spiky and bristling"? Oh, I do believe you love them all as much as I do, Princess! You unpack my thoughts so plain!'

Ouallada examined the contents of her heart and found nothing there but a slight residual hatred for the suitors, a resentment of their privileged births and the small use they had made of life, whiling away their time all sniffing after the same rabbit. 'I can weed out the Bishop, if you think he's out of place in the garden.'

But Aude only said, 'Not at all, not at all,' colouring a little as if she nursed a secret fondness for the irascible old devil.

The Old Railing Bishop (as he was referred to by his rivals) was not truly old, except inasmuch as he was fifteen years older than the others. He was not a bishop, either, having thrown up Holy Orders for the allure of the secular world. Hard to see just what facet of the secular world had lured him, thought Ouallada, for he seemed to hate almost everything.

He eschewed the silly fashions brought back to France from the Crusades. He wrote poetry attacking the politics of the day, the secularity of the day, the vices and tastes of the Franks, and the soft-underbelly of their popular heroes. He was tolerated, for the ironic reason that acerbic, carping verse was in fashion just then. Also, being older, he had a certain air of wisdom, and the reputation of being a demon with a mace. Even though he had left his calling, and could have carried a sword and lance, in this and in every other respect he conducted himself as though he were still one of the fighting bishops, confining himself to the one weapon - unless, of course, one counted the lash of his tongue.

People had asked his opinion on their verse before now and lived to regret it. Approbation could be measured only in how far he refrained from abuse. He awarded twelve pejoratives for every 'fair', a dozen vituperative snarls for every grudging nod of his large, shaggy head. Whether he still wore a tonsure was impossible to tell, for either his hairline had receded to embrace it or his hairline had simply receded to the crown of his large, sunburned skull. The depth of his forehead was further exaggerated by the fact that his eyebrows were usually drawn down into a scowl. His nose had been broken at some stage, presumably by someone who took exception to his advanced critical faculty; the original Norman column had been depressed, exaggerating the flute of his nostrils and making the tip of his nose turn slightly upwards. On the rare occasions of his smile, the face transformed itself beyond mere amusement to a misleading ingenuousness.

Ouallada ben Zefir was not misled. She neither sought his praise nor invited his opinion of her work. His hatred of women was reputed to outweigh even his hatred of the times. But just once - on the occasion of the butterfly poem being delivered at dinner - flushed by triumph and flattered by the applause of her peers, Ouallada did glance in Foulque's direction. He returned her an unpleasantly rigorous stare: she had noticed before how his brown eyes had a quality such as one saw in pictures of God, deluging the Earth in judgemental light, pinioning Man where he stood. Perhaps just this once, she did raise her eyebrow a little as if to say, 'Well, monk? What exception can you take to that?'

Just at that moment, Aude asked outright: 'And what does our Railing Bishop think to the Princess' exposition of Love?'

He tossed up his head, like a cow emerging from the manger at the sound of a milk pail. But his eyes never left Ouallada. And even though he addressed himself to the Lady Aude, he went on looking at the other girl. 'She has as fair a grasp of the language as any foreigner can hope for,' he said.

The rest of the audience, accustomed to Foulques' asperity, thought it a poor jibe. They were frankly disappointed that he should find nothing more offensive to say. They groaned and jeered. He waited for them to finish.

'I don't refer to her nativity as much as her strangeness to the subject,' he expanded. 'She is a foreigner to the country of Love. Those who write about Love should first have visited it. That's all the opinion her efforts wake in me.' He appeared to mumble, but every syllable and consonant reached the rafters, lifted the starling droppings in the angles of the wall, shifted the soot in the upper storeys. His was a poet's voice, powerful and resonant. He could not have delivered a sneeze without making it sound like rhetorical punctuation.

Ouallada's heart diminished within her, shrank down and then expanded with a sudden painful rush of resentment. 'If I were to write on my own behalf,' she said, rising on the balls of her feet to project her voice over intervening heads, 'Monsieur Foulque might have grounds to query my art. But I meant only to sketch a picture of my *sister's* affections.'

He inclined his head as if conceding, and it was with palms raised in conciliation that he said, 'Quite so, quite so. It is simply that my lady employs a physician for the sake of her health, a chaplain for the health of her soul, a gardener for the welfare of her vegetable plot. It merely astonished me that she should employ the blind to read what is graven on her heart. To talk of Love without having been there is to describe Arcturus without ever seeing it. Without ever touching ice.

'Oh, but surely, sir!' she retaliated instantly, feeling her cheeks flush. 'Anyone who has met *you* has travelled to Love's Arcturus and knows the pangs of frostbite.'

La Belle Aude laughed with the rest, then pushed her lips forwards in an affecting mouet. 'My poor, dear Bishop. Come here. I won't have you made fun of! Indeed I won't! You're much the cleverest man here. Much. And I *know* you're acquainted with passion. I *know* you are. The Princess Ouallada is new among us. She hasn't heard you sing or she would not be so cruel.' It was said banteringly, implying no censure of Ouallada at all, but only a wish for no one to be excluded from the happy society of her court. Like the kind child among ruffians, she would allow no friend of hers to be bullied. 'Come here to me,' said Aude again, crooningly.

It seemed for a moment that Foulque would not move from where he sat hunched over his dinner. Then he swung first one great booted leg then the other over the bench and stamped up to the dais where Aude sat nibbling bouchets of herring off a little three-legged table beside her. She signalled him close, then closer still, signing that she wished to whisper in his ear. Ouallada noticed that he shut his eyes tight against the proximity of her face - perhaps just against the smell of fish on her breath - and that sweat sprang quite miraculously from his temples. Born of what? Irritation? Distress? Anger? 'Why do you stay here,' she wanted to ask, 'if you dislike us all so much?' She could not imagine what Aude had found to say to him.

'Of course, he's quite the cleverest of men. He's studied absolutely everywhere. And he is *original*,' said Aude later that evening.

'But not the greatest aid to digestion,' said Ouallada.

'Oh, don't you think so?' she asked, genuinely surprised. 'I wouldn't be without him for the world! In every bowl of fruit there should be a lemon, don't you think? ... He said that, of course, not me. In every bowl of fruit a lemon. The sour among the sweet.'

Not for the first time, Ouallada was reminded of the room's warmth in contrast to the frosty, moonless night chiselling at the castle wall; of the bright colours and soft textures in contrast to the blackness outside lousy with draughts, slimy with filth and evil spirits; of the wealth of meat hung in the cellars, like Egypt prepared for seven years of famine. She felt the roof shielding her from lightning, snow and war. 'Yes, but what lemon once it's brought to your table refuses to ripen to a sweet ness?' She meant it as a slight on the Bishop, though it came out sycophantically and brought a feline grin to Aude's face.

Just then there was a deep, embarrassed cough beyond the door curtain, and Aude summoned Foulque into the room. For a fraction of time, Ouallada saw the face as it might have looked before irascibility took a hold - the grey flecked eyebrows raised in anticipation, eyes wide open, the mouth slightly ajar and smiling. Then he caught sight of her and quite perceptibly reeled away as if he had collided with an invisible barrier. He had clearly expected to find Aude alone. The eyes lifted to the ceiling where he seemed to look for some emergency source of patience, and he drew a couple of deep breaths.

'Ah, Foulque! My dear friend!' At once Aude sat down on the edge of the bed and extended one foot towards him. 'Do help me off with my shoes, won't you?'

He stood looking from one woman to the other. 'Princess, have you no fiddle to tune?' he asked.

'None, sir, that would hold its note till morning,' she said obstinately. She glanced at Aude, but Aude did not wish her to go either. Indeed, she patted the bed beside her indicating that Ouallada should come and enjoy a more sisterly closeness.

As Foulque, with uncharacteristic clumsiness, struggled with the buckles of her shoes, Aude stroked his hair and fingered his ears, trailing her fingers round his jawline.

After her shoes, she had him unlace her sleeves at the shoulder, then untie the cords which gathered her skirt, then uncinch the hoop of padding that cushioned her hips - a pallid thing like a great fat slow worm. 'That's enough,' she said, all of a sudden. 'The Princess can help me with the rest.'

He did not get up from his knees immediately, chafing his palms up and down his thighs, his head bent so far forward that neither of them could see his face.

'Aren't you afraid of him at all?' Ouallada asked after he had left the room.

'Me? I'm not afraid of anyone!' she declared, bright with hilarity, proud of her daring.

Ouallada wanted to say, 'You should.be. You ought to be.' Instead she said, 'He frightens me.'

Unfortunately, such was the concentration of artists at Haut-Béziers - bright geraniums crowded together on one narrow window-sill - that it was impossible for two who disliked each other to avoid daily contact. Sometimes one would detach himself to execute some pilgrimage of love, some family business or some feat of heroism to enlarge the fame of La Belle Aude. Sometimes another would arrive and adhere to the group like a piece of flotsam gathered into a raft of river litter awaiting a change of current. But there was little to break up the agreeable household with its seasonal diversions of hunting, bowling, chess and jousting. The gradual disintegration of Jerusalem's Christian kingdom, viewed from afar, had lessons to teach, but only as a Greek drama does, all real action happening off-stage, out-of-sight, fetched in the mouths of messengers.

More exciting by far was the thought of an *assais*, for there were more than a dozen hearts fixed on the lady of the house and until she gave some intimation as to where her affections would light, all those hearts were held in a planetary orbit, all bliss trapped within the bud, all tragedy still unfurled.

'Like dogs when a bitch is on heat,' said Foulque splenetically to himself one Sunday. Aude had snagged her dress on the lock mechanism of the chapel door and ten young men crowded round her with sympathy and advice.

Ouallada overheard him. 'Then why stay in the kennel?' she snapped. 'What brought you out of Orders, sir, to bless us with your oh-so-merry views on the world?'

He turned, startled at being overheard. She wondered whether he valued his board and lodging enough to ask her not to repeat his comment, but he seemed unabashed. 'The Council of Tours is what brought me out of Orders, young woman,' he said. 'I grew tired of the hot pursuit of ignorance. So do you think I'm any gladder to see stupidity here, among laymen, rather than there, among monks?'

'You'll have to explain, sir. The Council of Tours? I don't believe I was born.'

'It forbade the study of Law or Science - for fear that "knowing all, we might be as gods" ... But then I suppose you worship at the feet of Saint Norbert, like all the other good, pious little *fraus*.'

'Ah, the Holy Norbert. He is a very ... energetic gentleman, you must allow him that.'

'And God sent him two helpmates to prosper his work: women and fools. Women thrive on ignorance and fools depend on it. Forgive me, but I'd throw Norbert to the lions and beatify Hugh of La on myself "Hear everything and then you will see that nothing is superfluous."'

'Is that where you studied? Laon?'

'Hugh of Laon studied in Saint Victor's in Paris. He was *born* at Laon, for God's sake ... Or for the Devil's sake, if you'd believe Saint Norbert. Yes, I studied at Saint Victor. Here and there. The Episcopal School at Ile de la Cité. Montague Sainte-Geneviève. Chartres.' He tasted the words - indulgences of his youth, happinesses choked off by the Church's recent hard-line suppression of the New Learning. Perhaps he hoped to shock her by naming them: other men used dirty language in front of a woman in order to be shocking. At least Foulque's offensiveness had dignity.

He did not appreciate that he aroused only envy in the soul of Ouallada who, having tasted knowledge at the hands of Oriole and the bear, would have given her hair to study at Chartres.

'Chartres? Did you hear the lectures there on Plato?'

'Plato, Aristotle.'

'And Donatus?'

'And Priscian.'

'Cicero?'

'And Boethius.'

'Pythagoras?'

Hand over hand they raced each other up the Tower of Knowledge.

'Euclid.'

'Ptolemy?'

'Seneca.'

'Peter Lombard?'

'Yes. Even the Bible. I admit it!' He gave a short, unwilling laugh. 'So. You've climbed the damnable Tower of Babel too, have you, and read them all?'

'Jesu no, of course not. How would I? I'm a woman.'

All his sarcasm came rushing back. 'Ah, but I remember now! You have glanced inside *The Book of All that is to be Known*, haven't you? I forgot that advantage you hold over us all.' Still, he did not directly call her a liar. 'I see I must enrol you an honorary man among my acquaintances.

And he did so, scrupulously annotating his vast mental library with a memorandum, so that never again would he make the mistake of treating her as a woman.

Now, when he looked back towards the chapel and saw Gaston Mauriac kissing the hem of Aude's dress, he made no attempt to conceal his disgust. 'Women are all jakes and jades,' he said.

Her anger returned too. 'Well, then, might you not *go home*, sir, rather than suffer the daily trial of closeness to us all?'

'Go home? Where's that?' he said. 'My grave?'

'All right, then. Should you not go in quest of a lady who *does* please you? An exception to the rule?' She was aware of being blithe and brittle. She had walked around the corner of the chapel path before she realised he had come to a halt. At last his face appeared, scowling but with bewilderment and not temper for once. There was even a trace of pain.

'What do you mean, go in quest of one? Isn't this one enough? D'you think I'd inflict this torment on myself a second time? Do you know something I don't, then? Are you privy to her secrets?'

'Whose? Aude's? But I thought she was a jake and a jade!'

'So she is! So she is!' he blustered. 'Do you think I'm cursed with blindness as well as love? What difference does it make? It's a poison. It's a contagion. D'you think distaste's an antidote?'

'You're in love with Aude? Just like the rest?'

He struck his fist against the church wall - a blow so hard that a string of bloody drops welled up along the side of his palm. '*Nothing* like the rest! How, "like the rest"? Have you never heard my verse? Doesn't it speak a thing to you? Are you deaf or foolish? Far more than the rest! Sulphur past fire more than the rest!' She recoiled from the sheer noise of his bellowing, but walking backwards brought him pursuing her down the path, his consonants wet in her face. 'Do you think age damps it? Do you? Do you think an intellect arms against it? Do you think a grey beard keeps it at bay?'

'I'm sorry. I'm sorry. I'm new to the place. I didn't mean anything of the ...'

'Love's a worm in the gut ...'

He seemed suddenly to recollect whom he was talking to, and cut himself off as short as if he had crammed a rag into his mouth. 'Didn't I say you were a foreigner to the country?' he muttered.

'You make it sound like a place where I'd rather moor offshore,' she said in quiet conciliation.

He dropped his head forward as he had in the bedroom that night - caught his breath, then nodded. 'Sail right on by, while you still have the option.'

He smiled ruefully, put a comradely arm around her shoulders and drew her away from the irritating sound of shrill laughter around the chapel door.

'But Love's the centre of our world,' she said, as one professional *trobar* to another.

He wiped his face on the cloth of his sleeve and breathed in deeply through those wide-flared nostrils. 'Ah yes, my green young friend, but next door is Hell. Next door is Hell.'

CHAPTER TWENTY-TWO

The Clap-Net

'Would Foulque ever have made a bishop?' Ouallada asked her patron as they lay in bed together, to keep warm.

'Christ, yes. He'd've made a cardinal for sure if he hadn't fallen in love with me. Not that he has the rank by birth, you know. He's a poor relation. But what a relation he has! Only a merchant who's as good as bought himself the rank of a duke, that's who. His uncle would've bought Foulque advancement in the Church, as high as he wanted to rise. Meant him to, of course - to win a voice in the Pope's ear, for the sake of the family, you know. But Foulque fell in love with me instead.'

Aude was a little selective in what she remembered of Foulque's past. She recalled that he was landless, but not how his family had been ruined. His uncle - the same one who had placed Foulque in Orders as a child, with the hope of him rising - had annexed his own brother's castle and estates, had dispossessed Foulque's father. The sort of thing Aude recalled was the moment Foulque had first seen her and become trapped, like a wasp in a cup of mead. She failed to remember that he was also seething with indignation at the time - against the short-comings of the Church, its legal immunity, its pride in ignorance, its lack of penitence for its many sins. Foulque was incensed by it, but then Foulque was incensed about so many things that Aude had never taken any great note of the particulars. Only his romantic enslavement could she remember in every detail.

'He just watched. For week after week, he just watched me from the back of the room,' she said. 'Never smiled or bowed. I swear that man seems to look quite through to your worst sins ... but then it was his place to once, I suppose ... Then all of a sudden he marches up to the fireplace and takes hold of a tabor and beats it so hard the ducks leave off laying for a week, and he sings me this song about how I've made him mad as Legion and tied him up in chains of Love. It was quite alarming, I promise you!'

'But you don't care for him, sure?'

'Don't I?' Aude sat up in bed, genuinely wondering. 'How should I know? How shall I know *who* I love till I've put them all to *assais* and tried their love to the bottom? ... You're probably right, of course. But he isn't a faller yet. Oh, he's such a *monk* still, you know. I used to think he'd cling to his vows in or out of the cloister - I'm sure he meant to. But one by one I'm bending that stiff neck of his. Men are like horses, don't you think? They have to be broken in before they're ridden ... And how can I tell which is going to be the best until they've all been broken? It's a great quandary ... So you don't like my Foulque, then? No, I suppose you wouldn't. He said you didn't know anything about ... '

'It isn't that.'

'You think he's too old?'

Ouallada hesitated to malign one of Aude's admirers. But the feelings welled up so strongly within her that she could not help blurting out her chiefest objection. 'It seems to me that a man who's broke faith with Holy Orders can't be relied on for a constant heart. Not in anything.'

Aude broke out laughing - a great generosity of laughter overspilling with bounty, and once again Ouallada was put to shame, thinking that Aude could find good in everyone. 'Well, aren't you two the comicalest things! That's just what *he* thinks, too! If he had the power any more, I swear he'd damn himself, bell, book and candle! I can't think why, though! Not when every other priest I know is far easier in judgement on himself! No, his uncle put him in Orders and his Orders put him to vowing vows. But *me* he chose of his own accord, and the vows couldn't *help* spilling from him. Isn't there all the difference in the world? Oh no, I haven't any doubts about Foulque - not for a moment. He'll love me till his last breath's spent and probably a good while after. Shall I prove it to you?'

It is not so very strange that ordeal should count for so much. In a land and at a time when a man's guilt could be proved by Ordeal of Combat, where witches could be found out by Ordeal of Fire and Water, where God's liking of one knight above another could be proved on the field of tourney - what other way could there be for a lady to give her heart than by testing her suitor's mettle? She might have tested him in bed, but that would have rewarded the undeserving. She might have required him to prove himself by glorious deeds, but that fashion had come and gone somewhat, devouring thousands in Crusade slaughter: an extravagant test of the heart. How much more civilised, how much less wasteful of feminine chastity, is the courtly *assais*. It mostly proves a man as an apple is proved, by paring; proves a man not by what he is prepared to do, but by what he is prepared *not* to do; by what he is ready to go without. Gold, which is soft and simple, yields its secrets to one assay. Man is a much more complex enigma, however: his assay calls for more skills than mere metallurgy.

Aude displayed a real aptitude for the science of *assais*. She knew how to temper her *assais* to each particular man. The test might begin the same, daring him to look not touch, touch without grabbing. But beyond that, she tailored the affliction to each suitor's nature.

Gaston Mauriac, who had such a passion for his horses, she required to go on foot for one year. Auxerre d'Impt, who had the finest mew of falcons in the Languedoc, she commanded to loose his birds along with a cageful of songbirds, and to shoot any falcon which dared to menace its weaker sisters. (An *assais*, said

Foulque surlily, framed to try the falcons rather more than Auxerre). Simon Bobignol, who was vain to a degree and owned a wardrobe of clothes more lavish than Aude's, was expected to wear hessian every Sunday. 'She's afraid he'll outshine her at Mass,' said Foulque sourly. For him, no further *assais* had so far followed the one in Aude's bedroom. 'Had the man shown insufficient restraint while assisting Aude to undress,' Ouallada wondered. Was it unchivalric for a man to sweat with desire?

'I think you overlooked a vital thing,' Ouallada said coldly to her father next time he came and sought her out, secretly.

Like a bad dream he crept into her awareness as she sat one day by the Fountain of Morgan la Fey. (Aude was in the grip of the Arthurian cult and had relabelled the countryside.) Oriole was aggrieved: 'Who was that with you? Who was that here just now? Don't deny it. I saw someone with you just now.'

'That was Gaston Mauriac,' she said impassively, her two hands plucking up grass with a rhythmic ferocity and tossing it into the water. 'He says he loves me with a *practical* love. His heart's Aude's but his body's mine if I want it. Says he'll probably die if I don't.' She was still shaking a little from the encounter.

'You can do better,' said Oriole dismissively. Her father was maggot-white, his hollow cheeks stubbly, his earlobes like the drops from melting ice. 'He's a fourth son. Hasn't above five thousand ēcu to last him a lifetime. Did he bring presents?'

She put out a hand into the long grass and picked up

a carved wooden model of a horse, its rider inlaid with mother-of-pearl and some precious metal. 'He doesn't mean it. He's bored. He'd as soon be hunting, but he's sworn to go on foot, so he's bored.'

Oriole looked pleased. He crept closer; close enough for her to smell him: an insanitary brown and yellow smell.

'There was a thing you didn't teach me, Father.'

'Then it's no use to you. I'm sure that whore of a mother taught you all there is to know about lying on your back, if that's what you mean. Look what it won her, then shun it.' He crabbed round her, his knees up by his ears, his shirt-end dragging through the grass where it spilled out between jacket and hose. There was no need for him to look so decayed, she thought. He took enough money from her.

'I didn't mean that. I've no taste for that. I can see the beasts doing it in the fields. I don't hanker after that.' He beamed with self-congratulation that he should have made such a sweet amputation of her more useless, womanish characteristics. 'But you left me lacking Father. That's all I'm saying.'

'How, "lacking"? There'll be better than Mauriac. Time to move on, I think. Leave this place. That Aude woman casts you into shadow.'

'You forgot I wasn't bred to it. You forgot, it's not in my blood. You forgot I'd have to be noble to make any sense of it.'

'Sense of what? Chivalry, you mean? Being *trobar*? The Gay Science?' When he could stop himself laughing, he spat fulsomely into the spring. 'You stupid baby! Noble? Anyone can grasp it, bladder-brain. Anyone can carry it off. If that dog Amaury ... '

'What about Amaury?'

But he only swivelled his eyes uneasily and spat again, and tucked the wooden horse out of sight under his cloak.

She did not want the conversation to go on. She wanted him gone. She wanted to be free of his grubbing hands always searching her for money. She wanted to be free of the smell of beans fermenting in that little mound of a belly that protruded beneath his ribs like a moated tumulus. And yet there was no one else to ask, no one else with whom she could share anything real, anything self-revealing. 'I don't understand why they do it!' she burst out. 'It all seems just foolishness. Just a game. Like bear-baiting. Like pricking yourself with a pin to see how often you can do it. *What's it for, Papa?* Why do grown men do it?'

He howled in her face, hardly rising from his squat to dance in front of her like a deranged goblin, exhaling his hatred into her nostrils. 'For grown women! That's why they do it! If you don't see that, it's because you're not grown yet. That patron of yours sees it. That Aude, she sees it right enough. She works 'em all like fish on the line. You learn from her, girl, then you get from under her shadow, you hear me? It's small fry here. We can do better!'

There was no point in asking him any more. Once he began to talk of 'we' and 'us', she knew she had lost him to the realms of his imagination, to the empire he was building, turret by terrace, where they would one day live together in material bliss. She got up and left him there, beside the rill. She heard him call after her in that bellowed whisper he had perfected for bullying her in secret, 'Just think on! Keep clear of their pricks! If you must know what the hunt's all in aid of, lie with that lady of yours. Lie with that pretty Aude!' She shook herself involuntarily, like a cat climbing out of water, shaking his words off before they could soak in. Perhaps he was right, though, in saying she was too young to understand the chivalric ideal. She was, after all, only about seventeen.

Just to depress her further, she discovered, on returning to the castle, that the barbarous Foulque was still included among Aude's potential lovers. Ouallada passed him on the bailey-motte, burning off laburnum which had seeded itself where the castle horses might graze and be poisoned. He wielded the torch with all the energy and flourish of a fairground performer, grinding the flames home into the heart of each pretty plant. He seemed quite manic, his eyes so bright that she thought he must be feverish, and began to skirt round him. But he was not ill. He was happy.

He was glad to see her, too. 'Princess! Come with me! Quickly! Please.' He extricated his feet from the clutches of ground elder and leapt down the slope. It was novel, at least, that he should be so civil. She waited for him to take her by the arm and hurry her towards the gate. 'Aude won't break it to me till she has you by her. She has an *assais* for me.

"For you?'

'What, is that too big a surprise? Too improbable for you, is it? Do you think I can't answer the challenge?'

She hung back against his pulling. 'I just wonder you should want to,' she said.

But he looked at her as if she were mad, as if his delight had been visible for all to see, a long way off, coming towards him. How could a man want something so much, the face said, without his wish coming true?

Aude had simply been savouring the details of an exquisite test tailored to the very proportions of her victim. Withholding from him the details until her sister-in-amour should be on hand to enjoy it, she had in fact grown so excited that she fairly fell on them when they arrived, caressing their faces, leading them by the hand, stroking the breast of Foulque's sheepskin waistcoat and fondling his beard. He flushed to a very strange colour indeed, and his pale brown eyes looked over the top of her head, brilliant with defiance; as if to say, 'Well? You thought I hadn't a chance!' Ouallada suddenly understood, though, why she had not recognised his happiness when she first saw it outside. Though it was in his eyes, he had not once smiled.

Now his eyes fed on the sight of Aude, wandering over her features like bees drunk on the nectar they found there. You reveal yourself, my dear Bishop, Ouallada thought sarcastically, but could not muster the energy to say it out loud. A kind of fascination kept her watching, too: watching those eyes, that face. So soon after talking to her father, even Foulque's face compared surprisingly well with those shrunken, crab-apple cheeks, those unkind, withdrawn eyes huddling back in their sockets. Perhaps Love softens the hardest of them, thought Ouallada, and never touched my father.

'Do you recall, sister, how the Bishop recited to us all the other night from *Tristan and Iseult*?'

He winced, aggrieved. 'Must I ask you every day not to call me that?'

Aude broke away from him and swept in a great circle about the room, her fingers pressed together at the tips, her lips pursed equally tight, though they curved upwards in a beaming grin. 'Oho, and are you so changed since your former life? I can't think it. I do believe your heart's still perfectly given over to the Church and not to me at all.'

His brows constricted, like a man with a headache. 'How so, since I've quit the Church and yet here I stay at your service, like a ship run aground?'

'Oh really! Just because you can recite poetry about a pair of lovers, do you suppose we think you've left your real love behind you? You're still in love with the cloister!'

Elation was turning to desperation. 'No, lady. Or I might still enjoy the promise of salvation rather than just the broken promises of women. This morning you promised me an *assais*.'

'Oh fah!' She dismissed his conscience with a happy laugh. 'Foulque. Dear, poor Foulque. Always dwelling on Hell and damnation.'

'Because my mind is always on you, lady.'

'Prove it.'

He started, as though an explosion had been set off behind him. She had not been teasing him; there really was to be an *assais*, and an *assais* raised a man up from *fegnador* to *precador*. He wiped his face with his hand. 'How, "prove it"? What splendid torment have you conjured up with your friend here, to afford you both a half-hour's amusement at my expense?'

'Well, if you don't want ... '

'Tell me. Let me be the judge.'

Ouallada felt suddenly awkward. She suggested she should leave, but Aude would not hear of it. She was far too excited by the originality of her *assais*, and perhaps a little afraid of Foulque's sheer physical bulk should he fly into one of his notorious rages. As a result of her excitement, she mistimed her *coup de grâce* with a clumsy, gauche, 'Would you enjoy a lovers' rendezvous?'

'*What?*' he said, and she quailed quite visibly.

'I said, would you attend on me at a lovers' rendezvous?'

'I'd keep your secrets better, sister, if I heard less of them,' said Ouallada nervously, and again tried to leave. Aude caught hold of her from behind, and held her close round the waist, fingering her bodice, scratching her nails across the stiff buckram stomacher. 'Don't go. I want you as a witness to the Bishop's cowardice when he fails me. I may need you to console me in my disappointment, Princess.'

'I shan't disappoint you,' said Foulque so sharply that she broke off and contemplated him for a time with her head on one side, smiling thoughtfully. She was wonderfully beautiful: could flex the collar bones of her shoulders so precisely as to allow her breasts to brim their bodice to the very lading-line of desire. One shade more pink of the areola and Goths and Vandals would have overrun the country. 'I shan't disappoint you,' said Foulque. 'Name the place and time.'

'A church,' said La Belle Aude. 'And not until you have built me a bower inside it. A Crystal Cave! Like the one where Tristan met Iseult. With a bed made right on the high altar where we shall ... well, where we shall become Iseult and Tristan, Tristan and Iseult. A Crystal Cave, Bishop Foulque, in place of the Holy of Holies. In my rustic chapel. You know? The one in the wood.'

He turned from purple to white, like a man does who falls from a high building and hits the ground: ruddy then pallid as the blood ebbs away. 'Christ Jesus,' he whispered softly, then turned on his heel and left the room without another word.

Aude d'Haut-Beziers was confused. She had expected something - a yeah or a nay - and did not know how to interpret his leaving. She tried to cover her confusion with a cheery laugh, but Ouallada was too shocked to join in.

'Aude! You want him to desecrate your own chapel? Suppose he does it? Suppose he builds you a bower?'

'Oh fah! Falalah!' She pranced self-consciously about the room, flicking her fingers through the ends of her silver-gilt hair. 'None but the Bishop would think twice about it - "desecration", I mean. These old superstitions! This dry old popery. It's all simony and sin, you know. Oh, shame on you, Ouallada! How can you be so old-fashioned? It's simply not the fashion hereabouts to mind about such things! Gracious, no! Hugo says the Roman Church is quite simply a culture foreign to the Midi. Always was!'

'Isn't Foulque a Camargais ...?' Ouallada began, but Aude was not listening.

'We're not bound by all these dismal superstitions any longer! Not we artists. Foulque yes, but not us!' Her tone was so shrill and brittle that Ouallada was left in no doubt Aude was daring herself almost as much as she was daring Foulque to blaspheme in the house of God, to desecrate the sanctuary of her church. She was still saying how little she feared Divine Wrath when Ouallada interrupted her with another consideration.

'In the story, Tristan and Iseult made love in the Crystal Cave. Do you really mean to ... '?

'Oh, he won't do it,' said Aude categorically. 'He won't build a bower. Can you see Foulque building a bower?' The muscles of her jaw were rigid with nervousness. 'He won't do it.' Realising this would mean Foulque valuing God's good opinion more than hers, she insisted. 'He'll fall on his knees and beg forgiveness of me and say he's too afraid of the Devil stealing his soul. And anyway ... If he does ...'But the sentence trailed away for lack of knowing what she would do.

Foulque would never do it. Ouallada had to agree. No one would do such a thing. But Foulque least of all.

Why should she say that? There was no more cynical or rash man in the Rousillon than the Railing Bishop. The stupidity of the Church had driven him out of it, and his passion for Aude had replaced his vocation. Still. He would not do it. No one would. Besides, the idea of that thunderous black-and-grey head growling from the rear of a sparkly faery grotto was too absurd.

It was warm, stepping out of the round tower: warmer out than in. The sun seemed to pin her against the masonry. 'Where are you going, Bishop? Are you leaving altogether? Have you given us up?' Ouallada called out to the figure on horseback by the gate.

'I'm going to market,' Foulque blared back, wrenching at his horse's bridle so hard that the beast staggered.

'What, to buy a present? She won't negotiate, you know.' Ouallada was glad. She had not been at ease thinking of Foulque as a genuine contender for her exquisite friend. Such ferocity alongside such delicacy. The lion alongside the turtledove.

'To buy bloody birdcages,' he bellowed, and the pigs in the run slithered in their manure and stampeded up and down. 'Blasphemous bitch,' he said aloud, but not to her, not to any listener. 'Blasphemous bloody bitch.'

After that, he was the butt of every courtier's joke, as he came and went with birdcages, lopped branches, osier baskets of grass and buckets of water; building his lovers' bower to resemble the one described in *Tristan and Iseult*. He might have been building a siege engine to judge by the speed and desperation with which he passed to and fro, absorbed past all consideration of food, rest or conversation. If people did not move out of his way, he barged them aside, his eyes set on some imagined prospect, his mind fixed on some future time. It was hot summer weather and he drank whenever he chanced on a cup of wine. On an empty stomach, it had the effect of fuelling both thirst and obsession, like a shipwrecked sailor drinking seawater. Once, when Ouallada collided with him in a doorway, he grabbed her by the biceps and lifted her clear off the floor, demanding to know where he might find nightingales. 'Nightingales!' he yelled. 'Where round here? Where do they sing?' She had to name the place and give him directions before he set her down again, and then she had got no more than ten steps towards safety when his voice stabbed her in the back, a voice mortified with self-disgust, *'I don't even know what the vermin look like!'* She turned back.

His doublet was spattered with long leaves of green

lime, like exaggerated tearstains, stuck tight by a tacky gum that he found repellent to touch. So he held his hands spread a distance in front of his breast, as if his body disgusted him without his being able to slough it off. He saw her turn back.

'And what's a siskin?' he asked in a whisper, so that she laughed and offered to show him the way to his nightingales and siskins.

He made a clap-net, too, look like a weapon of war. Wielding the great racquet of netting he approached the task of bird-catching like Orion the Hunter, club at the ready and a host of monsters to subdue. She thought he would blunder through the copse frightening away every living thing, emptying the trees of birds. But of course subtlety of movement is a knightly accomplishment and stillness a specialist art of the monkhood. Consequently, he had soon closed his clap-net around the struggles of a drab little bird, an ugly, bristling hawk-moth and a detritus of leaves. 'Come here,' he told Ouallada. 'Is this the thing? Is it?' His whisper had the martial authority of a trumpet.

She went closer, thinking she really ought, as Princess ben Zefir, to pretend an ignorance of Frankish wildlife and the practices of poachers. As a child she had clapped up birds to eat and birds to sell into captivity. She knew, for instance, that nightingales would not sing in cages: just pine and die. She knew they had mistimed their ride, too, relying on a long summer dusk when there was in fact rain coming in from the Cevennes. The trees shivered. The light began to fail.

He reached into the net and took out the bird. The

moth seized the chance to escape and fluttered into her
face, making her shut her mouth and eyes tight. 'Is this
a nightingale?' he said. 'Please.'

'I can't see.'

He held the bird between careful, nervous hands; held
it close to her face. The bird stretched its neck and filled
his palms with yellow excreta: she could see that much
in the twilight. And yet he did not let go. His fingers
touched Ouallada's cheek. His eyes waited, hopeful, for
her answer. They glittered in the darkness, very large
eyes with very dark lashes, drinking up the last light, as
certain constellations absorb the light of the surrounding
sky.

'No,' she lied. 'It's a female blackbird.'

The nightingale fluttered away between their faces,
upwards, against the artillery of unfletched rain that
suddenly began to fall. He dropped his hands to the
ground and squatted there, his head hanging forwards,
wiping his palms over and over and over again on the
moss; over and over and over.

'Why do it if it gives you no joy?' she asked; though her
voice was low, some kind of animal shifted uneasily in
the leafmould.

'You've read Andreas. "The essence of Love is desire."
It's not supposed to be comfortable. One doesn't become
... acclimatised.'

'And is it making you grow to greatness? Your *ascesis*?
Your self-denial? Are you climbing the Ladder of
Perfection?' Perhaps this man could give her what her
father could not: some insight into the workings of a real
troubadour's mind.

But he stood up instantly and laughed out loud, a

bark like a wolf stepping in a trap. The trees overhead rattled with birds and rain. 'Ladder of Perfection? *Ladder of Perfection*? Mudslide, you mean. I'm on the mudslide to Damnation. I studied under Peter Lombard, remember? "Desire's a punishment laid on Man for the Fall." Desire's a taste of Hell, to whet your appetite for the eternal meal of brimstone.' He towered over her, swinging the net to and fro to capture a flock of leaves, a skein of raindrops.

'Oh, but Lombard was a theologian. You'd expect a theologian to say that!' she said, trying to sound cheerfully dismissive.

He opened his hand and let the handle of the net go in a gesture of resignation. 'But *it's* my opinion too, Princess. It's the opinion of my conscience. Which is all that signifies.'

'But surely, if Desire's sent by God, then it can't be avoided!'

The space between every branch end was teeming with bats. He watched them as though any or all 'of them might be nightingales, the rest of his life given to plucking them out of the air. He smiled absently. 'Certainly it can't be avoided, no, or I'd've found the way before now.' He watched so intently that he only blinked when the rain running down his face overfilled his lashes and he could no longer see.

Ouallada was suddenly reminded of an earliest memory - of watching her mother combing her stook of shining black hair; combing it until sparks of light cracked around her head, some blue, some white - a halo of sparks, an evanescence of spangling, Looking at Foulque now she thought he must be charged with the same power and that if she were to reach out and touch him, there would be a pain to match.

'I'll help you catch your nightingale,' she said, but stood on her hem in getting up, and overbalanced. He reached out a hand to steady her. And she found she had been right. About the pain.

As a child, she had clapped up birds to eat and birds to sell into captivity. But she had never guessed before how it felt for the clap-net of Love to close around you - how the shock could confuse all your instincts, how the mesh could confound all thought of escape.

CHAPTER TWENTY THREE

The Crystalline Cave

She helped him find a nightingale for his collection. And a siskin and a calendar lark too. For though now, more than ever, she did not want him to succeed in his *assais,* she suddenly knew how he felt and could see that failure was unthinkable.

' ... Their loyal subjects were the green lime, sunshine, shade, brook, flowers, grass, blossoms, leaves, slender nightingale, thrush, blackbird. Siskin and calendar lark vied in eager rivalry,' the narrative read. 'Their high feast was Love ... '

Their high feast. Aude intended it to take place on the high altar of Haut - Bezier's woodland chapel, in 'a Crystalline Cave'.

A Crystalline Cave? It defied Ouallada's imagination,

but Foulque did not need her help there. He knew where to find crystals which would refract the rays of the low sun shining in through the windows. He knew that if he sent to the Camargue - to Lattes or Maguelone - there would be oddities of crystals to be found among the shovelled salt mounds - polygons of perfect geometry, oddities of precipitation available for a few sous.

The thrushes mobbed the lark, the blackbird squirted its yellow unease all over. The chaplain mobbed Foulque, calling him a demon. But Foulque only bent his neck under the invective, and went on decking the place with blossom and flowers. He wrenched whole boughs off the trees without recourse to a saw. He strewed the floor with herbs, grinding them furiously under his boot with the excuse of freeing their scent. When it came to removing the heavy gold crucifix which stood on the altar, he held it between his hands and stared at it like the souvenir of an old love.

Ouallada, kneeling awkwardly in the cave-mouth, securing bird-cages to a baton in the roof, watched him through a hole. His lips moved but she could not hear any words. He was praying, but it could not be for himself, since La Belle Aude had commanded him, as adjunct to his *assais*, to replace, in his worship, every 'I' and '*me*' with '*she*' and '*her*'.

'To prove that he places my salvation above his own,' she had told Ouallada, her voice shrill with hilarity and daring. It occurred to Ouallada that this particular sin would place Foulque outside a state of grace, since he would be incapable of making any penitential act. Still, she comforted herself that, as a theologian, he must have found some let or waiver; no one would tread the world in such peril. It would be like crossing an icebridge carrying a basket of fire.

The crystals had arrived from Lattes - great ugly outcrops of opaque salt presenting shineless facets to the sunlight which streamed in on to his tableau. He laid a quilt over the high altar with gentle, meticulous hands, and the chapel was full of the sound of his breathing. Ouallada pretended to be sorting the best boughs of blossom. They had their backs to one another. 'It can't be wrong,' she said. She had been rummaging through her disorganised scholarship like a thief through a chest of valuables. 'How can the same thing be a sin that's at root of all the finest things in life? Someone said that somewhere. Innocent babies born of it. Heroism. All sorts of good things. From physical love.' She did not believe it, but at least she had found some grounds for him to carry a clear conscience.

The throstlethrush in the cage he was holding suddenly took fright, as though it sensed violence in the air. It clattered against the bars. 'You talk like the peasants hereabouts,' he snapped. 'Enjoy it and it can't be wrong.'

She filled up with indignation. What was the matter with the man? Did he not *want* an excuse for the sin he was about to commit? 'Maybe peasants are forced to think like that,' she retaliated. 'Joy doesn't come to them often enough to question it. Unlike their grand sisters in their great castles.' And the siskin jumped up and down from its perch, its little claws scrabbling on the bark floor of its cage. Their backs were still turned on one another.

'Are you disparaging my lady?'

'What if I am? You do it. Can't anyone else?'

'No one. Not till he has cause as good as mine.

'Best call me out, then. What? Swords here and now in the chapel? You're good at blasphemies, you!'

Neither of them knew where the outburst had come from.

What was he doing building a bower when she would have settled for a haystack? What was he doing dirtying his soul, when she would have carried it to Jerusalem and back for washing? She took her passion away to a safer distance - out of the chapel - out where God would not see her jealousy.

But her father was waiting by the door.

The chapel stood in the centre of a clearing, on the nearest piece of flat land to the castle. Given the undulations and corrugations of the wild, red countryside, there was a half-mile walk back to the round tower. Beggars and pilgrims often drifted through the trees to foregather at the church and await Aude's charity. It made an ideal place for Oriole the Minstrel to harangue his daughter.

'What's going on in there? Where've you been keeping yourself? Why are you spending so much time with this one? I don't like churchmen. Churchmen can't be trusted. Too many coils in their souls. You'd do better to keep away.' Her father's aggressive face lurched at her like the skulls wielded by hell-fire preachers, precisely when she least wanted to think about sin.

'He's not a churchman, Father. He's a *fegnador* to Aude. He just dresses like that.'

'I know a churchman when I see one. I've seen him up here, day after day, turning people away, bolting the doors. What is he, then, an architect? He's a churchman.

I know the look.'

'He's making something, Father. Inside the chapel. - Don't do that. If I had anything, I'd give it you. Aude's too busy presently to think of gifts. Don't paw at me like that.'

'You're my cub to paw, aren't you? I fed you out of that paw. No gifts? I told you. It's time to move on. Somewhere a *trobar's* better appreciated. Somewhere you're not so thick on the ground, you singers. Too many splitting the harvest, that's what ... What's he making? Making what? I heard hammering.'

'A thing. A bower. For the Lady Aude.'

'A *bower*? A love-nest? Christ-on-the-Cross, the blasphemous lecher! What you doing keeping company with a blasphemer like that? Eh? What kind of demon-worshipper is he, then? What d'you want with his kind?'

Again and again she tried to pass him to right or left, but he jigged to and fro in front her. The ride leading from chapel to castle stretched away like the path to Salvation, steep and narrow. All the way along it, he would cling to her, paw at her, this leech, this bat. Knowing she could not listen to one more slur on Foulque without retaliating, she turned back into the chapel and banged the door behind her. Oriole could not follow her in there.

Foulque was startled by her return.

'I came back for a first impression,' she said nonsensically. 'To see the thing as a whole.'

There it stood, like a mouth in the act of devouring the holy altar. An arch of crystals and pyrite spanned a cascade of white flowers and blooms which spilled down the altar steps. Ivy coiled its way up every column and across the roofbeams while, from the hooks where lamps and sensors more commonly hung, swung birdcages, their occupants huddled on the floors, silent as nauseous seagoers riding out the draughty swaying and the piercing cold. Even now, in summer, the chapel struck cold: it was the only thing preserving the blossoms from turning brown and the ivy from shrivelling.

'Those birds,' he said despairingly. 'Not a note.'

'Have you fed them?' asked Ouallada.

'Fed them?'

'Fed them.'

'I should feed them, shouldn't I? I should've done, shouldn't I?' There was something childlike about his disappointment.

Ouallada found seed and fed the birds. She was aware of having lost Foulque's attention altogether. The imminence of his fondest dream raised around him an impenetrable hedge, like the roses that grow up around bewitched castles. He was trapped inside, with his hopes and guilt and obsession. Ouallada found that she was watching her own tragedy unfold without the power to intervene. Her hands seemed pinned to her sides, her mouth sealed shut. She knew that he was happy: if not happy then tormented by the prospect of happiness. A whole lifetime's celibacy, building up behind a higher and higher dam of restraint, was about to be breached. A love which had been distilled over long, patient years in a damp cell was about to be fulfilled. His failure as a monk was about to find the only compensation it had ever sought.

The other knights-*trobar* relieved the frustrations of their ascetic love with the peasant girls in the villages.

Anything can be had for an ēcu or a piece of cloth - even for the fun of it, with girls who believed rape and unkindness were the only sins. There were no peasant girls for Foulque, and no easy peasant theology. He was also about to commit a mortal sin.

Still. Ouallada had grown up with her mother's brand of Christianity, gleaned piecemeal and haphazardly, without instruction. One could sin, Kadija had told her, then apologise to God and he made right again.

So that night, Ouallada followed the Railing Bishop out into the clearing and found him sitting in the blackness holding a missal to his face without the smallest light to read by. She said, 'You can do penance after, can't you? There's no harm, is there? You can always do penance.'

He did not seem surprised that she knew exactly what he was thinking. But perhaps he thought his sins so scarlet that they glowed in the dark. 'No.' It filled the courtyard, that 'no'. It ricocheted to and fro, making the tethered horses restless. 'No, I can't. I learned that theology from my ancestors. It never did stand up to inspection. It's a bequest I turned down when I was ten. Sin and do penance: that's the family way. That's the Nerra way. I've done without it this far. I don't mean to take it up now.'

'I don't understand,' she said, meaning that she knew nothing of his past.

'You wouldn't,' he said, in the old, bitter tones. 'None of *you* would. You spiritual peasants. I wouldn't expect it of you.'

'Oh, it's a terrible story. Quite terrible, poor man. It's

quite the reason we have to treat him very tenderly,' said Aude that night when Ouallada asked about Foulque's past. 'His uncle put him in Orders when he was only a little boy - as a safe place to put a nuisance heir - then went about putting Foulque's father out-of-doors. I mean his own brother! He burned down his house and nailed his hands, or did something frightful which meant he couldn't write after - and the man was a great scrivenor, they say. Threw the wife into an icy lake - for a joke, he said, though everyone knew it was to kill the next child in her' cos he'd got none of his own the right side of the blanket. Brought all manner of lawsuits to seize the brother's land, and when he couldn't, finally, they say he locked the poor man in a dungeon and tortured him till he signed it all away. His own brother! I mean, you know the kind of man. A great embarrassment in a family, but so very ... *powerful*.'

'You said the brother couldn't write. How could he sign away his land when he couldn't write?' said Ouallada, sceptical of what sounded a ridiculous assortment of myths and lies.

'Well, I suppose anyone can find a way of signing if it keeps you from lying in a coffin full of adders, no matter what's been done to your hands! Couldn't he? But Foulque's father - well, you can see the family nature - it's said he didn't - wouldn't - chose to die sooner than sign ...' And Aude broke off for a moment's contemplation of the ceiling. 'So his brother came into all the land anyway, since Foulque was conveniently in Holy Orders and couldn't inherit. Had no children of his own. Two wives he put away - one within a year of marrying her. Oh, it's a wicked story. I don't wonder the Bishop is a little ...' Her voice trailed away. It had been many months since she last recounted Foulque's history, and hearing it again, even out of her own mouth, always gave pause for thought.

'The poor man,' said Ouallada, her heart laid open with a cleaver of pity. 'The poor, poor man.'

'Well, he isn't though, is he? Poor. In that case,' said Aude obscurely. ' ... Tell me again. About the Crystal Cave.'

For the third time during its month-long construction, Ouallada described to Aude every detail of the crystalline grotto.

'So it's finished, then.'

'He says not.'

'But it'll wilt if he leaves it.'

'I have told him that.'

It was the childlike purity of Aude's appearance which contributed most to her spectacular beauty. But that same child in her was incapable of deferring a treat, an excitement; the naughty indulgence, the little – oh-so-*little* sin. 'Tomorrow I'll go to see it.' A peachy blush suffused chest and throat and rose into her face.

'Go to see it? Inspect it, you mean?' said Ouallada. Invisible hands took hold of her, quite without warning, and shook her till her teeth rattled. She went rigid with fright.

'I mean visit it! Visit my Tristan in our Crystal Cave of love ... Princess, will you come and read to us? *Tristan and Iseult*, I mean? Or sing? While we embrace?'

'Embrace?'

'Oh *do*! Please do! It will be such a glorious pinnacle in the Romance of my life - of all our lives. A tribute to

Poesie and to Love. Won't it? Won't it?'

What did she foresee? What did she envisage happening in her Crystal Cave, that silly, yellow-haired woman with the plucked temples, the browless forehead, the choir of *fegnadors?* Was it an icy sunlit pinnacle where a serene white hand would be laid in blessing on her brow? Ouallada had grown up in stables, had slept under hedges, balanced on the drystone walls of meadows at dusk. The images in her mind were put together from far earthier memories: the quick clumsy lunge, the struggle and resentment, the undignified assertion of strength over weakness, the shove of heavy flank against flank and the stamp of hooves. Hot breath turning the cold air to steam. Those were the things that came to Ouallada's mind while Aude spoke of the Crystalline Cave. And yet they were both thinking of the same thing - of Iseult keeping tryst with her lover in a cave.

'Oh Christ, I never thought ...'

Aude looked at her quizzically, her head on one side, her mouth tightly closed in a contented, feline smile. But she was absorbed in contemplation of her triumph, raising her imaginary *fegnador* to the rank of acknowledged lover with a kiss and an oath of fidelity: her lips even pouted to meet the imaginary kiss.

Ouallada had somehow thought it would go hungry, that blaspheming wattle mouth on the chapel's altar, with its drooping lascivious tongue of flowers! Up until then, she had managed somehow to fool herself that somewhere else, in some spot properly intended for such happinesses, she would be the one to swallow up all the pain and potency, lick up all the sheer blessed sweetness of Foulques Nerra.

It was only a want. As a child she had frequently longed for food without getting any, craved warmth and stayed cold, prayed for gentleness and received none. Why then should wanting a man bring gratification any the closer? And yet it seemed impossible to want something so much without drawing it to her. She wanted to demolish the Crystalline Cave and smash all the birdcages, yelling *'Leave him be! Leave him his soul! Leave him for me, you bastards in your round towers and mansions! You never gave me anything when I was a beggar. Leave me just this, just this one man. Is it too much to ask?'*

Instead of yelling, she said nothing. Only two choices remained open to her: either to go to the chapel or to refrain from going. Aude wanted a witness to her *jeuc d' amour*; could not imagine theatre without an audience. She really ought to observe the etiquette of secrecy, but that was rather too much to ask of a woman so accustomed to admiration - to have her *plus grand éclat* go unseen. But if she expected Ouallada to spread the word, to let the other suitors know they were runners-up in the race, she could think again. Ouallada would conceal Foulque's rendezvous as close as if he had committed murder and depended on the discretion of his friends for his life.

Even so, how could she stay away, who had subjected all those birds to their captivity, who had condemned all those flowers to death by picking? Besides she had been asked to sing.

A song! She would write a song. A *winileodas* – a 'song for a friend', revealing her love as she should have done before. If only she had known about it.

What good would it do, other than to spoil his great moment of triumph? She wrote her song, then vowed not to sing it.

The chapel was ringed by bird song. Every larch was flexing under restless birds. The sun falling obliquely between the trees cast cage bars of light on the church itself. And a big cow ready for milking had strayed into the church porch. Ouallada saw that the door was already open.

The awful possibility of the cow pushing its way into the church emptied her mind of anything else. Hanging her bagpipes over one shoulder, she ran at the cow, punched at its flank, sank her fingers into the dusty flesh of its neck and pulled; she pushed in front of it and put her shoulder to its nose. 'Go away! Get out of here! Out!' The exertion squeezed the bellows of her pipes - the gasping drone and the cow's amicable regurgitation broke the sacred silence and the peaceful rapture of the lovers within.

'Princess, is that you?' Aude's voice was tightly strung with happiness, like a string tuned to too high a pitch so that it hums of its own accord. Such a small, tender voice, praised by a dozen men for its sweetness. Still it was enough for the cow to take fright and back out on to the grass. Drops of milk fell like semen across the skirts of Ouallada's gown.

Inside the chapel, the mouth of the Crystalline Cave was camouflaged like the opening of a bear trap, draped with branches to conceal the people inside it. Ouallada sat down in a pool of sunlight nearby, but the light could not keep her from shivering. The pipes groaned and droned. Her fingers fumbled the chanter and she could not find its holes. The bladder engorged under her arm, the short wooden pipe trembled and kicked a little against the passage of air. She focused her eyes so hard on the spots of milk, that the weft of her skirt made bright jagged patterns on her eyeball. The taste of blood told her that she had bitten into her cheek.

This is the blow with which the drummer slits
his tabor and deafens even silence.
This is the note the singer shouts so loud
that his throat tears to the very cleft of his heart.
This is the dawn in which the singing bird is shot
through with arrows and falls in rain of blood.
These are the words that fill the world with emptiness
like a breaking vessel ...

'Brrrr!' A shrill, happy, joking noise. 'Before you begin, Princess, a blanket for the love of Venus!'

' ... I love, though I am not loved.'

There were no blankets, but there were cloaks: two cloaks lying heaped together on the stone flags, their swirling folds like knees over-riding one another, brown over ecru. A piece of armour whose purpose was not plain - a side vent or a throat guard or some such - lay on the ground. It occurred to Ouallada that she had never seen, Foulque in armour.

The summons to a lovers' rendezvous required it: the uniform of love, the carapace of the passionate soul in its breeding season. Ouallada told herself that she longed to see Foulque in armour, tried to fill her mind with the longing, since she feared, more than anything in the world, to draw back the branches from the mouth of the cave and see him without it. Out of armour, out of sheepskin, out of the dark wool fustian he wore as if to camouflage him from the eye of God. She was shocked and horrified, ashamed and embarrassed to find pictures in her mind other than of Foulque in armour.

She bundled up both cloaks in front of her - would have liked to cover over her head with them rather than see beyond that baffle of branches. rather than see Foulque in the arms of La Belle Aude. 'Your cloaks, sister. I'll lay them here, by the door?' Her palm caressed the brown cloak, for it was surely his and might never come within her hands again.

The merest kick of a man's boot tumbled the branches away from within, and she was confronted by the sight of Tristan and Iseult enjoying their lovers' bliss. Tristan's tourney armour was lying about like the golden calf newly smashed, but he reclined on the quilted altar still fully dressed in his under-wadding, whereas the lady in his arms was whitely naked, clinging to him for warmth as much as gratification, her toes tensing and relaxing, tensing and relaxing, her nose a little red with the cold. There had been a great many embraces, for her golden hair clung all over the wadding like fissures crazing it.

Ouallada must have looked for a long time to see such things. She saw, too, how Iseult was enraptured with her first taste of Love, but that Tristan's face was puce with discomfort, like a man with his bladder full. 'I have poetry enough of my own, Princess, an' it please you to go away,' he said in a breathy, strangled voice.

'Indeed, my lord,' said Ouallada, but no sound came out of her mouth. She coughed and said again, 'Indeed, my lord. If I'd known it was you, I would never have trespassed to bring my song here and trouble you with it. Never.'

Her face shone so radiantly that Gaston Mauriac believed he had conquered the hearts of two ladies that morning.

He frowned a little at Aude's wish to cover herself up against the cold, and his fingers drummed on the dome of his shiny helmet while Ouallada clumsily put back the branches round the cave-mouth. 'More music, Princess!' called Aude in a sleepily sensual voice, but Ouallada felt no compunction in gathering her bagpipes into her arms and running for the door.

She could have run to the top of the Black Mountain; she could have run downriver to the sea, treading from wave to wave. She could have danced with David before the altar of the only true God, in praise and thanksgiving. For Aude had fouled the Crystalline Cave like a bird fouling its nest - but *not with Foulque*! She had made Gaston Mauriac her Tristan and laid his body and soul on the church altar as an offering to the Devil.

Foulque's soul was still intact. Foulque's chastity was still out there somewhere, in its armour, unlaced. Foulque's hopes lay as dead as the songbirds in their wicker cages. God had kept Foulque whole for her: the only part broken would be his heart.

That last thought, coinciding with the bang of the church door closing behind her, shook all the fine grains of happiness down within her. Sharp hard grit rose up to the surface instead. The sight of the man approaching across the grassy clearing made her hate the Lady Aude with a sudden, seething pain.

She was running so fast that she actually collided with Foulque; his hands lifted her back off his feet. He looked nothing like Gaston Mauriac in his armour. Leather and iron interlaced one another less like a suit than a study in sinew and bone, and he wore no cloak at all, either of brown or ecru. He had the look of Lucifer contending with the idea of rebellion, the ambition as huge as his eyes, the horror compressed, compressed, compressed until it could be swallowed out of sight. He was larger than life with triumph. When she put out her arms to bar the way, it was like barring a river's way to the sea.

'Don't go in, Foulque.'

'Don't go in? What do you mean, "Don't go in"?'

'Aude's there ahead of you.'

'I'm late, then. To think I could be late ...'

'With someone else.'

And then his face fell apart - subsided into lines and shadow, like Lucifer falling into the dark. Falling into the fire.

She saw the rage kindle in him just in time to leap backwards into the porch and close the door of the chapel between them. Even though she had thrown the bolt, the impact of his shoulder against the door made her shoes slip on the pavers and her teeth bite into her tongue. 'Don't, Foulque, don't!' His mace hit the door and sunlight flew between the timbers like splinters from the wood. When he saw that even his friend, his ally, Princess Ouallada, would not obey his demands to open the door, he circled the chapel building, laying his club into the stonework, so that plaster sprang from the wall inside and powdered Ouallada's hair.

Just then the lovers in the Crystalline Cave laughed. A shameless, muffled laugh. What would they have done, wondered Ouallada, if I had not bolted the door?

But they did not realise their danger. Or at least Aude did not, to whom the beating on the wall only confirmed her beauty, her desirability, her right to have the whole world in love with her. It was what any chevalier should do whose heart she chose to break; he should weep and howl and beat with his mace on the impenetrable ivory of her tower. It was mere etiquette for Foulque to run mad.

The lovers chose not to emerge from their bower; its brushwood only heaved a little like the fabric of a beaver's den, then settled to a quietness as Ouallada skirted the interior wall of the church shadowing Foulque's progress on the outside. 'Foulque, don't! Foulque, be calm! Don't torment yourself! Don't you see? Have you lost all judgement? It's for the best. Think, Foulque, think! Remember how wrong ...' The explosion of noise and shivering plaster shook her words into an incoherent jumble. To Foulque, outside, her weak, squeaking inaudibility was only the yelping of a dog sent in to torment a bear and madden it more. As she reached the leper's window, where a gap of one cubit let in the keenest draught of all, Foulque's fist shot through the hole and grabbed her by the skirts, making her cry out with alarm. It was a hand backed with fine, dark hairs; the radiant pattern of bones below the knuckles fixed itself in her memory. The hand pulled the threads of her open-weave dress into a crinkling that showed forever after, like the scar of a burn. She took hold of the wrist between two hands and tried to restrain him there, in the one spot, for long enough to reason with. 'Foulque, listen to me! Listen, man! It's no great matter! There are worse things in the world. Listen to me! Listen. If Aude doesn't love you, it doesn't mean there aren't ...'

Bending at the waist to keep possession of his hand, she glimpsed his face through the hatch, a madman's face capable of murder but not of reasoning. Her hands were pulled into the rough stone orifice and out into the sunlight, grazing her forearms and pulling her face – smack - up against the wall. She was obliged to let go.

But perhaps it was the sight of those two hands reaching out of the church wall like damaged rosebay willow that finally stayed Foulque's rage. He stood a little way off - she could see him through the leper's window - feeling the exhaustion settle on him of such a huge physical exertion. It made him reel a little.

How could Aude lay such grief on a man, on such a man? Why should she want to? It was past all comprehending for Ouallada, but no longer seemed so to Foulque who sagged visibly beneath the weight of understanding. La Belle Aude had chosen a lover and it was not him; had never been him. His eyes glanced guiltily back along the side wall of the chapel haphazardly pitted as a citadel is by siege engines. He was picturing the things he might have done - like blinded Samson - while the fit of rage was on him. But if he was grateful to Ouallada for preventing him, he never said so. Her presence as his humiliation was enough to make hers a face he would avoid wherever possible. He turned and walked back through the forest, dragging his mace along the ground so that its head gathered round it a raft of twigs and leaves and unspeakable loneliness.

When La Belle Aude emerged from the Crystalline Cave she was not quite as radiant as before. In fact she looked dishevelled and a little afraid. She kept her cloak pulled round her and her knees slightly bent, as if braced to keep them from shaking. And she never once looked Gaston Mauriac in the face. She said she was very cold. Mauriac, on the other hand, had lost that look of physical discomfort along with the leather codpiece which allows a knight in full armour to relieve himself during battle.

When Ouallada was called on to help Aude dress, she noticed an almost perfect reproduction of Gaston's wadding latticed on the lady's chest. The very lack of bliss in Aude's face was what goaded Ouallada to say, 'I congratulate you, sister, on this your hour of hours. Love's apotheosis.'

Aude's eyes travelled to and fro between narrowed, defensive eyelids, then her mouth moulded itself into a smile. 'What? Ah yes. Bliss. Perfect bliss. The Chaste Embrace. The purest joy lovers can ever hope for.' She failed to notice the grazing to Ouallada's forearms; seemed in some discomfort herself which made her clench her knees together and bob a little. 'Naturally you're sworn to secrecy. No jealous gossiping now, sister. Just because you haven't the joy to match mine? No gossiping. No betraying my lover's name.' Little by little, she clambered back into the vocabulary of chivalric love, filming over whatever unpleasantness had momentarily confused her. 'Oh, we are so much in love!' she confided to Ouallada, laying a sisterly hand on her wrist. 'Is he not magnificent? ... The Chaste Embrace, remember. If you should see that peevish old bishop.'

Gaston Mauriac, now under plume and plate, prayed self-consciously, on steely kneecaps, a prayer of thanksgiving to the God whose altar he had just helped to desecrate. Any amount of contradiction could be compressed into a trobar's behaviour providing enough weight of poetry was brought to bear on the lid.

Ouallada too shook off some of the day's rubble and crawled out from under its ruins. She mustered her blessings together. Foulque's soul had not been tainted. Foulque's heart had not proved an acceptable gift; he was therefore presumably still in possession of it. And Foulque's admiration of Aude must surely have suffered an agonising death. So was Ouallada not a happier woman now than she had been at daybreak? Upheavals always leave the spirits flagging a little.

She owed it to Foulque to reproach Aude with her monstrous cruelty. 'I can't help feeling pity for poor old Foulque Nerra,' she said later, casually, afraid of betraying her own love.

'The Bishop? Oh, I'll make fair reparation to *him*,' said Aude archly, assembling a wad of rags to cope with a quite unexpectedly early and violent menstruation.

'*Reparation?*' Ouallada laughed openly with disbelief 'What kind of reparation could you possibly make ...?'

'Can't you guess?' said Aude with such blithe and elegant serenity that Ouallada's blood turned to water during the space left for theatrical effect. 'Why, I mean to *marry* him of course. If he fulfils his last *assais*.'

CHAPTER TWENTY FOUR

The Assais

Whatever entered in to Aude within the Crystalline Cave of Love - whatever demon profited from the blasphemous rendezvous - she emerged from it the masterpiece of sin.

'I am right in thinking, aren't I, Bishop, that you are all the male family left to your uncle, Barral Nerra?'

The whole court had got wind of the extraordinary rumour - that Aude planned to marry the Bishop if he passed one last test of merit. No one believed it. They barked with laughter and countered with the rumour that Gaston Mauriac had received the kiss-of-acknowledgement: altogether a more likely tale.

But strangely Mauriac seemed to have slipped in the lady's esteem. He scurried to and fro, anxious, twitching like a rabbit as he tried to catch her eye and failed. Still, no one believed she really meant to marry the Railing Bishop - not until she asked him about his uncle, at dinnertime, in plain hearing of everyone.

Foulque Nerra was an extremely peculiar and unhealthy colour. His cheeks and ears were hot and his mouth ashen, while the grizzled hair over his ears and collar was wildly dishevelled. His hands were bandaged in lengths of rag, for somehow he had blistered the palms and torn the blisters. Chopping wood, perhaps. He gave the impression of being too angry to speak, and yet he had heard the rumours like everyone else. That she meant to marry him. That she might intend to marry him.

'He hasn't a son, if that's what you mean,' he muttered into his trencher. 'That doesn't mean he'll name me for his heir.'

'Has he named another?' asked Aude brightly, and when he shrugged as if the matter was of too little consequence to think about, she was able to tell him, 'I've looked into it. He hasn't.'

'He's shed two wives. He may yet take a third,' said Foulque, his eyes on the wall opposite him and never once on her. 'The country-side's a-teem with his bastards, too.'

The more delicate gentlemen at table would no more have mentioned such things before their *domna* than presented her with a dead rat. 'Oh *la*!' they said, rattling their cheeks at him in disapproval. 'Oh la!' But in truth they were not shocked by Foulque's rudeness. It was how they knew La Belle Aude would never marry him.

'Foulque dear, come closer.'

He hesitated. Ouallada bit her lip. As she saw it, this was the first and most perfect opportunity, since the events in the chapel, for him to approach the dais and lay hands round Aude's white neck; to throttle her for the wrong she had done him. Ouallada prayed to God he would not, so that she would not have to see him die on the points of a dozen eager swords. And for what? For a jilt?

God was good. God was kind. Foulque approached the lady, bent his knee before her chair, his eyes shut and his nostrils flared. He tolerated her mouth to touch his ear as she whispered to him.

A spasm went through him like the palsy. A whole roomful of men and women started at the sight, and drank up their wine and snatched at their bread and pulled little pieces off to be seen to be eating, to be seen to be indifferent. But look how she ran her hands over his hair! Look how she searched his face for an answer! Look how his eyes widened without seeing. 'God knows, you have cause enough to do it,' said Aude. 'I looked into it.'

He leaned away from her sharply. 'If you know I'm heir, then you know it's all yours in time. You only have to wait ...' he said in his incompetent whisper.

'On the contrary. You shall have it all, provided you don't wait. That is your *assais*, after all.'

Then he started to deny her, like Peter denying Christ, over and over and over again. 'No,' he said. 'No, no, no, no.' He half-climbed, half-fell off the dais and off his knees, and fled the room backwards, still staring at her, still saying it: 'No, no, no, no,' while Aude smiled, a serene, confident, complaisant smile and blew him teasing kisses off her fingers' ends.

Ouallada got to her feet. Gaston Mauriac was shouting a protest. The room's noise rose and rose to a roar of delighted excitement. Romance was afoot. *Assais* were being fixed. If Foulque were to fail, there were others even now vowing to put up a better showing, to remain gallant in the face of their challenge, however hard; to handle themselves better than Foulque had done, clattering and jabbering his way out of the room. They laughed at his humiliation. But they asked in their hearts what could have pasted such a look to the face of the Railing Bishop. Cowardice was hardly the man's forte.

And then he was back again - before the meal had even finished - before the evening's music had even begun. He came only as far as the door and he made so silent an entrance, carried himself so erect and expressionless that one of the women said afterwards she had mistaken him for a ghost. 'The spirit of the Grey Bishop!' she laughed.

Ouallada did not take it for his spirit, but for his body devoid of spirit. Somewhere outside in the darkness he had dug a hole such as the wolf digs to bury its afterbirth, and interred his conscience, his reason, his qualms before packing the earth back into place. 'Very well, lady,' he called from the doorway. 'I'll perform it. You shall have your heart's desire, though it cost me my hopes of Heaven.'

'Fie, Bishop!' she simpered, reaching an open hand towards him as though to present a gift past value. 'And I thought I was the only Heaven you craved!'

'Why would anyone want a woman like that?' Ouallada asked when Foulque finally confided to her the proposition in hand.

'Anyone would not,' he said, winding a spare rein between finger and thumb into a tight, tight scroll. 'But I do.'

'It's damnable, Foulque. It's damnable.'

He shrugged as though damnable sins were loaves of bread, to be picked up two a day. 'I'd best make a bliss of the time left to me then, hadn't I? My damnation was always sure. I never had such hopes of the bliss before.' And it was true that he was a man freshly charged with energy. The balance of his life had taken on a new shape, and he packed his saddlebags like a cartographer about to map a new continent.

'But have you ever killed a man before?'

It was a foolish question. He had been a fighting cleric even before he left Holy Orders, and his mace must have accounted for dozens of infidels and free-company men. 'Battalions of 'em. With less cause and smaller relish,' and he cinched his horse so violently that it staggered to and fro, crossing its big feet. 'Now I come to think of it, I have plenty of crimes to lay at my uncle's door.'

'I'm coming with you.'

'You? What for?' The suggestion took him completely by surprise.

'To be the voice of conscience in your ear.'

'Oh, then you can sleep up a different tree from me.'

'All right, then. To be a friend on the journey. Because I ... Because you're a man in need of a friend. Because I ...'

While Ouallada struggled with the terrible admission

of loving him, and could find no words to say it, Foulque guessed at quite another reason for her wanting to make the journey. His energies were given over to gratifying the whims of a designing woman. So he had stopped believing that simple motives existed any longer in the world. 'She sent you to watch and keep commentary, didn't she?' he said all of a sudden, nodding his big head as he thought he recognised Aude's handiwork. Aude had sent Ouallada as a commentator, to relay in letters the progress and merits of her amour - errant on his last great adventure.

The fact that the object of his journey was to murder his uncle Barral, and so grasp his huge inheritance, was neither grisly nor vile enough for her to cover her eyes. She wanted to miss not a minute, not a move, not a single bestial thrill. 'She's told you to keep me company. Well, then. Who am I to turn you off?'

Ouallada let him think it. It did not matter how she succeeded in staying by him, so long as she was there. They left Haut-Beziers for the Camargue with a train of four horses and a chorus of thunder muttering ominously in the hills behind them. The rain overtook them at nightfall when they hobbled the horses, rolled themselves in gabardine, and lay like individual wormcasts along the grass. There, at close quarters, they watched the rain crawl down the grass stems like tears down eyelashes.

A grass snake, bright as the green flash at sunset, moved by a yard from Ouallada's face and brought a primordial sweat to her hands and feet. She recalled, in that instant, the story of Foulque's father, closed in a coffin of snakes by his own brother to elicit a signature he never made. It was right that such an uncle should die. Where was the sin in it? A work of justice, not felony, to rid the world of such a fratricide. Thus the serpent grass snake whispered its comfort in Ouallada's ear.

'Is it true your uncle killed your father, Foulque?'

He did not answer at once. She thought perhaps he had managed to go to sleep the instant his head touched canvas. It did not seem very likely. The night was damnably cold.

'That's only rumour,' he said at last, his voice cracking a little as if the rain had penetrated to his vocal cords. 'It was never proved. His body was never found. I do know our family was a lifelong affront to Barral.' The hiss of the rain seemed to encourage him into confidences he would never otherwise have spoken. Perhaps he thought his words were being blotted out. 'The bastard arranged a marriage for my sister to a Cypriot: she was drowned on the voyage. He had me placed into Orders - out of the way of inheriting and breeding, you understand. And to make reparation to God for some or other bloody sin. There were always plenty calling for atonement. When my parents stood out against it, he perjured himself in the ecclesiastical. Said my mother was a perfect.'

'A what?'

'A Cathar. A heretic. Zoroastrian. A ...'

'Yes, yes. I understand Cathar.'

'My uncle acted as lawyer in her defence - "negotiated" a penance whereby she gave her firstborn to God and the Church as down-payment against forgiveness. He never wanted something but he got it, my uncle. No one gainsaid him ...'

She thought he had finished. She clutched the endictments to her breast, one on top of another, comforting herself that the man Barral deserved to die. '

... Except once.'

'What did you say, Foulque?'

'Except once. My father defied him once. Not at the end, I don't mean. I can't witness to that. But once before that.' (The man was mustering his grievances, mustering his motives for murder.) 'He was forever away on pilgrimage - to Compostello - to Jerusalem - all over. Once when he was away my father began a house - a fortified house. To fix an edge to our estate after all the encroachments and raids and slipped boundaries ... When Barral came back he burned it to the ground. Nailed my father to his own door. Crucified him. He could never walk again with any ease. Never write again either. And my father was a poet. A better one than me. A poet, yes.'

Ouallada held very still, as if to move would alert him to the presence of someone eavesdropping on his thinking aloud. They lay like the shrouded dead, side by side, exchanging the memories of lost lives. 'He deserves to die,' she said, fierce with relief.

'And be judged,' he replied. 'But not by me.'

She sat up, and her hair escaped and stuck itself to the muddy exterior of the gabardine sheet. Pools of collected water spilled off her shroud. 'You mean you're not going to kill him?' The delight in hearing him say it! Not that the uncle did not deserve to die, but that he would not risk his life and soul attempting the execution.

'Oh, I shall kill him,' he corrected her, from within his canvas ", cocoon. 'I just don't deceive myself that I'm the Flail of God. I know, I know. You'll say it's for Love, and Love excuses everything. What crap. I'll pay for it in Hell,

I and my Queen Macbeth. I and my ... wife. But at least
I'll have her. At least she'll be mine.' He said it as though
he were talking of a cancer, something attached to him
irrevocably that could not be cut away; something
infinitely repellent.

'Then don't do it, for God's sake!' As she shouted it,
the wind and the rain combined to snatch the words and
leave the lips cold that spoke them. 'For God's sake! You
won't do it, then!'

He rolled over and the wrappers parted to show
nothing but his eyes. 'For God's sake I'd leave it undone.
It's not for God's sake I'm doing it. It's for her. My "lover"
so-called. My obsession. My *raison d'être*. My *domna*. My
senhor. My god-outside-Heaven ... You people, pah. You
velvet-and-silk troubadours. You talk as if fidelity's some
great virtue - some great edifying endurance test. That's
crap too. Fatuous sophistry, that's what that is.
"Fidelity"? It's just a symptom of the disease - like loose
bowels or a sweat. A man in love doesn't keep faith: it
keeps him. Sinks its teeth into him like a wolfhound; the
flesh is off his bones before it ever lets him go.'

She did not know what to say to him. She did not
know what to do for him. If he had been a dog, her dog,
her only beloved dog, she would have knocked out his
brains with a hammer to put it out of its misery. But
people are not so readily parted from their miseries.
Besides she could not contradict him. She believed what
he said. Otherwise she would never have been there, on
that terrible journey, riding towards murder and
damnation.

When she was sure he was asleep, she got up and left
- her father had taught her how to lead a horse away

without waking those nearby. In the morning Foulque would think she had gone back to Haut-Beziers, too shocked and disgusted to bear him company another yard of the way, or too wet through to bother. Instead she pressed on in the direction they had been going. She had never needed a moon. No one needs a moon to find their way to Hell.

'Where are you going? What's happening? Have you quit Beziers?' yelped Oriole.

'Jesu, Father, you frightened me half to death. I thought you were a footpad. Have you been following me all the while?'

Oriole leaned forward over his mare's neck, plucking at his daughter's cloak. His heels hammered continuously into the dusty horseflesh behind his saddle but the mare did not react; she was held to one speed by the mule tied on behind, its back festooned with the minstrel's instruments. Oriole never played these days, but his instruments followed him round like the impedimentia of war. 'Of course I've been following you! Did you think you could slip out of my eye? Are you moving on? Who tells me anything?'

'I'm going into the Camargue.'

'Stinking place. Flies. Mosquitoes. Salt,' said Oriole. 'No one wants to go there. Where in the Camargue?'

She did not want to answer. She did not want to tell him anything. He always came with his questions, like a whelk gatherer, trying to prise off something of value. 'To Arles. Near Arles. A place near Arles.'

'What, with that bishop villain? With that blasphemer?' He tried to snatch at her reins and they jostled against each other, horse against horse. His leg was hurt more than hers by the crush.

'Do I look to be with him? No, not "with" him. Ahead of him.'

The mystification Oriole had felt at a distance deepened to fright now he was close up. His daughter's taciturn surliness was hiding something disastrously counter to his interests. Unless he wrung some kind of explanation from her, she was about to do something on her own initiative, something outside the Plan.

'Anyway, don't call him that. What right have you got to call him that? We never led such very pious lives, did we? If we'd had to suffer the things he has ... '

'Suffer?' He gave her such a push that he all but unhorsed her and she was left clinging on to mane and saddle. She did not mind. It was confirmation that she need give him nothing, tell him nothing. 'Suffer? Some stuffed, fur-lined prelate? Some unchurched aristocrat idling his days away making love to that woman - that *doll*? What's he know about suffering? Have you forgotten everything your mother and I went through to raise you to where you've reached?'

'Let Mother lie. She'd not've raised me a charlatan if she'd had her way. She'd not've let me come to this.'

'Come to what? What? Jesu! ... You're in love, I can tell! You can't hide it from me, chit. You're in love with that Devil's prelate, aren't you? Admit it. You think you love him, don't you? Confess it!'

'There must be worse sins you could lay on me, Father. It's not a crime: Love. Not a blasphemy.'

But Oriole was standing in his stirrups, his fist hammering the air, ranting, tossing his head until thought curded inside it into wordless abhorrence. 'If he's had you, I'll kill him! If he's spent you, I'll take the cost out of your pelt! If he's ... You fool! You thankless wretch of a penny whore! Who is he? What is he? Could've had a prince, but no, you had to lust after some penniless monk in league with the Devil!'

He was riding his horse into her, like one ship ramming another, trying to break something underwater, trying to smash her into pieces small enough to give him no more offence, slapping and cuffing at her. She might ride off - outstrip him, burdened as he was by his pack animal. But he would only follow her, catch her up, spoil her plans. When he began to damn Foulque for his landless insignificance, she suddenly saw a chance to silence him, to pacify him, even to choke him on an apology and send him away reeling at her good news.

'If you must know, Father, he's heir to nigh the largest fortune in the Languedoc. On his way there now. To stake his claim. His uncle's near to death, you see. Very near. *And I'm his closest friend.* Does that please, Father? Does that part his hair differently? Does that paint his portrait in a better colour?'

The jeer, the sarcasm fell on a hide too thick. But her father was silenced. Finally, he let his own words fall with the steady plop, plop, plop of the dung falling from his mare. 'What kind of fortune? What's his .blood? What's his name, then, this monk?'

Ouallada straightened her back, let the fantasy of what she was saying blend with the truth, until she almost believed it herself. 'It's a name you'd best know in connection with the Counts of Anjou,' she said haughtily, 'though the family fortune's grown from salt. His name is Foulque Nerra, father, and I confess I love him, though you are the first and only man to know it.'

The look on her father's face was past all forgetting. It was as if the man fell away from behind the face; it was the face of a hanged man where the noose breaks the fall of the body but not the soul. At first he seemed to be shrinking, but then she realised that he had stopped and that she was moving away from him, leaving him behind on the road. She thought she heard him say, '*Never*,' and wondered at the man's snobbery - that even the largest fortune in the Camargue should not be enough to satisfy his greed for nobility. She hurried on, not looking back for fear he was following, after all.

What he had actually said was: '*Nerra.*'

The name struck him like a blow. It choked him as though he had ridden into an ambusher's wire stretched across the road. He put his hand up to his throat. The cords of his cloak pressed intolerably on the arteries of his neck: he plucked at the knot with fumbling fingers. '*Nerra.*'

'*And I'm his closest friend.*' It was not true, of course. But she would make it so. Ouallada was minded to do Foulque such service as only the best of friends might do. She had almost enjoyed lying to her father, for he was the one who had made a liar of her. And as with all the lies in her life, while she told them, they became almost real. She had enjoyed tailoring the truth to a lie. For it was true that Barral Nerra would soon be dead and Foulque made heir to his fortune and estates, happy in his imminent prospects of marriage. And she was the friend to help him to it.

Rather than see Foulque murder his own uncle and damn his soul, *she* would murder Barral: murder him and account him well dead, and her soul well spent. An excellent rate of exchange, really, considering the base stuff from which she was made; given the small intrinsic value of her soul.

Men did not make *assais* of their lady loves, but Ouallada, being a troubadour and in love, would make secret *assais* of her love for Foulque. She was almost entirely sure she could carry it through to the end, if God would just make her cruel. As Barral was cruel; as Oriole was cruel, as Fate and Love themselves were cruel.

CHAPTER TWENTY FIVE

Barral in the Dark

Barral Nerra, hearing of the death of his former wife at a convent near Florriac, went on pilgrimage all the way to Arles-sur-Tech. He took with him a train of one hundred companions. Each pilgrim was allowed only one gill of the holy water which miraculously filled the sarcophagus of Saints Abdon and Sennen each year. But by taking a hundred companions, and pooling their allowances, Barral brought home enough liquid to steep his bedsheets in forgiveness, just in case there was a need. He felt no direct guilt over her death, but one could never take too many precautions with suicides, their access being so good to the Devil, and their influence so lasting. Alazais' restless spirit had visited him in more than one dream, and he did not feel it wise to embark on a third marriage until he had taken adequate precautions.

After killing his brother, much more drastic penances had been called for, naturally. He had not intended the fool to die, of course - just to take fright, having a lifelong aversion to snakes and the like. As he had told his confessor: 'There wasn't a poisoner among them - just newts and toads and slowworms and such.' His confessor had agreed that it fell a long way short of murder, to shut a man in a box with grassnakes and frogs. But then Barral had never found much comfort in confessors. So he had been back to Jerusalem to be flogged in the Chapel of Thorns and to endow some frescoes in the Templum Domini. Immediately after, he felt much better.

Unfortunately, while visiting the precincts of the Holy Sepulchre, a cat had scratched his leg, and the wound had ulcerated. He lost the leg in Tripoli, on the return journey. At the time, he had resented the size of God's punishment, and yet on reflection the merchant in him could see that, *pro rata*, the settlement was fair - a leg for a brother.

So that when his brother came to him now in dreams, wreathed in snakes, and poked toads and crayfish in at the bottom of the bed, Barral would bawl at him indignantly that they were quits, even, all-square. After ten years or so, it became easier not to sleep. It had made Barral a great patron of the arts, that small nightly dilemma. In order to keep at bay the queue of dream-visitors who waited in the anteroom, he employed a host of minstrels and glee-maidens, whores and priests and puppeteers, readers and talking birds.

It was easy, therefore, for Ouallada to gain access to the primary bedchamber at Castle Etangs-Nerra. She found there a man confined to bed by the sheer insupportable weight of his own flesh. It would have taken hoists and winches to raise Nerra, and then his one remaining leg would not have held him. Crutches carved as immaculately as the arcades at Mirepoix leaned against the wall: a wonder of woodcarving. But Barral never ventured out of his bed to use them. The room smelled so much of urine and suppuration that Ouallada involuntarily screwed up her face.

'It comes up from below,' said the old man in the bed. She could only see his forehead and eyes over the height of his stomach. 'I keep telling 'em to clean out the kitchens, but it keeps on coming up between the joists. That smell.' The rim of his mouth had fallen in like a decayed rabbit-hole: morsels of his dinner lay like droppings by the lower lip. His eyes were milky blue and desolate.

Ouallada had brought a rebec fiddle with her from Haut-Beziers. It was small enough to carry but large enough to accommodate a narrow-bladed knife within the body. As she tuned it, the knife shifted inside: she could see it through the holes fretted in the woodwork, turning on its haft like a compass needle. The blade came to rest pointing at Barral. She wondered how well defended his vital organs were by the great cladding of fat he wore.

She had forgotten to think what she could sing to the man she was about to murder. But it was necessary to sing something; the woman attendant who had brought her was still in the room, lighting a succession of lamps and candles. The light of each illuminated the presence

of more - the task of lighting them all seemed endless.
The sound of priests intoning prayers in a chapel nearby
made it harder still to call to mind a song. So she sang
the one which had made her despise the rest: the song
she had written for Foulque.

    …These are the words that fill the world
     with emptiness, like a breaking jar:
     That you whom I love are removed so far –
     far as the past which cannot be reclaimed,
    far as the morrow which is never breached,
     far as Lucifer fell beyond God's reach.
    Still, as the Earth is bound by singing spheres,
     So will I bind you within the compass of my song
     And hold your name where I can hold no longer
     the company of my friend …

The old man exploded in a rheumy eruption of coughs.
'Very nice. Very nice, I'm sure. You must have something.
Come here. Let me look at you. Very pretty. Very. Such
lovely hair. Lovely. Always liked dark women. Closeness.
That's right. You're quite right. That song of yours. Well,
it touches on things. It does. It does. Closeness. That's
what matters. Not hanging back by the wall. Curtseying.
Wagging two fingers at you from the far end of the room.
That's not a blessing. Call that a blessing? Standing
closer would be more of a blessing.' The pipes of his throat
were yellow and white as tripe, beneath a white stubble.
His breath already smelt like the exhalations of a grave.
On his chest a huge golden crucifix with ingots linked to
its arms was pressing him to death.

    'You're a sick man, Barral Nerra,' she said while his

hands held the fall of her hair, sorting the strands between thick fingers: an embroiderer selecting silks. The hand tightened on her hair.

'Me? Not me. I've raised an army of priests and barbers to keep me in good health. I'm in good health, me.'

'An army? To fight off Monsieur Death?'

He shot her a look of such abject reproach that his eyes bulged in his head, currants in uncooked dough. 'I'm a pious man, me! I'm not afraid to go before the Judgement Seat! Listen! Listen to those priests groaning on for me. House is full of 'em. Jerusalem, too. Normandy.'

He still had hold of her hair. She prised his fingers open one by one to recover her hair out of his grip, and as she did so she said cruelly, 'I'm a singer myself. One thing I know. It's very well to be told to sing, but no one can tell you who you're singing for. Maybe in their hearts they're saying the Mass for themselves. Maybe they do it for their friends and relations.'

She could see it accorded with his view of priests, his contempt for them, his faith in them. He gripped the pillow on either side of his head and pulled on it so hard that it doubled over his face and burst a length of seam, spewing out clotted feathers. 'Have something. You must have something.' Perhaps he thought it would give her a more sanguine outlook. Perhaps he thought she represented all those watchers, those invisible watchers behind the window hangings, above the bed's canopy, outside the door. He felt their eyes continuously, lascivious demons watching him shed one day at a time of his remaining life, watching from their hiding places, ready to come out when he fell asleep, to steal one or two more of his covers. In his eagerness, he swept money off his bedside and on to the floor rather than into her hand. So he thrust the candle-holder into her palm, the candle stump still in place.

It was a squat, ugly, valuable thing, encrusted with candle wax. She tilted it between her hands, the candle rocked, too small to fill its socket. She could picture dropping the liquid beeswax on to his eyes, to seal him up, as the bees seal their hives with the gross, maggoty queen inside still pupating. She let the candlewax drip, drip, drip down. Then she took the candle from its holder and stuck it in the puddle she had made on the table, so that it stood as it had before.

She could picture driving the ugly, cruse-shaped holder into his wizened mouth, choking him on his own, obscene wealth, gorging him on his own greed.

But his hands enfolded one of hers, folding it around the metal gift. He was trembling. 'Such a pretty song. Such a pretty voice. You don't know it yet, but songs can be quite ... *speaking*, you know. Quite speaking. I've always been a very cultured man myself, and I like the best. Nothing but the best, me. I've studied these things.'

He took the candle-holder back and thrust it into the opening of her sleeve where it dropped leadenly down into the inaccessible cuff. She would have to be rid of it, or it might incriminate her.

'I know your family a little,' she said.

'Family? Mine? The Count of Anjou, you mean? I thought there was noble blood in you! I knew it! I'm never wrong.'

'Not the Count. But I'm acquainted with your

nephew, Foulque Nerra. He's a fine scholar - and poet.'

'My nephew? Nephew? Do I have a nephew, then? A bastard, you mean, sure!' Such a litter of sins swirled in the cold, inclement winds of the Past that Barral Nerra could no longer see as far back as ten years, let alone thirty. A little boy cloistered against his parents' wishes. A little boy cloistered, like, a gratuity slipped God out of the back of a hand. He struggled to remember, but there were mice in his brain these days, eating into his memory, nibbling away at the grains. 'He could have it all, for all I care. I'm not a material man, God knows. Not a man who treasures up, lays in ... who lays up treasures in ... Did you say "a poet"? Didn't know there was another poet in the family.'

Suddenly Ouallada had decided. On her way downstairs from the bedchamber, she planned it all: how she would intercept Foulque, make him sue for reconciliation with his uncle. Even if it were refused, he had only to bide his time; Barral was halfway to his grave already! If he were to die of natural causes, would Foulque be any the less his heir? Would his prospective wife be any the less rich? They must simply wait a while for Monsieur Death! There was no need for murder. Not by her. Not by Foulque.

'What did you get from him? What did he give you?'

Like the pain from an old injury, her father always came suddenly, unforeseen, making her faintly nauseous. As she stepped out into the evening air, he grabbed the back of her cloak.

'I thought I'd seen the last of you,' she said, remembering the uncharacteristic sag of him on that rainy road, the look of a man finally overwhelmed by events. Hand-over-hand he pulled himself closer, up the fabric of her cloak.

'When you're just set to spin straw into gold? Come on. Come on. You've been with Nerra. You must have money.' He fumbled upon the candle-holder, and almost thrust his head up her sleeve, delving with a desperate, swirling arm.

'Be careful. You're tearing the seam!'

'I need it. I need it. Give it me! What is it?'

'A thing. Nothing. Have it. Take it. Here. Take it.' The candle-holder fell between them like some piece of coke from a dead fire.

'You have been with him, then? You've seen him. He's alive? You got in to see him?'

'There's plenty there to be had, if that's what you mean. But you'll have to sing to him yourself if you want any of it. I'm not going back there. Don't worry, he likes minstrels. They cover up the silence.' All she wanted was to get away from this importunate beggar and to find Foulque - tell him there was no need for a killing. It all seemed so simple and obvious, if only she could shake off this impediment, this small-minded man with his heart set on trinkets and pennies. So her eyes were not on Oriole; she looked beyond him and away down the side streets. She did not hear what he said; her ears were listening for the sound of horses' hooves in the little passageways. There was hardly a section of her brain left to wonder where her father spent his money that his need was never any the less.

'You've just come from him. Just now. What did you play?'

She wanted to scream with frustration, to drop the cloak off her shoulders and run, leaving the wretch yammering in the roadway. 'A *winileodas - a* lament. What does it matter what I sang? He liked it a lot.'

She should at least look at him. She should. She ought. He was the one who had taught her. *Winileodas!* How could she even know the meaning of the word if it were not for him telling her? Had he not devoted years to guaranteeing her success and admiration? She ought at least to look him in the face and see how important it was to him. Well, she deserved the reward of ingrates. Let it fall to her the way it would. At one time he would have said she was the most important project of his life. But now ... Suddenly he was seeing her from a different viewpoint - higher up - from the battlements, as it were. And she was small, diminished, nothing but that silly, grubby bastard of Amaury's. All along he had hated her. Should not have gone to the trouble of hating her. Too small, too expendible. Still, now he saw why he had kept by her all these years - supported her with advice and wisdom in return for paltry trinkets and insults. Now he saw why he had kept this 'thing' seven years. It had its uses.

'I meant, what instrument,' he said. 'What instrument did you play to him?'

'Well this, of course. If I was carrying any other, you'd know by now, wouldn't you?' she said, slapping at his hands. 'What? D'you want my instrument now? I never thought you'd strip me of my tools as well. But here you are. Take it! You'll have me making bricks without straw next, you Egyptian! Go on, take it! Anything if you'll just let me go. I'm in such haste, Father!' As the rebec changed hands, it bridged for a moment the gulf between master and pupil. 'I'd stay and tell you why, Papa, but I'm in such haste as I never was in all my life. I'm sorry.'

'Go on, then,' he said. And she flew away from him like a stone from a catapult. Soon she was no more than a point of colour in a grey town encrusted with salt.

The clutter of houses that had grown up around Barral's castle had no rhyme or reason. It was full of cul-de-sacs and alleyways stopped up by the later addition of a stable or by some forge's stockpile of cauldrons. Upset by the argument with her father, Ouallada paid too little attention to finding her way between the jumble of buildings. She got hopelessly lost. The dark was against her. It fell like a veto, forbad anything but to find an inn and to sleep. But Oriole had taken her every last coin. A fine princess he had reduced her to! There was nothing for it. She would have to retrace her steps and claim to have been robbed. (It was true, after all.) Now she thought about it, why not let Foulque find *her* rather than go in search of him? She would go back to the old man, lend him the closeness he craved, and wait for Foulque to arrive. That way, she could sleep warm on the floor of Barral's stateroom, or in the troubadour's chamber.

As she approached the fortified gatehouse of the castle, she thought that one of the guards called out to her. It was dark, but he seemed to be beckoning to her, or pointing. She turned in his direction.

'Yes, that's her!' repeated the soldier, his eye-whites

showing with the intensity of his stare. From out of the guardhouse behind him four more men came running, their mouths full of bread, their knife-blades stringy with supper. 'Are you sure?'

'I'm sure! I'm sure. For Christ's sake! Don't let her get away! It's her! That's the witch that did it!'

They fell on her like grain sacks from an overhead winch. All her wind was knocked out of her. She felt the pats of horsedung on the road subside under her, soft as molehills. She felt the tips of their knives prick holes through the precious fabric of her cloak.

She knew then that she had come too late. Barral Nerra-des-Etangs had already been murdered. Deaf now to the singing of his monks, his soul had fallen through their interlocked, praying fingers, and was plummeting down to Hell.

Up in his crystal cave of whorled wax and wavering flame, Barral Nerra lay belly-up, like a beached whale, his head hanging over the edge of the bed, the gut string of a rebec wound so tightly round his flacid throat that it barely showed. Death often shows more in the face than at the point where it is inflicted.

CHAPTER TWENTY SIX

Ordeal

It was the justice of God and not Man she had meant to
shield Foulque from, but she was ready to do both. So
when they said she had strangled Barral Nerra, she did
not deny it. They said her singing had been nothing but
a murderer's pretext, and in a way they were right.

Foulque arrived within two hours of the body being
found. No sooner had the castle snatched in a breath to
cry that it was fatherless, than a fighting bishop arrived
to tell them they were not. If it occurred to anyone that
the death had been wonderfully fortuitous for Foulque,
no one said so. No one felt such a fondness for Barral as
to wish him alive again. They simply ran an eye over
Foulque, and cast their worries in his lap. Some people
remembered how Barral had cloistered his brother's

firstborn; when they discovered Foulque was that selfsame child, they somehow assumed he was still a cleric. Like Ouallada, he neither admitted nor denied it: he simply allowed the assumption to stand.

He had dignity and natural authority, and a voice which could quell a room of babblers. And at the news of his uncle's death, he displayed a certain quality of religious ecstasy that dampened his shining scalp with sweat. They were exceedingly glad to be able to bring before him the perpetrator of the ghastly murder.

After that, it was sheer *mardi gras*. All of the small Camarguais world attempted to cram themselves into the castle's great-hall. Those at the back shouted for those at the front to sit down. Those wanting to bear witness pushed and shouldered their way through, braying with self-importance. Some called themselves witnesses just to reach the front of the press.

Barral was laid on a table-top and carried in to bear silent witness to being dead. There was a counter movement against the general flow, as spectators struggled to move away from the trestle and its body, not to be touched by it, not to incur bad luck. Then suddenly everyone was on tiptoe, straining to see.

'This is the woman, sir. This is the mad woman.'

'But this is ...'

Ouallada and Foulque looked one another in the eye and, just for a moment, she brushed her fingers against her mouth: keep silent. He said, nevertheless, 'I know this woman. She is Princess Oualada of Bamberg. She's a poet.'

'That's right. That's right!' They congratulated him on his fore knowledge. 'That's how she won entrance to your uncle's room! She sang to him. She was heard singing. She played, too. A viol.'

'A rebec,' she said. 'It's true.'

They looked at one another, but with a kind of unwillingness to focus.

Foulque was fond of Ouallada and was horrified to see no repentance in her face: he wondered if her pagan blood truly made her a different breed of beast. That she could commit murder and not repent it.

And Ouallada did not want to breathe deeply, for fear she smelt sulphur on him. For this was the man she had come too late to snatch back from the edge of the Fiery Pit. This was the man who had committed murder for love of La Belle Aude.

Their misconstruction of events was mutual and complete.

A commotion near the door barged the crowd against her, and she was obliged to step closer to him. 'Is it true,' he asked; 'that you took a string from that rebec and strangled the man Barral Nerra-des- Etangs?'

'Did what?'

'Show me your hands.'

Her hands jumped in his open palms; she watched them as if they were creatures independent of her, trembling and jumping in his palms. He closed his hands around her wrists. 'He was strangled with a wire?' She whispered the question to him alone, indifferent to the concerns of the court but quite transformed by the news. He felt the change pass through her hands.

'The instrument was found close by.'

'Then it wasn't ...'

'And now we have her accomplice!'

The crowd ruptured in two, and a pair of soldiers thrust Oriole at Foulque as they might a mastiff at a bear. He was bloodied and bruised - seemed to have been pulled out of shape so that his limbs were of different lengths. The red stubble on his cheek looked like rust. Already they had deduced his actions of the night before.

He had sold his horse and pack animal and bought opium from the apothecary. He had tried to sell the very candlestick that had stood beside Barral's bed before he died - an ugly thing, chased with the heraldry of the Counts of Anjou. When the murder was discovered, this unsalubrious stranger to the town was almost as easily found as the Moorish woman.

Oriole stretched out a finger and pointed at his daughter. With one eye shut, he took aim along the length of his arm, over the age-nobbled sight of his knuckle. And with his mouth so contorted that his lips turned inside out, he screamed, *'I had it from her! I had it from her! I've done nothing. I had the thing from her! Ask her! She'll tell you!'*

As clear as if someone had called it in at the window, Ouallada recalled the words: *'Ouallada will be our salvation, you see if she isn't.'*

'It's true. I gave it him. I gave him the candlestick.' She waited for him to be shamed into penitence. She waited for him to admit, 'She gave me the rebec, too, and I took the wire and I strangled the old man.' But she knew he would not say it, for she knew her father through and through; knew that the truth to him was a maleable thing, changing from moment to moment. To himself, he was probably already innocent.

Foulque let go Ouallada's hands and stood up out of

Barral Nerra's chair. When the hubbub was slow to quieten, he picked up a box of chess pieces that lay on the floor beneath the chair, and shook it: a wincingly loud rattle that made even Ouallada step back from the noise. 'You were in receipt, even so, of stolen goods,' he said, 'and therefore have blood on your hands. You may yet be this woman's accomplice. '

'No! As God's my witness! It lays all to her. I did nothing. I did nothing! As God's my judge!'

'Then may God judge aright, when you prove your innocence by Ordeal of Combat.'

It doesn't matter, thought Ouallada. It's of no consequence.

Foulque had done nothing! Foulque was as she had wished him: guiltless, innocent of murder. What was more, events had brought him both the woman he loved and the lands to which he was entitled. Nothing else mattered, she told herself, though her ribs were too rigid with fright to let her breathe, and the room reeled.

It was true when they said she was guilty. Inasmuch as she had brought her father here - implied to him that Barral's death would make her heir to a fortune, she *was* guilty of the old man's death. She was her father's accomplice. And if she were to deny everything, to cast the capital offence all on to Oriole, he might blurt out something about her which she did not want Foulque to know. So the truth was no great loss: she would not trouble to mention it.

'Against who?' shrieked Oriole. 'Combat with her? You heard her! She told you! *She* gave me the gold thing. She told you she did it! - But, yes! All right, I'll fight her. 'Fore God! And push the lie between her teeth.'

The room stirred with amazement. The man was plainly mad. What better to expect of a man who used opium?

'Fight a woman?' said Foulque impassively. 'What an extraordinary notion.'

'Oh, she can handle a sword and dagger, that one. Didn't she kill old Nerra? Didn't she throttle him? She's no fieldmouse, that one.'

Foulque blinked away the interruption and waited, with his eyes closed, for Oriole to finish. 'Since I am chiefly wronged, I shall be your accuser. You shall fight me.'

'*No!*' said Ouallada.

What new sensations were left to devastate their tedious daily routine? One souzerain dead, the next in combat with a vagrant! There was uproar. A bailey sergeant went to stab Oriole under the ribs and be rid of him. Oriole ran and took refuge behind the trestle bearing the body. 'What about her? She told you! She good as said she did it! *She told you I never killed him!*'

'No. No, no, no, no, no.' Now she kept on saying it, until the clamour in the room died down. 'No, no, no, no. I never said that, jongleur. I said I gave you the candle-stump, but that was all I said. I gave you the rebec, too, and you did the murder. And 'fore God and these people, I'll fight you in combat to prove it.'

'Why couldn't you say it before?' Foulque shouted at her.

'I'm saying it now, aren't I?'

This was better than dog-racing. Mothers sent their children running home to tell grandparents to come at once and to fetch milking stools to sit on.

Foulque hustled Ouallada aside – in as far as that was possible with moonish faces pressing in all around, staring, passing on a commentary to the faces behind. 'What are you doing? What are you thinking of? Don't be ridiculous. You can't fight in combat! Why didn't you deny it before?'

'He's right. I can handle weapons,' she said.

'Better than I can? You fool. *Why didn't you deny it before?* How can I help you now? Why in hell did you offer him combat?'

She pursed her lips obstinately and looked his face over and over, finding the crannies where doubt lingered. 'Sooner me than you,' she said.

Then she added the quick lie, 'Because I know he did it, and you don't. A man can't fight to prove a thing he only half believes. I can fight in good faith. 'Fore God. Believe me.' She could not add any gesture of tenderness. She could not kiss the bewilderment out of his eyes. For then she might imply a conspiracy between herself and Foulque which would damage his hold on the estates of Etangs-Nerra. So she knelt and kissed his hand instead, as a devout country girl might request a bishop's benediction. He looked to right and left of him. Faces were gawping, hungry for confirmation of a day's sport. His hand hovered indecisively over the nape of her neck, picked up a strand of her hair and fingered it. He was black with rage. The sign he made in the air was more of an incision than a blessing, a curtailed slash consigning her to her fate.

'Prepare the combatants,' he said, and the crowd broke into a cheering, jigging mob.

The cause was quite lost sight of in the excitement. In

fact an opportunist taking hurried bets on the outcome of the fight backed into the trestle table, and Barral Nerra's hand was dislodged from his chest. As it fell, and the arm swung like a pendulum, a ruby ring slipped off his finger. He might have been misconstrued as offering a bet himself, but then no one would have taken it. For Barral had insider knowledge. He already knew the outcome of combat - knew which of the prisoners had strangled him with a wire, and which therefore God would favour. And everyone knows what a sound fellow God is with a pick horn.

One last stir of excitement. 'Keep off. Let go of me. What are you doing? My Lord Bishop! My Lord Nerra, help me!' The one called 'princess' tried to rise from her knees but was being held down forcibly and her head pulled backwards by its mane of black hair. There were calls for a razor.

The barber, engaged just then on shaving the vagrant minstrel's head, flourished his blade and promised to come as soon as he could. Foulque gave orders for his uncle's body to be moved to the lantern-of-the-dead beside the churchyard. Then drawing his cloak around him, he left the room.

He tried to fix his thoughts, as a paliative to ugliness, on his *domna*, his belle Aude. But her image would not crystallise in his overheated brain and kept melting away to a brownness. He tried to construct her out of her many perfect parts – sky-blue eyes, bird-small features, cumulo forehead rising to a corona of blonde ... But it would not shape into the dearness of her face. All he could see was that thick, black hair dropping down like the tail from a flayed horse, like the manes of those hundred horses he had once seen burned to death in a pit for the spectacle of it. There was nothing he could have done to save her hair, of course. It is a requirement of Trial by Combat that the protagonists should go shaven into the pit.

She had been right to doubt his conviction of her innocence. His powers of observation told him that those two prisoners - that man and that girl - were conspirators of some kind, despite their mutual hatred. Surely Aude, cherishing him dearer in truth than he ever guessed, had asked her friend the Princess to do the killing in his stead: had asked a pagan to do it, who had no soul to endanger. Nothing else made any sense at all.

Oriole was singing. Ouallada could hear him in the next cell of the donjon, singing. It was the strangest of noises. She would have liked to sing in *tenson,* supplying his every second line, out-rhyming him. But there was no music left in her. Brought to this dark place, she felt like a plant in a pot that had used up all the nutrient in its soil, turning back to earth. Perhaps the power of song had been in her hair, like Samson's strength. Perhaps her Love had its seat there, too. Perhaps now that they had turned her into a sexless thing, she could feel nothing at all for her *senhor*. Not like the man in the next cell. He was singing a love song for a woman.

'Opium, Father?' she called out to him. 'What did you want with opium? No wonder the money I gave you was never enough.'

The song faltered and there was a brief silence. 'I commonly use it. Opium is the pillow of poets and wise men. I learned the practice from a knight of distinction in the East.' The voice was strange. For all it was distorted by calling, it was distorted even more by a quite grandiloquent refinement, a courtly enunciation nice to the point of lampoonery. 'He was a faithless knight, mind. No steadfastness in his love. He waned as a troubadour - waned to nothing.'

Wherever Oriole was in his fantasies, he was certainly not penned in an underground cell, ruing the loss of his hair. Something - whether opium or madness - had liberated his spirit into a realm of troubadours and fayre ladyes.

'Why did you kill Barral Nerra?' she called, and he answered without hesitation. The answer made no sense to Ouallada, but it was perfectly coherent, and again delivered with the mannered deliberation of a court chronicler.

'Oh, it was the very least I could do for her - for Alazais. He never paid, you see. The *other* paid; I saw to that. God saw to that. But Barral never paid for what he did. For fetching her down. For letting Herm near her. For believing Herm's slanders. For putting her off. Do you know? He *beat* her in plain view of the world. Did you know that?'

'No, I never knew that,' said Ouallada, sunk in darkness.

'Beat her like a mongrel dog, when she could have called down angels to trample him if she'd been minded.'

'I didn't know you knew Barral before,' called Ouallada.

'Still, God sent me back to end it,' he went on, no longer hearing her. 'He made it plain enough - couldn't make it any plainer. Laying it out before me. She pointed him out, that bastard brindling daughter of mine. She was all set to mate with a Nerra, you know? Both sprung from the Devil. Might've known they'd cleave to each other, wheeling round in the world's drain. One bad drawn to another. Should've drowned her the day she was born. Well, so, I'll put that right today. Ended the old man. Now I'll end her. For you, Alazais. For you, my exquisite. You hear? Do you hear?'

'I hear, Peter Oriole,' said his daughter.

The arena was thrown together out of lengths of wood-weave fencing used for temporarily penning sheep. There were fluffs of wool still caught in the hurdles. As the crowd pressed forward during an ordeal, there was a tendency for the arena to shrink in size.

The combatants were each given a pick made from deer horn, a wooden club, and a single vambrace such as archers wear on their forearms. There was to be no referee other than God, though His name was bandied about a great deal. His presence was invoked by the clergy, His help begged by the fighters and the proceeds of the betting men left inside the church for safe-keeping.

The removal of the combatants' hair was a shrewd element of tradition, for it rendered them somehow less human, more beastlike. Often it made them indistinguishable, though hardly so this time, given that one was a yellowing, thin man approaching old age, the other a half-caste young woman. They had found her some men's clothes to fight in, but there were still a great many lewd jokes shouted as she was fetched in a cart up to the sheep-fold.

Ouallada looked about her for Foulque. There was something she had most urgent need of, which only he could supply. All her flow of thoughts had fused together in that one need. Allay that panic and he would allay all the rest. But his face was nowhere to be seen.

Oriole, now that the dungeon walls were removed from round his fantasies, was a tower without scaffolding: he looked prone to collapse. That expensive addiction of his to opium, the vice borrowed from his betters, had eaten into the very mortar of his constitution. He turned the pick over and over in his hands, uncertain even how to hold it. Then they brought him out his daughter to kill, and though he told himself she was no great loss, he suddenly could not remember what else he had to lose. There had been a lump of gold yesterday, and a pile of musical instruments. A while earlier there had been a bear and a rented house and a chest filled with some other man's wedding garments and an expensive minstrel's livery. Where had it all gone? Even the pretty daughter he had embroidered and chamfered and polished and groomed for the maintenance of his old age had been mauled and shorn into that bald, sexless creature over there with a horn pick and club like his.

Now if it had been a tournament field, under a sky fretworked with banners, between panoplies of silk . . . if there had been the bray of trumpets rather than the scream of gulls ... if there had been heralds in chevroned liveries, with parrains bearing fasces of lances, ah! then he could have shown his mettle. Then he could have summoned the strength at long last to break out of the carapace that had crushed his life down to the significance of a landcrab.

They stood looking at one another for so long that the

crowd began to jeer and complain and demand that the Bishop come and put them to it. When Foulque came, he was even dressed as a cleric, his leathers laid aside in favour of gown and hood, his face shaven, his hair brushed into docility in the nape of his neck. He had added the authority of the Church to his strong right arm.

Ouallada had wanted something of his: that was her need: some token, some favour. His pen, his knife, his glove. Now there was nothing to him but the smooth, impenetrable disguise of a monk. How could she face an ordeal like this without a token? Though she told herself it was superstitious, the superstition went deep enough to paralyse.

They were wagging cut twigs under his nose, begging Foulque to make the villains fight. But how could they fight? Ouallada looked down at the pick in her hand and shook her head. No. Foulque must intervene. She must tell him the true facts and have him settle it somewhere else, somehow else. She walked wearily towards him. 'Foulque – sir - we can't do this. You see, this man is my fa - '

His face filled up with alarm. 'Behind you!' he said, and she turned just in time to see Oriole reach his best speed and start to fetch down the pick from behind his head, shouting, '*Alazais!*' She crouched down in abject fright - the horn brushed her back, but his impetus pitched them both, along with the fence, up against Foulque. Reflexly he fended them both off his legs, obliged to let his hands emerge from his sleeves. Closed inside one was a piece of blue ribbon. Ouallada had it out of his hand so quickly that even the cutpurses in the crowd did not appreciate the sleight of hand.

She had it: some part of him! The energy flowed into her as though she had drunk blood. She locked her antler into the angle of Oriole's and wrenched it out of his hand, flinging it back into the centre of the arena, then got to her feet as he scrabbled after it. Amaury had taught her that all was lost to the fighter who could not keep his footing. She adopted a swordsman's stance, her knees bent, her weight evenly spread, the piece of horn held in both hands in front of her. *Alazais, indeed.* Who was *Alazais?* Not Ouallada's mother, that much was sure; not that benighted woman gathering stones in the winter fields of frozen blood; not that black ewe tenderly guarding her litter of brindled lambs while they vied for her warmth under a minstrel's cart. Alazais? Who was Alazais? Alazais be damned, and be damned to him for his 'Alazais'.

'For Alazais!' Look at her, striving to remember the techniques that bloody Amaury had taught her - using them against her own father - rebellious and obdurate to the last. All along she had been Amaury's in blood and in heart. All along Amaury had allowed Oriole to feed and clothe and educate his own spawn. Oriole's children would have been white, like Alazais, golden like Alazais, looking only to him as Alazais had. 'For Alazais!'

She could see that his legs were spongy, his footwork slow. Time and again he scuffed the uneven ground with the side of his shoe, tripped and had to recover himself. Time and again he signalled his intentions in his grimacing - gave her time to jump out of reach of his lunges and slashes. Then his fingers would touch the ground and his breath would come and go, unsynchronised with his panting, along with sobs of sheer exertion.

She shouted too, to cover the sound of her heartbeat and the curses he threw at her. When the horn picks tangled and they wrestled head to head, she could smell a stale, yellow stench out of him like badly cured vellum or unwashed breeches. He drove her backwards, for all his wrists were as thin as hers, the skin on the back of his hands inelastic. His breath smelled of yellow tallow as he grunted into her face, in a childish, singsong bleat, 'I sang for God, I did! In the face of the King. I sang for God. I'm safe from devils like you!'

'Only the dead are safe from devils,' she said, and instead of pushing him away, she pulled him on to her. A spit of horn caught him in the diaphragm and made him cry out. She let go of her antler, scrabbled for the club by her feet and lashed out at him - weak, ineffectual little taps, but enough to make him stagger. She reached out a foot to trip him and then, with her eyes shut and her thoughts all thrown like firewood into a fire, she brought the club down on him over and over and over again.

His antlers were across his body. She drove their spikes into the ground, pinning him inside a cage of hollow bone. Little by little she smashed the cage into jagged fragments that lodged in the folds of his clothing or sank their claws into his chest. Her eyes so tight shut and her efforts so intense, she lost her target and some blows fell on his legs and some on his hands and some on his boots. At last her grip on the club grew so weak that it flew off into the crowd and struck the gambling man.

She could not get air enough into her lungs; her arms and legs were turning to water. She would soon be at his mercy, trapped inside her perfidious, female body. Her eyes were full of lashes, so tightly had she screwed them shut. She peered about her for the other club - his club - stumbled over her father and waded through air as dense as water, to pick it up. Then she used it to lever herself to her feet - the man on his feet always has the advantage; Amaury said that - and sobbed and panted her way back to her opponent. Broken free of his horn cage, he was crawling on hands and knees towards the hurdles.

Sometimes a fight could last half a day. Though years seemed to have passed, there had been barely an hour of weary pursuit, of lifting of a club too large for her to wield, of grunts and obscenities and counter-blows to her legs, hands snatching at her ankles. When she could no longer lift the club, she stamped and kicked, holding her naked head between her two hands as though she were holding curtains of hair out of her eyes. In fact, for the most part, her eyes were shut, and she was seeing not him but herself, shorn and bestial, returned to the peasant dogfight which was her birthright. Of all the wrongs Oriole had ever done her, this was the worst of all: that he had made her grotesque in the eyes of Foulque; that he had made her ugly.

She finished astride Oriole, slapping at his face with her fists, sobbing, 'Where's my hair? Give me my hair! Give me back my hair!'

'Craven. Craven. Craven.'

She held the strip of ribbon between her two fists as if it could be tapped for a drop more of the vigour of hatred. But it gave her nothing more. For she realised just then what it was - Foulque's gift from La Belle Aude - her colours, her token, her blessing on the man she intended to marry.

'Why her? Why her? Why her?' she asked, beating the question home with weary blows of her fists. 'Why Alazais? Who's she? What's Alazais? Why not Kadija? Why not Ouallada? Why not me? Why not me? Why not me? Why not me? *Why couldn't you love me, your own daughter?*'

'Craven. Craven. Craven,' said the face beneath her, in a voice like a caged bird's. 'Craven! Craven!' He wrapped his arms over his face, knowing he was blind but need not acknowledge it while his eyes remained covered. The crowd picked up the cry: *'Craven! Craven! Craven!'* and all the hurdle fencing collapsed inwards.

Impatient hands pushed Ouallada aside, and two men, their belts embellished with squirrel tails, took hold of Oriole by the armpits. 'What's your name?' they kept asking him. 'What's your name?' his reply was incoherent. "Oriole." Is that all?' they said.

Condemned by his own cry, he was dragged away, face up to the sky and only his heels touching the ground, through the press of the crowd which gave way, the better to view him, then closed rank again. There was a single cry - from not very far away and quite distinct - 'Alazais!'

And then he was of no more interest, all attention reverting to the arena.

One of Oriole's boots lay on the grass, and a length of pale blue ribbon dislodged from his chest as he was carried away. Bishop Foulque stepped forward into the arena and picked up the ribbon, his fingers feeding it to and fro from left hand to right, right to left. 'The woman is proven innocent by Ordeal,' he said unceremoniously.

'No! no! Didn't you hear her? She's his daughter! She

said to him, *"Your own daughter"*, she said. Didn't you hear her, Lord Bishop? They were in it together. Don't let her get off, the blackamoor! She's a devil, she is! A fiend! He maybe got her from the Devil!' He saw them decide against her in their hearts, condemn her, out of fright and bloodlust.

'Prepare a bonfire,' he said. 'I shall speak of God somewhat, then you may have her after to burn.'

He turned to Ouallada, the ermine of his hood-trimming gleaming like the living animal 'Your father, Princess? The Sheik Obeid ben Zefir is fallen on hard times, isn't he, since his conquests in the East?'

As if cued to appear by the mention of its name, Oriole's head appeared just then, raised up on a pole, and the pole driven unsuccessfully into the ground. It keeled out of sight again, the earth too hard and salty to bear such fruits. Ouallada only glimpsed it for a moment: for long enough to see that the mouth was open and silently singing. Unaccompanied. Solo. Solus. Alone.

CHAPTER TWENTY SEVEN

Transported to Hell

An execution is always an occasion, a break from routine, an opportunity for grand speeches and lavish tears. The best sermons are preached by the light of bonfires, raking over the coals in a spectator's heart till he burns with gratitude at escaping such a fate. Death is brought close - close enough to smell it, to hear it rustle with the mice among the faggots, to see it moving about on the other side of the smoke. Executions bring out holiday clothes and holiday processions. An execution is a pageant and a play, with orange scenery and properties brought from the very treasure chest of the church - chalice and pyx, crucifix and relic - to be paraded through the streets. Even the faggots and the prisoner take on a kind of holy, processional significance.

So all to church for the address of a condemned 'princess' by the new Lord of Nerra-des-Etangs.

Executions bring forth good rhetoric as surely as they bring forth viscera and screaming, and a hot, righteous rejoicing in the belly of those watching.

It was traditional that the condemned should be incarcerated, for the duration of the harangue, in the base of the pulpit. So the shaven girl encrusted with her own and her accomplice's blood, was thrust into the small dark cupboard, her legs tied together at the ankles and a bundle of firewood in her arms as a reminder of her imminent tryst with the bonfire. Then the Bishop Nerra mounted his rostrum to preach the Exhortation to Repentance and to move the strong to tears.

'Men and women of Etangs-Nerra, I know you!' he said, and the jostling for floor-space, the chivvying and chastening of children, the shared recollections of the Ordeal all came to a sudden stop. His voice impaled them, as did the light falling in punitive rods through the windows of God's house on to His assembled People. 'Do you think yourselves safer than this miscreant whore? Do you call yourselves redeemed? I look down from here and I can see the Devil jump from back to back, small as a flea, gorging himself on your blood, tasting of his cattle that he may know which he will feed on in Hell. Already he has tasted the sweetness of Lust and the sharp spice of Unchastity. There are fruits for him here already stuck with lies, each one like the black clove; there are joints for him here that will baste themselves as they turn on the spits of Hell. For they are made fat by gluttony and usury.'

Hands swatted at necks but killed only lice, not the crawling fear he cast over them. 'Call yourselves sinners?' he asked as they scratched at their matted hair. 'My little children ... there are sinners casting shadows in this world that make you shine in my eyes like a host of candles. I have been to the lands of wickedness and I have seen the children of the golden calf, and I am happy now beyond the power of telling to rest my eyes on the white fleeces of a gentler flock. Even here, in our own land, there are heretics calling themselves "pure" and "perfect" who deny the Saviour seven times a day. But not my flock.'

He tossed them between Heaven and Hell like flapjacks. Just when they felt the heat scorch their souls, they found their heads knocked against the floor of Heaven. It made them dizzy.

'Take this woman. This creature penned at my feet. I feel her evil. I sense her there: a grub pupating in the bark of the tree, I the wood-pecker sent to devour her.' The beading split from the crown of the pulpit, and he leaned over and banged it against the ugly carvings at the base. A shrill cry of alarm came from inside. Otherwise, the prisoner was silent. She did not shout denials of her guilt or drown out his preaching with howls of repentance. 'This woman. This murderess of my uncle - oh, pour lime on the place where you bury the ashes of this fiend! For she was a princess and moved among copper and silver, in shoes too precious to tread on aught but carpets; a thing so unused to hardship that the very air she breathed must be perfumed with almonds and civet. Do you know, they oiled her body with the milk of she-goats and dressed it in damask and silks. *She wore flowers in her hair.'* And when he said it, men who had never tasted luxury were translated to foreign harems. 'Not for her the ignorance of the heathen! Her mother knew the mercy of redemption, and she was swaddled in the bands of Baptism. No! This one *chose* the ways of perdition, and her ear delighted in the Devil's music as she tuned her song to his fiddle. I have watched this woman move among the shoals of men, silent as the lamprey, boring into righteous flesh, tempting them to crimes of luxury, to acts of venial wickedness. She haunted the dark places her complexion fits her for, as the lizard blends itself with its surroundings. There are men among you who have known passion and sinned for the sake of it. But I say to you that this woman's passion is for sin itself, and her lover is Evil!

'And did she think to overleap the outcome? Did she think to maul and to murder and to mar, then leap up and snatch at the sun's rays and climb them to Heaven? Oh! Would that I could deny her that chance, for the stench of her, as I stand here, shrivels the charity within me and clouds my sight with loathing! And yet...

'And yet God's love is open to all that repent. He is infinitely forgiving. And so I must exhort you – woman – dray - coiling viper who wrung life from the Lord Barral and tears from his people - do you repent of your gall, of your guile, of the day you were born and the tally of days you have added to the misery of this world? Will you take yourself out of it in humility and truth? Will you beg these people to pray for your soul, and welcome the purge of fire, so that your filthy soul may be burned clean and Satan turned out-of-doors? Speak, sinner, that you may be found human, after all, beneath that black hide! The Holy Spirit beats its wings against your cell, child!'

For a long moment, the only noise in the church was the crack of the wooden beading against the base of the pulpit, and the skittering of its fragments as they broke off, inch by inch. Then Foulque incited the chant to begin, starting in a low, rythmic mutter which only the front row could hear, and allowing it to wash back through the church, accumulate the stamp of feet, the occasional hysterical shriek. *'Repent! Repent! Repent! Come out! Come out! Repent! Repent! Repent!* He had raised them all to the station of summoners, and their unaccustomed power dazzled them.

So too did the phosphorous. Its searing flash pierced a black hole in every retina, and the pupils of every eye shut down against the light.

Then a stream of smoke - grey interwoven with red - belched out of the little door at the bottom of the pulpit, and stormed the congregation, submerging the first few rows in acrid smoke and reaching out into the side chapels and the great roofspace over the nave. Through the tears in their stinging eyes, it seemed to the worshippers that the angels supporting the hammer - beams writhed and fluttered and coughed into their trumpets.

A stampede to escape began. A chevron of compressed humanity drove the uninformed ahead of them: 'Get out! Get out! A fire!' And though it had occurred to many, it took the new bishop to confirm their worst fears. He waited until the church doors were both pushed wide, then shouted, *'Satan is come for her!'*

Satan inside the church? Impossible. Had demons lurked there, all through the sermon, prising loose the flagstones beneath their feet, forcing an entry to carry away their prize? It filled them with the terror of swimmers who see shark moving below. Afterwards, people described seeing demons with green legs and goats with bloody horns. At the time there was only the wish to get away, rapidly followed by the desire to see what had become of the woman in the pulpit.

They re-mustered in the porch. Men poked their heads round the door. Their wives pulled them back, then crept in under their arms and advanced over the flag floor, eyeing the beams overhead for jibbering demons swinging by prehensile tails. There was a smell of rotten eggs.

The base of the pulpit stood open. Like the Disciples on Easter morning they looked inside, their hands clamped over their mouths and noses. On the floor, where the murderess had squatted, lay two thigh bones and a twist of charred cloth.

'Jesu. She's carried off to Hell!'

The dawning realisation that their new bishop and souzerain had been standing perched above the conflagration made them cross themselves afresh, and one matron who had found him particularly attractive, ventured up the twist of wooden steps to the drum of the pulpit, thinking to find his remains still smoking. 'Sir! Lord Bishop? Sir? Your reverence!'

But there was no trace of him. The same combustion which had propelled the murderess to Hell seemed to have tossed Foulque Nerra up to Heaven. The matron cast about for a sprinkling of ash to revere as a relic and preserve her family against bad luck.

'She was unrepentant,' said a voice from the echoing recesses beyond the rood screen, and Bishop Foulque moved out into the public gaze, his face and hands stained with soot, his shining head peppered with ash.

'Or was she proud and left repentance too late? Let us learn by it, my excellent good people, and live mindful of the demons at our elbow waiting to wrest us away to eternal torment.'

Just for a short time, while the veil was torn that divides the Living from the Dead, a religious devotion gripped the castle community of Nerra-des-Etangs. It carried the people dancing through the streets, speaking in tongues.

It would settle. Gold-dust cannot be kept in permanent suspension. It sinks down again to the riverbed. But for a time they were God's Chosen People, the ones visited by pillars of fire and smoke. They racketed about the town shrill with self-congratulation: it was *their* church which had been chosen by God for His Great Example.

Meanwhile, in the church itself, silence recuperated. Starlings twitched the bell ropes, and the smell of phosphorous and sulphur settled in the cobwebs to be eaten away by spiders. Foulque Nerra went to the pulpit and, lending bulk to brute strength, he shifted the thing two feet back to its original position. He was then able to lift the small stone access to the crypt. 'You can come out now.'

She did not. She could not. The ladder would not stay still, but bumped and rattled against the stone curbing like two skeletal brown arms reaching out of the grave. And her legs had no substance to them.

Foulque stood astride the opening, reached down a hand to Ouallada and pulled her up. As he set her down on the church floor, she subsided on to her haunches, hugging her knees, and jibbered with unwarranted cold.

The soft flap of his woollen skirts moved around her as he tidied the church scrupulously of all trace of his sermon. He gathered up the pieces of broken wooden beading bit by bit, counting them every so often in his open palm.

'That was very clever,' she said. 'I never knew you dealt in alchemy as well as verse.'

'Who, me? Of course. I'm of the *Scientific* brotherhood, don't you recall? That's why the Council of Tours ... disagreed with me so. The ban on the sciences. No opportunity for me to entertain my public with magic tricks. And see how they love it, too? Of course, charismatics are the fashion of the age. I think they're all side-show charlatans, myself'

They lapsed into a silence so dense it seemed to stifle Ouallada.

'I didn't kill your uncle,' she said at last.

'I know that. I saw your hands. The wire would've bitten in as you pulled it tight. I regret you were put to ... all this.' He dismissed, with a gauche wave of the hand, his manmade miracle. 'The blood lust was up, though. They'd've burned you in any case, and maybe gone on to deduce us confederates, you and I. Mere self-preservation, you, see.'

It was meant to ease the crushing onus of gratitude on her for saving her life, but she still could not look at him. She crouched there, tracing an inscription raised in bronze beneath her feet. *Inh toml qi cb* ...

'I'm just sorry I didn't prevent the Ordeal. You should have let me fight your fa ... the killer.'

'I told you. I knew he was guilty and I was innocent. And he tried to put the blame on me. I had cause to fight him. Anyway. Now you can go back to Haut-Beziers and -'

'I could have judged the matter better if I knew why your father should want to kill Barral Nerra.'

'My father?'

He was angry with himself for letting the mutual deceit drop, but then deceits pestered him, like wasps, and the temptation was to swat them. 'Yes. The Sheik Obeid ben Zefir. He's clearly fallen on hard times, the sheik, since you were a child of his tents. I'd heard opium wasted a man, but to drain him so of his colour?'

Her back stiffened. She came close to resenting the imputation. It was such fabric as her childhood was woven from. 'My father knew Barral, seemingly. In his youth.'

'Ah yes. I forgot. My uncle was a much-travelled man.'

'I think they must have loved the same woman.'

'Ah. Love. The all-purpose devil. And you, when you saw that your father's life stood in jeopardy, were prepared to keep silent and let the axe fall on you.'

'Oh, but I thought you - ' She broke off, and he looked at her squarely for the first time, his eyebrows raised. She did not finish the sentence. How could she say, 'I thought you'd done the murder; it's only you I'd die for'?

And so the amazement disappeared out of his face as he found another way of interpreting her silence. 'You thought I would extricate you. Whereas no one would extricate your... esteemed father.'

She nodded. The Truth seemed so very much more complicated than this simple account of events. She would have needed more words at her beck.

'Then he proved to be unworthy of such a daughterly gesture, and you turned harpy and tore him in shreds. I swear, I never saw such savagery. Still, I'd've killed him for you if there'd been a need.' His voice was unshocked, slightly mocking, as if the antics of his fellow human beings were consistent only in their foolishness. She did not know whether she was talking to a man or a monk.

'Your kindness has already outrun my means to thank you, sir. I'd best not stay any longer to endanger your repute as a miracle worker.'

'No. No, you're right.' He seemed suddenly nervous. He crouched down a few yards from her and tried to lay the pieces of beading out in the right order so that the splintered ends would fit together. 'No, you'd best get back to Haut-Beziers and deliver the news.' She looked at him blankly. 'Well? She sent you, didn't she? My lady *domna*? To see the job done? What will you tell her? Have I snatched you out of the claws of Satan to have you spill my guilty secret in my lady's lap? Will you tell her it wasn't I who killed Barral?' He was afraid of her. She was capable of telling Aude that he was not the murderer. Ouallada had the power to declare the *assais* failed.

'Go back to Haut-Beziers? Like this? How could I?' She meant more than the labourer's leggings, the shorn head, the smell of crypt and blood that clung to her. But he only waved his hand briefly in front of his face and said that cap and gown could be found; it was surely not impossible to find cap and gown and to pretend ...

'I'd be immensely obliged to you, sir,' she said. 'And of course I'll simply tell the Lady Aude that Barral is murdered and you are made Lord of Nerra-des-Etangs.' She looked for his face to crumple into a smile, but it remained as stony as ever. He simply nodded to acknowledge his indebtedness.

'We'd best go now, then,' he said. 'While the town's in frenzy.'

'*We?* You're coming too? But you're established here! You can't leave! Send for her.'

'Send for her?'

'Your hand's on the great "salt-cellar of the Camargue", isn't it? Send for her to come here and marry you. She's bound to come. She's given you her promise ... It's really very fortunate the way things have come about, don't you think? The thing done and no blood to blot your good fortune? All very propitious.'

'*Send* for her?' The notion was plainly unimaginable. Graceless past all gaucheté. It caught him unawares and made him laugh. 'Send for her? I don't really think so! Besides, there is a small – ah - impediment to my staying here. Or even coming back. Until I've seen my Prior and set things to rights.' His large, doleful eyes flickered in her direction, full of guilty admission. 'You're aware, I know, that I'm somewhat ... *lapsed* as a man of the Church. Otherwise we'd hardly be having this conversation. What you may less immediately call to mind ... ' He pulled at his nose sheepishly. 'For some years now it has been, in fact, a crime to impersonate a priest. Punishable by death - at the discretion of the court ecclesiastic, I daresay. But you see, not only would it - how can I say? - *embarrass* me a touch, in the person of 'Bishop Foulque", to bring my wife here - yes? - I'd also run the slight but considerable risk of being hanged. So you see a short adjournment to the pastures of Haut-Beziers seems not only pleasant but advisable.'

As Ouallada and Foulque travelled back into the central

Languedoc, it was as if she reclaimed her disguise from the branches of each tree they passed. Never once did he refer to the man whose head stood on a pole beside the gate of Etangs-Nerra. He gave her money to buy a dress. She managed to find a woollen helmet that fitted close to her head so that she looked no worse than a victim of some sickness that had caused her hair to fall.

Of course, as far as he was concerned, her return to a dress invested in her no more femininity than before. He had merely rescued a colleague, a fellow troubadour, and though the kindness might seem so huge that Ouallada's love redoubled within her each time she thought of it, it was no more than he would have done for Gaston Mauriac or Auxerre d'Impt.

The closer they came to Haut-Beziers, the more anxious and absorbed he became at the prospect of what lay ahead. When his horse actually strayed off the track, she was loath to call out and tell him: he had so often scorned 'the per *cuda* ramblings of absent-minded fools'. The horse decided matters by coming to a halt. Foulque was obliged to get off and lead the animal back to the road. He coughed and scowled as he remounted, but about a mile farther on, he caught her eye and, with a sheepish sort of a smile observed, 'There's a good deal to be said for the joys of anticipation.'

'The journey as opposed to the arriving, you mean?' and he nodded. 'The hoping as opposed to the having?'

'Ah. Aha, well. Perhaps that's to press a theory too far.'

If she had really been a man, as he treated her, she

could have asked in the crudest terms, the question that raged in her head: 'Are you truly still a virgin? At your age?' Half the priests in France could not have said so much, and they still toddling in the skirts of Mother Church. But coming from a woman (as she persisted in thinking herself) the question would have been outrageously immodest.

Just as it would be to remind him his bride was not a virgin.

But he knew it, didn't he? Did he not care, so long as Aude have not given her *love* to Mauriac? The questions tumbled through her, all unanswerable. What did it matter, she concluded, and followed on, in tow behind him, resolving to break away as soon as she was new rigged and seaworthy. Before the wedding, if that were possible. Until then, she would keep a quiet tongue in her head and quash her private thoughts.

'Doesn't it worry you that she lay with Gaston Mauriac before you?'

She blurted it out, so loud and inarticulate that he stared at her wide-eyed and ran a hand several times over his head. He opened his mouth as if to speak, but when nothing came out he kicked his horse to a gallop and raced off ahead. He rode directly at a grassy hill so steep that the beast could only buck and scrabble so far up the slope before coming to a halt and sliding back down on its hocks. By this time Ouallada had caught him up.

'A tapeworm can gnaw on a man without killing him, can't it?' he shouted at her. 'I can stomach it. Don't I merit one small *detraction* from my earthly blisses? You think I haven't deserved ... ' He swerved his eyes to survey the familiar, lovely landscape of the Orb valley and the sky warping it with corrugating heat. 'Don't you think I've detracted from God's joy in creating me? Given Him grounds to regret breathing the breath of life into me? Hasn't He good grounds to set a curb on my happiness?'

'No,' she said involuntarily, and then, 'No! Since you ask me. No. In my case, as you said to the pleasant people back there: God is infinitely forgiving.'

He dug his spurs into his horse again but he was also unknowingly hauling on the reins so that the beast only crouched down in abject confusion. 'I was play-acting back there. Don't you recognise satire when you see it?'

'You'll never starve for want of work as an actor, then. Your theology sounded plausible enough from where I was sitting.' He finally managed to break away from the spot and put on speed, but at first she kept level with his horse's tail, shouting into his slipstream. *Don't you believe it, then? Nerra? That God forgives?*

He let the words fly back to her over his shoulder, angry that she should have soured his day of triumph. 'If there's one thing my ancestors taught me, it's not to use God like a royal warrant: a free pass to ride roughshod over my neighbours and my conscience! The third Count? You recall my royal ancestry? He burned down cities then put it right with a penance. Barral Nerra? He nailed men to their doors then went on pilgrimage. If there's one thing I learned from my antecedents, it's not to pretend sins can be shed like that - like a crab's back - the better to grow bigger ones below. Me, I carry my sins with me where I can keep close reckoning.'

She could not sustain the pace, and he pulled away

from her, reaching the top of the rise first and so catching first glimpse of Haut-Beziers. At the sight of it, he punched a clenched fist hard into the air over his head with surfeit of feeling. He might have tricked the people of Nerra-des-Etangs into seeing miracles, but he had tricked himself into believing a much greater one: that all earthly happiness lay in the I possession of La Belle Aude and was within reach now, just beyond that outcrop yonder of marriage vows.

As the door of the great-hall opened and Foulque Nerra humped his saddlebags and rolled tarpaulin over the threshold, the room fell silent. He felt the stares keenly, and his colour rose. He stopped in the doorway, half-blocking it, half-holding it open for Ouallada. 'You tell her,' he said in a low voice. 'She sent you to keep a watch on me. You tell her it's done.'

Ouallada squeezed past him and, knowing he would never notice it, let her fingers trail across the sheepskin of his waistcoat. After that nothing remained but to approach Aude, where she sat at the topmost table, and to say, 'The *assais* is done', and offer congratulations on a fortunate marriage.

As she came closer, she could see that Aude's face was powdered with ground silver and glittered with every turn of her head and with the suppressed laughter of her twitching cheeks. 'Princess! Where have you been? So long gone from us!' She stood up and pushed her face forward for Ouallada to kiss and then, seeing that the woollen cap concealed no hair, thought better of kissing a possible source of disease. 'My dear, dear Princess. You've not been well!'

'I -'

Ouallada turned round and walked back down the room, every step an ordeal under the public gaze. 'You say it,' she whispered bad temperedly to Foulque. 'It's not for me to say. You say it.'

So Foulque lumbered himself and his baggage farther into the room and dropped it all down behind the door. A lady in a samite dress burst into uncontrollable sniggers and was shushed by her companion. Foulque scowled and straightened his back. His stacked saddlebags slithered one over the other and spilled their contents. The woman in the samite could not be restrained from snorting into her cup.

Foulque started down the room and, to force a path through the sheer density of silence, began his formulaic address as he walked. 'As you know, mistress, when I left my former life, I commended myself to fortune, gave the rein to my steed and let it carry me where it would. It bore me here, to discover a love more precious to me than Heaven, and I courted that love, as Love itself commended me to do, in verses and song. My lady took pity and inclined her ear. She set me *assais* to try and temper my love - for God knows it was a love always conducted in temper.' His walk brought him to the opposite side of the table from her, and he leaned his palms down among the dishes. 'And now I present myself, Foulque, Lord of Nerra-des-Etangs, and crave ... ' There was no formula for the proposal of marriage: it was not a troubadoric principle. '... and crave the reward of your companionship during all the remaining days of my life.'

Why must she do it to him? thought Ouallada: make

him speak in formulae, who despised cliché; make him speak at all, who preferred silence? But she persuaded herself that it was natural for Aude to enjoy her last moments of actual power: the scope of a married woman is, after all, a circle drawn on the ground for her by her husband. At least Gaston Mauriac was not there. And ultimately the triumph was Foulque's who had fulfilled his *assais*.

Aude cupped a pair of hands over her grinning mouth in a show of horror. 'Christ, you did it, then! What a monstrous man you are, to be sure!' She said it in shocked delight, and with a dramatic shiver. 'Everyone said you'd baulk at it. But you did it! Well! What a wealth of money and land you have now! We must all treat you with great respect, mustn't we? I'm very happy for you, dear Foulque. What a difference from before!'

'I have nothing but what you can call yours, lady. That most worth having, I had before, unless you prize a man according to his purse. What I most wanted, I left behind me here, in the safe-keeping of your heart: that's to say, your promise.'

'Such a pity you were gone so long,' she said as if he had not spoken.

'A two-weeks, madam? It seemed a long time to me, but ...' He scented a danger. Even from the doorway Ouallada could see it. On the road back he had always known when there were wolves running. Now his head leaned slightly back, his nostrils stiff and wide.

'Ah, but so much has happened since you left! Such interesting visitors! Such wonderful debating! Let me introduce you to Deacon Gislebert, who is perfect.'

Foulque's eyebrows soared as he turned to address the

shabby individual dressed in gunny and frieze and seated on a stool at the table's end. 'Perfect? Oh, happy man that anyone should impute it, let alone it be true!'

The deacon, a pallid man with a straight, lipless mouth like a sword scar, smiled without parting his gums.

'I mean he's *a* perfect - a saint! - a minister of the new religion. Oh, the windows he's thrown open for us! The light he's let in!' (She seemed less than enraptured now, though could have been describing a genuine emotion that had come and gone. As Gaston Mauriac had come and gone.)

Foulque no longer spoke or moved. His stillness made the rest of the room seem wriggling, fidgety, wormy.

'Auxerre and I were totally and completely moved to ecstasy! Not just us - oh, everybody! I mean moved to the bottom of our souls! Truly! Deacon Gislebert blew into our mouths, you know. To impart the Holy Spirit. He can do that, you know! He's in direct communication with - Well, the problem is, Foulque, you're just such a very ... *Christian* man. I mean, as Deacon Gislebert says, all carnal love is a sin, but if it must be, then best between two like-thinking people, don't you agree? And unmarried, too. Or there's all that tiresome forswearing to be done ... And you gone so long. Deacon Gislebert says that marriage is defunct - a scab over material filth. "No marrying in Heaven" and so forth.' Gislebert scratched his head, as if he had been slightly misquoted, but did not contradict her. 'So I've acknowledged Auxerre d'Impt as my *drut*. - Of course, we shan't marry either, so you mustn't feel cast down – disparaged - nothing of that sort. You see, of course, that I couldn't tie myself now, in any case, to a papist. Leave alone a murderer.'

An orange hit Foulque in the back, and the whole room burst out laughing, a deafening, crescendoing Babel of collapsed sobriety. He was the butt of a joke. The Lady Aude had never intended to marry him. And what a topical joke she had made of it! The lady was to be congratulated with laughter and applause.

It did not seem possible that Foulque should know who had thrown the orange. And yet when he drew his sword and flung out the full reach of his arm as he turned, the flat blade caught the very man across the face, leaving a white pennant edged with blood on his cheek. The room protested at Foulque's lack of humour. It also delighted in seeing the Railing Monk restored to character. The guests laughed and screamed alternately as he broke up the food and tableware all along the top table. Only when he lifted the board clean off its trestle and overturned it into the faces of Aude and Auxerre did they worry that some real harm might be done. The board was heavy and Aude lay pinned beneath it, her face as round and silver as the plates alongside it, her arms raised defensively.

'Come away, Foulque!' said Ouallada from the other end of the hall. 'Come away and be glad. Save your injury for your verses, man. You always meant to sing her through the land, didn't you? We can sing songs that'll make La Belle Aude famous through the Languedoc. The famousest whore ever to jilt an honest man. The silliest trollop ever to spit on salvation.'

They left to the shrill protests of Aude, her dress spattered with food and her hair pulled about by her own hands. 'You won't do that! He won't do that! He doesn't hate me, do you, Foulque? You've sworn to love me always, haven't you? Anyway ... one word about me and I'll tell how you murdered Barral for his land!'

Foulque turned and pointed at her with a gloved leather hand that silenced her with its sheer menace. 'Ah, but I didn't, you see. I am become a liar in your service, ma'am, but not, thank God, a murderer.'

Even after the door shut behind him, Aude continued her tirade – half-taunting, half-afraid - while the silver shimmered down from her face like moondust from the perfidious moon. 'Not one song, you hear? By all the Codes of Love, I forbid it! One slur and I'll know you never really loved me at all, deceitful man! Not one word, you hear? Either of you! Not a word from either of you. Well! Now we all know where the *Princess's* hopes are laid!'

CHAPTER TWENTY EIGHT

Ships of the Desert

He did not hear Aude's jibe. Ouallada heard it and was glad she had made her love so plain to Aude, but there was no possibility of Foulque hearing it. His ears were full of roaring, his vision blurred. The ground heaved under his feet and dissolved into something resinous and gummy, seething and bubbling, choking him with the acrid vapours of melting matter.

Ouallada tried to take hold of his arm to draw him away towards the horses, but he shook her off with such violence that she felt the sprain in her hand for days after. 'Don't touch me! Don't you know I'm come down from Satan? Don't you know I'm kin to the Devil himself? I do! I know it! I feel very present proof of it right here!' and he beat on his sternum as if he might dislodge the

Devil like a plumstone out of his windpipe.

'I don't see it. Satan would've given you more wit than to let the woman pillory you twice over.' She staggered under the weight of their joint luggage. 'Get on your horse, will you? Do let's leave this place.' The sound of laughter was still loud from inside the building: perhaps Auxerre d'lmpt was standing at the window now, giving commentary on the last antics of Aude's court fool.

'Go to Hell,' he told Ouallada.

'And meet your ancestors? No thank you.' She ran and fetched his horse to him, and put the reins in his hand and flicked the ends in his face. 'You have estates to see to ... You've no business to keep you here. With these Cathars. With these *Zoroastrians*.'

He gave another roar and then, like an animal trapped in a net, submitted to helplessness. Once in the saddle, he dug in his heels and rode at a gallop until it seemed he would kill the horse beneath him as proxy for La Belle Aude. When Ouallada caught him up, he had come to a final halt at the crest of the hill overlooking Beziers town. The distressed breathing of his animal cut twin craters in the ground and raised plumes of red soil which stuck to the sweat streaking its cheeks. There was foam in Foulque's beard, too, and his eyes were bloodshot with the sheer exertion of hatred. He stared ahead of him without seeing the rise and plunge of the green, oceanic landscape.

Ouallada stopped a short way off 'What will you do now?' she asked.

'Hunt whale out of Bayonne.'

'With your bare hands, I don't doubt it. And after you've extinguished all the whales?' She waited a long time for him to speak again.

'Go back. Sue for re-admittance. To the *vita apostolica.*'

'Go back to being a monk? I think I preferred the whaling.'

'Well? Why not? How did I profit from quitting the Church?' he said, adenoidal with sarcasm. 'Tell me that, if you can.' Then he waved her foolishness aside with one hand. 'Oh, I don't mean go back into cloisters. Events have rather robbed me of that for a peaceful bolthole, haven't they? But a fighting bishop ... I daresay the Bride of Christ won't turn down a dowry the likes of Nerra's salt. I'll bribe my way back. My lands are probably my one great entrée back into God's livery.' He was blushing as he said it. In truth he was neither sure of the Church welcoming him back nor his wish to be re-submerged under brown monastic mud.

'Don't do it,' she said. It was an abject request. She dared not look him in the face when she made it, but let her eyes rest on his horse which had begun to shiver as it cooled in its sweat. She shivered in fellow-feeling with the horse.

'Ah! I see.' He coughed awkwardly. Nothing in the big world had accustomed him to the etiquette of giving and asking for gifts. 'Naturally I shall make good to you such possessions as you've been ... parted from by recent events. Instruments. Clothes ... A house somewhere, maybe. If I'm allowed possession of my lands, there are some in Normandy, I hear tell. You're welcome to 'em. Normandy. Ha! What man would ever want to find himself in Normandy, for God's sa... I really must make shift to clean up my language before I confess my sins to my Prior.'

'And do you think that'll be enough? For him to grant you absolution? For impersonating a priest?'

'Oh, for that ... I daresay. There's a penance to cover most crimes in these forgiving days.' He made the times sound like the heyday of Sodom and Gommorah.

'What do you mean, *"for that"?*' she burst in angrily. 'Whatever else have you done wrong? The world's full of monsters, but you go on thinking you're the worst man ever to draw breath!' She was horribly certain that the Church would take him back - embrace him in the lighted doorway, then shut the door against her. He looked at her in alarmed astonishment, unable to understand what new offence he had committed. 'I'm sorry, Foulque. Pay no notice ... May I go with you?'

'To visit my Prior-Confessor? I don't think ...'

'Just to have company on the road, I mean. With my hair, you see ... Until my hair grows down, I'm neither one thing nor another, and I'm loath to go back to "wand'ring the world", as they say, until I'm more plainly the shape of a person.' She jostled and bustled him into agreeing, with a torrent of barely comprehensible reasons for not being left behind. None was the truth, but then the truth was no longer compatible with Foulque's future life.

'It's not quite so simple, my son,' said the Prior of the Premonstratensians at Toulouse.

'Is it not?' said Foulque. 'I ventured into the dark forests of the world and found them full of wild beasts. So I've returned to the shelter of Castle Church wiser and more penitent than I formerly was. It seems the most logical ... '

'Ah, logic,' said the old man, as if it were not a subject of his immediate acquaintance. 'Tell me truthfully, Foulque, what do you think of the English *lex episcopi*?'

'As little as possible.' He scowled obdurately, a weighty, immovable object of furniture in the centre of the round, bare room, while the Prior walked around him, frail and pale and agile. He was a white haired, wraithlike man, his arms bare and fleshless, his open-weave habit showing a shadow of similarly cadaverous legs. He unravelled conversation from within himself, spun his arguments like one of the spindly spiders that weave their webs in the corners of windows, pale to be indistinguishable from the light. And yet Foulque was in awe of him. The slight jingling of his metal accoutrements were witness to the uncomfortable shifting of weight on his haunches.

'Oh, come now, Foulque, you're not among your wits and sophists now. Consider the English attitude to crime. Manslaughter punished by banishment - at the very worst. A priest seduces a girl then kills her father when he complains - and what's his punishment? To carry a small brand through life to boast of his immunity. No mutilations. No executions ... '

'They'll meet with impartial justice on Judgement Day,' said Foulque petulantly.

'And so you think all's well in England.'

Nerra wrestled visibly with the temptation to condone the corrupt English episcopal system, then remembered, only just in time, that it was the sin of the Lie which above all had driven him back to the refuge of the monastery. 'You're right, of course, Father. But what are you saying? What's England got to do with it? You mean

a cleric ought to pay for his crimes? You know me, surely?
I'm content. The branding iron holds no terrors for me:
God knows I've got no looks to mar. And mutilation
might've come to me any time in battle. If that's all that
stands between me and readmission ... '

'You're right, Foulque, I do know you. You're a man
who doesn't just bear with suffering, you invite it. All
your life you've been trying to atone for other people's
suffering by mortifying your own spirit.'

'Oh, now that's cra- ... arrant nonsense.'

'Is it?'

'Well? Aren't we all supposed to atone for Christ's
suffering?' and his metal jingled like the hawfrost on a
blackthorn.

'Christ's, yes. But your earthly father's?'

'That's a damned - ' The two men looked at one
another, acknowledging what a gulf had opened up since
the outraged young philosopher had stormed out of his
cloister accusing the Church of wilful ignorance.

'That temper of yours,' said the Prior at last. 'I'd as
soon you offered up that violence inside you, Foulque
Nerra. Offered it up, and left it behind you, buried in the
soil of some useful cause. Then come back and tell me if
I may absolve you of your broken vows and your crime of
impersonation.'

'I never broke my vows of chastity, Father. Except in
contemplation, maybe. And if I'm re-admitted, all my
estates will be knit to the Church.' But it was the last-
ditch defence of a defeated man.

'Pray don't try to bribe me, sir!' said the Prior,
suddenly filling the room with the authority of anger.
'And though you may not have broken your chaste vow,

you have most certainly broken the Commandments most venially!'

Foulque was too shaken to speak, though his lips formed the word 'How?'

'In swearing your love for a certain young woman over and above your love of God. *The Lord saith, Thou shalt have no other god before Me. And thou shalt love the Lord thy God with all thy heart and with all thy soul and with all thy might!* Do not suppose, *'Bishop'* Foulque, that because the Church presently abjures the pursuit of science, it goes entirely ignorant of everything in the outside world. I have kept trace of you, my young fellow, and I know your comings and goings, your risings up and your sittings down!'

There was another protracted pause in which the motes afloat in the sunbeams flurried and swirled then sank slowly downwards into a restored quietude. 'What do you want me to do? Do you have a particular "cause" in mind?'

The Prior at long last seated himself on the stool opposite Foulque's, tidying his habit over his knees and breathing out deeply to exhale the demon Anger. 'You're aware that Saladin has offered the Franks a truce.' It was a startling change of subject.

'I know we refused it, too. We thrashed him at Montsigard in seventy-seven and now the Templars have made an alliance with the Assassins, we're better placed to beat him than ever.'

The Prior winced. It was not received Church opinion to approve of the Templars' wild alliances, made without reference to Pope or King. 'Do try to think like a good Catholic, Foulque, even though it comes not as second nature to you ... Anyway, there are other reasons why we refused a truce - reasons which even you may not know of. There are raids planned on the Lakes of Suez, for instance. One on Taima in Hejaz. And one by Reynaud de Châtillon.'

'The Prince of Antioch.'

'Well, formerly, yes. He's the Prince Consort of the Lady Eschive of Transjordan now. But you have the man, clearly. His sight is set on Mecca and Medina.'

'Is it, by Christ!'

'No, Foulque, by ship, although I trust by. Christ's inspiration. He is constructing ships now in the Crac of Moab.'

'That must be thirty miles from the Dead Sea!'

The Prior laughed softly, dabbing his mouth with a square of cloth. It was plainly an effort for him to suppress a lively interest in the politics of Outremer and a pleasure in surprising even Foulque Nerra. 'But Mecca and Medina are not on the Dead Sea, you recall. He is headed for the *Red* Sea. Carrying his fleet by camel. When I heard tell of it - no, don't ask how - I thought at once of you.'

'As the only other lunatic of your acquaintance.'

'As a man with a partiality for hopeless quests.'

'Carry a fleet across a hundred miles of desert?'

'You see? The prodigious folly of the project commends itself to you already. The narrow possibility of success. Confess it.'

'It can't succeed! What when he gets there? Where can he make a base? How many men does he have?'

The Prior shrugged. 'You have the full sum of my intelligence. But since you're clearly afire already with the venture, I rest my case, Foulque, and I decline to readmit you to Holy Orders. Visit me when you return. If you return. I do like to hear of these things.' He got up and went towards the door. 'I'll appoint a steward over your estates until such time as the matter is decided."

'Wait! Father! Send me on martial pilgrimage without absolution? All right, I agree! But you won't reinstate me before I go?'

The Prior looked at him with ill-concealed affection - his protégé - that darker, more virile side of himself, roaming the world beyond the singing purity of the cloister. He raised his hand in benediction. '*Absolo te*, Foulque Nerra-des-Etangs. But for many, many years I used to do that daily. And I never once saw you lay aside your guilt. No, not once, though a thousand angels bellowed their forgiveness at you through a thousand trumpets. And I do not - I repeat not – re-admit you yet to Holy Orders. Go away. Go somewhere. Do something to make you like yourself the better. *Au revoir*, though we meet next in Heaven.'

'*Au revoir,* Father, though we meet next in Heaven.'

Ouallada was sitting on the grass outside, her back against the monastery wall, watching the bees carry their *trobar* compliments from flower to flower, wandering the silly *trobar* round, being kissed bare of their golden pollen by the lascivious labia of field orchids. Foulque had gone into the monastery, leading his horse behind him. If re-admitted, there was no actual need for him to come out-of-doors again: not unless he was sufficiently aware of her presence to remember that she was sitting there, waiting to hear the outcome.

When he came back through the gate, his led horse stretching out its neck, slipping on the stone flags at the pace of their departure, he did in fact look at her as if she were an unforeseen complication. 'I am sent on a penance of martial pilgrimage. To Jordan,' he said peremptorily. 'I must levy a few good men out of the étangs.'

'May I come too?'

'Don't be ridiculous.'

'I can use a sword!'

'I've seen the level of your fighting prowess, if you recall ... And before you say it, I have no need of music.'

'Everyone has need of music.'

'I can make my own, then.'

'Not as good as mine, for all you're the better poet.'

'The camel is largely deaf to the Frankish scale, I believe.'

'I wasn't going to sing for the camels ... And I can spy.'

He paused, one foot in the stirrup, to turn and look at her. He had quite forgotten she was a Moor. .

She said brazenly, 'Well? Wasn't I born in Outremer? It's time I went back there. Why shouldn't you benefit from the services of a squire? And one who can pass hither and yon among the enemy. A runner. An ecurie.'

'You have the tongue?'

So it was for this that her father had bred her to be a liar. Not so that she could survive and thrive, but so that she could pitch herself into a foreign desert and be buried by dunes in the company of strange animals and stranger men. So that she could look Foulque Nerra in the eye and say, without compunction, 'Naturally, I speak it.'

'What when your hair grows down?' he huffed, bad-tempered to the last.

'Shan't it grow as I tell it?' she retorted. 'It's my hair.'

He mounted up, letting his crotch slap down into the saddle as men always mount at the start of a long expedition. He looked her up and down, and conceded, in the most graceless way he could find to concede, 'It's true, you have no breasts to speak of If you choose to go, there's nothing I can do to turn you off - Only I warn you: it's a madman's plan, for the prize of a few days' glory and a sure death.'

She looked him in the eye and said, with the conviction of a life-long liar, 'It's time I sought out my own kind. I can always leave you along the way.'

The Crac of Moab stood far beyond the Jordan, on the borders of the Kingdom ·of Jerusalem and Transjordan. By the time Ouallada and Foulque and his small muster of Camarguais knights reached those ancient lands of Gilead and Ammon, the fleet was all but complete. A dozen woodwall galleys lay about piecemeal, a keel here, a mast there, and acres of curved plank pallets which would one day join together into hulls. Camel dealers were arriving earlier and earlier in the day with larger and larger strings of camels. The news was out that Reynaud was buying livestock.

Reynaud Châtillon proved to be no idealistic hothead, either. Though he spoke of raiding Mecca and Medina, his vision of victory incorporated the seizure of Bab el Mandeb, thus taking control of international trade routes between Egypt and Asia. He had had seven teen years, as a prisoner-of-war, to formulate his plan, and although it was audacious, it was not beyond all credibility. The rewards of success would be materially immense.

Reynaud was also a born pirate, and felt the need to break out of his small dry princedom, to pillage somewhere salt-wet again.

He took it hard that Foulque should know of his plan and expect to participate. He at once assumed Nerra wanted a half-share of the prize, and to share Reynaud's throne with him on the shores of the Red Sea. But Reynaud needed the manpower, so he agreed to tolerate the man's presence.

The fact that Ouallada was still with the Frankish party when it reached the Crac of Moab owed much to her art of keeping silent. Foulque did not exactly lose sight of her among the impedimentia of battle, but she became no more than one moving shape in a caravan of moving shapes all corrugated by rising heat, reduced to a black anonymity by the brightness of the sun.

At first, before her disguise was proven effective, she felt in more danger from her fellow countrymen than the raiders behind the rocks or the scorpions under them. They talked about women like a strain of unreliable, disease-ridden cattle, and had nudes painted on their shields 'that they might always be under their mistresses in Jordan as they had been in France'. They grew mawkish and wept when she sang, but then it was a form of relaxation, to cry; it washed the dust out of a man's eyes.

There was little time for rest at Moab, but Ouallada was glad of that. There were women there, and baths. Women are more observant than men: less easily convinced that a page is male, just because she claims to be. In the event, the only comment which Ouallada raised among the women (for all she sang nightly) was a word of regret, that Bishop Foulque should prove a pederast. Such a very striking man, and so stirring in his warlike *sirventes*. How might he have moved the ladies if he had had a mind to!

'What d'you mean, he's a sodomite?' Reynaud de Châtillon snarled at the Lady Eschive. 'He's in love with some heiress in the Languedoc. His squire told me.'

'Well, then, why does he never sing of her? And why does he keep that pretty black squire so close? It's plain the boy's sighing after him. Boys don't do that without encouragement.'

Châtillon, who had observed none of this, herrumphed through his gout-misshapen nose - a habit his wife said he had picked up from the camels. 'Certainly they do. There's a dozen boys've idolised me in my time. Beside, it doesn't signify. There's plenty fighting men obliged to take their comfort where they can. It don't signify their breed.'

Even so, he kept closer watch after that on the squire who sang so very sweetly about a France Châtillon barely knew. He took more interest, too, in the fighting cleric, for fear he endanger the expedition with any sins too objectionable to God. There proved no truth in Lady Eschive's scurrulous imaginings. Though Foulque's jongleur did look fondly at him from time to time, the irascible old bear never looked back.

'Give us a song about your lady-fayre,' Châtillon suggested mischievously.

But Foulque only said; 'My mistress is the war, Prince,' and sang a *sirventes* instead.

The journey south was a jaundiced fever - a yellow

miasma of sand, and a sweat that crawled with imperceptible slowness over the ridges and dunes of the earth's body. The camels, stacked with the sections of ships, looked like huge living engines of war, half-hide, half-wood; monsters of a strange, exotic anatomy with prowed sternums above their heads and bony excrescencies bulging from their flanks. The scorching updraught melted their legs into insubstantial trickles of brown, so that they seemed to float over the sand, shipwrecks being shifted from one resting place to the next by each successive tide of heat.

Châtillon tried to travel at night rather than day. Then the sound of the fleet was just as unnerving, the creak of spars and leather, the chankling of bridles and the jingling like treasure of sacks full of nails, bolts and dowelling plugs. The fleet went dressed overall with knightly pennons never stirred by breeze, only by the refraction of troubled light. Some of the weaker beasts foundered, driven feetfirst into the sand by sheer overloading. One was throttled when the ropes securing its cargo held fast and the superstructure itself capsized. Three stampeded away, dragging their handlers like sea-anchors.

Bedouins rose out of the sandy swell and attacked this phenomenon of walking carpentry. The raiders saw nothing they coveted but a platoon of camel and several dozen chain-mail byrnys. The wood, they supposed, was another Christian haul of True Crosses, or Noah's ark rediscovered yet again.

The bedouins along the desert trails had no largescale vision of politics or war and did not pass on what they had seen. They felt no allegiance to the general Arab cause which despised them as gypsies. Some even joined the expedition, as guides.

The wooden walls bleached. The rolled sails filled with sand and grew heavier than cabers of timber. The sharp-tipped nails bored holes through their hessian bags and trickled away like flecks of dried blood. At night, as she lay with her face to the fire and the camels knelt in the sand, Ouallada dreamt she was sleeping in the ruins of some neolithic earthworks with broken wooden pallisades, and that the pallisades were falling in on her, crushing her legs. In the morning, her legs even bore the bruises. The blood vessels broke beneath the surface of the skin and day by day darkened into yellow and purple mottling. It looked as if her legs were turning into leather, and the texture of the skin was as rough and scuffed as a pair of long-boots. She loathed herself.

Bad enough that Foulque should have seen her shaven-headed and reduced to a beast in the arena, armed with horn. But for him to see her in the very process of decomposition, before her soul had even fled her body, made her cry helpless, wasteful tears - tears that only added to her body's thirst, tears that rolled down and stung the open sores around her mouth. Perhaps females shrivelled and dried up much faster than males under a desert sky.

Ouallada kept silent, ran no risk of letting her legs be seen, showed no sign that the jolt of her horse's every stride felt like so many nails hammered into her flesh. She saw the sores flaring round Foulque's mouth as a wicked injustice to him. Her own she also saw as an affront to him and kept at a distance, he on one side, she on the other of that moving pageant of bizarre floats.

Long before Aqaba was reached, the singing had stopped. Tongues were too dry, lips too cracked, and the desire for sleep too great. The caravan lapsed into a deeper and deeper silence. Often a man would not speak from one day's end to the next, his thoughts all sunk in the accomplishment of the journey. Ouallada practised the juggling she had done as a child, but with knives now instead of balls or cups. The blades cut through the air making bright crescents in imitation of the moon, sparkling with the reflection of the stars, bloody with the red light of the fires. The camels watched her superciliously, their legs folded under them like paraplegics discharged from the army. She too expected her legs to snap off at the hip any day now. She was a tree dying back from the trunk, all her leaves withering, all the sap retracting to the core.

'Oh Christ, my legs!' said Reynaud de Châtillon suddenly, his voice booming across the desert. 'Another day of this and I'll never walk again!' The murmured assent grew into a communal groan, and fifty men eased themselves gingerly in their saddles, gratified that they were not alone in their affliction.

Next day they were in the Bay of Aqaba, standing on an empty beach, paralysed by the sheer anticlimax of success. No army of opposition lay among the couch grass of the dunes; no fleet of sails out at sea greeted the flap of their bleached banners. A flotsam of broken fishing-pots and fraying twists of rope were the only signs of life. A sea so seemingly viscous as never to break or foam, pressed itself against a few bare mottled legs, the knights lifting up their mail byrnys and white surcoats like maidens coyly raising their skirts. Seagulls shouted, rose up into the air, but re-settled farther down the beach.

The gulls were the only witnesses to the assembling of Châtillon's fleet amid the pitchy smell of hot caulking, the hollow percussion of ten thousand nails being driven home. The Prince-Escort of Crac of Moab prowled among the great ribs of his fleet, stepping from spar to spar, like Jonah in his whale. Foulque Nerra-des-Etangs, on the other hand, was arranging for barrels of seawater to be boiled free of their salt so that the shipwrights might have something to drink in the midday heat. He got no thanks, since the desalination process smacked of science and was therefore thought to be ungodly. Many would not drink what he brought them, and one knight told him that, as a cleric, he ought to know better.

They took the island offshore - Jazirat Far'un - opposite the city of Aqaba itself. And from there they conducted a ferocious *razzia* out along the coast. Raids on ports and forays to pirate ships from under Egyptian merchants astounded an enemy unable to guess where their attackers had come from.

On the eve of setting sail from Jazirat Far'un, Foulque abruptly said to Ouallada, 'You'd best stay behind.'

The terror permanently swarming within her like bees increased to a roaring in her ears. 'Please, no!'

She did not know what she had done to deserve such a punishment. Had she not walked a plank one span wide over water more alive than any river or lake she had ever seen? Had she not put out from shore and felt solid timber creak and reel under her feet as she rode over fantastical kingdoms of sea snakes and shark? Had she not concealed her sea-sickness like a pregnant whore, so that he should think her stronger than the men who retched over the ship's side? Had she pretended so hard to be familiar with the vast, brawling sea only to be marooned on an island and left behind?

Foulque did not directly accuse her of being a woman, but he muttered gruffly, 'You lack the skills.' He was pulling on his byrnys. The mail mittens wagged above his head like hands waving goodbye. 'You'd be an impediment. You'd do as well to stay here and wait for us to come back.'

'And will you do that? Come back? You won't come back this way!' she said.

His head was inside the hauberk: he felt able to say, without apology, 'Probably not. Châtillon means to move on from place to place. Raid and run. Egypt. The Hejaz. On to Medina across the Hejaz desert.'

'Then why say I should wait for you?'

He seemed in difficulties. 'Wait for news. I meant wait for news. Naturally, if Medina falls, you may want to ... renew your acquaintance with us. We'll all be rich enough then. You said you might leave us once you got among your own kind.'

She went and tugged on the long tails of hissing mail until he was able to shrug the last folds down over his shoulders, and his head emerged close to hers - the unshaven cheek, the dishevelled grey curls, the big purple vein pumping in his throat. He settled the cowled collar of mail more comfortably around his neck, not turning his face full on to hers when he glanced at her. 'I wish my hair would grow as readily as yours,' he mumbled. 'You'd best do something about it again.'

'Do you have no faith at all in Châtillon's plan?' she

asked.

After a moment he said, 'As God wills it. But no. No, not a lot.'

Ouallada returned to where instruments lay strewn about, her reeds in pots of water, the leather connections in tubs of oil like old rheumatic joints. 'I should like to rest,' she admitted. 'My legs ...'

'Mmmm. Yes.'

'You too?' She was surprised. He had never mentioned being troubled by the mysterious malady.

His white surcoat fluttered over him like a fall of snow obliterating a fortress. 'Oh, nothing that a taste of sea air won't right,' he said dismissively and picked up his mace. 'So. You stay and have a rest. Integrate. Settle. For a time anyway. You can have my share of the Egyptian loot. Would be against my vows to keep it, you see,' he added hastily. It was as if he considered himself a monk again already.

'I can cook.'

'What?'

'Or stir the blood with rousing music.'

'I really don- '

'Whither thou goest, I shall go.'

If a fellow knight had said it, he would have understood it perfectly. Knightly comradeship was as binding as religion. But coming from a woman it bewildered him.

Seeing the uneasiness in his face, she lost the courage to speak of love. She had come as close as she dared to her declaration. So she explained away her eagerness to go with him with yet another lie. 'I can't stay here. They'd

kill me for a collaborator. You look at me and see black.
They would see mixed blood. You forget. I know these
people. Shall we go aboard now? I do so like to be at sea.'

CHAPTER TWENTY NINE

In the Hejaz

Like Vikings they pitched through the coastal ports of Egypt. Like Goths they destroyed and pillaged the coppery bazaars and marble villas. The smoke behind them smelt of sweet, spicy fragrances, each looter dropping more than he had ever owned. The tarry, seamed bellies of the ships strained with a gluttony of plunder - so much so that it endangered Châtillon's long-term plan. Then hiding their booty in insecure citadels, with untrustworthy guardians, they travelled on into the Hejaz desert.

'Some of their wealth Reynaud spent buying the loyalty of bedouins to guide him, for there were no maps, either Christian or heathen, to make sense of the shifting landscape. After the sea, where the wind and currents had been their allies, the desert was a hostile enemy. It shortened their stride, it slowed their step, it tripped them and filled their clothing with a worthless gold-dust. The bedouins fawned on them face-to-face, but spoke in low voices among themselves, at camp fires of their own, laughing in short, sharp barks as their eyes darted towards the Franks. They renegotiated the price of escort time and again, watching where the money was fetched from as if to rescue it from the vultures after the Franks had become carrion.

Châtillon's troupe had certainly become a strange sight. The success of the *razzia* had decked out plain knights in silver and gems with glittering bridles and footcloths of ludicrous delicacy. Their saddles were bossed with copper, and their horses' tails knotted with ribbons which quickly became tangled, stringy and of a uniform dung colour. Their clothing grew increasingly Egyptian, each man binding a turban round his *châpeau de fer* to keep the sun from heating it to incandescence. Even Foulque adopted the kefieh to keep his brains from scalding, though his puritanical plainness showed itself plainer and plainer along-side so much conspicuous wealth. His only treasure, pillaged from the bazaars of the coast, was of musical instruments - syrinxes, rahabs and zejels - which he seized ostensibly for his half-caste jongleur but on which he, as often as not, impaled the tedious hours of their endless journey. The sinful science of music still held its allure - a thing he would have confessed had there been anyone to hear his confession. As it was, he was pressed, against his better judgement, to absolve the sins of rapists, gamblers, fast-breakers, oath-breakers, sodomites, gluttons and dying men, none of whom truly repented anything but leaving' Aqaba for the Hejaz.

Ouallada did not make her confessions to him. They would have shocked him. Though she believed herself to be dying, cankering from the feet upwards as her legs turned into leather, only the Christian half of her felt condemned. The other strain - the African - thrived in the African sun. They had always told her there was more wickedness in her than in white women. She had not questioned it then, and now she knew it to be true. Now, when she saw Foulque pull off his coif, she wanted to taste the sweat that trickled down his throat. When he sat in his white undershirt, the sleeves rolled back to the elbow, she wanted to finger the black hairs of his forearms and curl up in the angle between his thighs, and rest her head against the quilting of the gambeson he wore beneath his mail. Whereas she had thought she loved him for the virtues of his character, now she found her imagination was filled with his nakedness, with an unignorably blatant lust which made her blush when he looked at her, and prickle with heat whenever he passed close by. In fact she earnestly believed him to be wrapped in some corona of fire, for she knew when he was standing behind her, knew when he was absent. The magic even extended to his name, for when she heard it mentioned, the words alone made her heart contract and her pupils dilate and her fingers rush to hide themselves in her disgraced hair. She did not deceive herself: she was not of the *trobar* breed. Abstinent passion brought her no spiritual fortitude, no mystical energies or courage. Whereas a chivalric man would have grown stronger by the torment of *ascesis,* she felt more exhausted by each successive day, like a plant in terracotta attempting to grow and finding itself rootbound, choked. On the contrary, if she could have closed her mouth over his, she was sure she could have drunk in the succour to keep her from a desert death.

Almost unbelievably, they found themselves within a few days' march of Medina. Châtillon was almost hysterical with the success of his project. But though his army was still large - still threw up a column of sand behind it by day and of torchlight by night - no one knew how he thought to capture the city of Medina for God, for Fame, or for any longer than a day. Some of the ships had been broken up and reconstructed into siege engines. But they were such an impediment to Châtillon's speedy progress that they had had to be abandoned, left stranded on sand-dunes. He had left men behind, too - those wounded, those sickening of the heat, those who questioned the wisdom of the attempt on Medina.

Thus Prince Reynaud hasted towards his magnificent impossibility. Surprise was worth a thousand siege engines, he said. And since they had surprised themselves so much already, might they not surprise Medina all the more? With the smell of sandalwood and cinnamon already drifting to them from the city, the army of Reynaud de Châtillon struck camp, half the men singing a Kyrie, the rest competing with a Gloria, hurling the music at one another like abuse.

Ouallada had slept late. Generally she dressed early (inasmuch as anyone dressed or undressed) so as to smother her shape in baggy outer garments. Generally she rose before the knights, rose even before Foulque, though he was the first of the fighting men to get up and pray. Not this morning. She woke late, so waited wrapped in her blanket on the ground, until all the men cabined by the windshields had sauntered away to their horses. All but Foulque. She waited a little longer, looking up at a cobalt sky, while the heat of the coming day seemed to swell out of the ground, billow down the canopy of the sky, incandesce the barren hills to either side.

Not that she had to conceal her sex from Foulque. But she did not want him to see the ugliness of her legs, their yellow and purple varicose geology of pain, or the effort it cost her to pull on her short-boots. Besides, her lust had made her, like Eve, ashamed to go uncovered. So she waited for him to stir, watching the silhouette of his body and face as though it were her skyline. His eyes were open and yet he did not get up. He did not see her watching him; his eyes were fixed on the sky above him. It occurred to her suddenly that he was dead and she sat bolt upright and shouted his name.

Caught unawares, and flustered, he sat up as suddenly as she and, clasping the sleeves and body of his unfastened gambeson, he got to his feet. But he promptly fell sideways again, sprawling in the sand.

'Foulque!' She sloughed off her blankets and ran, though he was already waving a dismissive hand in front of his face. 'This heat. Too quick to my feet.'

But his legs would not hold him. 'Cramp,' he said. 'Cramp, that's all,' but he did not rub in the angle of his knees, and when she began to do so, chafing her hands over the quilted leggings, he pushed her away with a violence that was not modesty or bravado but plain, undisguisable pain. 'Don't touch me, for Christ's sake.'

He caught sight of her own legs - looked while endeavouring not to look. 'You too, then,' he said. 'It's damnable, isn't it? This desert worm?'

She tried to help him up, his arm over her shoulder, but he was too heavy for her and she only fell, with him on top of her. The desert sky to either side of his head put on vulture wings of blue. Châtillon left behind his impedimentia - stranded his useless fighting machines in the desert when they became more handicap than advantage.

The sailcloth windshields rattled between the poles rammed home into the sandy dirt, screening them for the present from the others. But at any moment, the ordnance crews would rip the screens down. Foulque's immediate fear was the shame of being found out: a chevalier incapable of mounting up. Again and again he told Ouallada to fetch his horse, fetch it so that he might pull himself into the saddle. But she was preoccupied only with her stupidity: she who had watched him night and day; she who had concealed her own discomfort for fear he thought less of her. 'I didn't see! I didn't realise! I never knew!'

'I should hope not!' The monk in him was still aghast at letting slip his private gift of pain. It was a thing to be borne with fortitude and offered up to God, a thing he should never have allowed to be seen. He dragged himself towards the billowing screens, filling his clothes with sand, and grasping a pole, he pulled himself to his knees. His face, grey and mask-like, he quickly found it unbearable to squat, and leant forward on to his fists, panting like a dog. She saw that there was nothing she could do for him so kind as to roll his gambeson up over his shoulders and help one arm at a time into its sleeves. But when she fetched him the mail shirt (which he rolled at night for safety and slept with under his head) they were both obliged to admit that its weight was an impossible burden. It lay between them as they knelt face-to-face, each leaning on the unstable, flapping windshield. Little by little, the realisation came to him that he was incapable of continuing on to Medina, except as a passenger.

Suddenly, the face of an *equipeur* appeared over the sailcloth and asked leave to collapse it.

'Never mind that,' said Ouallada brusquely. 'The Lord Foulque is ill. He needs a litter. See to it.'

The youth looked Foulque up and down, blowing out his cheeks at the enormity of the request. Then his face disappeared from sight. The windshield rocked to and fro in the soft ground, until finally it listed so far that the whole desert beyond yawned into view.

The army was assembled, its knights mounted, its camels belching and roaring. Reynaud de Châtillon, resplendent in his newest white kefieh, ambled his horse towards Foulque. He was leading Foulque's mare by a headstall, the great mace dangling from her saddle as a swinging pendulum, its shadow moving to and fro on the bleached ground. 'An indisposition, monsieur?' he enquired with gratification.

'Of a few days,' replied Foulque. 'I shall catch up to you.'

'That would be best,' said Châtillon, smug at the thought of Medina's laurels falling on a single head - an unshared triumph. 'I would never forgive myself if I were to carry you into mortal danger when I might leave you safe behind me to recuperate.' He emphasised the words with gratuitous pleasure: *'carry you ... behind me.'* 'I'll leave you a guide to care for you.'

'I pass my men into your command, of course, temporarily,' said Foulque. 'My jongleur, too, as a chronicler of events to come.'

Châtillon inclined his head graciously. Then dropped the halter of Foul que's mare and returned to the head of his expeditionary force, the sole sun in his sky once more, untaxed by the difficult mathematics of dividing glory in two.

The soft ground muffled their departure like snow, but the dust and sand raised by their hundreds of hooves fell more like volcanic ash on to Pompeii - stifling, horrific, too much of an inundation to fend off with arm or hand. The two left behind were grizzled by it - their hair, their clothes, their lashes - and kept their mouths shut tight against the pervasive grit. Not one of the Camargue men stayed to express his loyalty, his good wishes, his esteem. Their heads were all too full of Medina.

But Ouallada did not go.

'I shall never be missed,' she said, checking over her empty clothes for scorpions before slowly dressing. 'Sir Reynaud has a poor ear for music, don't you find?'

Foulque struggled to deduce the motive behind her staying, but had not the mental energy to succeed. He simply watched from below lids heavy with dust, as she drank her morning ration of water - how the drops escaping at the corners of her mouth cut furrows through a mask cast in reddish sand. He could no longer remember how she had looked when they left Haut-Beziers. But there was another face he could remember, coated in silver and creamy with fard.

The bedouin left as their guide humbly suggested they return the way they had come. It was like suggesting a man return through life to the scenes of his greatest mistakes. No, said Foulque, was there nowhere closeby where a man might find hospitality? Was there no bedouin settlement? The guide expressed himself delighted: his own uncle was encamped nearby. He would go and ensure a welcome, and return. So the bedouin took the camel carrying Foulque's collection of musical instruments and promised to return by nightfall. They watched the sun glint on a copper-bodied tambour the shape of a ship's bollard as it rolled over and back, over and back on the camel's swaying rump, secured by a leather strap. The taut drumskin, stained by the grease of Ouallada's hands, gaped at them like a dirty face gazing back.

They knew he would not return, but it was not until nightfall that they admitted as much to one another. At last Ouallada began to pluck the windshields' poles out of the sand and to dismantle its component parts.

'What are you doing?'

'Making a travois,' she said. 'Can you read the stars for direction?'

'They say you deserve long life and prosperity ... but they aren't prepared to commit themselves in the present state of political uncertainty. And they have nothing whatsoever to say to a Premonstratensian.

'Damn you. I thought you studied astrology in your days of loose intellectualism. '

'Oh, I did. And I can name the constellations well enough. But to tell you where they stand in relation to

Bethlehem - or even Medina - I'd need the help of an unseasonal Christmas star. Didn't your mother reveal the secrets of the desert to you?'

'Only her breast,' said Ouallada irritably, lashing poles to the saddle of Foulque's horse by the stirrup leathers. The horse looked over its shoulder at her, baring its teeth, and swung its rump so that the sledge trailing insecurely behind it swung against her aching legs, broke free and fell flat amid plumes of moonlit sand. As she began again and again, she was sobbing with frustration and misery, while Foulque made no attempt to help her, but sat back serenely against a pillow of sand, watching the sky. An inundation of stars more stifling than the army's dust was precipitating on to the Hejaz desert.

In her exhaustion and fright she called him idle, ungentlemanly, a craven man who had given in to Fate, a man typical of his sex. How should she - a princess - know better than him how to construct a travois? Why shouldn't he do it? No! He saved his soft-skinned hands for plucking syrinxes. Not far from here lay Eden, sealed up and empty. When Eve and Adam were evicted, was it Eve who had carried the spade and hoe and built a sledge to carry the children? No doubt about it. Adam would have sat contemplating the apple core.

When the travois was finally rigged, she returned, keyed up to the sharpest excesses of bad temper to tell him that his carriage awaited him if he would only deign to mount it.

She found his eyes shut, his legs sprawled apart in the sand, his crucifix in one hand and a length of ribbon in the other, his arms crossed on his chest. And she realised that with her noisy and insensitive construction project she had interrupted the man's preparation for his own death. He had died unshriven, thousands of miles from the fraternity of saints who might have eased him, on a travois of plainsong, up among the friendly constellations of a French heaven.

She howled like a wolf. She fell on her knees and plucked at his clothing. She shouted his name into his face. She coiled herself, foetal, into the angle of ground between his elbow and his side, holding very still, hoping to snatch hold of the cart-tail of Death before it left her too far behind and alone.

No undertow sucked out her soul. No slipstream swirled her away to oblivion. Only the irreverent sound of the horse rattling its ears made her uncurl and look about her. No other living thing stirred, in any direction, as far as the moon could show her. No damning angel. No bullying father. Not one needling blade of grass. Not even God was there to disapprove. So she clasped both his hands, kissed his mouth, then lay her head on his chest.

Only after a matter of minutes did she hear the remote thud of a heartbeat, echoing through her head like departing cavalry. She knotted her hands in the sweat-stained gambeson and even lifted his shoulders a little way off the ground, so incensed was she at the everlasting unfairness of life. Even here - even in the bottom of night's cauldron, in the ashes of a burned-out landscape - there was no peace to be had. Even here, even before she was permitted to lie down and sleep the final sleep, she was saddled with trying to keep Foulque Nerra alive.

Without means of navigation, there seemed no

purpose in moving from the one spot: in a hostile wilderness it was as good a place as any. But then sheet-lightning flashed on the skyline. Any good crusader, any obedient pilgrim knew God's staff-of-office when he saw it. Lightning. She cursed the portent. She cursed Man's whole abject subjection to signs and symbols. Then she watched for the next flash on the horizon and set her face towards it and drew herself an arrow in the sand to follow after the flash faded.

She tried to drag him to the travois, but he was too heavy for her. So she leaned into the mare, backing her laboriously closer, until the stretcher lay alongside him, and somehow, by grubbing the sand and pebbles from under him, contrived to get him aboard it. All the while, she remained furiously angry, cursing inanimate objects, seeing malice in the whole material universe.

Little by little, as the work and the petrifying cold sapped her of everything, she perceived how useful the anger had been: a rattle to shake in Death's face: a burning branch to keep off the wolves of Night.

The night desert was peaceful. Its cold finally excised all thought from her brain. She crouched on top of Foulque's horse, steering it between the rocks and potholes that might roll and wrench the travois free of the stirrup leathers. And she composed verses that concerned bodies other than hers, other than his - bodies she remembered from a time so long ago that it lapsed almost into myth: as long ago as Haut-Beziers.

Shortly after dawn, one stirrup leather broke, throwing such a weight on the other that the saddle was dragged round under the mare's belly. The travois turned over completely, Ouallada was dumped to the ground between the horse's legs and run over by the empty tangle of poles and sailcloth as the beast took fright. She was dimly aware of the sound of something heavy and metallic rolling away into the shadows.

She got up and ran to Foulque; he was as hot and inert as a joint of meat fallen from a spit. He opened his eyes and looked at her, but he called her Aude and spoke Latin, and said that his Devil's blood was boiling in his veins, that his feet were turning to hooves. So she went after the horse, since there was better hope of fetching it back from its predicament than him from his.

It led her a chase over a rocky outcrop, goaded on by the poles and ropes clattering behind it and the elaborate saddle hampering both stride and breath. It led her through a heath of huddled *had* bushes and spiky aristida grass. It led her across a carpet of green colocynth, its fruit scattering their black seeds. It led her towards a grove of cypresses and acacia.

In the solid black disc of shadow beneath the dense acacia boughs, the horsemen were not immediately visible. They might have been goats or gazelles. When she saw that they were tribesmen, she still hoped they might be bedouin.

But she could not delude herself for long. Saracens on horseback shortened their reins but stood still and waited for Ouallada either to run or to approach. She walked forwards. Perhaps half a mile she covered before lying down on her face on broken ground, in the full glare of the sun, in front of the acacia trees and cypresses. Some part of her waited, listened while they called out to her in Egyptian Arabic. She hoped that perhaps her Moorish blood would make the language plain to her, like the Holy

Spirit translating tongues. She recognised the salutation they threw at her as the ones the bedouins used, night and morning. If only she could have memorised the correct reply. Instead she must feign deafness or say nothing at all, if they were to mistake her for a Moor. She raised her eyes to meet those of the lead horseman, seated on a chestnut stallion.

He wore a zardiya of shimmering silver laminae mail reaching to his feet but split to the waist to reveal stockings and leggings. His splint armour was chased with Arabic lettering and his *baida* inlaid too with golden writing, though the chain-mail which hung down over his face in battle was folded back now and hid much of the decoration. He raised his little convex shield, a baffle against the sun's dazzle and so light and pretty on his arm as to look ineffectual. A scabbard of red Moroccan leather hung from a cord round his neck, and the flattened pommel of the sword was inset with jewels. A *tabar* with semi-circular axe-head hung from his saddle. Here was Sheik Obeid ben Zefir come from out of her imagination: a fiction made flesh, a joke made by real life at the expense of the story-tellers. This was how she had always imagined the father of her invented childhood. Only now, confronted by a man whose language she could not speak, in a landscape whose insects she could not even name, did she finally surrender all hold on the title of princess. She shrank in the sand, in fact, to the dimensions of a dung beetle.

She said, 'I deliver up to you my life and confide in you the life of my friend yonder. Not for the price he warrants as a hostage, though God knows he might raise a great ransom - but chiefly as a poet. The world has too little beauty to spare his loss, and I have too little art to prevent it. Please help him.'

A general jabber of aggression greeted her French. But the officer on the chestnut only raised his shield a little higher to study a broader landscape. His jaw was cushioned from his chest by a huge bush of black beard and the rims of his eyes were so dark as to look painted, iconic - an impression assisted by the stillness of his features. The tip of his long, large nose, was pulled in tightly to overarch his moustache, much as his horse's short, handsome head was pulled close to its chest by a martingale. The movement of his lips barely showed amid the beard when he said, 'Your master is a poet?'

She praised God for the gift of tongues. She wanted to say, 'How do you speak French? Did God send you? Are you a Christian? Like me, a Christian?' But she curbed her speech into a pattern as formal and formulaic as the Psalms. 'He is. To any with ears and to all with hearts,' she said. 'As a hostage he would grace your hearth. When you've come to know him, you will barely want to part from his company, though the friends who crave his return are as many as the stars.'

'And you are? His squire or his son?'

'His jongleur merely. His singer of songs.'

The Arab drew his *saif* and examined its double-edged blade honed to an edge as thin and irregular as a nibbled wafer. The signals he gave his horse were invisible, but the stallion sprang forward as if to trample Ouallada. Its shadow splashed over her, cold as water. The Saracen tested his sword's sharpness in the air above her head. But though she drew in her fists to her body, she did not squeal or run: her legs would not have carried her, in any case. 'Come,' he said. 'Show me.'

She walked behind his horse, but pointed the way, telling herself it was not treachery, not real treachery to lead the enemy to where Foulque lay; telling herself she had no alternative. A covey of horsemen followed behind her - four horsemen armed with throwing lances: four, like the end of the world. The rest remained behind in the shady groves, the murmur of a hundred soft voices, the tinkling of a hundred bridles, and still the clicking of crickets was louder.

'Why do you walk so?' asked the Sheik, as Ouallada stumbled along, buckled as a cranefly. 'You have the Unbelievers' disease.'

'Would that I had more in common with my master,' she said.

'It hindered Reynaud of Châtillon and his companions, this sickness. '

When she did not respond, he asked her directly, 'Was your master valued so highly by Prince Reynaud that he was left behind to die?'

'If you ever meet the Prince, sir, pray upbraid him with it.' Her feet trod the black seeds of the colocynth into the soft ground. They moved through the aristida grass and passed between the *had* bushes to where Foulque lay sprawled in the dirt.

Even such a short absence was enough to shock Ouallada on her return: she had not realised to what depths of squalor the men of Châtillon's army had fallen. The mouth caked, the face parded with sores, the leather boots scuffed dry and crazed, everything eroded by the desert wind. Foulque had, in some moment of consciousness, dragged himself as far as his mace which had fallen from the horse when the saddle failed. His fist was closed around its chain, his face half-buried in the gravel. Lying within the shadow of the chestnut stallion, he was barely recognisable as a human being. Leave alone the wonder of the world.

'This is your master?' said the Saracen dubiously.

'Yes. Would that I were his equal as a poet. Then my words would make you hold his life as dear as I do.'

'And yet Reynaud de Châtillon left him behind.'

The four horsemen shifted their grip on the light, wood lances, to make javelins of them, lifting them to one shoulder. Ouallada went and stretched her body across Foulque's.

She felt the same thud of a heartbeat shaking her frame, except that this time the heartbeat was hers. 'Don't ask me to speak well of that particular man. All my praise is used up for my master. You must judge Reynaud for yourself'

'And how should I do that?' said Siddi Yusif as-Shafih al-Umdan. 'Salah-ed-din Yusif ibn Ayyub, ruler of Egypt, cut down the pirates of 'Aqaba last evening. As the corn before the reaper. May Allah ever thus dispose.'

CHAPTER THIRTY

The Enemy

'May Allah light the candle of pity in your heart to spare the life of Foulque of Nerra,' she said, as formulaic as in a troubadour's *tenson*. He did not reply directly.

'*Dabbus*,' he said, pointing at the mace. 'No sword. Your master is a rabbi, then - a holy man.'

'A priest, yes.'

'But a poet, too?'

'It's not impossible,' she said belligerently.

'No, no! Not at all: Sheik Yusif dismounted and, spreading his voluminous robes as wide as possible, plunged his head in among the festooned folds of black wool like a bird preening under its wings. 'There is the notable example of the Bishop of Clermont. And the Monk of Puicibot. - Even Foulquet of Marseilles after his great disappointment. Here. Have this. Eat it.' He produced from the magical depths of his cloak, a large orange - the first she had seen since' Aqaba.

Did he think she was a monkey to be tempted away from its master with a bright toy? She tucked down her head, refusing to move from shielding Foulque, refusing to make way for the *saif's* blade, for the sword-thrust through Nerra's defenceless body. He threw it to her and it rolled close to her temple, a shiny globe of gaudy colour. 'Eat it. It will help your legs. What you lack, young person, is fruit and greenstuff.'

'In that case, let it help my friend and master.' And she pressed it against Foulque's mouth, tore into it and squeezed the juice triumphantly into Foulque's mouth. 'There now! You've given him food! He's your guest. You can't harm someone you've fed. Isn't that right? You people? We people. You can't offend against hospitality. That's your religion!'

The Siddi Yusif was amused. His round jaw bounced on its cushion of black curls. 'Please. Please. I would call that merest good manners, young person, religion or no. And I have no intention of killing your master. I greatly prize poetry.'

The Siddi Yusif as-Shafih al-Umdan greatly prized not only poetry but literature in general - in the decoration of his ceilings with phrases from the Koran, in the mosaic perfection of his marble floors, in the lace-like handwriting and illumination work of his scribes. In his palace at Umdan eighty women were employed on copying manuscripts for inclusion in his library - a treasurehouse of two thousand books all bound in leather or kid. The only foul smell occasionally to reach Foulque's sick-room was the boiling down of camel hooves for their glue as a means of binding books.

'What's that smell?' said Foulque.

Though she knew he had been awake some time, she had allowed him to keep silent until he could orientate his thoughts, accustom himself to the room and to being alive. It was a strange enough prison cell. They had been allotted an airy room canopied with cotton cloth so that it had the feel of a tent, the continual flutter of a bivouac.

'Attar of roses,' she said. 'They say it's beneficial to health.'

'No, the other. There's another smell.'

She sniffed the air. 'Frankincense, I dare say. The Siddi Yusif trades in frankincense - up the Darb al-Haj to Damascus and Baghdad. And in mother-of-pearl to the furniture-makers in Bethlehem. When the ways are open, I mean. Can I fetch you anything?'

He did not reply, but sat up, his knuckles white where he grasped the edge of the bed-roll. He looked like a frail old bird of prey waking to find itself in a golden cage. 'This isn't Medina, then. I thought perhaps ... I don't recall ... We're taken prisoner, then?'

'And kept alive by the kindness of the Siddi Yusif as-Shafih. It's a place called Umdan.'

He let this knowledge percolate through the haze of nausea, pain and sleep, 'Any news of Châtillon?'

'His force was wiped out by Saracens the day they parted from us. Not Reynaud himself, they're saying now. But the rest. All the rest.' She concentrated fiercely on sewing together two pieces of leather, not looking his way. 'He's a remarkably civilised sort of a man, this one.

I've never met anyone quite like him ... And he's nursed you like a brother.' She broke to him, little by little, how Yusif had sent his physician with medicines of powdered gold and rose-jelly, had bombarded their quarters with oranges, limes and lemons, with sherbet drinks and Egyptian beer which, though he did not drink it himself, he thought might slake a Frankish thirst.

When she had finished, Foulque growled, with a kind of surly repugnance. 'Don't let's praise God's enemies too highly. I owe you an apology, Princess. I admit I used to doubt your claim to know the language hereabouts. My apologies. I always thought you had more the look of a Spanish Moor. Have you asked him what ransom he's seeking?'

'He said - I'd best try to remember it was very prettily put. He said that his hopes of gain travel no further than to see your health restored and to hear your poetry.'

'Tell him I'd sooner sing for the Devil ... and keep that robe tight closed, woman. God knows what end you'd come to in a place like this, if they knew your sex.'

The 'place' he spoke of with such ignorant disparagement did indeed harbour a harem. The gauzy, sugary scents of the women inside permeated all the corridors approaching that maze of filigree metal and pierced stone screens. Sometimes, when the afternoon heat silenced the palace at large, a murmur like bees in acacia would still drift from the cooler interior - that inner afforestation of columns less troubled by heat than the outer, male preserves. Two of his wives, said Siddi Yusif, were creditable poets - better than many men, he had told Ouallada, and sung their *maouchahs* in a high, clear voice.

'You should hear them, Foulque!' she reported back to him, in those first waking days when hers was the only face he saw. '*Maouchahs*. Little lyrics crammed full of rhymes. "Embroideries", they call themselves. And that's how they sound - so many threads interweaving. Even without understanding ... '

'But you *do* understand,' Foulque interrupted her irritably. 'You have the language, whereas I...'

'No.'

'What d'you mean, "no"?'

'I mean the Siddi Yusif speaks French. He keeps teachers to tutor him in all the languages: Italian, Greek. I don't ... it won't handicap you not to speak the language. And he asks if you won't match him line for line in a *tenson* this evening.

'She held her breath as he lay back on his bed, his scowl directed at the canopy, the arches and consoles sculpted with bas-relief animal heads and flowers. They were exquisitely beautiful. She could feel his struggle to make sense of the anomaly; how Moslem barbarity could be compatible with such beauty. 'Tell him I'll stir as far as to thank him for his trouble, but I won't make poetry with him.'

'You must not judge all Araby by the bedouin,' said Siddi Yusif that night. 'He is a savage. A Visigoth. An ignorant tribal lout interested only in fighting for the sake of the plunder it brings him. You will find the intellectual Moslem despises him. He - how do you say these things - he keeps his loyalty in his pocket. He can be bought.' He was leading them through the passageways of his long, pillared library, scuffing the heels of his cloth shoes as if to polish the floor by continual coming and going. 'Here we have the *Book of Similes* by Ibn Abi 'Awn; and here Abu Hilal al'-Askari's *Collection of Concepts.* And here some works of your own Marcabrun - my own struggling translations, I fear. Presently I am studying your Saint David's Book of *Psalms* - hence my interest in the *tenson* form. Though truly my chief art lies in the *casida.* You know of this? One rhyme throughout?'

'I've heard tell,' said Foulque. He walked between the shelves like a man in a dream - a man with gold-fever buried alive in a gold mine. Words were piled by the million to left and right of him. Knowledge, debate, poetry and science were ranged about him like siege engines ready to batter their way through his flimsy resolve. Ouallada could see that it frightened him, this glimpse inside the Enemy's armoury. The Christian army had Saint Norbert, preaching obedient simplicity. The Infidel had this.

'Naturally I admire Arnaud Daniel,' Yusif was saying, 'But then, of course, the *sestino* deals in conceits, and Arabesque literature places a great value on all things elaborated: the decorated phrase: the protracted metaphor ... Shall you sing for me, tonight, Lord Foulque Nerra-des-Etangs? Pray do not tax yourself if you are still frail. You have been very ill - scurvy, malaria. They are not shaken off like a quinsy. How are you feeling now?'

She knew exactly how he was feeling. She could read it in the way he held himself, shoulder raised belligerently, fists clenched behind his surcoat, his head jutting towards the spines of different books as though in search of the one titled in a language he understood. For decades Foulque had done battle with the Church, defending his greedy acquisition of knowledge like a beggar defending his plate.

'I don't believe that's possible, sir,' he replied. 'The state of enmity that exists between our two races forbids such fraternising.'

'Oh!' exclaimed Yusif, snatching apologies out of the air with both fists. 'Your sickness has been so long in the mending, and I have been remiss not to bring you news. A truce is agreed!'

'A truce?'

'Indeed! Indeed! You recall that Salah-ed-din Yusif ibn Ayyub extended the hand of friendship a while ago, but your rulers saw fit to refuse it? I daresay the ... misfortune met with by Sir Reynaud Châtillon's army has made them think again. A truce is agreed. So, my honoured visitor, pray consider yourself my guest. Your need for rest and recovery are all that prevent you from leaving my home.'

Foulque was powerless to know what to say. He considered the possibility that as-Shafih might be lying. He considered his own attitude to a humiliating truce. He considered the possibility of relating to his host as a fellow human being. All these dilemmas were written in his face. 'The King of England has nine books,' he suddenly blurted out, to everyone's surprise. 'Makes much of it, too. As proof of intellect and breeding.'

Siddi Yusif shrugged and made a gesture with his large hands which dismissed his library as valueless. 'A wise man may derive more from nine books than a fool from two thousand,' he said self-deprecatingly. 'I thank Allah hourly for entrusting such riches to such an unworthy custodian.'

Foulque was undermined by his illness, not only in strength but in resilience to the charm and courtesy of Siddi Yusif. If the man had merely been clever, then he could have been written off as a Faustus, a necromancer, an eater of the Tree-of-the-Knowledge-of-Good-and-Evil. But as-Shafih was deeply religious, rose in the middle of the night to pray, knew the Koran by heart.

'Such a waste to see a good man damning himself,' Foulque observed to Ouallada. 'Languishing in error.' But he did not preach to the heathen, for there was no resource of energy within him, no combative desire to do battle with the mullahs, to fell their prayer-spires with his Christian mace.

Just once, in *tenson*, Siddi Yusif began to praise Allah, and Foulque to counter in praise of God. But the psalmic structure soon made it seem as if they were lauding the same God:

'The Lord is the fountain of all Truth.'
'He who drinks shall have Life Everlasting.'
'His Law shall endure for ever.'
'For lo, He is with us even unto the end of time.'
'Thus will I sing praises to Allah!'
'It is our joy and our duty always and everywhere to give praise.'
'His hand is mighty on land and shore.'
'The winds and the waves obey him.'

It was Foulque who called a halt, finding the idea too blasphemous of error and truth interweaving themselves like a woman's plait.

462

But the more Foulque found to admire within the collonaded walks and peristyle courtyards of Umdan palace - and in Yusif himself - the deeper he sank into thought. One night, when he had sat experimenting with oriental scales, until each note dripped like water-torture on Ouallada's ear, he suddenly laid aside the gittern and said, 'Some of these religions make themselves right plausible, don't they?' She smiled compassionately and nodded. 'It's no wonder my Lady Aude fell prey to those Zoroastrians.'

'*What?*' She reeled as if he had pushed her.

'I mean, if a man the stature of as-Shafih can persist in Error, it's no wonder a cunning villain can turn the brain of a silly young woman. One with no experience of the world, I mean, is it? There's no sin in being misled, sure?'

'Then Eve didn't sin.'

But he was too busy re-opening a door he had locked shut within himself; too fascinated to find the key still in his pocket. Next morning he told Ouallada he had dreamed an Arthurian dream in which La Belle Aude was imprisoned by Falsehood in the Tower of Darkness, calling for the help of a pure knight. Though he was too sheepish to recount the dream in full, Ouallada read it in his face. Foulque's love, smothered (as she thought) to extinction, had flared up again into a blaze. Like a child rediscovering an old toy in the bottom of a chest, it brought him real delight. The laughter at his expense was forgotten, the treachery. The Aude of his imagining was beset by evil advisors whispering foul lies in her pretty ear. In short, he went back to loving Aude like a lost man finding his path again out of the desert.

'What do you think? What do you say?' he kept asking Ouallada, and for a few days she felt an exasperation with him that extinguished all her admiration. It was then that she felt the emptiness he had been feeling. It was then that she understood his preference - a chestful of passion in place of a gutful of ice. He was right. Better to be in love than out of it.

'What do you think, Princess? What do you say?' He pressed her time and time again.

'I think you're in danger of forgetting,' she replied frostily. 'Your Prior sent you here on a pilgrimage of atonement - to win re-admission to your Order. You don't sound to me like a man who wants to be a monk again.'

He flinched at the home-truth, waved an inarticulate hand around him - not so much at the sophistication of an Arabian palace as at the infinite sophistication of Life itself 'There's so much to it!' he pleaded. 'So much *to* it. Why give us enquiring minds if we're not meant to use them?'

She could not argue. She no more wanted him swallowed up by Mother Church than by La Belle Aude.

'Well, that's one thing at least that sets us Christian men above the Infidel!' he laughed. 'We know the true value and merit of a lady!' He even took hold of her hand when he said it, and pressed his forehead to it in salutation. The forehead was hot: she could almost feel the poetry fermenting inside it: not *sirventes* any longer, but lovesongs. And all in praise of Aude.

Yusif as-Shafih was also in love. So that when Foulque burst out with one of his wild, impassioned exclamations of verse, stamping one foot as he extemporised, the Siddi rose from his leather-bound chair and strode down the room to embrace him. 'At last! My brother, Foulque! Most excellent fellow! I marvel that you have kept your tongue still until now, in the service of such a lady!'

Foulque emerged from the embrace flushed with the release of pent-up emotion. His head still nodded a little with the frenzy of the rhythm, and the toe of his boot tapped the floor. He shook himself as if he had just made confession and felt cleansed by it.

Yusif went on, 'It pleases me! Oh, how it pleases me! Though to tell the truth, I was among those who said "nay" when others said "yea, they must be lovers: the great troubadour and the beautiful jongleur".'

'The colour drained dramatically from Foulque's face and he looked about, as if for an escape route. He gulped, quite audibly, and when his voice emerged next, it was hoarse and strangled. 'What do you take me for? We don't do that manner of thing. That's an Arab trick.'

Yusif looked baffled. He had gone to urge Ouallada to her feet, to have her join hands with Foulque. He grabbed both their wrists and was so excitable (and so strong) that it took some time before he felt them strain against it. 'What's the matter?'

Foulque glared across at Ouallada, his eyes large with anger and his nostrils flared. 'It's a *boy*!' he said, and his voice shook.

'Well, of *course* it isn't a boy,' said Yusif 'Ah, I see my grammatical error. I should have said *jongleuse*. You took offence at my poor grammar. Jongleuse, not jongleur.' When Foulque held his ground, Yusif said, 'Come, come man. Don't tell me you were fooled by her clothes. No! I won't believe it. We have discussed many, many times, my mistress and I, what should be the purpose of this disguise. It's not possible anyone should be fooled.' He laughed softly at the improbability as he unfastened Ouallada's coat and had servants lift it off her shoulders and carry it away. Then he set about illustrating the curves of Ouallada's body by gathering the back of her blouson into his fist.

'Don't touch her!' roared Foulque, snatching up a cruse lamp in a threat to engulf the Siddi in burning oil. 'She is Princess Ouallada, daughter of Sheik Obeid ben Zefir of the Tuaregs, and she is under my protection!'

A sadness crept into Yusif's eyes like a single cloud into the sky, and he wandered off back to her chair, unintimidated but slightly hurt. His big head shook with disappointment. 'Ouallada,' he mused. 'Are you named for the renowned daughter of the Caliph of Cordova? Ah yes, now there was a woman worthy of poetry. Untrammelled by convention - like yourself. And her own poetry was excellent. My beloved is a poet, too, you know? An example to most men. A moon among stars - it's widely acknowledged.' His easy, rambling conversation was intended to defuse the situation in the room, but curiosity suddenly got the better of him and he went trotting back towards Foulque. 'Do you truly mean to say that your love is for another lady than this one? I am astonished, I admit it! It must be a lady indeed who can wake more fire in you than this "princess".'

Foulque was rendered speechless. 'Look. You people ... ' he sputtered, grasping for an amicable way of expressing himself. 'You people have different ... You hold ladies in a different ... We Franks ... we men of honour, at least - we're raised to think of them as ... as ...

inviolable.' It came out of him with all the force of a rock from a trebuchet. His eyes were closed and his fists clenched. He opened them very gradually to see whether such a foreign concept as inviolability could possibly have struck home to a heathen heart.

Yusif had gone and sat down again and was looking at Ouallada with his head on one side, ruminatively. 'Ah yes,' he said with a vestige of wistfulness. *'Al-hawa al-'udri.* The chaste love. It is a virtue our poets too have prized for a thousand years. Myself, I mean to marry my love, but then I am only half-poet, half-Siddi and cannot aspire to such heights of spiritual excellence. Naturally I should have guessed, since you are a man of such character and breeding, that you would give your heart thus. But sir! You must own, the "Princess Ouallada" is quite worthy of a lover's attentions. I trust you will not blame me for my foolish mistake.'

Foulque deflated like a punctured bladder. His relief at the continuing safety of Ouallada was almost outweighed by his disillusionment. His last misapprehension of the scurrilous and amoral Arab had been taken from him. His last illusion in the superiority of his race had been buried under a thousand years of culture. *'Al-hawa al-'udri,'* he murmured.

'But tell me, "Princess Ouallada",' said Yusif, picking his precise way over the syllables of her preposterous title. 'Do you follow in the likeness of your namesake? Do you write love poetry yourself?'

'A little, my lord Siddi.'

'And will you grace this company with an example?'

'It would fall short of my Lord Foulque's, as an arrow falls short of the cross-bolt.'

'And yet there is room in any army for both archer and crossbow man,' he countered with his easy charm. 'But of course, I take you unprepared.'

On the contrary. Given time for consideration and no disguise to hide behind, she would never have volunteered a song. Something inebriating in the Siddi's compliments, the atmosphere of jarred sensibilities, an intuition that the time would never come again, goaded her to the brink of foolishness. 'I have a thing of mine comes to mind, my lord Siddi. A *winileodas*. A song for a friend.' And she picked up Foulque's cloak, went and stood to the windward side of a fireless hearth, and pulling the cloak round her, concealed her hands inside it along with every distracting detail of her appearance. Then she sang the song she had composed in the desert.

The closing of my lids unclothes you,
Your nakedness overclouds me, filling my sky,
And I thirst for your shafts of rain to prick me through
As sweat invites the horsefly,
My throat is ash-dry for fear of thee:
Unicorns clash horns.

And yet the shock of war I might absorb,
For such pangs are the miracles of pain
That bee stings bring with sight to the blind eye's orb.
Thou art the sky and I the plain,
And only ever between us the ripe citrus sun and moon
Ripe for crushing to a juice so sweetly moist
That we might drink, in kissing, a boon

As healing as wherein Mankind rejoiced
On the day God was born.

Foulque did not appear even to listen. He seemed wholly preoccupied, adjusting his preconceptions of the Enemy.

The Siddi Yusif as-Shafih also listened with only half an ear, for a letter had been brought him while she sang - a military communication. He was stirred by it, as if his chair had grown suddenly hot beneath him, untenably hot. His bushy black beard bristled, and his mouth disappeared entirely as he pressed his lips together in agitation.

'Tell me of Reynaud de Châtillon,' he said suddenly to Foulque.

Foulque was startled, 'Younger son of Count Geoffrey of Gien, Sometime Prince of Antioch through marriage to the ...'

'And does he have horns like a ram and jibber like a monkey? Is he a beast or a man or a fool?' They stared at him. 'Would that I had carved him in the Hejaz! Would that I had buried him in camel dung! The man's a goat. The man keeps his brains beneath his saddle. The man is a defiler of women.' Unconsciously, Foulque and Ouallada drew closer together into the middle of the room, as whispers in Arabic concerning the letter's content roused the room to excitable unrest. 'The truce is broken. The days of quiet are undone.'

'Can one man achieve so much?' asked Foulque diplomatically.

'Can one man be fool enough to outrage the sister of Saah-ed-din Yusif ibn Ayyub? As she travels unarmed along a neutral road? *The sister of the ruler of all the world?*' Sidi Yusif shook both fists in the air, bouncing in his chair, and gave a monumental howl of solidarity with his ruler's anguish. In that moment the Franks felt, for want of any weapon at all, like lambs amid a party of butchers.

In fact, quite suddenly after his outburst, Yusif was restored to calm. He had exorcised his anger and now it stood apart from him, a palpable presence in the room but nowhere to be seen in their host's benign, florid face. 'Honoured lady. I was distracted. I quite neglected to praise your excellent song. Please forgive me. Pray sing it again.'

'Another time, my lord Siddi,' said Ouallada nervously. 'I fear my voice would break at the sadness of your news.' With a glance she passed to Foulque the task of discovering whether their lives were forfeit as a result of Châtillon's outrage.

'I pray to God that Châtillon is powerless to harm the friendship between us,' said Foulque.

The Siddi rose from his chair and once more lunged down the room to embrace him. 'I hope so too. I do hope so, Foulque Nerra-des-Etangs, I do. You are my friends! You are my guests! You are as one of my household. Please accept this assurance.'

'And you are a friend to peace, sir.'

'I prefer it. I prefer it, I admit,' he said. 'But nothing good can come of this. There will be blood spilt. It is most regrettable. Most.' So Yusif as-Shafih retired to write to Saladin, asking what should be done with the prisoners he held. The day's entertainment ended as abruptly as the daylight, which night ruptured into a diaspora of stars.

As Foulque and Ouallada walked back to their quarters along moonlit pavements, the colonades which had given Yusif's palace its name had blackened into the bars of a cage - a pleasant, airy cage, but a cage nonetheless.

'I hope for your sake a new truce can be patched up,' Foulque said.

'And I hope it for your sake.'

'No, no, I mean - in the light of your song.'

'My song? What about my song?' Her heart staggered at the realisation he had, after all, heard it. *Your nakedness overclouds me.* What had possessed her to embarrass him so? To embarrass him with the knowledge of a passion he could not requite?

'Well, only that you've plainly learned a thing or two about the real nature of desire since I cast such slights on you at Haut-Beziers.'

'A thing or two.'

'And I just regret that you couldn't plant your hopes in more promising ground.'

'These things aren't of our choosing,' she said. 'I like the ground well enough.'

'Oh, so do I! Don't mistake me! He's an excellent man. I've laid aside my prejudices far enough to say that - at least, I hope I have. I like the man, I can say it hand-on-heart.'

'What?'

'But in the circumstances ... '

'What?'

He clearly decided, seeing how crumpled her face was growing, not to dishearten her any further. 'I just wanted to say ... I do wish you well of your love. If as-Shafih requites it, it's just one proof more of his excellent good taste.'

CHAPTER THIRTY ONE

Godsends

While the Siddi Yusif waited for instructions from Saladin as to what to do with his prisoners, he continued to treat them like friends of his dearest acquaintance, entertaining them with hunting, hawking and, today, polo.

The apron wall of the palace was built of brick of such antiquity that the Israelites under Moses might have baked them. The funnel kilns lay derelict as termite hills, here, there and everywhere. The walls had been blasted by sandstorms, too, to a stark, shiny whiteness, with a single stretcher of decorative red. Seen from a distance, raised up from the ground by heat-coggled air, it put literate men in mind of Troy, or Atlantis.

Foulque was thankful to be allowed to view Yusif's

fortress from outside. He had a great horror of confinement, and if the Siddi had held them prisoners under close arrest, he would have contemplated escape from the very start. Now that Saladin might require their heads to be dispatched to him at any moment, Foulque gave the matter of escaping serious thought.

To no great avail. For he had not the remotest idea where they were, or whose territory lay between Umdan and the sea.

'What d'you mean, you don't speak the language?' he had said when at last she admitted to it.

'You were right. I'm a Spanish Moor,' she said with wavering dignity. 'Besides ... I lied.'

'Why?' he asked.

'It's a congenital failing. I take it from my father.'

He had insisted, since the singing of the *winileodas* that she wear dresses, the better to appeal to as-Shafih. At the selfsame time, as-Shafih sent women's clothes to their quarters, requesting that she wear them. Foulque thought it a hopeful sign and congratulated her. Ouallada would far rather have continued to wear masculine clothes, for then she too could have ridden to hunt and hawk instead of finding herself allotted more and more often to the ladies of the household for them to entertain her. Yusif as-Shafih was of the impression that, given her sex, she must have suffered considerably at being kept from embroidery for so long. Several days, as long seemingly as the White Nile, passed in the resinous fug of the harem before Ouallada laid down her needle, shook off the polite, giggling ridicule of the dextrous wives, and fetched musical instruments from Foulque's quarters. After that, she entertained the wives rather than be subjected to their efforts at entertaining her. She had no doubt that they were cultured, literate women. Equally, she did not intend to stay so long at Umdan as to learn their wholly unintelligible language.

She would have liked to lie down to sleep at Foulque's feet wearing the pretty clothes. But unfortunately he thought it detrimental to her ambitions: as-Shafih would not like to think of her sleeping in another man's room. So she returned one day to find her couch expelled into the passageway, laden with her few possessions. It made her cry, that she should, of her own doing, have distanced herself from him. And that there was nothing, nothing to be done.

All Foulque's poetry had reverted to lovesong, Like water swirling round a drain, his mind swept in smaller and smaller circles, drawn towards the inescapable suction of Aude d'Haut-Beziers. He made Ouallada swear that if Saladin proved a gentleman too and spared his female prisoners, she would deliver to Aude all the written tributes of his heart. Indeed, their proliferation must have been another reason to move her bed outside his door: he needed the room. She herself wrote no more *winileodas*: she had shouted her love across the ravines of the world and the echoes had come back hooting with laughter.

It was an act of great personal esteem that Siddi Yusif should allow Foulque to participate in a game of polo at all, let alone allow him to play in competition, for his own team. The challenge came from Yusif's nephew who materialised one day with a household of eighty or more.

The Siddi himself did not play. He said he had damaged his back, though it may have been his politest way of avoiding personal defeat alongside his novice player. Still, large numbers of sizeable animals were wagered on the outcome - camels and cattle and horses. The nephew, an arrogant boy of around eighteen who coloured his thin beard with henna, pointed in Foulque's direction after offering salutation to his uncle, and said something overtly unpleasant in Arabic.

'What did he say?' Ouallada asked Siddi Yusif. They sat side by side on long-legged chairs on the sidelines of the marked ground.

'Oh, it was very insulting, dear Princess,' he replied. 'Pay no heed.'

'Never mind. There's an art in a fair insult. Lord Foulque would be the first to admit that.'

'"Green in skill, though not in years",' Yusif translated uneasily, then added in an alarmed rush, 'But we shall show him, shall we not? Your friend will make him swallow his insults.'

The first crack of stick against ball echoed off the fortress wall with a startling report, and Siddi Yusif as-Shafih settled back into his seat with a show of exaggerated diffidence. It would have been unbefitting to show excitement or partiality. Ouallada curbed her own instinct to stand on her chair seat and shout; it would have been difficult, anyway, in her women's clothing: linen pantaloons, a long embroidered kaftan, and a little red waistcoat sewn with mirrors.

'So, Princess Ouallada ben Zefir of the Tuaregs,' he said, deliberating over each syllable as if to savour its comedy, 'what more can be done?'

'Pray don't call me that. I feel sure it's an insult to your race or your intelligence, it was my father's silly invention. I wouldn't have used the name here, but I'm afraid my Lord Foulque ... I mean, he doesn't know me by any other name.'

The struck ball moved too fast for her even to keep it in sight, the lines of horsemen melting into chevrons, diagonals, starbursts before reforming around the ball. The white robes of the riders, galloping at full tilt, rattled like the sails of a ship.

'But does he truly believe it?' The full depth of Yusif's incredulity suddenly showed itself. Clearly Oriole had bestowed on her the most ridiculous assortment of names ignorance could light on. And yet Yusif had not laughed out loud or derided her in front of his household.

'Oh no. He knows it's a nonsense too, but somehow it sticks to me. He's a man of great chivalry, you have to understand. Like yourself He does not like to question a lady.'

'Unfortunately he is also stupid, yes?'

The ball had just passed cleanly between the legs of Foulque's horse, the opposing team passing to one another with insolent confidence. A third rider closed fast on him from the hind quarter and their bodies jarred, almost dislodging Foulque from his saddle. Ouallada wound her legs together inside the concealing kaftan. Foulque reined back hard and, turning behind the third rider, drove his horse directly into the press surrounding the ball, scattering them as he would have scattered enemy cavalry and wielding his stick like a mace. He hit the ball squarely on before emerging from the melee with a second mallet caught beneath his saddle flap. 'But not blind, I see,' said Yusif as-Shafih appreciatively. 'I had begun to wonder. Had not you?'

Ouallada, finding herself standing on the rung of her chair, sat back into its seat and glanced sideways. Yusif's ochre-rimmed, black eyes still moved with the play. 'I can only do so much,' she said. 'Beyond that, I'd only hurt my cause.'

'I too,' he apologised. 'I too can only do so much. The clothes you are wearing, for example, are the ones my second wife wore the day I set my face to marry her. The braid in your hair is sewn with propitious phrases from the Holy Book. And yet, and yet.'

'You are very kind. But I'm afraid it's impossible he should ever see such a dark star while the sun is out. You've never seen Aude d'Haut-Beziers.'

Yusif nodded lugubriously. 'Ah yes. The sun. I am afraid that for such men as Foulque, a Lady Aude is like the Dead: she can never grow old, never grow less. For she is as she always was - a figure of his own imagining.' He patted her hand affectionately and she was conscious of more filial feeling in that instant than in seventeen years' acquaintance with her father.

'You are a good, kind man, Siddi Yusif as-Shafih. I can understand how my friend mistook my *winileodas*.'

'Mistook it? This is what I cannot comprehend. How can one mistake such a song? How could you have been more plain?'

'Modesty, sir, I suppose. He did not expect anything in praise of himself ... So he took me to be in love with you.'

For the first time, Siddi Yusif's eyes left the polo field and turned on her, their bloodshot whites quite apoplectic with surprise. Then he began to laugh, with such a bark and a roar that the riders on the field looked up and missed their stride. A mallet-head missed the ball, so that for the first time in the game it came fully to a stop - a solstice in the heat of the game.

It was enough of a laugh to knock horses off their feet and unseat riders. So for a matter of seconds Ouallada saw nothing strange in the way the animals staggered and pitched, their legs flying out; ungainly. Then the wooden ball jumped spontaneously off the ground, was shaken into the air.

The bright wall of the fortress appeared to sneeze, a phelgm of mortar obscuring the figures along the battlements. A long pennon fluttered slowly down from a drunken flagpole, snagging against the brick, then breaking loose, snagging and freeing again and again. Before the flag even reached the base of the wall, the cupola of a minaret within the fortress precincts had swayed, capsized and crashed to the ground, crumpling like a tin bath, its copper leafing shaken clean off. The earthquake began as a noise and a dull misgiving. It rose to a drunken riot of the senses, the brain jibbing at the impossible. For the hills moved and the ground writhed, and all the vertical and horizontal wires on which the landscape was threaded snapped.

The polo ponies bolted, shrieking with terror, their ears flat; their nostrils drizzling white, their riders held prisoner within the hugely moulded saddles. Riderless horses criss-crossed their path, turning back again and again from a danger whose source seemed to be always in front of them. They were thrown suddenly off-track by spontaneous plumes of eddying dust spat up by the demons underground. The greenness of Wadi-al-Umdan was erased little by little by the uniform yellow haze rising up like the winnowings over a threshing floor.

People ran in all directions - away from the fortress wall or back towards it for the sake of relations and property. Children running in search of their mothers, were pursued and intercepted by their fathers to stop them re-entering the palace. The spectator chairs, ranged out for the comfort of Siddi Yusif, Ouallada and a dozen old men of rank, began to sway and rack, then to lift two feet off the ground and walk, until the joints gave way or they overturned. Siddi Yusif leapt out of his chair at the very first intimation of movement - but into the path of a riderless horse which bowled him over and over before itself losing its footing and falling. Ouallada, on the contrary, clung to her chair's arms like the witch of Endor in her burning tower. There was a hiatus of thirty seconds, then the fit began again.

Foulque dropped his reins and let his mare run, rather than wrench at her head and pitch her off her feet. But when the earthquake paused for breath, he manoeuvred her in a half-circle towards the spectator seats. He rode out of Ouallada's blind quarter and snatched her, his insecure grip slipping and slipping higher and higher up her body until her kaftan was bunched round her face and her feet were scuffing the ground. Just before he dropped her, he succeeded in bringing his horse to a halt, and set Ouallada down in front of a vicious, mad-eyed, riderless gelding, its double reins hanging down.

'Get on! Get on!' Foulque bellowed. Such was his restored strength that his legs had the power to right his horse's stagger, to hold the vertical even when the walls of the world were listing. When the owner of the gelding came roaring towards them, his fists in the air, Foulque swung his polo mallet and caught him square under the chin and threw him on his back, unconscious, though his hands and feet twitched with the sheer vibration of the ground.

She had felt like this at sea, robbed of all firm footing, suspended over dark, preternatural regions, about to plummet down. Gulfs did not open in the ground, but the dry earth crazed into mosaic shards and subsided into shallow dips. The fortress itself groaned like a live thing, the lines of its face distorted as if by a stroke. The handsome stretcher of red brick twisted into a grotesque grimace.

'Can we get away?' she shouted across to him. But the very sky seemed to be grinding against the warped earth, filling the air with noise. Under cover of the bilious yellow dust, Foulque rode due north, leading Ouallada's horse by one broken rein. The earthquake had made things plain. It was his Christian duty to try to escape.

If they had stayed, Yusif would have spoken a word to Foulque - taken him aside and told him his mistake. So to Ouallada the earthquake was as inevitable a sign from God as it was to Foulque. Give up, it said. She submitted now completely, consoled to think of God taking such care to keep His bishop out of her grasp. It awed her that angels and earthquakes should have been assigned to the cause.

And yet Foulque had not forgotten to take her with him. He had not thought her a piece of baggage to be left behind, like his instruments and his mace and his reams of song.

They rode ten miles without stopping. By that time, their mouths were full of sandy dirt, their lungs full of grit. And the spent earthquake had taken on the quality of a nightmare half-remembered. Birds were still settling out of the sky like ash, and the ground seethed with ants displaced from a million nests. But the sky was a placid, stationary blue. And the acacia trees threw long, steady shadows pointing back the way they had come.

'Should the shadows point that way?' she called, chiefly to remind him she was there. It seemed the height of disrespect to ask it, but weren't they riding west rather than north? Beyond the next wadi they turned south.

His horse fell in beside hers. 'I'm going back,' he said. 'I don't know where I am. I've brought nothing with me. No water. No night cloak. We'll freeze come nightfall.' Both horses nodded their heads up and down, as if hasty to agree. Bred in Yusif's stables, solely for polo, they had speed but no stamina. They were already thirsty from the game, already hankering for their stalls.

'Well, then. Back to Umdan,' she said, though inwardly she wanted to hurl clods of dung at him and shout, 'Why didn't you think of that before? They'll cut us to pieces if we go back now!'

She could see, in her mind's eye, Yusif as-Shafih pick himself up, realise that his prisoners had fled, feel betrayed by those he had treated with trust. She could imagine affront turning to anger, anger to pursuit. The nephew's retinue would join in, relishing the sport. She became persuaded of a great galloping force of men about to sweep over the ridge behind them.

But she stiffened her resolve not to call him foolish,

stiffened her back, too, and fell in behind him without a word. Sufficient that he had felt the need to try to escape.

'It was the earthquake; you see.' He had taken off his kefieh and was rubbing his hands to and fro across the top of his hair made dark again with sweat. 'I took it for a sign from God.'

'Ah. I see.'

'The chance came, you see? A call to action.'

'Well, then. I expect you were right. God's chance for us to get away,' she said peaceably, fingering her horse's mane. The desert around them was turning purple. She still envisaged battalions of Arabs sweeping in waves over the near horizon, so real in the imagining that she held her breath.

'But that's not in my theology! What was I thinking of? God wasn't in the earthquake! God wasn't in the wind or the fire! God was in the small voice after the wind and fire and earthquake!' He held his hands out towards her in strenuous appeal, a debater losing his own argument.

'Foulque, could we talk about this somewhere else?' she asked.

'Besides, I don't believe in a Zeus armed with thunderbolts.'

'No. Well. Of course not.'

'I don't believe in symbols written on the sky and saints lifting sieges on horseback.'

'Oh, really? They do say that lightning ...'

'I don't believe God takes a personal hand in your safety or mine.'

It was a shocking, heretical thing to say. It prised the roof off the world and let in the rain. Her peasant blood roared with outrage. But she said, 'I see that. Yes, I see that, I suppose. Why should He?' She felt like a flea on the body of the world, waiting to be crushed, for when he said it, she believed it. God had not sent the earthquake. Nor would His hand shield them when they surrendered themselves back into as-Shafih's custody. Foulque's Christian God was confined, a thousand miles away, within clammy, monastic cells. Foulque's personal God was dying within him, smothered by the books in Yusif's library and the prospect of another Crusade.

Ouallada nodded. 'Yusif's a good man, Foulque. He likes you a lot. You make him laugh. Maybe he'll keep us back out of Saladin's hands. Even if he is told to give us up. He's not so very partial to Saladin, you know? To the Kurd. A Kurd ruling Egypt. He resents it. I've heard him say as much.'

He could not fail to hear the fright in her voice. He reached out and gripped her upper arm. 'A Kurd, absolutely. And I'm sure the sight of you will buy us both a pardon. As I'm sure Yusif will never part with you to Saladin. I saw him – today - during the game - his hand on yours. Come on, I should never have parted you from your lover, I'm a fool in the van of fools.'

They broke into a sprightly canter. It was only ten miles, after all, that they had come. Every ridge, as they climbed it, revealed another familiar undulating mile of scrub and tussocks. Everything was familiar. They covered twelve, maybe fifteen miles of 'familiar' ground and never once crossed their own hoofprints. They climbed thirteen ridges of sandstone or sand and still did not find the Fortress of Umdan. It was as though the Palace of Columns had sunk into the ground, fragmented to sand by the earthquake and blown away along with horse men, horses and howling children. They began to see that the landscape repeated itself as regularly as the trees in a forest, and all that changed was its colour, as the sun sank.

'The great thing is to get back before they're put to the pain of looking for us,' they kept saying, but they both began to think that pursuit and capture might be their only means of seeing Umdan Fortress again.

When at last the noise took substance, the noise Oullada had been dreading, it was somewhere ahead, somewhere out of sight. She reached across and snatched the white kefieh out of his hands. But she was hardly tall enough in the saddle to make the signal of surrender plain, and she threw it back for him to tie to the polo mallet and raise it up high.

The drumming of hooves seemed to have begun a thousand miles away, and the jingling of bridles to come from another quarter entirely, so distorting were the landscape and the evening breeze. It seemed to be an army of ghosts approaching, audible without ever coming into sight. Whatever size of troop had Yusif mounted to recapture his hostages? Foulque and Ouallada let their horses come to an uneasy halt when, at last, the sound seemed to surround them entirely.

With a rushing noise, the army's leading horsemen topped the ridge ahead of them. Fifty, Foulque counted, before the first banners came into view - gauntlets and flowers and wolves and castles, lilies and leopards and lions. And soaring and swaying in the background, blurred by their own dust, a host of inanimate giants rumbled along - a city of wooden buildings, a skyline of siege-engines - beffrois, mangonels, arbalasts and espingales rolling and rocking, some with the tiny figures of carpenters still hammering, hammering within the uncompleted guts.

'Look!'

First he, then Ouallada lifted the palms of their hands towards the sky and hailed God with a yell. God with the thunderbolts in His fist. God who sent earthquakes to deliver His servants from captivity. 'Who says we weren't meant to escape!' she shouted delightedly, above the din of stirrups on metal-shod boots. 'They're Christians!'

Foulque took off the white linen coif he wore under his helmet and thrust it into her hands.

'Oh! Can I still not be a woman?' she asked, slow to pull it on.

'Be as you choose, Princess - if you trust the honour of the Frankish soldier as well as you trusted as-Shafih.'

She tucked away her long, thick hair, distributing it evenly under the coif so that it gave the impression of a larger, masculine head. She dropped down into the dirt the little red jacket sewn with mirrors, which Yusif had given her to stir the affections of her friend. The rest of her clothes were so torn and dirtied by the events of the day that they could have been for male or female. And though one of the first men to reach them mistook her for a piece of loot stolen from the enemy, he only asked if there were 'many good slaves to be had locally'.

CHAPTER THIRTY TWO

Engines of War

Leo de Montpellier and his men, with whom Foulque and Ouallada now found themselves, felt unconstrained by truces or diplomacy, by nice details such as whether their country was officially at war or not. They allowed their campaign, on behalf of the Duke of Poitiers, to take them where it would, ambushing camel trains, lending their swords to tribal feuds, dealing a little in slaves and other perishables, razing Moslem villages to the ground. The Duke himself was not among them, but home in France, zealously' campaigning for a Third Crusade.

Before Montpellier turned for home, there was just time to besiege the Fortress of Umdan and discover whether the rumours of fabulous treasure there had any foundation. And although the earthquake had been taken by some as a warning to turn back, others had said it was God (in a kind of forward action) shaking down the walls of Umdan: they were in a hurry to see if this were true.

The building which ultimately came into view looked so serenely white, so still and impregnable that the earthquake, the polo match, the dust, the sound of screaming might all have been a dream. Umdan had not, it seemed, fallen at the blast of God's ram's horn. Furthermore, there was no access to water outside its walls.

A prolonged siege would be impossible. Leo de Montpellier resolved at once to storm the white walls. Leo de Montpellier was given to acts of resolution, though he frequently changed his mind a short while later. He was the Duke of Poitiers' right hand in the desert, and he was not slow in imparting this to Foulque Nerra. Foulque was similarly quick to notice that Leo was, in fact, left-handed.

Foulque found Montpellier's men an undisciplined rabble, called them hyenas and crows, surveyed their slovenly dress and rudimentary hygiene with disgust. Ouallada could see no difference between them and the pack of ruffians who had followed Châtillon. 'You're comparing them with Yusif's men,' she said, watching him eat right-handedly, scrupulously avoiding his plate and millet with the left. 'You've become an Arab.'

But he had forgotten where he learned such habits. 'Speak for yourself. Better yet, keep your mouth closed. These barbarians would cut your throat if they thought you held the Enemy in good regard.'

'Don't you, then? Must we go back to thinking of him as a godless brute? You and I, I mean? Should I have left behind everything I learned in Umdan?'

Relations between them were strained. For Foulque wanted to be a warrior once more, a Christian warrior with undivided allegiances. He needed it. He could not afford to adopt a new outlook, nor even hold to some middle ground.

'Tell them, Foulque! Stop them attacking as-Shafih,' she begged.

'Tell them what? That the Enemy's civilised? That the Pope's in error? That Châtillon should have handled Saladin's sister like a gentle man? Or that there are books in there? And staunch men and delicate lovers? It's a war, Princess. It's been going on one lifetime and it'll last out another ... Oh, you can try to tell them that Yusif's a fine fellow. But it won't stop them. And it won't keep him from lifting up his sword against us. He's a soldier. We're all soldiers now there's a war again. Tell them you're enamoured of the Siddi, why don't you? They'll either cut your throat for it, or use you to fetch as-Shafih out of his fort and cut his. If you want to stop a war, madam, don't stand in front of it. Choose a side and hope to win.'

'You think I love as-Shafih,' she said. 'But it's not true.'

He clapped her on the back so hard that yellow dust was dislodged from all the creases of her clothing and the body beneath. 'Brave fellow. Well said, boy! That's the thing to hold in mind,' was all he said, alerting her to the fact that Frankish soldiers were walking nearby.

She tried to say only one thing more. 'You saved my life just now. I'm grateful.' She said it awkwardly, stiltedly.

'Don't mention it. Squares the score between us. I imagine I've owed you a life since the sickness brought me down in the Hejaz.'

'Self-interest entirely,' she said.

He seemed to derive some comfort from being released from his indebtedness. Small things such as that matter to a knight on the eve of battle.

Foulque believed himself descended from the Devil. And while he had tried, and tried with all his heart and with all his mind and with all his strength and with all his aspiring soul to cling to the skirts of God, to climb the long Ladder of Perfection, once his grip slipped there remained nothing but the long unbreakable fall all the way back to Hell. No middle rung. He was tiring, too, ageing and tiring: too tired, perhaps to attempt the climb to righteousness again. Easier to pull on his byrnys, his *casque de Croisade* with its depersonalising nosepiece, and drop into the flyblown latrines all niceties of reason and philosophy. To him, the transformation seemed complete. He could even smell, next morning, a pitchy combustion around his tent. Foulque the demon was fully restored to his rightful nature.

The smell was actually that of Greek fire, a mixture of pitch and crude oil simmering in braziers along the walls of Umdan. A large purchase of Sudanese '*abd* or slave mercenaries had been promised freedom in return for a night spent filling the ditch around the fortress - filling at least an area sufficient to allow the approach of siege engines. They were of a colour camouflaged by night. Only the incendiaries lobbed in earthenware vessels over the gleaming wall threw sufficient light to make their baskets of white rock shine. Comet-tailed with phosphorescent light, the missiles, big as wine tuns, had flown with a noise like thunder all night, lighting up the siege camp and killing three horses as well as several dozen *'abd*. Nevertheless, by morning the fifty-foot ditch was already reduced to a shallow indentation.

Two beffrois had been made ready - siege towers three storeys high, the topmost level roofed against arrows and with a drawbridge ready to drop across the battlements. Foulque began to climb one of these towers. He climbed right to the topmost platform.

'Foulque! What are you doing!' Ouallada yelled up from the ground. When he did not reply she ran, head down and on legs nightmarishly slow, to Leo de Montpellier's great vanity of a tent.

'Come quick! Come please! Foulque Nerra's climbing the beffroi!'

Leo de Montpellier put on a silk surcoat which matched that of his horse, mounted up, shielded his body from head to foot behind a long shield painted with pretty chequering as were his crupper and saddle flaps, crowned himself with a quilted circlet of red felt, and spent some time settling his helmet on to this soft upholstery. Then he trotted over to the beffroi and squinted up at its summit. 'Foulque Nerra-des-Etangs, what in devil *are* you doing?' he asked and his open mouth showed that all but his incisors had been removed by dentistry. Leo of Montpellier did not believe in being troubled by pain. 'That's no job for a knight. No knight is required to dismount, as you know. Pray don't set a poor example to those of your own rank.'

The beffroi began to rock along. Its big wheels settled

into the sandy ground wherever it came to a rest and needed scores of men pushing on rear shafts, and the 'abd pulling on ropes to the fore to make it lurch forward. Foulque spread his feet wide and gripped the rail, his face set on the fortress.

'He's not a knight, strictly speaking, sir,' Ouallada excused him. 'He's a cleric.'

'That's no excuse for him to behave like a bloody sergeant! I need cavalrymen! I lost cavalrymen the other day. I need horsemen. Come down from there, Nerra! Come down and find a horse!'

The forty or more infantrymen cramming the various platforms wore the blank expressions of men committed beyond their capacity for fear. As the hide blinds were dropped down to protect them from arrows, they fell perfectly silent like birds in a covered cage.

'Not a knight, you say? I didn't know that,' said Leo, and let his horse drift sideways away from the tower. There was such a press of men aboard it that even if Foulque's mind could be changed, he would be hard put to clamber down again. Ouallada resolved to mount the tower, too, and to keep him company in one last foolishness. But to her astonishment, she found that the wheels, as tall as she, were already rolling as fast as she could run. The teams of men bent over the shafts were racing their rivals, racing the other tower, all their attention given to competing, so as to forget the hail of arrows and fire to come. That was when Ouallada broke off her chase, when the first hand-thrown grenade of Greek fire burst its earthenware egg at her feet and hatched into an ugly phoenix moulting liquid heat.

At the first volley of arrows the Sudanese dropped

their pulling ropes and scattered, the tower continuing by its own momentum. On the roughcast in-fill, the wheels jolted so sharply that the shoulderblades of the men pushing lifted and their roar of exertion broke up into groans and grunts.

As Foulque dropped the drawbridge, the scene it had obscured from him was laid bare. A double row of twenty Saracen archers awaited the tower, but he was perched fully ten feet above their heads and had an aerial view - such as dreams allow - of a frenzied busyness. Boys with ladles spooned a soup of incandescent pitch into terracotta plantpots. A miraculous bonfire built of seemingly incombustible metals burned with a white heat on the parapet of the white wall. And beyond, the whole palace was revealed to him.

The earthquake had devastated it, like a box of chalks shaken to uselessness. Keystones lay blocking every archway. The rubble of the beautiful harem quarters had sunk down into a puddle of ruptured aquaducts and fountains, and the palace surrounding it had been gelded of all its towers and minarets. In fact the shining helmets of the knights ranged along the parapets were the only surviving domes of the city. Among them was Yusif as-Shafih's.

All of a sudden a huge beam of timber secured by chains loomed over the battlements - a vast baulk of wood made from several tree trunks chained together and larded with dripping rags. The first of the siege towers, with Foulque aboard it, crashed up against this buffer. The drawbridge, instead of overhanging the battlements, stopped five feet short and with such a collison that the men inside the tower were pitched off their feet. They fell on top of one another or piked over the railings. The only man other than Foulque to be riding on the uppermost storey was catapulted clean over the front of the tower and dropped the twenty feet or more on to the baulk of timber fending them off from the fortress wall. There he crouched like a panic-stricken cat, on all fours.

The second beffroi had sufficient time to stop short of the wall and to avoid contact with the buffer, though the men aboard found themselves pelted with shards of white-hot metal from the mangonel on the parapet. Its soaked hide cup steamed and charred and wagged like a defiant fist above the castellated wall.

The peculiar stench of vinegar superseded even the pitch as the second beffroi unfurled its felt blinds, hiding its occupants from view behind vinegar-soaked curtains. The metal shrapnel hit the felt with a stinking hiss, then fell to the ground where the pushers on the shafts cowered under their shields. It was one of these deflected slugs of incandescent pig-iron that fell and jammed the wheel. After only a few seconds it had bitten through the axle, and the tower lurched sharply over, immobilised within ten yards of the wall, listing wildly, its belfry almost nudging Foulque's tower, and with men sliding out beneath the curtains of felt, leaping or falling to the ground.

Foulque was lying on his face, where the force of impact had thrown him, reaching down a hand to the infantryman clinging to the timber buffer. Their fingertips failed to touch. 'Jump for the tower! Jump out to it!' shouted Folque, but the man on all fours was paralysed with fear. He was still there when the Arab boys on the wall lobbed their grenades of Greek fire down on to the petrol-soaked rags coating the buffer, and it and the topmost storey of the siege tower were both engulfed in flame.

A hundred years before, watching Fulk Nerra, Black Count of Anjou burning his wife to death, the impressionable onlookers must have seen something the same: a pyre of flame igniting, a gout of black smoke breaking away, elongating into the likeness of a human form, winged and fleeing. The burnt woman's soul flying back to Hell.

Ouallada saw it. Watching what she took to be the death of Foulque, she saw the black smoke-shape break free leap up and away above the envious fingers of reaching fire.

A moment later, through a rent in the dense black smoke, she saw Foulque himself jump, with all the inaccuracy and inelegance of a ship's rat, from the summit of the burning tower across to the second belfry and cling perilously to its curtains of vinegar-soaked felt. Somehow his boots found purchase on the timber of the drunken, foundered siege engine, and he pulled himself on to its listing top platform, his surcoat and kefieh on fire.

Across the smoky gulf alive with arrows, shrapnel and terracotta grenades, Yusif as-Shafih watched Foulque make the leap and wedge himself in one corner of the sloping platform while he tore off his surcoat and threw his helmet aside. As he did so, he was looking all the time at the defenders on the wall, trying to place as-Shafih. When the two men's eyes met, they acknowledged one another, Yusif with a salaam, Foulque by crossing himself. It was a statement of loyalties - a crossing through of former lies.

'At the barriers at noon, Foulque Nerra-des-Etangs,' said Yusif as-Shafih, and the men at the mangonel turned at the sound of his voice.

'At the barriers,' said Foulque, and all the men beneath him, scuttling down their broken tower like squirrels down a lightning tree, looked up amid the monumental din to wonder who had spoken.

She resolved, while they waited for his return from the wall, to tell him that Melusine his ancestor, had not been a demon - just a gout of black smoke, an optical illusion, an unfortunate woman butchered by her husband. She had not flown back to Hell, to orchestrate from there the wickedness of future generations of Nerra blood. It might make a difference to Foulque to know that he did not have brimstone in his veins. But with the chaos and confusion of battle, the news of jousts at the barricades, the necessary ritual of burying the dead, she was not able to find the time, and ultimately it slipped her mind.

'Fight at the barriers? You and the Sheik of Umdan?'

'I and the Siddi Yusif, yes,' said Foulque, galled by the need to ask permission of Leo de Montpellier.

'It's not really that manner of a siege, man,' he said dubiously.

'What kind of a siege?'

'Well, the recreational sort. With diversions. Jousts at the barriers. All that. I mean, we can't afford to dally, you know? No idea who's at our back. And water's in short supply. You troubadours, you think everything can stop for a musical interlude and a passage of arms.'

'Not for recreation.'

'Beg pardon?'

'Not a joust for recreation. A joust for the city.'

'Christ Jesu! Then I should certainly fight him. Why should he wager that? He'd never honour a wager like that. You don't know these people like I do ... No, no. I wouldn't trust him to hold good to the bargain. I mean, Chivalry, it isn't to them what it is to us Christians, you know.'

The loss of two siege engines in a single abortive assault was a source of personal grief to Montpellier. He had been lucky enough never to see one bum before, its tower rocking in the orange heat, rocking and sloughing its felt in great rags of fire, the skeletons of trapped men dancing in the up draught, their skulls jammed between the rungs of the ladders, their weapons all welded together at the base. Montpellier's previous conquests - villages and minor forts - had succumbed to slaughter and rapine without much resistance.

His sergeants were muttering now that the expedition had overshot itself. They began to glance over their shoulders, expecting to see Egyptian forces coming to end their run of luck. Montpellier, like his sergeants, was losing his nerve. He had swum as far out into enemy waters as he dared, and began to feel the tide turning.

And now this Camarguais madman with the black squire came and said he wanted to fight as-Shafih at the barriers for possession of the city. It smacked of David offering to fight Goliath, and who cares to fly in the face of biblical godsends? Not Montpellier. Only one small problem remained.

'I hear you're not actually, in point of fact, at this moment - a knight. Is that right?'

'No, I'm a cleric. I mean, I was ... I'm a mace-carrier, me. Never wore a sword.'

'But you say you know this man.'

'I've had a year to study him. Learn his strengths and weaknesses.'

'There seems only one answer then. Here. Here. Here.' He pushed his own equipage at Foulque - helmet, sword and spurs, as if he wished Foulque to carry them for him as far as the horse. He dropped one of the spurs and as Foulque knelt down to pick it up, Montpellier struck him a blow in the side of his neck with one fist.

'What the ... '

'Do you swear to love and serve God and the King?'

'Are you trying to knight me?' Foulque stood up so fast that Montpellier had to move his chin sharply out of the way.

'I really think you ought to swear .. .' Leo complained.

'I already swore. On several occasions. For instance, I swore to re-enter Holy Orders when I get back to France.' He added ferociously, 'I'd sooner you didn't honour me beyond my means to satisfy.'

Montpellier sucked his lower lip into a shiny pucker. He was much younger than Foulque and felt a certain lack of presence while the man was standing up in the same tent. He was also conscious of having hit Foulque in the neck as hard as he could, to give an impression of superior strength. And now the man was holding his throat: Leo hoped he had not lessened Nerra's chances of winning the combat. 'A mace,' he added, taking his equipage back out of Foulque's arms. 'A mace, you say.

We must find you a mace.'

Not that Montpellier had the smallest intention of letting the outcome rest with Foulque's mace. He told his sappers to continue tunnelling under the wall, using the combat as a source of diversion.

'*La ilaha ilia 'llah,*' called Yusif as-Shafih from a distance, raising his short lance in salutation. When Foulque did not give the required response, the Siddi's second shouted it out like a taunt: '*Allahu akbar!*'

'Christ is risen,' called Foulque in defence of his faith and, holding his mace halfway down the chain, lifted it over his head. Leo of Montpellier had no sense of ceremony or moment: it was left to Ouallada to call out, in response, 'Christ is risen indeed!'

The two men who were to fight kicked up their horses to a walk until the animals were shaking their heads at one another close-to.

'Risen in dogma, perhaps,' said Yusif quietly. 'But in deed?' He was magnificent, in chased gold *baida*, plumed with a banneret of white cloth and the woven mail of his forefathers. His cloak encompassed his horse entirely, so as to give the impression of a centaur. Two *parreins* bore along behind him pennoned lances painted with Arabic characters. He streamed with words, each gust of wind rattling fresh prayers out of his lettered clothing. Even his horse bore legends from the Koran around the perimeter of a footcloth which swept the ground. He looked his opponent up and down, pointedly recognising the Arab horse of his which Foulque was still riding. 'I see little of Christ among those who visit my land wearing His device.'

'Pray don't look for an exemplar in me, Siddi al-Umdan. I take too much after my ancestors who come of different stock. I am descended from a demon.'

'If that is intended to frighten me, I have to say, Lord Nerra-des-Etangs, that you are more primitive a race than I thought.'

'I said it by way of an apology,' he broke in, aggressively. 'I've seen over your wall. Is your loss very great?'

'My wife. A daughter. My men were mostly out-of-doors. As you know.'

'If grief had hands, I should lift the stones that fell on them.'

'Thank you. But it was the will of Allah. I bend to the will of Allah in all things.'

They were both silent for a time and then Foulque said, in an embarrassed rush: 'I took it for a sign, you see. The earthquake. That's why I shunned your hospitality. I took it for a sign.'

'To rouse you up from here where you'd lain down so comfortably with dogs.'

'God knows. No. To act. To do. Simply to act. D'you see the arrogance of the man? To read a personal message from the Almighty in an earthquake? An earthquake especially for Foulque Nerra, eh? Why not Montpellier there? Or Saladin. Or you, now I come to think. You see how I lack the modesty for my priestly vocation, Siddi? I don't believe I shall return to it.'

'Then you share the opinion of Salah-ed-din, monsieur, for he sends word you shall die on my swordpoint in recompense for the outrage to his sister.'

Foulque laughed to himself, a private joke not

intended for sharing. He lifted his face towards the sky and screwed his eyes up against the sun. 'Of all crimes. As God wills it, then. Either yours or mine.'

The barriers were a clutter of massive timbers - a lattice of cabers and beams, some sunk end-on into the ground, some nailed on the diagonal to form a barricade against cavalry assaults on the gate. The space contained by them formed a corral within which the siege army and the men mustered beyond the fortress wall became an irrelevance and war was reduced to a personal scale.

'He's a great man, Salah-ed-din,' said Yusif surprisingly, on the point of turning. 'He has a vision. Of a united Arab people. Above tribe. Above territory. Soon he will sweep away you crusaders with a wave of his hand.'

'But he won't do it soon enough to save you,' said Foulque softly, indicating with the smallest of gestures the desolation beyond the wall. 'He hasn't come in time to help you.'

'No. No. And if I win here, on the field of combat, I do not delude myself that Montpellier will honour the outcome. I believe,' said Yusif slowly, contemplatively, appearing to look directly at the sun, 'I believe - little as I care for my brothers of the Israelite persuasion – I shall be forced to borrow a tradition from them. Make the Jewish Pilgrimage.'

'What's that? What's it mean?'

'Oh ... It need not concern you. It is quite foreign to your culture.' He became suddenly animated, gathering up his silver-studded, double reins. 'First I mean to salvage the sport you robbed me of when you left our polo field so ... abruptly. First we shall have sport here at the barricades. You and I. Hector and Achilles beneath the walls of Troy. '

Foulque restrained him a moment, putting out both arms as their horses passed side by side. Yusif received the embrace, even returned it with unfeigned affection. 'You have my respect and my gratitude as a gracious host, Siddi. If I kill you, I shall never speak ill of you after.'

'Nor I of you, Foulque Nerra-des-Etangs.'

'But I shall kill you if I can, sooner than see a hundred men more die in taking the city.'

'And I you,' said Yusif 'My need is equally great. Let me tell you one thing, so that you shall not die in ignorance of it. No man should die in ignorance of such a thing. You mistook your squire when you said she was in love with me. It is not me she loves.' He swung his horse away, describing a full circle, to have the advantage of charging at full gallop on an almost stationary target. He drew a sword with a huge jewel inset in the pommel and a handle wrapped in red leather, and the blade dissolved in the brightness of the sun. He had already given himself the advantage of riding out of the noon. 'It was not I whose life she saved in the desert!' he shouted and brought his sword down across the red blazon of Foul que's shield with a blow that shivered a bloody splinter clean out of its face. Foulque's mace was still hanging down, lifeless. 'It was not I for whom she put on men's clothes and made nothing of her sex!' Foulque leaned away from the blow and his horse turned, answerable to the merest thought. The tactics were common enough: to mar an opponent's concentration. Although Foulque was startled, the reflexes learned in twenty years' campaigning did not desert him. As Yusif executed a turn, so did he, describing a circle wide enough to close on his opponent from the left-hand side, making any sword stroke by Yusif awkward and dangerous, across the horse. He barely seemed to raise his forearm before the mace began to whirl, a Catherine wheel of grey light, an orbiting planet shifting its orbit with every circuit, from low down beside his knee up to his shoulder and then over his head. The little round shield Yusif raised over his face was bent and folded by the impact - a drum note that galvanised the Franks and had them standing at full stretch to see as-Shafih fall.

He did not fall, but as he passed by his *parrein*, laid hold of a lance, and came at Foulque again before he could turn his horse to receive the charge. Rather than receive it side-on, he dug in his heels and fled, pursued by Yusif up to the very barricades. By weaving in and out between the trellis of beams, he left no clear target for the lance point, and both riders lost momentum, their horses slowing to a trot.

'Are you blind or unnatural that you can let such a love go unrepaid?' called Yusif

'If it existed, I should thank the lady and have her place it in safer keeping than with the Church.'

'Oh, and if her only rival were the Church, she would have conquered long ago!'

Foulque's thighs drove his pony on, drove it on, into the very face of as-Shafih. Watching from a distance, Ouallada had the impression that the mace was cutting sinuous incisions in her eye, etching the sight of him on to her retina. Fear and desire so mingled in her that she almost envied Yusif his destruction at the hands of such a man.

'As you say. My heart is already given elsewhere,' said Foulque, conjuring up the thought of Aude to enhance his fighting power.

But Yusif only shook his head and grinned, his own carriage fluid and relaxed, plying his horse's head to left and right and left in a dancing dressage. The white plume of words rose straight up from his helmet in a fountaining brightness. 'I know it. Yes, your heart is quite given over to hating yourself, Foulque Nerra-des-Etangs. In that I can never match you.' His horse suddenly sat back on its haunches and virtually sprang forward, Yusif's lance dropping, dropping to the level as he closed the space between them.

Only by fetching his mace up high to meet it could Foulque deflect the impact and point, and even then the entanglement fetched both men off their horses. Yusif's lance snapped, but the mace was pulled out of Foulque's grasp and he found himself weaponless, getting to his feet, face-to-face with a man whose sword was half drawn. Rather than run, and feel the edge between his shoulder blades, he leapt forward, knotted his fists in the white folds of Yusif's surcoat, lifted him off his feet and threw him on his back. As a move, it had neither skill nor merit, but an unforeseeable fluke made the Siddi's horse shy, at that very moment, from the striped shards of the broken lance, and jump backwards, catching Yusif in the face with a hoof.

He got to his knees - almost to his feet - but being unable to see, fell back on to one hand, the other stretched out towards Foulque. Then he rolled back in a foetal position on the ground, with bright red blood glistening in his beard. Foulque dived headlong for the dropped sword, got two hands to the hilt and, at full stretch along the ground, managed to hold the point to Yusif's curled back, though he had no more reach left to drive it home.

It was at this moment that Montpellier's watchman blew his horn.

Rising above the horizon, like an Arabian ifrit come to intervene, a cloud of flying sand blurred the sky. *'Riders!'*

No one laid claim to shouting it first, but at once everyone was shouting: 'Riders! Riders!'

'To arms!' yelled Montpellier, though the men around him had already scattered to their tents. 'How could it happen? Why wasn't I warned? To horse!' yelled Montpellier. 'Knight the squires! *Knight the squires!* No horse without a rider! Give me more knights, for Christ's sake! *Give me more knights!'*

Ouallada, paralysed with uncertainty, was the only one left standing close by Montpellier. He caught her by the shoulder. 'Don't you have a horse, God blast you?'

'Yes, sir! At once, sir!' She ran out, beyond his flailing arms.

'Where are you going?'

'To get my horse, sir!'

'Before mine? Get mine first! Where's my bastard squire? Where's my boy? I'll break his neck for him, that craven runt!'

All over the barren, open ground - the one-time polo-field - boy squires appeared to be sinking under the weight of their knight's panoply, falling to their knees and casting the equipment aside to raise prayerful hands to Heaven. Ouallada was not immune to the wish that she too could fall down and beg God's intervention - cry out, 'I'm a woman! I'm a woman! Tell them, Lord! I'm a woman!'

Spreadeagled on the ground, his arm at full stretch, unable to command that last span of blade to pierce Yusif's side, Foulque was not even conscious that the spectators' attention had turned away from the barriers and out towards the desert. But he did have time to realise that he was about to kill with a weapon to which he was not entitled. He drew up his knees under him and threw himself forwards, his body on top of as-Shafih, pitching the sword beyond anyone's reach. He seized Yusif by the leather shoulder-straps of his breastplate, but the man was limp, a raggy, torpid deadweight. 'Do you cede? Do you cede?' Foulque panted in his face.

'Enough. It is enough,' said Shafih, his eyes rolling away into the tops of their sockets, but he did not mean that he had ceded defeat, only that he had achieved what was necessary, allowed sufficient time to elapse, killed time. Just as Montpellier had told his sappers to go on digging, as-Shafih too had viewed the combat only as a diversionary tactic.

As Ouallada grabbed the reins of Montpellier's horse, it snapped at her with protruberant yellow teeth, rolling its Frankish eyes. She kicked it in the knees: if she had been tall enough, she would have sunk her teeth reciprocally into its dusty neck. Jumping and tugging and cursing and praying, she watched the sky fill up with the dust of an approaching army, turning the blue to green, to fawn, to brown. Day was turning to night. And when, finally, she got back to ranting, impotent Montpellier, her only thanks were to be knocked to the ground. Even when she got to her knees he struck her again - a fearful blow with a big mailed fist, in the angle of her neck. 'D'you swear to serve God and the King?' he bawled at her, the veins bulging in his temples, the spit streaming from the corners of his mouth while the horse wagged its head up and down between them.

Fearing he meant to kill her on grounds of her colour, she swore a more fervent oath of allegience than ever came from a pure-blooded Frenchman.

'What's your family name?'

No time to spray him with exotic inventions. No time for 'ben Zefir of the Tuaregs'. She thrust a good Frankish name at him, the one her father had died in. 'Oriole, sir. Oriole.'

He misheard it, of course, mistaking birdsong for something grander, something more pretentious and vainglorious by far.

'Arise, then, Sir Gloriole, *and get on a bloody horse, for Christ's sake!'*

'Enough time. It is done,' said Yusif, and perhaps because Foulque was lying on the man's heart, he understood him almost at once.

'What's done, Yusif?' he asked, kneeling over him. 'What's done, you mad heathen?'

Yusif rolled his head sideways and his eyes cleared, appraised the wall of flying grit storming in from the desert. 'There's a sandstorm coming,' he said with interest. 'To cover our faces.' He looked his opponent over briefly. 'I would tell you to cover your eyes, Foulque Nerra, if they weren't blind already ... Our mail, look. It's knit. Tangled.'

Foulque knelt up awkwardly, shaking his gloves off so as to extricate the brass laps of his own mail from the delicate links of Yusif's byrnys. As he did so, the Siddi drew a small dagger from inside the armhole of his breastplate and opened his own throat just below the ear. A jet of blood spurted high, high in the air, and fell in very fine droplets of darkest red across Foulque's hair and arm and hand.

Nerra all but ran to the city gates. They hung closed, but unlocked, and he had only to shoulder them ajar. The fortress community of Umdan was peculiarly silent by contrast with the noisy confusion of Montpellier's panicked army. The inhabitants had gone into the cool green shadows of their houses to make the 'Jewish Pilgrimage': to kill their wives and babies before forfeiting their own lives to the vicissitudes of Fate. Saladin's forces were busy, none free to send on missions of rescue to out-of-way settlements. There were more important events afoot. So to the people of Umdan had remained the choice of how to pay the price, and their pilgrimage had been made within the span of time that Foulque and Yusif as-Shafih had fought at the barriers.

The knowledge fell on Foulque as though he alone had walked through the ruined streets slitting the throats of babes and sucklings. He went and sat on the low wall of a fountain whose statuary was draped in black to signify pollution. Threading the water, like the blood vessels in an eye, were a million tiny worms, plague red. Lifeless flies floated on the still pool, as though they had gorged overmuch on the dead.

'*Salaam aleikum,*' he said to the city at large. 'Peace be upon you.'

Ouallada was reduced to speechlessness - not by awe or surfeit of delight or even the pain in her neck, but by the sheer absurdity of the thing. Montpellier's stupidity stupefied her. At the back of her brain, her father's voice whispered, 'What gain? What profit?' But she had no answer to give him. What gain? What profit? From being knighted by mistake? There was none. For she was no more knight than she was Ouallada ben Zefir of the Tuaregs. She was no more a knight than any of the tufts of whirling sand which had been mistaken by Montpellier's ignorant Europeans for an approaching army. She would have to say something, draw his attention to his mistake. But not yet.

When the day ended, flayed out of the sky by a great gale of blinding grit, Leo of Montpellier already had to confront the fact that he had knighted two score squires in order to do battle with a sandstorm. The Enemy which had thrown him into such panic was nothing but a cloud of grit inhabited by dead locusts, flies and the nasty black seeds of the colocynth melons.

Further to vex Montpellier, they did not find treasure of great worth inside the walls of Umdan. For by the time Foulque had pointed out to them that the Arab mind might measure wealth in other than money, Siddi Yusif as-Shafih's library was well alight, its two thousand books spiralling up as ash to enlighten the flies which attempted to mate with each black particle.

'He knighted me,' said Ouallada as they walked, if not side-by-side then on a parallel course around the curtain wall. The burning buildings loosed an acrid stench of disappointed malice, as the army strove to find victory among the ruins. 'Montpellier knighted me.'

'Mm? Yes, he's partial to it, that one. The smallest crisis and he knights his squires. Fifty at a time.'

'But what do I do, Foulque? Do I tell him? Or just let it lie?'

He was wholly occupied with his own thoughts. She could bring only a tiny part of his mind to bear on the foolishness of the situation. 'Oh, tell him, tell him. He'll be glad enough there's one less knight to account for to the Duke of Poitiers.' He walked along the parapet, his face towards the desert, his hands brushing each other, palm over palm, again and again, almost as if he were washing. His surcoat steamed in the early sun where he had washed it yet again at the fountain to try to take out Yusif's blood.

'Come with me, won't you? He may be angry.' She was not afraid, in fact, of Montpellier, did not think there was anything left in the world to frighten her. But she wanted to prise Foulque out of the black mire into which events had sunk him. She wanted to break in on his thoughts which seemed to exclude all comfort.

Suddenly he scowled across at her and said, 'Are you in love with me?'

There was no time to lie. 'Yes, Foulque. A long time now.'

He assimilated the answer and nodded. 'As-Shafih

said as much,' then lengthened his stride so that he quickly left her behind, alone on the fortress wall, amid the indelible stains of spilled and extinguished Greek fire.

CHAPTER THIRTY THREE

A Love Returned

So she was obliged to confront Montpellier single-handedly with the news that he had knighted a woman by mistake. By the time she did so, their ship was sailing the last few miles into Marseilles harbour. She had come to think of it as unimportant alongside the fact that Foulque now shunned her company. She might have left it unsaid altogether, if Leo had not persistently called her 'Sir Gloriole'. In the midst of his regret at knighting forty boys unnecessarily, he adopted a stubborn kind of favouritism towards Ouallada whom he had at least knighted personally.

So when she came to him and said that he had made a mistake, he spent the first ten minutes contradicting her, believing she meant the mistake in *general* rather than any *particular* mistake.

'You see, I'm a woman.'

'You're what?'

And she pulled off her coif - by now so disgusting that it had raised a rash across her jawline and neck. Her black hair tumbled down, standing away from her head in odd, painful kinks where she had packed it, fresh-washed, inside the linen hood. It reached far beyond her shoulders.

'That doesn't prove anything,' said Montpellier, reduced to foolish ness by the shock. 'Hair doesn't prove a thing.'

'But I assure you, sir, I am a woman. Have been since my cradle.'

Rage took over from astonishment. 'And you let me knight you? When you knew all along you were a woman? You still let me knight you? Rutebeuf! Come here, Rutebeuf! D'you hear this?'

'I'm sure I shan't miss that to which I was never entitled,' she said, as carefully as though she were balancing her way along a high wall. 'I realise it was a mistake pure and ...'

'D'you hear this ... this ... this *blackamoor*, Rutebeuf? Says she's a woman! Says I dubbed a woman knight!'

'I'd not meant to make it so public ...' she said in a discreet whisper. But he fumed and spluttered the news to his second-in-command and to his chaplain, demanding to see them outraged, too.

The chaplain was of the opinion that it simply could not be. No more than a woman could become a prelate, could she be dubbed a knight. Rutebeuf, Leo's second-in-command, hedged his answers round with diplomacy, knowing that Montpellier did not like to see even his disasters discounted as being of no importance. 'It seems to me a purely *administrative* error,' he said between stiff, prim lips. 'It simply cannot be ratified in practical terms ... I mean, does she own a sword?' They were all of them inclined to pretend she was not present at all and represented a purely theoretical problem.

'Oh yes, I own a sword,' said Ouallada sadly. For Foulque had brought her, without explanation, Yusif as-Shafih's *baida* and jewelled *saif*, the spoils of combat.

'But she's never trained in combat, sure!'

'Yes. Truly, I have. And fought in combat, too.' She had not begun by meaning to make their life difficult, but somehow, once they started to discount her life, the recollections which came to mind refused to be ignored. She remembered the horn pick and the club with which she had killed her father; as good as killed. Maybe it was her father's ghost which egged her on. 'I did receive a knightly education, too, sir, in carving at dinner, and Latin, and heraldry and horsemanship.'

'Who from? The same as taught you to whore with milord Etang-Nerra?' said the chaplain drawing in his fingertips against his belly and shuddering theatrically.

A sea of red overwhelmed her. 'Have a care, sir. As a man of God it ill becomes you to offer insults to a maid, and since I'm a knight now, you dishonour the brotherhood of knights to say it. I am not Foulque Nerra's whore, nor ever was.'

The chaplain snorted and Rutebeuf stamped his feet on the hollow deck, feeling the cold. 'Well, a maid of any decorum might prove her breeding by letting a silence fall over such an indignity as this. Hardly seemly to be thought a man, I would have said.'

'It was a mistake, that's all. A stupid mistake,' the chaplain puttered angrily.

'Hold your haste, sir!' Montpellier bridled. He did not care to be told he made 'mistakes'. Great men are permitted to be eccentric, but not wrong. Besides, he had spoken certain magical words, and to say that those words accounted for nothing - could be waived - was to diminish his magic and theirs. 'Such things cannot be unsaid, being said in the eye of God and deeply sworn.' And with this grand but unhelpful piece of rhetoric, Leo de Montpellier took himself up to the prow to recover the status of a figurehead.

It was left to the chaplain and Rutebeuf to grimace at one another over the top of Ouallada's head and tacitly agree that drastic measures were called for. 'It can't be let stand,' said Rutebeuf 'The damage has to be kept to a minimum.'

'I've got no wish to damage Sir Leo - and nothing to profit by it, sirs,' said Ouallada. 'I simply thought it best to tell him ...'

'I draw the limit at killing her,' said the cleric.

'Oh, out of the question,' Rutebeuf agreed. 'But I can think of a way or two to ... neutralise the problem.'

'Neutralise?'

Grapples from the Marseilles tugs came over the ship's side nearby where they stood, raptor claws of metal.

'Leave it with me. It can be done before we dock.'

'What done? Done what? I told you. It's forgotten. It's nothing,' said Ouallada regretting her momentary vanity.

'Your opinion, young woman, is not germain. Unfortunately Sir Leo, your commander, *does* set store by his...error. The matter is out of your hands.'

She turned and fled along the deck, weaving between the shabby, boisterous troops with their eyes all set on the land. Her long hair cracked in their faces, brushed them like a living thing which startled them, being so out-of-place and unfamiliar.

The sand shifted and reformed itself within her boots into small ridged dunes that bruised the soles of her feet. 'Neutralised?' How 'neutralised'? When she looked back, colliding with chevaliers and making them curse, she could see the chaplain standing on his toes to keep track of her, a look of serene composure on his face. Rutebeuf was nowhere to be seen.

She wanted to search out Foulque, to ask his help, to tell him the presentiment she had of an imminent unpleasantness. But when she found him, he cast on her one of those haunted looks of intense embarrassment. She knew that he was looking forward to docking almost as much to put distance between them as to re-embark upon his courtship of Aude. So she merely curled up within his sphere of influence, so to speak, trusting to the fact that however great his dislike of her, he would let nothing very terrible overtake her.

'Shall you go back to Toulouse? Back to the monastery?' she asked.

'Out of civility,' he said, so sharply that she doubted he knew the meaning of the word.

'But not to be re-admitted to Holy Orders.' She was quite desperate to know what he was thinking, and no closer to knowing it than when they walked the walls of

Umdan watching the library burn.

'I've been thinking lately about the Cathar persuasion.'

'What, the Zoroastrians?' She laughed out loud.

'They're not entirely the same thing. At base they are Christians, after all.'

'And just what have you been "thinking" about them? How to confute them, all those heretics and charlatans?'

He frowned at her noise and looked around him, unwilling to attract attention by it. No one was eavesdropping, but a lad of about sixteen in a green doublet was peering down from the deck above, apparently trying to study Ouallada with myopic eyes. He did not seem to know whether or not to like what he saw.

'The notion of the Demiurge appeals to me,' said Foulque stuffily. 'And it's born in on me that this material world hardly bears the hallmarks of God's final purpose. On the contrary, the soul is pinned to the earth by its appetites.'

'Oh Nerra! Who do you think you're talking to? This is Ouallada! This is me! 'Sir Gloriole', as ever was. Keep your wordmongering for your Prior. I'm not impressed. What you mean is, your lust for Aude d'Haut-Beziers is worth sliding even into heresy! What you mean is you're too fond of your ... your *obsession* to let her play on her own at being a heretic!'

The waterfront was lined with women - wives, whores, mothers, casual spectators drawn by the sight of an unfamiliar sail; fishwives, children, tradeswomen, ranged like skittles on a shy. 'The world's full of women, Foulque! Look! Just look at them! The whole country's aswarm with them, Foulque! Why her? Why Aude? Why one silly woman in one silly acre of the big womany world? Why? If you've got to spend yourself in the fairground, why her? Why not one of them? Enjoy yourself! Compare. Look around at the others. See how she compares with the rest. Not well, if you'll take my word. But look for yourself! Taste! Don't just sink your anchor in the one spot because you always have! Don't! At least find a good Christian! Forget Aude. She's just one among the millions!'

The youth on the deck above had been joined by a friend and they were discussing Ouallada. They cast an eye over Foulque, too, and he bridled at that, half-rose to his feet and asked them if there was something he could do for them. They murmured vaguely between themselves, failing to answer.

'And had you anyone in *particular* you'd sooner have me favour?' he asked her pointedly, as he sat down again.

'Well, damn you,' she said, slapping his face. 'Damn you. Damn you. Damn you.'

Which eased him slightly of his awkwardness: he was accustomed to the dislike better than to the love of women. He said, 'It's just that – presently - since our stay with as-Shafih - I find myself ... cast adrift a little. From the certainties of my childhood. You see? One faith seems to have as much to commend it as another. As much and as little. Only Aude is constant. Only my love for Aude. That's where I've sunk my anchor, as you say. That's where I'll ride out the storm. You see? So I'm obliged to look over the Cathar faith with less jaundice than I formerly did. You see?'

His paternal condescension rested on her like a ton

weight - crushed all the spirit out of her. She nodded submissively and resolved to let him go to his own destruction and humiliation as some dogs throw themselves under the wheels of carts, for the fun of it.

The youth in the green doublet had suddenly appeared beside them. He waited politely for Foulque to stop speaking before putting his hand through Ouallada's arm. 'Very well. I agree. I'll take you,' he said.

She looked him up and down. She was taller than he by a span. 'Take me where, boy?'

'To wife,' he said, and picked up her bundle of goods, his eyes gleaming at the sight of as-Shafih's jewelled sword.

'Will you so!'

'So long as I can have in writing the promise of some land.' He did not say it to Ouallada but called it out to the chaplain on the upper deck. When she did not move from the spot, he tugged on her like a recalcitrant mule - took hold of an elbow and a handful of hair and even clicked his tongue in encouragement.

'Do you know this person?' Foulque enquired.

She tried to extricate her hair. 'I don't have that honour. But I fear I may require you, Lord Foulque Etangs-Nerra, to inform him that I am not disposed to company just now.'

What had promised comedy suddenly degenerated into an unpleasant degree of violence. A pack of youths with foul mouths, their clothes smelling of sea-sickness, crammed themselves into the companionway and took hold of Ouallada by whatever part they could reach, chanting a crude version of a wedding song. Rutebeuf had raised a section of the latticed deck to expose a rope locker, and into it they shipped Ouallada, amid the marlin spikes, tar brushes and coils of hemp. When the cover would not go back into place, resting on her arched back, her bridegroom jumped on to the hatch. 'I seize on this woman!' he yelped, while the chaplain endeavoured to restore order and correctness to the procedure. 'And I make her my ...'

'Pray let us do this thing in reverence and with due respect for the law,' said the chaplain severely.

'Oh pray just let's do it and have it done,' said Rutebeuf. In his opinion it demeaned the whole chivalrous ethic almost as much as mistakenly knighting blackamoor women. 'Let's just marry 'em.'

Meanwhile, Foulque moved with the slowness of a bear newly emerged from hibernation, delving about among his packs and bundles, shrugging on his sheepskin waistcoat. He joined the crowd of young men and curious sailors trampling around and across the locker. Strands of Ouallada's hair were being walked to a different, lighter colour where they protruded through the lattice. Her face was not visible below in the dark, her cell too confining for her even to turn over and see the sky. 'You'll need a guardian to give the bride away,' said Foulque ponderously.

Rutebeuf was embarrassed. 'Oh. Ah. We thought she was your ... We didn't know you were in place-of-parent. We thought she was your ...'

'Certainly not,' said Foulque blackly.

'Do I get a piece of land?' the bridegroom bleated hopefully in Foulque's direction. For a piece of land and a house and the title of knight, he would have married any of the rats which shared the bilge space with Ouallada and the tar brushes.

'In the face of this congregation, do you take this woman .. .'

'A piece of land, you say?' asked Foulque, placing a paternal hand on the groom's neck. 'Do you mean beyond and above the land she already owns in Normandy? I made the gift myself, you see. I'd like to know, if you lift the burden of knighthood off this lady's shoulders to wear yourself, into what hands my family lands will be passing. Do you have, for instance, lands of your own?'

The boy filled up with pleasure. His eyes were starry and his face was flushed. 'Got a quarter share in my father's feu.'

'And of course there are six feet more.'

'Six feet?'

'The plot every man is heir to. Though in the case of sailors ... '

He broke off to lift the squire by belt and collar and pitched him over the side of the ship - flying and flailing and somersaulting his way downwards, his cries garnered up by the gulls. The water received him greedily, closing its mouth over him before blowing a lascivious kiss up at its benefactors with gleaming, spray-fringed lips. 'The Princess Ouallada ben Obeid has my protection, sirs,' said Foulque, 'and I take it amiss that she should be made currency of barter. Is that plain?'

His audience were lining the rail, looking for their friend to surface. Foulque and the chaplain regarded each other over the open locker, as Ouallada climbed out, smeared with tar and peppered with rat droppings, retching and sobbing.

'The anomaly has to be rectified,' said the chaplain down his nose.

'Not by seizure and rapine, I think,' said Foulque.

This latest offence by the Church decided Foulque on his course of action. He would have decided on it anyway. He was fully primed to disembark from the great ship of Catholicism and set foot on the foreign islands of Heresy. And all because he needed to return to Aude, needed to return to the pursuit and worship of Aude, needed to think that just once, just once in his life, he had not chosen wrongly when he crowned her queen of his heart.

Ouallada thanked him, not once but a dozen times. Finally, when he could not bear her gratitude a moment longer and they were safely ashore, he turned on her furiously and said, 'We are entirely even now, miss. I had my life from you in the desert. Now you have your maidenhead to do with as you please. May it bring you joy and sixteen children. And wealth and repute and the esteem of peasants. Now, do we have to protract our acquaintance another infernal day?'

She reined in her horse and let him gallop out of sight. She thought she must have drunk dry the bilges of the ship, for she was full to the crown with saltwater. It strained in her throat, it pricked at her eyes, it trickled down her cheeks dirtier than her grimy skin. Filthy tears. Pernicious tears. Tears full of lost opportunities; tears full of selfishness and jealousy and resentment; tears as hot as lust itself.

'Let him go,' she told herself. 'Blasphemer. Fool. There are men in the world as many as women. He's only one of a million. Why one silly man? Compare! At least choose a Christian, for Christ's sake!' And she believed it just about as much as he had believed the same argument. 'Let him go and be damned.' And at the word 'damned', her face crumpled and allowed yet more of her filthy, despicable tears to escape the hatch where she had thought to batten them away.

There was nowhere to go. There was everywhere and anywhere to go. France lay at her horse's feet like a field ready for gleaning.

Unfortunately, her knighthood also lay beneath her on the road, a shadow so securely sewn to her that one swift pull was not enough to detach it. Even now, the chaplain was repeating to Rutebeuf, between anthems of the *Te Deum* in Marseilles Abbey, that 'the anomaly must be rectified'.

'I'll send out spies to note where she comes to rest,' said Rutebeuf 'She's not the hardest fox to run to ground. And there'll be plenty ready to seize on her for a knighthood.'

'Especially with lands in Normandy,' the chaplain reminded him.

'And an arse like Mount Horeb.'

'I wouldn't know,' said the chaplain primly.

'Wouldn't you? What, not for a piece of land in Normandy?' said Rutebeuf with a jab of his elbow.

News of Foulque's exploits in the Hejaz and Umdan had lost much of their relevance by the time he recounted them to his Prior at Toulouse. Though the old man asked animated and pertinent questions, it was out of civility more than curiosity. For his abiding interest in the struggle to secure Jerusalem could bring him no further joy. Some of the man's resilient spirit had been crushed by the more recent news of Saladin's Revenge.

Salah-ed-din had mustered an army of one hundred thousand men and marched against Tiberias on the Sea of Galilee. Securing the watered valley, he obliged the opposition, led by King Guy of Jerusalem and the ubiquitous Reynaud de Châtillon, to keep the upper ground, unwatered, unfed. Their twelve thousand horsemen and twenty thou sand *enfants* were half-crazed for want of a drink when, under an outcrop of wind-worn rock known as the Horns of Hattin, they con fronted Saladin's forces.

Yusif as-Shafih was avenged that day; the people of Umdan were avenged, and Saladin's sister, too. Reynaud de Châtillon was paid back, at a blow, for the piracies of a lifetime. (At two blows, actually. As the captured King Guy received a bowl of iced rosewater in Saladin's tent and passed it on, to Châtillon, Saladin drew his sword and cut off Reynaud's arm sooner than have him drink and thereby claim the asylum of Moslem hospitality. A moment later, his head too was off, and Saladin's anger at an end. 'A king does not kill a king,' he reassured Guy of Jerusalem.)

By the time Foulque reached home, in ignorance of all this, Acre, Jaffa, Caesarea, Sidon and Beirut had all fallen. Even the once impregnable Crak des Chevaliers had been captured. The Christian world had shrunk, as a man's heart contracts with the sadness of old age. At least that was the Prior's experience of old age: an inward contraction and diminishing of optimism. He continued to trust in God and the ultimate triumph of Heaven over Hell, of course, but the tunnel of remaining history seemed to him to have been stretched; not he, nor any man yet born would live to crawl to its end.

So Foulque's other news struck the Prior as appalling, but not unbelievable - his decision not to re-enter Holy Orders; his determination to damn himself among the Cathars. It was just one more grief for the Prior to offer up to God, in the hope that the Almighty might make better sense of it all.

'And is that what your journey taught you?' exclaimed Aude, bright with mirth. 'The truth of the Cathar teachings? How funny! How comical! To go to the Holy Lands to become like us who never strayed from here!'

'I discovered, lady, that the only lodestone of life lay here, in you, in loving you. Everything else is compromised. Only you remain the one true element at the core of my being.'

Haut-Beziers had come to resemble the Siren Rock of legend, strewn with repining sailors powerless ever to leave. Aude's admirers drooped about, looking dissipated and overfed, while two cadaverous *perfecti* in black robes ranged about among them, preaching total abstinence. Four great murals had overrun the walls of the great-hall, depicting the vileness of the flesh as well as certain disembodied heads witnessing to fleshless rapture with big, beaming smiles. There was a brightness representing God, and a giant serpent, encircling the Earth, with its tail in its mouth.

Aude was frightened by the arrival of Foulque. It was entirely possible he had come back to wreak vengeance for the jokes played at his expense. Not for the first time, she regretted abusing their rendezvous in the chapel, in the Crystal Cave of Tristan and Iseult. Keeping it would have defused the man, given him, no excuse to come back like this and trouble her.

Since then, she had slept with many men, and a perverse curiosity remained about Foulque who was, after all, *different* from the rest and might have shown her a different kind of passion. She had given her favours without marrying, for she had wholly embraced (as she embraced every fashion) the religion of the Cathars, including its corruptions and abuses.

All sexual relations were of the body and, since the body is vile, even marriage could not be said to hallow the act. Besides, a man needed the sanction of his wife when he came to make his ultimate act of commitment, his *Consolamentum*, and if he were not married, there was no such problem. As a result, marriage had largely fallen into disuse in Beziers, Lavaur, Albi and the like.

The indigent missionaries of the faith took it quite literally, on the other hand. They really did abjure all comforts of the body, and worked for their neighbours for nothing, subsisting on bread and water. What chance did the Catholic priests have, sitting in their comfortable priories, of recouping their scattered flocks?

Still, saintly example could only teach so much. Even among those persuaded of Catharism, only a few tried to measure up to live the Perfect Life. Most fallen angels (as Catharism deemed Mankind) put off making their *Consolamenta* until they were on their deathbeds, foreswearing the flesh just in time to part from it. And in case of sudden death, there was always the *Convententia*, undertaken in advance by way of insurance: a declaration of intent. It did not offer quite the same perfect consummation of bliss in death - not a direct reunion with

God - but it was enough to set a soul on the right path, up there, along the Way of the Stars.

For Aude, the appealing element - mischievous novelty - had rather bled away over the years, for the faith had spread far and near. The Bishop of Carcassonne was a Cathar, elected by a Cathar people. Aude, if she had dared give it thought, was a little disappointed that it had become so commonplace, a little peeved that it placed no store on social rank. She was just a little weary of ex-bakers and trouserless saints visiting her house to preach endlessly, over meals they did not eat, about the foulness of women. She was even a little bored that talk among the troubadours had given way to discussions of God's relationship with Harmony and how the principles of the Universe hung on the musical stave.

Foulque re-entered her world like a draught at the opening of a door, that whips up all the strewings. Her fingers closed tight round the arm of Auxerre d'Impt, and she said, 'What does he want here?'

'You once told me that if I took upon me the faith of the Credents, I should be welcome again in your court,' declared Foulque.

A hesitant twitch of the lips flowered into the brightest of smiles. She invited him close. Her face was so sprinkled with silver, crescents of the denser dust reshaping the high and low contours of her features. Her cheeks were hollower, her cheekbones higher, her temples projecting a narrower forehead of glistening flour-white skin. 'Can you sing still?'

'My throat's not been cut,' he said, and she shivered as she expressed her delight.

Behind his back, her aspirant, discarded or current

lovers looked at him as malevolently as dogs displaced from the fireside, but in front of his face they vied to outshine one another with the extravagance of their greetings, introducing themselves with panegyric laments at their own earthly shortcomings. They were vile sinners, they said, were victims of fleshliness, were almost as hateful in their own sight as in the sight of God. Such was the fashion. Aude meanwhile stood a little behind Auxerre, her fingers intertwining in front of her bodice.

Foulque did not seek to outdo them in rhetoric. 'I fear I've lately lost the art of the pretty word. I don't doubt it will come back to me after your Deacon has breathed a portion of the Holy Spirit into me. After all, God is Harmony, is He not?'

The two cadaverous deacons closed upon him, one enthusiastic, one suspicious; their hyena instincts saw the first stagger of a weakening bull. Aude shooed them both away. 'You mustn't mind Foulque,' she said. 'It's just his manner. We used to call him the Railing Bishop, but see! He's given up even his dyed-fast popery to seek the Consolation of the Pure.' And she emerged from hiding to seize Foulque's hand and draw him to a chair by the hearth.

'Does this stranger think the Consolation's to be had for a knock at the door?' demanded the suspicious perfect. 'Is he willing to serve a year - maybe two - living the Cathar life? Does he know he might still be found wanting as a trustee of the Spirit? Does he think to shoulder his way into God's presence with his mace and his mail?'

'Oh hush tush. Peace now, Deacon Ligaud. Foulque

here is the humblest man I know - aren't you, my dear? And the gentlest.' She sat down at Foulque's feet, stroking the backs of his hands, turning her face up towards him. 'And besides. Foulque doesn't strive after *absolute* perfection - do you? Not *complete* perfection, do you? We're not all as blessed as you, Ligaud, with saintliness. Foulque shall take his *Convententia*, yes, he shall! Then you may take as long as you like, Deacon, to teach him the difference between the Bad Life and the Good. I mean, I myself have been a Credent these two years, Foulque, and still I don't feel know enough to take the final step! Yes, make him one of us, Ligaud. Do! do!'

'And does he know that the touch of woman is vile?' said Deacon Ligaud with heavy sarcasm, looking at their joined hands. He had come to perform the monthly service of *Apparelhamentum* before Foulque's - arrival wished now to be gone, but was kept from leaving by the last ritual.

'I do know it,' said Foulque. The look which passed between them entirely altered their relationship. 'I am Foulque Nerra-des ... I am Foulque, formerly called Etangs Nerra, though I've shed my lands of late in payment of a ... spiritual debt, as it were.'

'Oh!' exclaimed Aude and let go his hands to make a fluttering gesture of exaggerated amazement.

Ligaud signified, by mounting the dais, that he was ready to take his leave. The household turned dutifully all in the one direction, as though about to say their Creed, and the room was briefly silent. Then they all bowed their heads, joined their hands and made three genuflexions. A ragged recital jerked and halted along until everyone was speaking in unison. 'Good Christian, give us God's blessing and yours. Pray to the Lord for us, that God will preserve us from the Bad Death and bring us to the Good End in the hands of faithful Christians.'

Ligaud signalled to his postulant to bring the household Bible from Aude's small side-table, and while he did so, said, 'God bless you and keep your souls from the Bad Death and bring you to the Good End.' Then he stepped down to bless, with the Kiss of Peace, Auxerre d'Impt, who passed the kiss to the man beside him. It was transferred thus throughout all the men present. Using the Bible to sanitise his kiss, Ligaud passed it to Aude d'Haut-Beziers who kissed the book with a sensual rapture. But instead of distributing this sexless Kiss of Peace to the other women, she skipped over to Foulque and, with a mischievious giggle, planted the sacred kiss squarely on his mouth.

'It is good of you to see me, Father,' said Ouallada kneeling down on the grass path of the priory herb garden to kiss the Prior's ring.

'Pray stand up, child. We shall walk, if you please. Standing aggravates the pains in my back.'

So they walked, through air so heavy with smells that it seemed to lean against her cheekbones and crumple them. 'Has Foulque Etangs-Nerra been here, Father?'

He was slow to answer. 'Are you trying to find him?'

'No. No. I know where he's going. He told me where he was going. But he said he might come here first.' Absentmindedly she broke off a sprig of rosemary and began picking off the needle-like leaves one by one.

'And if he did, young lady?'

'I thought ... ' She felt out of her depth, her head

swimming with the herbs' fragrance, her resolve ebbing away. She should have kept on her disguise, she thought now. 'I thought he might just ... unburden his soul to you. I know he holds you in great esteem, even if ... even though he ... *changed* a little while he was overseas.'

'The change was certainly very great,' said the Prior, taking off his straw hat and examining the inside with scrupulous care. 'And what makes you think that I could unfold to you what he spoke in the confidence of the Confessional?'

She pounced on the word, making him start. '*Did* he confess, then? Did he make Confession?'

The Prior raised the hat as though to put it back on, but held it in front of his face, the sunlight streaming through its open weave. 'I regret, you are right to doubt it. He has forsworn the observances of our Faith, mademoiselle ... I'm sorry, what name did you say?'

'Gloriole, Father. Gloriole. But he must've said something to you! He must've confided in you! He'd not have come here just to make himself offensive.'

The Prior Correau was clearly not offended so much as grieved. 'I blame myself,' he admitted. 'I had thought a journey of that sort - a challenge as demanding ... Well, I had thought the man would *find* himself Like John Baptist in the wilderness. And instead ...'

'Instead he lost himself. Like Legion overrun by demons.'

They passed beneath the dark shadow of a pergola entwined with laburnum, and the old man plucked down the medicinal pods, collecting them in his pocket. He did it without thinking: the pods would lie in his pocket until the next time he put his hand inside and wondered how it came to be full of laburnum. 'You ask, of course, entirely out of academic interest in his soul's welfare, I take it.'

'I ask because I love him, Father, as you perfectly well guess - probably hold me at fault for it. But my love's of the useless kind. It has no claws; it can't take a grip of him. I thought yours might catch deeper, that's all.'

'Peace, child. Peace. Don't upset yourself' He held up the long flap of his sleeve for her to wipe her eyes on. 'You mistake, you really do. I think Foulque's a fortunate man to be loved by such a ... feeling friend. And it wouldn't have surprised me in the very least to hear his affections had strayed from his vocation while he was in the desert. Indeed, I had great hopes of breaking the infernal shackle that binds him to that ... that unremarkable lady at Beziers. There are more ways than the cloister to reach the Gates of Heaven, you know. Unfortunately, you also mistake in thinking I could restrain him when he was bent on self-destruction.'

The crevice in her heart opened a little wider. 'So he came here as he said: just out of civility.'

'Oh, not entirely, child. He came to make gift of all his lands and estates to the Church.'

'To the *Church?*'

'Yes. I see you think it as strange as I did. In a man bent on joining a heretical cult. But he argued that the lands would have passed to the Church had he re-entered Orders, so that his promise was already given when he left to go abroad. He didn't feel he could break his word and hadn't the need of worldly goods, in any case, given his new, ascetic's religion. I tried to dissuade him. But you must see, my dear Mademoiselle Gloriole, that to a point I owed it to my church not to let such huge resources fall into the hands of Cathars. So I agreed finally to accept the gift. I see he may live to regret it - I pray he may live to regret every sorry aspect of it. But the man's acquainted with such depths of despair ... I tried and I failed, my dear Mademoiselle Gloriole.'

'Sir Gloriole,' said Ouallada vacantly, bewilderingly. 'And if *he* doesn't regret the gift, I'm sure La Belle Aude will rue it enough for both of them.'

'Well, that's that,' said Aude as the door closed behind the venerable Deacon Ligaud. 'Now confess it all, dearest Foulque - what's this nonsense about parting from your land? I'd have sworn you promised all those lands to *me*!'

'In marriage, naturally. But as you pointed out to me, you Credents ... we Credents don't observe the sacrament of marriage.'

'Oh well, that's not quite true,' said Auxerre d'Impt, thrusting himself concretely into the conversation by stepping between them, his back to Foulque. 'It's simply that a man must renounce his wife to make his Consolation. So it's best if he doesn't take one in the first place.'

'And if he has, his wife must give her permission!' laughed Aude loudly and skirted d'Impt and wrapped herself in Nerra's arm, declining to be separated from him. 'Which, of course I'd *never* give if I were married to any of my dear friends! I've had it explained to me ever so often and I know now that Death's quite the most wonderful thing. But oh dear, I'm afraid I just don't hate life as much as I ought. Is that very dreadful of me, Foulque?'

'You must be a real thorn in the side of *perfecti* like Ligaud,' he said.

'What?' It was a long time since an aspirant had said things to Aude that were anything less than complimentary. It took her some moments to readjust: Foulque could sound so venomous sometimes. She was still feeling her way with him, still nervous of some sudden violent act of vengeance for the mockery she had made of him. 'What can you mean, you dear, rude man?'

'I mean you tempt men to drop their eyes from Heaven and look at you instead.' A blush of satisfaction suffused Aude's cheek.

This acquiescence of his was almost too good to be true, and yet in her egocentricity, Aude had always half-expected him to return, to succumb, to be irresistibly drawn back to her. 'Do you have a song for me, Foulque?'

'A thousand and twenty, lady.'

'Well, well, one will do for today. Did you write it for me in the desert? I heard you went over the Jordan to kill blackamoors.'

'It was written in the desert, yes,' Foulque admitted, 'by rather the same process as a scorpion stinging itself to death.' And he sang, to the accompaniment of a huge bass tambor, his feet set square, reciting not singing, as though his verse were an incitement to violence, a *sirventes* rallying troops to a lost war.

The closing of my lids unclothes you.
Your nakedness overclouds me, filling my sky,
And I thirst for my shafts of rain to pierce the blue,
My lightning to rive you through and through.

My throat is ash-dry for fear of thy
Scorpions which are in me...

Aude was moved.

Primarily she was moved by great waves of self-congratulation which hit her like grit in a sandstorm. Here was a blessed relief from the philosophical conceits of her regular admirers. Here was a lesson for them in single-mindedness. Here was a reminder of the good old times when there had been Catholics and Cathars in equal number making their obsequies firstly and foremost to her. Even her body, which she allowed to act impromptu of late, told her Foulque should be rewarded, welcomed home, re-admitted to her happy domestic regime.

She took the drum out of his hands and, in its place, laid the great stook of her yellow hair. And leading him by this golden halter out of the great-hall, she climbed the stairs to her bedchamber allowing her breath to catch on her vocal cords and liberate small groaning sounds of uncontainable desire. As the exertions of climbing the steep stairs made her draw deeper and faster breaths, her moans grew quite audible to the men and women in the room below.

'I do believe it's time you received your sweet reward,' said Aude. 'The troubadour's kiss of acknowledgement.' She kissed him on the forehead, maternally, teasingly. 'Now I shall be your perfect and you shall make your genuflexions to me ... That's better: I never heard you laugh before. Dearest Foulque. People ought to laugh more. They don't laugh here as much as they did. People ought to laugh more. I do so like a good joke ...'

He made only one genuflexion, in order to take hold of her gown's hem and tear it along the weft. He tore it and went on tearing, and being cut on the bias it tore in a spiral, round and round her body, as a horn encircles a minstrel.

She would have him apologise later for the wanton destruction of a favourite gown. Presently she was inebriated with her own body's appetites. Later she would teach him in whose hands the power lay to make and mar. Sufficient for the moment to surrender to the anarchy of Satan with his rebellious angels, whom (the Cathars said) entered into the bodies of women to keep the fleshly world in thrall. Just as there would be sufficient time on her deathbed to renounce Satan.

In the meantime, she allowed Foulque the delusion of mastery, and did not resist the violence of his eager ignorance. There would be time enough to ease him away to a more manageable and deferential distance.

CHAPTER THIRTY FOUR

Perfect

'And what do you mean to do now, child?' asked the Prior. 'Will you go after him? Try to turn him from this latest foolishness?'

She shook her head. 'Not again. I've over-taxed his patience already. If you couldn't persuade him, I could only fix his heart on it. By the sea - that sea, I mean, down yonder - I saw these great worms - a million legs, sunk in the beach. You could fetch out their heads with a sprinkle of salt, but if you grabbed and pulled they'd break themselves in half sooner than let go their burrows.'

Prior Correau recognised the description of Foulque. 'So where will you go, mademoiselle?'

'To the land he gave me in Normandy, I suppose. I

have to live, and I'd as soon not live by lovesongs any more. I don't know, but I seem to have lost heart too much for lovesongs. Perhaps you can tell me - is Normandy very big, sir? Unless it's little, I don't quite know how I'll find the place.'

'I can't deceive you. Normandy is sizeable,' said the Prior. The sadness he had felt at Foulque's visit was only deepened by Ouallada's, and he was filled with anxiety for this unprotected woman travelling a thousand miles into unknown provinces and an uncertain future. 'My blessing and God's preserve you.'

She smiled at him, with all but her eyes, and thanked him several times over. Then the keys of the gatekeeper rattled in the lock and she was excluded once again from a community of men unsure just what function she fulfilled in God's overall plan.

Outside, in just the place where she had sat while waiting for Foulque to sue for re-admission, a pair of youths stood waiting for her. The woollen hose of one had shrunk and opened up a long gap between cuff and shoe which showed off large, raw anklebones. It was the seawater that had shrunk them: her prospective bridegroom was not accustomed to swimming in his drawers.

Ouallada clamoured on the gate bell again to gain sanctuary, but the gatekeeper had wandered away deep into the recesses of the priory. She backed away along the priory wall, the jewelled sword of as-Shafih scraping its hilt along the flints. She turned and ran for the trees where she had tied her horse - only to find her animal flanked by their two, her reins knotted together with theirs, the stirrup leathers buckled into theirs. With the noise of their shouting and panting and flatfooted running behind her, she clambered up the right-hand horse, squirmed her legs between the rubbing flanks and leaned forward to untangle reins.

'You! Stop! Or we'll marry you and hang you for a horsethief after!'

The horses barged together, flanks sharp with pricking hair banged together like boats, and her legs were squeezed so hard that the blood roared in the veins. She succeeded in drawing out her knife but, confronted by a twisted tangle of jerking leathers, cut through the wrong ones. As the horses grew more and more confused, as-Shafih's unsheathed sword brushed a sweaty flank. The beast jumped four footed off the ground, its back arched, its head between its knees. She was propelled straight upwards, and her head and shoulders smashed a lattice of twigs. The spiteful broken branch-ends took hold of her by hanks of hair so that it seemed she would be hanged, like Absalom, at the mercy of her enemies.

But they too had to contend with the bucking confusion of horses at the foot of the tree. By the time they stood below her, screaming obscenities, she was halfway up the tree and still climbing. When her bridegroom started up after her, she dislodged him once with a kick and once with downward slashes of as-Shafih's sword. There she sat, in the angle of trunk and branch, like a Moorish dryad ready to bring bad luck to anyone who touched wood.

'Well? Think you can stay there for ever?' blurted the bridegroom in the green doublet and shrunken hose. He grimaced up at her, his snub-nosed face contorted by a mixture of temper and short sightedness. 'We can wait! I can wait all night. All year, if you like! I haven't come all this way to leave you sitting in a tree, you bloody black crow! Get down here. Christ's blood! Ought to count yourself lucky I'm ready to take you!' Between bouts of insults he would mutter to his companion. 'Bloody old hag. How old is she, d'you think? What's she saving it for? D'you think she's baptised? Cut my throat when I'm sleeping, like as not.'

Not until the light was fading, and the cooling day put them in mind to light a campfire, did it occur to them - they could light a fire at the foot of the tree and flush her out of it that way. She allowed them to exhaust themselves gathering up tinder and trying to strike a spark, before she spoke - her first words, and so loud that they jumped and dropped the flame. 'Very well. I surrender. You win. Let's give Rutebeuf what he wants. I'll marry ... I'll make a marriage. You can have my land and much joy may it bring you. It's yours. You'll be doing me a service, you're right. Yonder. In that priory. Let's make a marriage, damn your eyes.'

'Hate,' said Aude. 'It's as if he hates me. I can't say it any other way.' She had come by a little black maid to comb her hair and sew her dresses and listen to her monologues without understanding a word. 'Hate. Almost like hate,' she said, but the maid did not understand the word and smiled agreeably as she brushed Aude's gleaming yellow hair. 'And he's written me no songs, either.'

He had written none even as a result of her taking him into her bed - a crisis which, in her other *trobar* lovers, had given rise to great outpourings of ecstasy. 'Too cocksure, I dare say,' she said and was pleased with the pun, in a disconsolate sort of way, wishing she could use it at dinner and knowing she could not.

They had noticed the difference: she knew they had. For even d'lmpt and Gautier had withdrawn to a sulky distance. Now they turned their backs on Nerra less out of disdain than like Gibraltar apes showing their backsides in submission. He had conquered where they had only explored. He had planted his flag where they had only mined and hunted a little. It would have to alter. She would have somehow to place a foot on his neck - to re-establish the correct alignment of the planets with her as the Sun shining down on the rest. All of the rest.

And yet she could not simply spurn Foulque, revoke her acknowledgement of him. He was too clever for that. He had ploughed her and sown deep. From one dishevelled morning till the scimitar moon cut off the Christian day, she thought of nothing but the smell of him, the weight of him, the beat of him like a great battering ram swung on ropes against the enemy's wall in time to a great skin drum. The Enemy, yes.

All day long the physical world reminded her of him - the shoulder of land pushing the river Aude aside, the trout in the river pushing against the flow, the prodigious looming belltower of Beziers' far-off church, the distant figures of riders on the road. For she always hoped one was him, could imagine that one was him, coming home early from his studies with Jean Ligaud in the religion of the *perfecti*. Coming home early. Preferring her company to that of the deacons and postulants.

'He's old, that's what,' she told her maid, who smiled and nodded exasperatingly. 'Already he can't love a whole night through.' But she knew it was not true. She knew it was not Foulque whose stamina tailed off with the dawn, but she whose appetite increased with every passing night, so that by morning she wished it to be night all over again. He came from the land of salt, and drinking him only increased her thirst. She feared the stories they told of sailors losing their wits that way.

She loathed the feeling of riding a horse with neither reins nor stirrups to steady her, to give her control. She resented his insolent power over her. But whatever grievance she felt towards him would apparently never match his against her. For he seemed to hate her. She could not find any other way of saying it.

Jealousy was bound to follow. Not only was it in her nature to want sole possession, but as the Codes of Love always made plain, once love has come, jealousy is never far behind. Even Aude (who was not particularly receptive to abstract concepts) could see the irony of her dilemma. Having taunted Foulque Nerra into giving up his religion, she now found herself envying the religion she had forced on him.

Most converts, after making their *Convententia*, were ardent in their observances for a season, then eased themselves back into the everyday business of sin. Some thought (since the next perfect they met could absolve them) to amass a few worthwhile sins in the interim. But not / Foulque. He entered into his studies with the same dogged diligence he had shown the ancient philosophers and the works of the saints.

She bitterly resented the time he spent with Jean Ligaud and the other *perfecti* in the ascetic squalor of their community. When he got up from her bed and washed himself, she could almost hear Ligaud clicking his tongue at the vileness of what they had done and see Foulque's shoulders bend beneath the reproach. Was it possible he loved Ligaud's God more than her? The mere possibility was unbearable. It tormented her. And because it was not her place, as the Loved One, to be tormented, she resolved to quash all rivalry.

She would make a joke of it too. To her maid's surprise, Aude suddenly laughed out loud at the hilarious prospect of the trick she meant to play on her lover.

'We'll soon see how much he hates the sins of the flesh,' she confided to her looking-glass, and her reflection grinned back at her, with white teeth and irresistible mouth. She noticed how a small bruise had blackened to a purple patch on her top lip and recalled how she had come by the injury. She had tried to detain him from putting on his clothes one morning, from buckling his great leather belt. An accident. An unintended clash of her mouth against the tail of the belt. He had apologised. But he had not unfastened again. Aude turned the mirror face down and abruptly stood up. She would have him kneel to her, before long, press his mouth where she had pressed hers, seek her blessing sooner than Jean Ligaud's, and give Ligaud cause to despair of his prize disciple.

She made the navette with her own hands - a local delicacy - a cake delicately flavoured with almond blossom. She selected monkshood for her purgative, because the name amused her. Life ought to be amusing.

She served the cake to Foulque at dinner, bringing him wine in a silver cup and several slices of the spongecake - as pink as her nakedness. Unfortunately, the poisonous monkshood sepels had sunk down in the cooking to form a purplish layer rather like a bruise: she was afraid he might avoid eating it. But he ate the cake, with the same absentminded appreciation he used in his lovemaking, catching the crumbs in the palm of his other hand. He did not seem to grasp what an extraordinarily open declaration it was of Aude's love, to bring him food baked with her own hand. Foulque's rivals watched in awe, never having seen the lady of Haut-Beziers grant such a boon. Either that was in their mind, she thought, or they had guessed her trick and were watching with the same delighted horror that she felt singing in her belly. She had made sure Jean Ligaud was staying overnight at the castle.

Only as Foulque sat stabbing the crumbs off his left palm with the tip of his tongue did it suddenly occur to her that she might have added too much monkshood. The thought struck her in the abdomen again, like a pang, as she lay in bed that night awaiting her lover. He did not come and he did not come. In the end he was so late that she met him at the door, frightened, thinking the effect had been over-quick. When he looked well, she was so relieved that she decided to forget the whole scheme. Perhaps monkshood was not as effective as people said.

The cramps struck Foulque soon before midnight. He was kneeling astride her at the time and, by the light of candles, she saw his face turn green as copper and felt his skin turn icy cold, except for the apex of his belly where the circulation struggled to counteract the toxins. Then he was overtaken by violent stomach cramps and uncontrollable vomiting. He fell from the bed, drew up his knees and, unable to catch his breath between spasms of sickness, writhed amid her discarded clothing.

'Oh God, you're dying,' she said, not having expected anything so violent, and she threw one of the bed blankets over him to avoid the sight, and sat curled up in the middle of the bed, her arms folded over her head. 'Oh God, he's dying!'

'Fetch some - ' He looked at her with eyes bloodshot from the strain of retching, and put out a hand towards her before drawing it back sharply. His nose began to bleed, convincing her more than ever that he would haemorrhage to death in front of her eyes. 'Ligaud!' he managed to say. It was that one word which brought her back to her senses. She even smiled.

'Yes. Yes. A perfect. I'll fetch a perfect.'

Jean Ligaud excluded everyone from the room while he made examination of Foulque, lifting him back on to the bed and pressing vicious knuckles deep into the man's gut to discern, he said, the full extent of the affliction.

'Oh Christ! Oh Christ!' groaned Nerra. 'Am I dying?'

Ligaud drove his fingers in at the solar plexus. 'Oh yes. I believe so, my friend. You haven't long. May God spare us time for the *Consolamentum*. Fetch a New Testament and a clean white cloth!' he called out to the crowd gathering in the next-door room. 'Foulque Nerra wishes for the final Consolation!' Then he strode about the bed, throwing the formulae of his faith at Foulque like logs on to a dying fire.

'My brother. Do you desire to give yourself to the Faith?'

'Yes! Bless me!' screamed Foulque.

'God bless you. Do you give yourself to God and the Gospel?'

'Yes!'

For Foulque, swamped in the panic of sudden, incomprehensible pain, the room around him seemed to be melting, the face of the perfect swimming on a molten torrent of furniture, fabrics and decomposing stove. The night sky rushed at him through yawning gaps in the wall. Someone brought a white cloth and spread it over the bedclothes - as though he were already dead - then laid a book on the cloth, which he could see rise and fall with the writhings of his body. The corner posts of the bed heeled like the masts of ships and Ligaud's hands were magnified to the dimensions of constellations.

' ... Do you wish to receive the gift of God and the holy ordination which the Lord brought from the Heavenly court to confide to the Apostles and which they transmitted to the good men through Holy Prayer by the laying on of hands, even until now?'

'I do, Jean. You know I do.'

'Do you promise ... '

The banality of the vows had no poetry to them, no comfort. They fell on him like jagged rocks. ' ... never go without breeches and shirt, never live separate from your brothers in Christ ... ' Even Ligaud hurtled through the list of luxurious worldly addictions that bound a man to the fleshly world, thinking at any minute for the demons tormenting Foulque to rend the life out of him. When he laid hands on the man, he believed himself to be wrestling with Satan himself in a combat for the soul of Foulque Nerra.

And Nerra believed it, too. All his life he had believed

himself trapped within his heredity, within a body and nature passed down genetically from the demon wife of Fulk Nerra III. As the poisonous monkshood griped, he believed himself the battlefield of angels, blessed and fallen, the odds hopelessly against the powers of good. And so he swore away his body's chains, as eagerly and easily as he had given up his ownership of Etangs-Nerra and the fields of Normandy.

'Do you renounce your wife?'

'I have no wife, damn and blast you!'

Only the bloody torrents rushing past his eardrums blurred the vows Ligaud shouted at him. 'Say after me! I promise to give myself to God and the Gospel.'

'...to God and the Gospel.'

'...never to lie or swear.'

'...never to lie - Oh Christ, the pain! - never to lie or what?'

'...or swear. Never again to touch a woman .. .'

Outside in the anteroom, the Lady Aude was weeping dismally into the sleeve of her smock, her ear turned towards the noise. She would have liked the comfort of an embrace, but all the men of her entourage were too spellbound by the sounds coming from the bedroom to pay her full attention. The imminence of Death has a mesmeric fascination. Even when, at the sound of his vow ... *'never again to touch a woman* ... ' she laughed manfully and danced a few steps to imply she knew better, they did not even glance round at her.

At last the curtain was drawn back by a haggard and white-faced Ligaud. He had taken off his own black *sadère* to lay over the newly baptised Cathar.

'He is peaceful at last.'

'*You mean he's dead?*' screamed Aude, and pushed past him into the room.

'Sleeping. Sleeping,' said Ligaud soothingly.

The room reeked. She covered her mouth as she stood by the bed looking down at Foulque. Then seeing the doorway full of her accolytes - some ex-lovers, some future lovers, some she meant always to dis appoint but never to part from - she spread her arms wide, allowing the candlelight to flatter her pose. A broad smile suffused her face. 'And tomorrow he will be fully recovered! Quite well again! Quite purged of all impurities! Ha! ha! ha!' They looked at her blankly. Even Auxerre d'Impt seemed to have forgotten her love of pranks. 'I peppered his cake with purgatives, don't you see!' she squealed, overbrimming with comedy. 'Just think how he'll rail when he finds he's made his Consolation because of a bellyache!'

One by one they did appreciate the joke. The laughs roared out of them like successive breaches in a dyke, until the room was bellowing with laughter. Perhaps in one or two the humour did not rise as high as their eyes, but Aude avoided looking directly at them, for she was intent on waking Foulque with the sound of laughing: that was how she had envisaged the joke running its course.

Somewhere in the brightness above the drowning depths where Foulque lay wrapped in a sailor's shroud of sleep, he did hear the laughter. He thought it the laughter of victorious demons, and was not surprised to discern Aude's laughter among the rest.

'I don't understand,' pleaded Ligaud, prevented from re-entering the bedroom by the press of men in the doorway. He had to call out to Aude over the men's shoulders. 'You mean you wanted to frighten him to Heaven? You wanted to frighten him into vows of celibacy? Gentlemen! Is this not a remarkable woman?'

Aude's face turned momentarily sour before its nose tilted once more in happy defiance. 'I'm sorry to disappoint you, brother. But I'm afraid you'll find there are some vows a man in love simply cannot keep! I did it to teach Lord Foulque a sense of proportion. Let him put first things first and the Last Things last where they belong!' (She was proud of the aphorism: she had thought of it all by herself and saved it up.) 'I think we'll find he's in less of a hurry for the things of Heaven, in future, and fonder of the people on Earth.' She picked up the black robe, which Ligaud had laid over the naked Foulque and, holding it between two fingers, dropped it on the floor. In place of it, she laid her two hands on him in mock ritual.

She expected the patter of applause which normally greeted her cleverest devices. But it did not come. Perhaps the men were too afraid of the perfect's anger. Or perhaps they were too envious of Foulque. For she told herself that there was not a man there who would not have welcomed one night's agony to be rewarded with such a laying-on of hands.

'If you think Foulque Nerra will break his vows,' said Ligaud, collectedly, 'you are more foolish than wicked. He's a perfect now. One of the Good Men. What possible enticement could *you* offer to compare with the certain hope of union with God?'

Aude drew herself up, regal with indignation. 'There's not a vow strong enough that won't break under the weight of True Love. I fear, Brother Ligaud, that's a thing a man of your class knows nothing of. This man has broken vows for me more often that you've broken bread. There's only one he'll keep, and that's the vow to love me till he dies. Which thanks to my dainty bakery, won't be tonight. Good night to you, Master Ligaud.'

She was quite right. About the effects of the *albigeoise navette*. By morning, Foulque was lighter by a stone and as weak as old age, but his system had ridded itself of the monkshood, and he knew he was not going to die. Not of eating poisoned cake.

He rose from Aude's bed, walked down to the Springs of Morgan le Fey and washed himself from head to foot, put on the black *sadère* Ligaud had given him, tying it with the *kosti,* the woollen belt. Then he fetched a paliasse from his own room and carried it up to the roof of the Haut-Beziers mansion. He refused help from the servants, ignored all salutations or comments from the knights. But by the time he had made the ascent, he was drained of all strength, and subsided under the weight. He had to recoup his energies before he could crawl out from under the mattress and organise himself a bed in the full face of the sun.

Uneasy waiting-women took word to Aude, but she did not go to him at once. Firstly she adorned herself - larded, farded, perfumed, clothed and decked herself out in preparation for a roof top tryst such as David kept with Bathsheba. He would be angry. But he would be weak, too weak to retaliate. She would explain that he had needed chastising for his neglect of her. She would reassure him that there were rewards to compensate for the tricks she had played on him, the lesson in manners she found it necessary to teach him. A little fright remained in her stomach, like the merest suggestion of monkshood poisoning, but then Foulque had always frightened her a little; that was all part of the man's allure.

The housemaids had not told her about the *sadère* and *kosti*. Her heart unaccountably took two steps back from the sight of him lying on his back like an ebony monument on a sarcophagus. One forearm shielded his eyes from the sun.

'Lord! You gave us such a fright last night, Nerra!' she said, overly loud, over bright, and sat down in the angle of his arm and body. He withdrew sharply from the possibility of her touch. 'What a wrack you made of my bedchamber! Lord! Such a *noise*! Such a fearful noise. So frightening. '

After a long silence he said, 'I thought I was dying.'

'Oh, I know. You wanted a perfect and your Consolation - thought we'd kissed our absolutely last kiss.' She leaned over him coquettishly and went to kiss his mouth. 'You must feel like Lazarus raised from the dead!' He turned his head away.

'Forbear, lady. As you say, I've sworn never again to touch woman.'

She giggled girlishly. 'Oh yes. Trust Foulque. Trust Foulque Nerra to vow vows and swear chastity! Such oaths! Such promises! Never to lie down without your breeches on, la! You'd've promised that friend of yours anything last night, wouldn't you? But first you promised me, remember? And who do you love more, Jean Ligaud or me? Who would you sooner lie with?' She sat astride him and plucked playfully at the knotted woollen belt.

She pictured herself - a kitten romping after mischief.

He clenched his fists and lifted them away from her, but there was nothing he could do to unseat her from across his hips; nothing short of touching her.'

The choice isn't between you and Ligaud. The vow was made in the face of God. '

She flicked him on the nose with her dress's tassles. 'Oh, but you've broken with God before now, for my sake, haven't you? And God forgives everything, whereas I ... '

'Get off me, lady. All's done between us.'

She bent her face down closer to his. 'Oh, come now. That was when you thought you were dying. Now you're going to live! How are you going to choose to spend the rest of your days - eating bread and water and sleeping in your trousers - or loving me as the gods of Love intended? I promise you, you are quite "perfect" enough for me, without you swearing away your manhood. Ha! ha! I can't imagine my Foulque living without the touch of a woman for the rest of his days - not now that he has the taste!'

He pulled his fist inside the black sleeve of the robe and struck her a blow that threw her on her back. As he got to his feet, the belt she had unfastened dropped to the floor and he picked it up and twisted it around both hands like a knotted garotte. 'I ought to kill you for the whore you are,' he said. 'Count yourself fortunate I'm sworn to keep hands off you.'

She stared at him, her mouth half open, her face bovine with bewilderment. All she could think to say was, 'But you swore to love me all your life.'

'And so I shall.' It did not sound like a declaration of love.

'And how will you do that? Live at the end of the lane in a ditch? With one shirt and dirty breeches?' Clearly he had guessed the cause of his illness. He was bound to be angry, wasn't he? But the more she talked, the more she believed in what she was saying. 'You? Keep always in company? You? Keep out of my bed when you might be in it? Keep faith with Ligaud sooner than me? Wait a week. Wait a month. Wait a year. Do you think you can deny your nature all the rest of your days? Or your heart?' She tried to sound both merry and cross, though she could hear the fright creeping into her voice.

He had gone to stand on the edge of the roof, looking out towards the Pyrenees, across the plunging undulations of red countryside creased like the blankets of a sickbed. 'It's true,' he said.

She tidied her hair. 'I know it's true.'

'It's true I shouldn't be alone. I swore to it. But I can't take a companion where I'm bound.'

'*You're going away again?*' For the first time she was genuinely afraid.' Where? Going where? You won't stay away. You never have. If you love me ...'

'You're right, Lady Aude. Nature does rule in me. I could not live the Good Life for long without failing in it. The prospect of living communal for one thing ... I think I'd run mad. Never to be out of the company of other men.'

Aude breathed a sigh of relief. Her heart steadied.

'I shouldn't have leapt so cowardly to my Consolation ...'

She went towards him, overflowing with sentimental and sexual consolation. 'You thought you were dying. It was a mistake, that's all. But I'm glad you've learned a lesson by it. I am quite content to have you in my bed, imperfect as you ...'

' ... But since I did leap to it, I shall observe the Endura with patience.' He turned on her a look of undisguised disgust. 'If only to be out of your noise, woman.'

She could not be sure she understood him.

She declined to understand him.

She went to find d'Impt and ask him - casually, conversationally, as if to settle an argument, 'What's the Endura?'

'Christ,' said Auxerre. 'Does he mean to keep the Endura? Now do you see what you've done with your foolish jokes, you stupid woman?'

'What's the Endura?' she demanded to know, stamping one foot in outrage.

'It's for those who make their deathbed Consolation and then find they're still alive. Some would rather make the journey they started out on, while salvation's guaranteed. Sooner than turn back and risk a worse end.'

'How? How "make the journey"? How?' she insisted.

'Have you never listened to a word the *perfecti* taught us? By fasting to death, of course. *Now* are you content?'

CHAPTER THIRTY FIVE

The Endura

She baked him fish and broth and custards, as if his appetite were a thing to be tempted, along with the rest of the man. But Foulque had no appetite either for food or for life. He had made up his mind to die the Good Death, and nothing she could do or say impinged on that decision.

'You don't understand! You think I've taken another lover! You think I meant to trick you out of my bed! It's not true!' Aude's metallic laugh ricochetted round the roof and came back to her untouched. It was a frightened laugh. 'I admit it! I was jealous. There now! You've made me say it. I was jealous of all the time you spent with the *perfecti*. It seemed to me you'd sooner spend time with them than me. You should be flattered that I *cared* what you do with your days, you should really!' Her confession fell on stony ground and died.

He reclined on one elbow, his face to the wall, his cheek already grey with beard and hunger. She tried to sound sententious, upbraiding. 'I only meant to show you how you were neglecting your lover. Setting other things over and above your duties to Venus.' But the words emerged as a mosquito whine, a panic-stricken childishness. 'Oh for God's sake, Foulque! It's only a silly vow! You made a mistake, that's all! You weren't dying, after all. So whatever you said - it doesn't signify! Of course it doesn't! How could it? Nobody's holding you to it! Nobody!'

It was very nearly true. Not even Ligaud rejoiced in the news of Nerra's Endura. Some of the deacons at the community said it would blow a clarion call to thrill through the ranks of the Blessed. But Ligaud secretly thought them fools and continued to wrestle uneasily with his Christian horror of suicide.

'Tell him, then! Tell him not to do it! Bring him to his senses. He'll listen to you!' the woman Aude shrieked at him, her hands all the time reaching out in an attempt to pollute his *sadère* with her importunity. Ligaud turned his back on her and climbed to the roof.

'What horror does the Good Life hold for you that you rush so towards the Good Death?' he asked Foulque, crouching on the roof, his knees up around his cadaverous jowls. 'Haven't you the courage to endure it for a few years, brother? The life of a man is over soon enough, in God's mercy.'

'That's right, Ligaud. I'm too craven to live the life I'm sworn to. So I'm taking the easier option.'

'I don't believe you.'

'Then don't hear my confession.'

Ligaud sat back on his heels, bewildered. 'Is it that you fear the lusts of your body will overwhelm you - that the temptations will be just too great, to sin? You must believe me, brother, the workings of the Lord are kind. You'll find, once you live in the community of perfects - frugally, like us - the flame subsides. It does subside.'

Foulque only smiled to himself and shook his head at some private thought which rendered Ligaud's suggestion ridiculous. 'I'd've thought you'd be rejoicing in the salvation of one sheep, Jean, sooner than trying to shoo it out-of-doors again. You of all people. You witnessed my oath.'

'I forgive you your oath,' exclaimed Ligaud rashly, all of a sudden.

'Only God has the power to do that, brother, and to be frank with you, I'm sick of asking concessions of Him. I'm heartily sick of being forsworn.'

At the foot of the stairs, Aude stood waiting to heap recriminations on Ligaud. 'You didn't try hard enough! You want him to die in the Faith! You think the Faith comes before everything.'

'*Yes*. Finally. Wonderful! The woman understands me at last,' said Ligaud exasperatedly, and though he returned in the afternoon prepared to lay hands of healing on Foulque, he found the doors closed against him and his presence at Haut-Beziers no longer welcome.

Aude's panic, meanwhile, spiralled towards hysteria, alternating between anguished prayer, rabid tirades and abject pleading each time the truth welled up before her eyes: Foulque Nerra genuinely intended to die.

Furthermore, she found that she was in love for the first time in her life.

She ate furiously, as if she might defeat the hunger in his belly by filling her own. Her hands were always full of sweetrolls, cakes, rollmops, apples. 'You're trying to punish me. You're trying to make me sorry for my silly joke. Well, you've succeeded! I'm chastened. Look at me, I'm humble.'

He blinked at her, his vision smudged and blurred, but made no comment on whether he saw humility or vanity.

'Oh, stop it! Stop it! Stop it now! You've gone on long enough! I don't know what you want me to say! Whatever it is, I'll say it! You've won it, whatever it is, this stupid game. Stop now! At once. Don't you see what you're putting me to?'

He groaned. After such a long silence, it took her so much by surprise that she clutched at her heart, and the herring in her fist broke off its head against her breast and fell in a greasy progress down her gown's front. 'You, you, you. Do you think that the great mechanisms of the world all turn with you for a pivot? Be content, will you? You asked me to shed my God for love of you. I did as I was asked. I became a Cathar. I joined your faith. I came to sit in your tree and I ate its berries. So pray don't tell me I haven't paid my duties to Love. In fact, pray don't tell me anything else about yourself. I find my curiosity to know is fully spent, mistress.'

She flew at him in a wild mixture of tantrum and fright, but his body was already so deep in the grips of fast that her touch alone caused him physical pain. He flinched from her exactly as a good Cathar should who has sworn never more to touch women and views them as the husks of God's fallen angels.

The old Aude, in the old order of things would have shut her gates against the Princess Ouallada, set the dogs on her, or at least treated her to the bright humiliation of insulting hospitality. As it was, she looked up from a plate of prunes and bacon at a face she could not immediately place, and then gave thanks to God. Here was a last potential intercessor between her and the man dying on her roof.

'Do something, Princess! Go and talk to him! Tell him I'm changed! I'm penitent! He can be as religious as he likes, if only he'll give over this spite!' There was a stillness, a slowness, a lack of excitement about Ouallada which, from the heaving decks of Aude's hysteria, looked heartless and cold.

In fact Ouallada, while she assimilated the news of Foulque's Endura, withdrew to the deepest, darkest caves of her brain and was powerless to move hands, body or face.

As they reached the foot of the ladder, Aude changed her mind, however, and in a last spasm of jealousy decided that Ouallada should not visit Foulque. It was, after all, her roof.

'I only came to tell him of my marriage,' said Ouallada, and Aude let her pass, so struck by the word (or by the way it was said) that for a while she could not get it out of her head.

'Marriage.' To think she might have been married to Foulque if she had not teased him so long with *assais*. One joke too many, she concluded. One joke too many. Or perhaps two, when she thought of the cake. And thinking of the cake, she crammed her mouth with brioche.

She was toying with the idea of convening a Court of Love to endict Foulque's behaviour and instruct him to pay Love the attentions owed it by a troubadour. The notion was an antique one, but then Foulque was an antique troubadour. He might respond. Duty might stir him where compassion could not. When Princess Ouallada came down from the roof, she might be prepared to advise on the etiquette of the proceedings ... Then Auxerre d'Impt, descending from the roof, said that Foulque seemed unusually disturbed by his visitor. Aude seethed with unease.

'Hello, Foulque,' said Ouallada.

Unsettled by her intrusion on his state of trance, Foulque could not recover his former stillness. Creases in his robe, pellets of horsehair in the mattress were now as fierce a torment to him as the bars of a griddle. D'Impt had placed a cloth over his face to keep the sunlight from damaging his eyes: if it had not been for his twisting and turning in search of comfort, Ouallada might have thought she had come too late and that he was already dead.

But he said, 'So you're married. I heard you below. Your voice always carried.'

'It was a matter of seizure. Not as I'd have chosen.'

'And I not there to protect you.'

'And you not there, as you say.' She went and sat down beside him, cross-legged, and drew the cloth away so that he raised his hands to protect his eyes. 'What's this I hear? Nerra on his way to union with Zoroaster?'

'I am become a Cathar, yes,' he said sharply.

'A suicidal Cathar no less.'

'You're not informed in the ways of the Faith. I would explain the concept of the Endura to you, but it would mean nothing to you, coming as a stranger to the theology.'

When she did not answer at all, he turned his head and looked at her from under his hand. The white lawn collar of her gown was blowing open and closed across her throat. Her loose hair, caught by eddies and swirls of wind, moved about her head in a cloud. She did not lift a hand to tame it; her hands remained unmoving, on her ankles, out of his vision.

'Please don't do this, Foulque,' she said quietly. 'In the name of friendship, don't. I've just come from Toulouse. I spoke with Prior Correau. In his name I ask it. Don't do this.'

It took him a great while both to assimilate speech and to formulate his replies. As often as not he did not take the trouble. For Ouallada he did. 'I'm afraid my mind is made up. It was made up for me. It's no great matter. Simply a question of timing. A little earlier than later, that's all. Don't put yourself to the trial of redundant arguments. I've heard them all, this last week.'

So she did not, but sat quiet, saying nothing, her back very erect so that she could see the view from the roof over its low perimeter wall. 'This puts me in mind of the Hejaz,' she said after a long while, 'when I built a travois and cursed you for not helping me more with the work. I curse you deeper now. Now you could save yourself and won't. Damnable, isn't it, this desert worm? Despair they call it. I'm acquainted with the symptoms.'

'As I remember, you gave me no peace then, either. And you delivered me into the hands of the enemy.'

'Whereas this time you've surrendered to her with your hands over your head . . . Mind you, if this show here was intended to humble your mistress and bring her to heel, you have succeeded. You can give over the lesson.'

'It wasn't my intention. I'm sorry if the lady feels humbled. Truly, I'm afraid without her pride, the lady must be hard put to exist. But I have every faith in its recovery. It's a hardy perennial, Aude's pride.'

That's bitter, from a lover. Poor Foulque. Did she shun you yet again?'

'Not at all. Not at all.' He said it out of cruelty, to persuade her he was not the man she recalled. He heard her swallow down the news, as though there were bones in it. 'We fed each other's appetites day and night for a pretty while - though it's indiscreet of me to gossip, isn't it? I'm falling away, you see, from the refinements of the court ... I must say, you don't seem very distressed by your enforced marriage. I'm glad of that, at least. Myself, it would choke me to finish in the wrong embrace.' He was resolved to kill any surviving trace of the love which as-Shafih had told him of.

But she retaliated with equal venom, 'So, didn't Aude's embraces live up to expectation?'

He set his face at the sky. 'I'm bound for the embrace of my Saviour now. In Heaven. Since that's the reward of the Good Death.'

Suddenly, without warning, she slapped him. In fact it was done at such an awkward angle, in such an untidy rush, that she brought her hand down across his nose and made it bleed. She looked momentarily at the blood in the palm of her hand then sprang to her feet as if to restrain herself from worse violence. 'Now I know you're lying, Foulque Nerra. For God's sake! If you're going to set such store by words as to *die* because of them, you shouldn't spend the telling lies - particularly to those who know better. Bound for Heaven, indeed! Bound for Heaven! Since when did you believe you were bound for Heaven? Where's that demon blood of yours, inherited from your great grandma? Where's that burden of sins you carried everywhere with you to be sure of keeping good tally of them?'

'I laid it aside in the waters of baptism,' he said with the flat petulance of a catechised convert.

'That's what you think!'

Auxerre d'Impt, returning to the roof out of sheer curiosity, had no sooner put his head above the trap than he pulled it down again, such was the danger from cross-fire.

'You think I know nothing of Catharism?' she stormed. 'I know enough. I know, for instance, that you need the permission of a wife before your make your *Consolamentum*!' The argument seemed so fatuous that he only shrugged. 'And though you ask it now, you shan't have it.'

He sighed at the prospect of her weary moralising. 'You mean that in God's eyes Aude and I are man and wife?'

'Certainly not,' she said crossly. 'God could never bring His eyes to look on such an aberration. I mean what I said. You're married already. I married you. By proxy, ten days since.'

'*You did what?*'

'That pleasant youth in the green scrim doublet with the complexion to match - the one on the ship? - he stood proxy for you. After all, it was the dowry he wanted, not me. I'm afraid I had to give him as-Shafih's sword and helmet: I'd only meant to part with the lands in Normandy, but he had me at a disadvantage. You're made a knight by it, you know? Leo of Montpellier will be hugely relieved. And Rutebeuf It didn't matter to him who the bridegroom was, provided the "anomaly was put to rights". No female knights to blot the escutcheons of Chivalry with horrid menstrual gules ... Your Prior made the marriage. Fine irony, don't you think? And remarkably charitable, given the slight you'd just done him. I do like Father Correau very much. He has real generosity of spirit, hasn't he? Not so generous, mind, that he won't damn you bell, book and candle if you persist in this .. .'

'Stop. Stop. Stop.' He tossed his head from side to side as if the words were stones falling in his face. 'What is this? What game do you think you're playing? Married? Christ, why? For what reason? I've got nothing! I gave it all away! Why me? Why, woman?'

'I was under duress. Sooner you than another of Rutebeuf's choosing. You're made Foulque de Gloriole, by the way - it's best you know your own title. The name's a slip of the tongue, but I suppose it's as good as any.'

'Oh, all very fine! Without asking me? Very fine, I'm sure!'

'Why? Men have seized on women before now,' she retorted, 'and for worse motives.'

'Well, I renounce you,' he sputtered. 'I repudiate you. I put you off!'

'You'd need the connivance of the Church to do that, my dear,' said Ouallada. 'A papal dispensation. And the Church might be a little hostile towards you just now. Your Prior, for instance; he'd disoblige you in almost anything presently, to keep you from damnation. He's really very fond of you ... I wouldn't have mentioned any of this, you understand, except to bring you word of your knighthood ... But it seems just as well I did, in the circumstances.'

'I don't want a knighthood! What good's a knighthood to me? There's nothing I want from you - except the peace to die in!'

'Well, you can't have it.'

'What d'you mean? What are you doing?'

She had sat down again at his feet, dogged, obdurate, her mouth pursed in stubborn determination. He raised himself up on his elbows and peered at her through the algaed brightness of decaying sight. 'I refuse to renounce you, husband. Your *Consolamentum* is null and void.'

She saw the old cunning defiance creep into his face. 'Then I shall go by the Way of the Stars.'

'Your soul migrating by gradual purgation from star to frosty star, as far as the Gates of Heaven. Oh yes, I understand that piece of theology, too.'

Above them, the first stars of evening hung in a greying sea of unfathomable depth. Their imaginations both quailed on the shore of such a sea-voyage.

'And I say you're out of Grace and must go the long way to your Cathar Heaven - you see how well I've studied? - by way of reincarnation.' Her voice was as icy, as penetrating as the evening draughts that chased one another across the roof.

'So be it,' he said and lay back, exhausted. 'Reincarnation.'

'So when you die, your soul shall pass into the nearest man or beast at hand, and toil through lifetimes of atonement, climbing back to perfection.' He was silent. 'So I shall sit just here.'

'What?'

'So that when your soul departs, I can seize on it and bear it in me. I did it in life: I can do it in death. It should weigh familiar enough. God knows, I've borne you inside me over enough miles and for enough years.'

A flock of ducks flew low over the roof honking out a ribald derisive laugh. It made them both start. The dusky sky filled up with bats and stars in equal quantity. The light failed to an extent where neither could any longer see the other's face.

'It's just a pity neither of us believes in all that,' said his voice out of the shadows. Then, 'Be content. Love doesn't last, you know. I based my life on the tenet that Love burns everlasting. Like the flame in the sacristy. But it was a false doctrine. I came back here because I vowed a vow. To love the woman for ever. But I couldn't hold to it.'

Ouallada lifted her forehead off her knees.

'Oh, I've done my duty by it. I've gone through the show and motion. Performed all the *assais*. Told myself it was just hidden from me for a while: it would flare up again. But it's a dead thing. I carry it around like a withered limb. No hiding it. I thought Love endured. But it doesn't. All the vows I made - all the oaths I swore - all the songs I sang . . . And still my heart strayed and my eye roved and I found myself feeling it all for another woman. That same madness. That obsession.'

She felt a shock and an outrage she had thought she was no longer prey to. She had directed his attention to the great army of women in the world and he had taken her advice and found another lover. 'So it's not the monk in you that declines to go on living. It's the disappointed troubadour. '

'Some part,' he said. 'Well? Love. If it's not a constant, what is it? Insanity? A prediliction to vice. Nothing else. That's all.'

'Oh, shame on you, sir,' she said waspishly. 'If you're going to summon up algebra! If Love's not a Constant, then it's an Unknown. That's all *algebra* will tell you. It takes a full lifetime to resolve that particular quotient. Isn't that what you're supposed to be - you *trobars*? - the 'finders out'? The explorers mapping a new territory? You and your new *domna* can find it out together. Even if Aude was a blind alley in the maze, you've no call to judge Love on the strength of Aude d'Haut-Beziers!'

His frown was full of impatience, but with himself not with her. 'I did try to go on loving her, you know,' he said. 'I did everything in my power.'

'I can witness to that.'

'Even after I ... after my affections wandered, I came back. I did as she asked me. Everything she asked me.'

'So very wholeheartedly, too, from what you say! I daresay you outran her. Like a dog fetching a stick from too far off.'

His head jerked away from her unkindness. 'Well. Well. No matter. It really doesn't signify. It's a travesty. Our *trobar* world. I've explored it and I have to report it's based on self-deception and poppycock. Though I suppose as a woman and a troubadour you hold it a blasphemy to say so. We worked up a beautiful artifice, we *trobars*. A great show of Fancy. Giltwork over something pretty base, as I guess. Pretty base.'

'Oh, I don't think you're right there,' she said without raising her voice. 'As a lifelong fraud and a charlatan myself, you've got to admit I'm well placed to judge a lie when I see it. And all in all I'd say it's an artifice, yes. It's a splendid artifice. But as I see it, it's more like the gold and silver and jewels covering over the True Cross. Well meaning enough. Even though the thing inside's a quite different nature of a thing. Quite different. They say, for instance, that there can't be love between man and wife. And yet here I am, wed to you and still beset ...'

'Would you be so good as to pass me a drink of water, Ouallada?' he said politely.

She had prided herself that she could keep up the appearance of collectedness. And yet she found, as she tried to pour water from a soft leather flagon into a metal cup, that it sobbed and gushed incontinently over her shaking hands, over the cup's rim, over Foulque. He sat up to drink it, closing his hands over hers to keep the cup still.

'Do you know how the Empress Catherine proved the True Cross was authentic?' he said, keeping hold of her hands. 'Before it was gilded and ornamented, I mean? When she first found it?'

'I suppose I must, if I could just ...'

'She laid the body of a dead man on it, and he was raised up to life.'

With a speed she could not pre-empt and a strength she had thought quite beyond him to summon, he put both arms around her and pulled her against him, the whole length of her body against the length of his.

'You see I'm the butt of a Divine joke this time. Married against my will to the woman I loved in secret. Despite myself. Against all my vows. The one I cursed myself for loving. A great joke on God's part, don't you think? Can't you hear him roaring?'

'You're forsworn, Cathar,' she said, when he gave her back her mouth.

'Yes. Now I've broken every oath I ever made. I'm a man of water. Don't look to me for any enduring continence.' He did not say it bitterly, but she knew it was the bitterest thing he had ever said. His body might be recovered to life, but his soul dragged behind it on a broken travois.

'As Euripides said, "'Twas but your tongue and not your soul that swore." Words. There's the other failing of the minstrel philosophy - that words are fit currency for the serious commerce of the soul. Even music ... only the Cathars would try and peg out the universe to dry on a five-bar stave.'

'No more oaths, then. And no more songs.'

'And no troubadours under our roof to tell us where love can and can't thrive.'

'Roof? What roof? I may be a knight, by your impertinence, but I'm a landless one, you know? The étangs are given to the Church. Normandy's given away for dowry.'

'Oh. Did I not say? Your Prior wants to give you a *salvetat* - in the Loire - an estate by way of a wedding gift. I think he believes you'll find God there surer than on a battlefield. - Or at the end of an Endura, come to that. As

Alcuin wrote to Charlemagne, "The voice of the people is the voice of God."

He held her off at arm's length and looked at her with a kind of baffled perplexity. 'Where do you have all this from, madam? Alcuin? Euripides? Algebra? All the little Cathar ins and outs? Who set you up to undermine me?'

'No one.' She ran her fingers over his face, as if the dark denied her too much of him. 'But someone once told me - I don't recall who. Was it you? It's the truth, so it must have been you. "Hear everything and you'll see that nothing is superfluous." So I suppose, truly, you were your own undoing from the very start.'

'I never thought otherwise,' he said, with a trace of the old bitterness. 'I never thought any different.'

CHAPTER THIRTY SIX

Newness of Life

His failure to persist in loving Aude, and even greater failure in outliving his failures, weighed leaden on the first days of that marriage. Foulque came to Ouallada like a drowning man, the errors of his life washing past his eyes in a suffocating flood. He made no further move to touch her, and Ouallada did not cling to him. She knew there was nothing to be had of the marriage unless and until he put the past behind him.

'You shan't hold him, you know!' Aude shrieked, snatching the pannier out of Ouallada's hands and throwing it on the floor. 'He'll come back to me. I've only to call and he'll come. You might win yourself a Christian surname by your tricks, but you shan't win his heart! That's mine. Always! Learning won't help you! Learning won't keep a man! You can't *talk* all night long!' She hit out at Ouallada, scratching her with little clawing paws, like a cat intent on damaging furniture. Ouallada walked round her, ducked past her, turning her back to escape the vicious, dirty nails. 'Do you really think he'll hold to a marriage got by trickery? You don't pen in a man of his kind! He'll come back to me!' She snatched up a pair of scissors. 'He'll come back here! He was happy here. We were happy. He won't stand for you making him a cuckold, you black whore.'

'Aude, give it over.' It was Auxerre d'Impt. He moved into the room with unaccustomed agility, and took the scissors out of Aude's hand. 'Give it over, woman. Nerra's leaving. Leaving you, leaving Beziers.'

'Only because she tricked - '

'Because he loves her, woman. Because he loves her. He's loved her ever since Egypt.'

'Don't be absurd. Were you there? You know nothing, you. What do you know about loving? You never did the things in bed that he did for me.'

'But now you've lost him, with your foolery, your damned silly *assais*. There'll be others. Leave him in peace now and let him go. You wouldn't like what he'd do to you for injuring his wife.'

They struggled hand-to-hand, Aude spitting in his face and kicking with her sharp little shoes. Ouallada moved away, against the wall, and stood with her eyes shut, the saddle panniers drawn up against her chest. Auxerre restrained Aude within the circle of his arms and lifted her away to the far side of the room. 'Finish packing, Princess. Madam won't hinder you any more.'

Ouallada was sorry to see so late the man's merits, his

loyalty to Aude despite a thorough knowledge of her slightness, her lightness, her silly, spiteful nature.

'She won't keep him!' screamed Aude, kicking her dress and underskirts into a froth of gold lace, drumming her heels against his knees. 'He'll come back to me if I so much as –

'Then be content, madam,' said Ouallada. 'Let us both watch and pray. The man has an estate to tend. With all his other lands gone, it's best he visits this *salvetat* of his as soon as possible.'

'Magic! You'll use magic! She'll use potions and filtres, Auxerre, you know she will! Her kind. She can do any kind of witchery once she has him away from here! She dogged him to the end of the world and back, didn't she?'

'I don't know what magic she needs, over and above her nature,' said d'Impt.

Ouallada darted forward and snatched up the raffia net holding the residue of her clothes and Foulque's, before running to the door. She had no hands free to wipe away the tears from her cheeks. 'You're very kind, sir. I trust you're right and that you won't ever be troubled again by the man.'

D'Impt called out to her as she struggled with the latch. 'Trust me, lady. He loves you with a passion that, for once in his life, is beyond even his power to mar.'

Even from outside, Ouallada could still hear Aude bellowing with outrage, vowing to summon a Court of Love and black Foulque Nerra with the stigma of the forsworn lover the length and breadth of France.

It would not matter if she did. The *salvetat* entrusted to Foulque by Prior Correau was on the northernmost extreme of the Languedoc, far from the blood-red soils of the troubadour realm. There would be little room for troubadours in such a place, few hearths which could afford to entertain knights-errant in fitting style. If Foulque were to prosper, it would not be for his *sirventes* or his good repute in the Courts of Love.

A *salvetat* is a fiefdom free of obligations to the Crown - untaxed, paying no market tolls, unlevied - a community drawn together by free trade. *Salvetats* were a social experiment so anarchic as to terrify some, so successful as to have injected new life into mercantile France. Foulque's land lay in a bow of the Sablois River, a tributary of the Loire, closeby Ormes.

There was no choosing who settled there. Craftsmen and hangers-on, artisans and dependants, freemen and dissenters drifted in like souls through the Gates of Heaven. They squatted in outlying villages, watching, asking questions, appraising the nature of the man given charge over the land. And when there was no rumour of drudgery, no levying of armed men, no talk of devil worship or heresy, they shambled and ambled over the boundaries and dumped down their osier baskets, babies, pannaged pigs and doorposts. Many came out of the Sologne, the sons of marsh-dwellers with the same taste as their parents for self-determination but less appetite for malarial, pestilential bog. They found untilled land watered by the convoluted river, quarries of schist and white tufa, forests overstuffed with game, and apple trees fruitless for want of husbandry.

Fruitless for want of husbandry.

They squatted on their portable belongings and looked about them for the flaw, the trick, the drawback that must surely attach to Gloriole-sur-Sablois. It all looked too good to be true.

Ouallada decided, on the day they arrived at the Black Boar inn, within the bounds of his new estates, to risk her everlasting exclusion from this Garden of Eden.

'There is no marriage between us,' she said as Foulque laid out the innkeeper's blankets on the plank floor of the empty upper room. The light of the room below made yellow perforations from one wall to the other - a constellation of lamplight - like the Cathar Way of the Stars, she thought, so very arduous and lonely. He stared at her. 'There is no marriage without consummation. Prior Correau was very plain on the point. I thought it would occur to you before now. Perhaps it did.'

'No,' he said vaguely. 'No. No. It didn't occur ... No.'

'I don't regret misleading you, then - winning you away from Haut-Beziers. But you know now.'

'Yes. Yes. I know now. Yes.'

'You never needed my renunciation to make the Good Death. You might say I lied.'

He had seated himself on the blankets, cross-legged, his panniers pulled into his lap. He unearthed, along with a shower of lesser items, which scattered round him on the floor, the black robe and woollen belt of a Cathar perfect. 'Should I burn these?' he asked her.

'No. Keep them. Everyone needs souvenirs.'

'Of my greatest failure?'

She went and snatched them angrily out of his hands. 'Oh no! You don't need any reminders of your failings. If that's all you can see in these, I'll keep them. As souvenirs of my greatest success.'

But he kept hold of one end of the belt, and pulled her off-balance as she went to move away. He reached forward along its cords and reefed her in. 'To tell you the truth .. .' he said inconclusively.

'I'd like that,' she said. 'It has novelty for me.'

'To tell you the truth, I think of little else but consummating our marriage. Despite. Aude.'

She ducked her head, as if he had shied something at her, something materially wounding. 'I know I'm not exactly the golden acme of beauty. I know I'm not Aude,' and she examined the back of her wrist as if it could reveal why the blessing of whiteness should have fallen only on Aude. 'But there's white bread and there's black. If you're hungry enough ... '

'I filled my belly with Aude,' he broke in in a rush. 'Gorged on her. That was when it ended. That was what finally ended it. Nothing left. That's how I see it, looking back. The beginning of the end. Not worth it.' He gave a wry smile. 'But I go on thinking.'

All at once she was reborn into the power of joy. So. After all those years of repressive abstinence, he had not found in Aude the magic he had expected.

Ouallada had learned a great many things from Foulque. She could have believed him now: that she was missing little by going without fleshly love. And yet for all her virgin ignorance, she knew that he was wrong. Whether by instinct, by Moorish magic or by unkillable optimism, she knew he was wrong. She stood on the wires of light stretched between the gaping boards and maintained a perfect balance on her platform of stars. 'You're afraid that if we lay down friends we'd rise up strangers.'

'No. Oh no.' But he was clearly grateful to her for putting it so concisely.

She sat down beside him. 'Foulque, my dear. I don't know really, but I can't help thinking - since it's proved so very ... popular over the years - that everything can't be learned by reading the one book. About Love, I mean. I think we'd be rash to trust for all our impressions to Aude d'Haut-Beziers. She may be very lovely, but she is only one woman, after all. And other lovers haven't felt as you do.'

He looked sideways at her, anxious, dubious. All the small crinkling hairs broken free of her plait and curling back from her hairline were illuminated by a corona of candlelight, and the updraught of air through the plank floor lifted and moved the curls around her forehead. He felt the same frustration at being unable to see her features as he felt when trying to study by too little light.

'Might we not ... ' she began. 'Would you think it too close a thing to science? To investigate ...'

'What? To explore it further, you mean?' he said frowning like a philosopher wrestling with an abstract premise.

'We are the discoverers, after all. The *trobars*. The finders out.'

She played her role well, tentative and uncertain. But he was not taken in. He could feel the certainty emanate from her like warmth. There was no moral doubt in her, no curiosity to sin, no shame, no hot mischief. There was only a desire so great, so moving that he might have been sitting beside the Loire itself, its dark, deep, shining, crestless currents dragging him out from the tangle of fringed margins. His moored soul swung so violently towards her that it made him dizzy. Lightheaded. He could steady himself only by placing his two hands on her shoulders, his fingers beneath the opening of her collar.

'The *winileodas* ... Your song in the desert.'

'What of it?' she said. 'Sometimes words are a relief. Second best, but a relief.'

'It was so very ... forthright. Passionate. A man might feel unequal to such very ... decided expectations.'

'He might,' she said, looking down. 'But he plainly doesn't.' His hands were joined by a web of laces, a cat's cradle of laces and within it her breasts. 'No more songs, then.'

'No more *assais.*'

'No more *ascesis.*'

'No more words in place of deeds.'

And the truth of it settled on her vocal cords, for she found herself quite unable to speak, the passageways of her throat engorged as though by unshed tears, the soft places of her body engorged as though by inexpressible emotions beyond-far beyond-the competence of the spoken word.

Foulque found as great a difference between love in the arms of Aude and in the arms of Ouallada as between sickness and health. With Aude, each encounter had increased his jaundice, wearied him, left him a little more nauseous, a little less inclined to exert the daily effort to stay alive. With Ouallada, his appetite and vigour increased with every day, as he discovered a youth he had never been allowed, an exuberance always forbidden him. There was no competition of wills, no scrabbling after the largest share of enjoyment, no shrill frolicsome childishness, no spiteful teasing. No comparisons at work in a half averted face. He found that virginity was not, as Aude had told him, a circumstantial triviality, but a gift of trust given as a student entrusts his ignorance to the keeping of a mentor.

He wrote no songs. When Love is there, hatched, in the nest, there is no time for singing, only feeding it with a tender, industrious diligence.

Ouallada wrote none either. She was so eager to cut free of the past that, given her way, she would have deepened and widened the Loire into an ocean, waded out and pushed adrift all the southern half of France, that it might carry its burden of blood-red soil and singers away beyond the catgut horizon.

Finding such intimations of Paradise in Ouallada's bed, Foulque cleaved afresh to the Catholic faith. He no longer craved a Heaven free of the flesh, a resurrection without either a body or the companionship of a wife. But though the Old Church fed him with forgiveness, washed out his troubadour mouth with Communion wine, Ouallada could see his back start to bend once more under the familiar weight of sin. He picked up, along with his old theology, the crimes of his ancestors, the mistakes of his youth, the guilt over the Cathar nails he had driven into God's hands. He was a man incapable of accepting forgiveness.

He even said to his wife, about the Gloriole *salvetat,* 'Here's my chance to compensate. Here's my chance to clear accounts.' To see how he worked was a measure of how high the mountain of sin beetled over him. And it had to be quarried away day by frenetic day, could not be mined by absolution.

He drew maps, he borrowed money, he felled trees. He appointed millers to their hills or leets, boat-builders to their timber, quarrymen to their cliffs. He commissioned fishnets and new vines, a church, a cornmarket, and a new bridge across the river. The river dismantled his pontoons and piles and smashed them into his barges downstream.

He built whole villages of hives, oversaw the construction of a little city of cane spires where the beans could grow. He hunted deer and coralled cows. And the wild sheep pillaged his pastureland, and pigs rootled their way through his beanfields.

All around, the forest pressed in, watching with haughty disparagement the burro wings and delvings of the little men and women. The little men and women retaliated, slashing and burning the woods, until the borders of Gloriole were ugly, seared wounds.

While Richard Coeur de Lion blustered and threatened his way out of Outremer, swearing to return in terrible wrath, Sir Foulque de Gloriole made war on starvation and want, along the shores of the Sablois River.

'The voice of God is the voice of the people.' Foulque had it carved over the door of the church, though the people who passed under it voiced the opinion that it might anger God, the King and the Pope, all three. It made them uneasy, they said. But he did not erase it.

As for Ouallada, she worked too, making candles, broadcasting sunflowers, plaiting rope, waxing paper for the windows, gardening, furnishing medicines out of the valerian and poppies that grew down by the river. But like a child of legend blessed by fairies, she always left her work to be home before Foulque, to be home to the fine, four-room, flintstone house Foulque had built her on the bend of the river. She would pretend she had been nowhere, done nothing. For however often she told him it was ridiculous, he treated her for the first time as if she were truly a princess. It were as if all the years they had spent together in flagrant breach of chivalric etiquette, must be overwritten with acts of attentive chivalry, with considerations for her comfort and welfare. But then Foulque was always compensating for something.

She fought against it, but inwardly she was grateful and relieved. For soon she found herself in the grips of a terrible weariness - as if all the risks, frights, hardships and travels had suddenly overtaken her, overwhelmed her with fatigue. When she began to be sick every single day, she said nothing to Foulque, but went and fell on her knees in the church, to beg for an extended lease of life.

'Don't part us yet, Lord,' she begged. 'It may seem from a distance that we've been together a good while, but if you could see us close up ... we've barely started!'

On the way back to the house, she stopped to gather fresh strewings from the riverside. The dead asphodels had turned all to straw in the summer sun, and could be reaped in stooks by a pair of arms.

Nearby, a woman whose baby Ouallada had helped to deliver (the women converged on one another at such times), was playing with the child amid the flowers, tickling its pink body with the green and yellow euphorbias it lay among. 'You want to go careful,' the woman called out. 'Lifting awkward like that. T'ain't the weight, 'tis the awkwardness. How many you after?'

'All I can carry, I suppose,' said Ouallada cautiously. She still found it difficult to understand the nasal northern accent - the *langue d'oil*.

'Aie me! I used to think like that. But it's the herb for me now. Six I got, and it's the herb for me from now on. It grows hereabouts, you know? Still, you're just starting, aren't you, ma'am? Don't pay any heed to me. The more we have of the likes of your knight, the better we'll like it. He's a right fine man. Merits seven boys - though God send you a girl or two for the company, manner of thing ... I'll be there, don't you fret. All supposing your good husband thinks we're fit to come in under the doorway. Me and all the women. Same as you did for me.'

An eager breeze flurred off the river and picked straws out from the bundle Ouallada was holding, whirling them round her head. 'When I bear a child, you mean?'

'When you bear that child there, yeah. Is it quick yet?'

Ouallada turned away towards the brightness of the river, using the breeze to cool her face. The core fell out of her bundle of grasses and scattered at her feet. The rest she loosed on to the river, opening her arms wide and wider still, letting her happiness whiten the river with asphodels interspersed with straighter strands of sunlight. The raft spread and disintegrated and washed downstream in wispy clumps. 'I'm with child,' she whispered to no one but herself. Even so, a big perch, with scarlet dorsals gaudy as a troubadour, came to the surface and gaped its mouth in wonder or silent singing.

She could not understand Foulque's reaction to the news. She had thought he would be pleased - almost as happy as her. But she laid her news at his feet and he seemed stunned, unnerved. He looked at her with wild, wide eyes, and went out of the house. For two days he did not come back. She asked the women what it could mean.

'He's maybe afeared it'll be black like an ape,' said one.

'He's maybe feared it'll take your love from him. They're born jealous, men are,' said a second.

'They are,' said a third. 'He maybe thinks it's not his - not meaning to offend, ma' am.'

'Not him. Thinks the world of her, he does,' said a fourth to the gathering as a whole. 'Reckon he's afeared it'll kill her when it comes, that's what.'

Ouallada was not partial to any of the options.

But it was simply that he did not believe her. It was as if he regretted her backslide into the habit of lying, and was trying to overlook the fault, hoping she would correct it of her own accord. He would not tolerate any mention of the child, would not discuss its potential life, whether in providing a crib or devising a name. She fell in with this harsh, dispiriting regime. She even concealed the swell of her belly as best she could, without understanding what horror it held for him. She offered him love in bed, but he turned away from her, as if she were not fit company while she persisted in her lie. Ultimately, however, it took no words to tell him, each time he looked at her, that she was with child.

Then the pains began, and the women closed on the house without summoning, like bees to a broken hive, and put themselves between husband and wife and jostled him aside. Only then did he fight his way back to her, through their slaps and angry flustering. He wrapped her in his arms and kissed the crown of her head, her face, her ears, and mouth in a panic so passionate that the neighbours fell back from it open-mouthed.

'For shame! Anyone would think you was lovers not man and wife!'

There it was again: the Code of Love. It flapped in his face like an enemy flag: *true love cannot exist between husband and wife.* Even if no one lived by it here, where life consisted of stone-clearing, sowing, reaping and harvest-home, it still crept in. Now and then tatters of Love's Code blew through even here - hints at a fairyland of errant knights and virgin lovers.

They threw him out-of-doors. His knighthood was of no use to him. His authority stood for nothing in a houseful of women who had given themselves free run of his property. They drew his water; they tore the bedding off his bed. They lit his candles and the logs in his hearth. They nailed a length of fishing-net to his ceiling to serve for a cradle. They searched his belongings for a suitable length of white cloth. He saw them, bent as hyenas, laughing over the carrion, bloody figure of his wife, and he fled the house and took an axe and went and attacked a tree on the forest's edge. A good old tree. A plane tree. The wedge-shaped incision opened little by little by little until with a shudder and a human groan it was impossible the tree should withhold its life from him another moment. A wetness of sap speckled all his clothes; the core of the trunk snapped through, and the hewn point of the upper section lurched towards him, the branches falling away. It nearly ran him through, that log sharpened to a point. He jumped aside, but the hewn tip with its starburst of broken wood-fibres drove between his body and his arm, filling his clothes with splinters, tearing his waistcoat free of its lining. As the felled tree slid down towards the river, its branch ends washed over him, feathering him like a bird with sticky green leaves. When he got back to the house, the neighbours thought he was dressed for a mumming: Jack o ' Green. They thought it some southern rite, some excess of the hot places, probably some tribal custom from the unchristian places.

'What have you done to yourself?' said Ouallada, from their big new bed. 'I thought you'd run away and left me, you were gone so long.'

'Only five minutes.'

'Nearer five hours,' said the women feelingly as they shut the door. They had not liked to leave Ouallada alone and had waited for him to return, but impatiently.

The baby was wrapped in the white linen kefiah Foulque had once bound around his helmet to keep off the desert sun. It made him look darker than he was, for his complexion was pale - somewhere between Ouallada's honey-colour and Foulque's summer suntan, and much paler than the colour that suffused Foulque's face in the agitation of the moment.

'Do you want to hold him? Your son?' she asked.

He snatched his arms away at the last moment, so that the baby was almost dropped. 'No. No. I'd stain him. I'd mire him up.'

'A few leaves won't hurt.'

He looked down at himself 'I didn't mean my clothes,' he said.

'Take him. Am I to do everything? Put him in his cradle if you don't want to hold him.'

'But once he had hold of the linen bundle, nothing could persuade him to set it down. He took the child to the window and pulled all the wax paper out on to the floor and looked and looked and looked.

'We'll call him Foulque, of course,' said Ouallada with the smug complacency of happy exhaustion.

'*No!*'

The baby started and flung its arms wide in alarm. Foulque turned his back to the window to stop up the draught, and tucked the kefiah scrupulously tight again around the little arms. 'No. Not Foulque. He's got none of his ancestors in him. Look at him. He's perfect. He's innocent. He's spotless. He's new. No casting back to the black Counts for him. Haven't I done enough to cut his ties with those bastards?'

She wanted to say, 'Your grandam was never a demon from Hell. Just a story. Just the superstitious myth of a superstitious people. Something to frighten babies with.' But she knew he was not talking just about the legend of the Nerras. The sin he wished to exempt his son from was his own.

Instead she said, 'He's your newness of life, Foulque,' and did not speak again until the words had sunk home.

His eyes turned in her direction. They wore a look she had seen in the eyes of pilgrims fresh from drinking water at the shrine of Abdon and Sennen; pilgrims returning from Jerusalem having knelt in the cave where Christ was born; pilgrims clasping their fragments of bone or wood or cloth left behind as litter by God's bodyless saints.

'He is, isn't he? Newness of life. That's what they talk about, isn't it? Newness of life. The Resurrection. Look!

Look, Ouie!' He showed her the baby, as if she might not have examined it closely yet, pulling apart the swaddling, spreading his fingers over the single span of its belly. 'This is the Resurrection! It doesn't mean the raising up of the body on the Last Day! Nor that reincarnation business - climbing about from beast to beast, phah! *This* is the Resurrection!'

'Hush, Foulque! Quick!' She took the baby from him and hid it, as her mother might have hidden a child from the spying eyes of malicious gods. 'I don't think you said that,' she said firmly. 'I don't think you meant to say that.'

He bowed to her caution. 'Well, then, maybe it's all the Resurrection I *need*!' he declared in his booming troubadour's whisper. His smile was so dazzling that Ouallada could not fail to see what she had done: how she had imparted the gift of life that day not to just one but to two men.

CHAPTER THIRTY SEVEN

Telling the Truth

It was no fleeting happiness. It survived and grew with the child, with Aigret their son. The incentive of each day was to see what new joy the baby would bring them. At first Ouallada's only fear was for the boy's survival: she moved his crib closer to her bed so as to be sure of hearing him breathe if she woke in the night. When he was walking, unsteady and rash, she saw the Sablois River as a great serpent writhing through her Eden, awaiting an opportunity to swallow Aigret down. The fact that no other children followed concentrated both the love and the fear, like sunlight through a burning glass.

Perhaps it was to pre-empt God from confiscating such happiness that Foulque first resolved to make Aigret perfect in piety. Or perhaps it is just the ambition of every father for every son: to see the boy succeed where he has failed. In any event, Foulque inculcated Aigret with the knowledge and observance of the Catholic faith from the first moment language had meaning for him - imposed on him a regime of praise, reined him in with notions of grace. Not for one minute was it a joyless exercise, for Foulque suddenly understood about praise. Exhortations to praise leapt out of the Scriptures at him as though written in red, while the punitive wrath of God blurred with his lengthening eyesight.

Foulque's impact on those who knew him in his later years was of a bright white man visiting the outreaches of his green universe with the regularity and momentous energy of a comet. His clothes were always stuffed with pieces of smoked fish his wife had prepared for him, with ducks' eggs he found in the grass for the baby, with grafting bandages and pouches of promising seed and lists of resolutions, as well as scribblings by his boy which he showed to everyone, including the priest during Confession. He was a conjuror, with delight inadequately concealed about his person.

Aigret was not primed to explode with the same force. He was a quiet, pretty, dark boy, broad built like his father but inclined to burn up his nourishment in nervous excitement: he carried less flesh on the bone. As a small child he washed a great deal, and when asked why, said that he did not want God to mistake him for a dirty boy. That made Ouallada cry, but not as much as she wept at Foulque's reaction: he was delighted.

'You're *glad* he judges a person's wickedness by the colour of their skin?' she stormed at him, taking him by surprise.

'Of course not. Of course not,' he said, catching her round the shoulders and kissing her. 'That's just childishness talking. I mean I'm glad he wants to please God - sees himself in the eye of God. Wants to do right by Him.'

She was comforted. But a shapeless, ill-defined fear entered into Ouallada which she put down to her own innate wickedness: she did not want Aigret to be a saint, to be good without flaw, to be perfection itself.

Foulque himself was not immune to hurt at the hands of the boy. For Aigret said one day, in a declaration of fervent infant passion for the father he adored, 'If you'd been there at the Horns of Hattin, Saladin would never have won. *You* should have gone! The Prince of Châtillon would've won for sure!'

Ouallada was angry. 'If your father had gone, then there'd've been another good man dead or sold into slavery! A hundred and fifty thousand ... ' she began, but Foulque put his finger to his lips. The loss of Jerusalem reflected on every knight in the realm. But when Aigret persisted - 'Aren't you sorry? Don't you wish you'd been there? Alongside Châtillon? - he found he could not say 'yes'. He could not stomach the thought of the man: Châtillon the rapist and killer of old men, who had surpassed himself in inciting the Saracens to war.

Foulque tried to explain to his little son, knowing as he did it that the boy was too young to understand. 'Châtillon swore to dig up Mahomet's body and scatter his bones. That's a very terrible thing for a Moslem to hear. In a way it meant they had to fight him, whereas otherwise ...'

'That's what I'd like to do! That's what I'll do when I'm

a knight! Dig up their stinking old saint and scatter him all around! Wouldn't that be fine, Papa?' And because he was too young to understand, Foulque simply nodded and let the matter rest. To a little boy's way of thinking, a pagan skeleton must seem a brave object of hatred. The issues were too complicated. He knew that he could not erase the myth from his son's mind, of his father changing the course of history had he only been at the Horns of Hattin. Perhaps a part of him did not want to.

His parents might have seen, from looking at Aigret, that he was already halfway to being an angel. Aigret's face, as it aged into manhood, was a winged face - eyebrows like raven pinions, large, slightly protruding ears, and wing-shaped cheeks upswept as if ready to catch some turbulent updraught of speech. His heavy black hair hung in two wings to either side of his brow, and a moustache came to his top lip as softly as bird-down, in the shape of a flying rook. He used his eyes, too, like a raptor - alert, piercing eyes, quick to see the scurry of a spider, the scuttle of a mouse, quick to judge right from wrong. All Ouallada's fears for his physical safety changed subtly, year by year, into the unspoken misgiving that Aigret would find himself too good for the world of Men.

They gave him everything they could afford or make without expenditure. They deprived him only of poetry and song, because Foulque said he must never be allowed to know the past which had brought them where they were. The life of the *salvetat* was sufficient in itself, hermetic in its isolation from the past, so low-built that it had no need of foundations in nobility or the blood-red earth. Still, Ouallada at least was sorry not to sing and play to her child, sorry that he would not hear his father's voice singing.

For all his pious ambitions, there was no risk of Foulque committing his son to the monastic life - giving him to God, as it were. His memories of the life were so unhappy that he would no more have wished it on his dear Aigret than imprisonment or exile. On the contrary, he wanted to show him, with that conjuror's flourish of his, all the great joys in store. He raced Aigret towards them, swooping him down to the market fairs on his shoulders, setting him to stoop on the pretty girls at the harvest dances. Aigret danced like a patten-dancer, with his hands by his side and his head still; danced and then expressed the opinion it was good exercise for the liver and kidneys; he sought nothing more of the pretty girls than to dance. Father and son made mutual discoveries about the taste of local grapes, but it was sober Aigret who steered Foulque home singing slurred snatches of his old *sirventes* while Aigret asked more and more searching questions about where and when his father had learned such songs.

Then one day, in the first week of the new century, Ouallada found Aigret writing a poem of his own. She was overjoyed. It washed over her, that springtide flood in which love for child and love for husband overlap in the resemblance of son to father. She wound her arms around his head - a laurel of praise - and read the poem over his shoulder.

Oh foolish wickedness! Oh damnable crime!
That men entrusted with a span of Time

Plucked from God's own garner store

Should spend that gift upon a whore

And count their time upon God's earth

A span of torment nothing worth,

Wounding the wounds of Christ with nails of scorn,

Goring his side with th'idolator's golden Horn.

Credent heretics lift up your eyes!

And cast them on the hills where dwells the Lord!

For the very Church you dare despise

Will send a second Flood, a Flood once heard

Will come too fast for those who hear to flee;

Will come in mighty wrath to wash you clean:

Oceans of words loosed by a Holy See,

Leaving but tears where heresy has been.

'What is this?' she asked, abruptly letting go of him.

'Haven't you heard, Mama? The Pope is finally going to crush those heretics in the Midi! He's going to damn them all to Hell.'

'Only God can do that,' she snapped. 'You shouldn't write about things you don't understand.' And she snatched the paper and screwed it up, her cheeks hot with fright, just as Foulque entered the room.

'What's the matter?'

'Mama, it's true! The Pope says heretics are traitors, and he's sending preachers to teach them the error of their ways. Tell her, Father! She doesn't believe me.'

'The Pope wants to confiscate himself some pieces of land, that's what the Pope ... '

'Mother!' Foulque's interdiction was so fierce, so adamant, that Ouallada's lips still moved after her voice fell silent. 'The boy's quite right. It's a canker that's spread far enough. Nigh the whole Languedoc is given over to the heresy. It's time to confute it. Not that the Cathars will listen. '

'But Foulque, I found him writing this. I don't know where he picked up these wild notions.'

Foulque shook out the crumpled ball of paper and held it at arm's length, casting a quick, sidelong glance over it. She saw some of the colour go out of his face, as when a smell summons up sudden unpleasant memories of childhood.

'I agree with Aigret. The Cathars are traitors. The new Pope's right to take a stand.'

'Yes, but Foulque, there's so much said in ignorance north of the Line ...'

He silenced her with a look of such tyranny that she felt he had stopped up her mouth and that all the words were glutting in her breast.

'And those troubadours,' said the boy disgustedly.

'What of them? There are Christian troubadours, too, you know?'

'Yes, but these Cathars ... Father Valery says they're all libertines and loose women.' He had no notion of what the words meant, but delivered them with the puritanical fervour of a little Saint Norbert.

Foulque at least had the good grace to laugh. He left the room laughing, and Aigret turned on his mother a burning curiosity to know why.

Ouallada, however, had not recovered her good temper. 'Your father used to move among poets a good deal,' she said picking up the ugly verse off the floor and slapping it down in front of the boy. 'He wrote some, too. So, pray remember: in the words of that heretic troubadour Miraval, when he turned his wife out-of-doors: *there's room for only one poet in a house!*'

She took issue with Foulque afterwards, that he should condone the boy's intolerance. She said the Languedoc was too complicated a sorrow for glib solutions. 'The Pope calls Cathar land "contaminated", then confiscates it, you know he does!' she said reproachfully.

'The boy's world is simple,' he replied soothingly. 'At this age he can only deal in Good and Evil. You're wrong - we'd be wrong to confuse him with petty side issues.'

'I don't want him to grow up thinking he hates an entire community of souls that stretches from yonder to the sea!'

'Not hates, pities,' he said, making the differentiation that was in his own heart and which he therefore assumed must be in his son's. 'Surely you'd like to see one Church again under Christ?'

'But what lengths will this new Pope go to to see it?' she wondered.

'Ministry and reasoned argument,' he said, putting an arm around her, soothing her like a child. 'What else? Aigret's eleven years old, Ouie. Eleven-year-olds see the world in black and white, wheat and chaff, saints and devils ... And the play on "see" was rather good, don't you think? In his verse?'

Ministry and reasoned argument continued in the Midi and increased in zeal. In an attempt to match the exemplary *perfecti* Cistercian monks wandered the blood-red countryside barefoot, living out their monastic vows as well as the Disciples. There was a largescale rustling from the Cathar flock. The King of Aragon even travelled to Carcassonne to preside over an amicable debate, Catholic vesus Cathar.

But Pope Innocent, unlike Foulque de Gloriole, had never set great store by the persuasion of reasonable argument. He had known all along that it would take more than barefoot monks to trample out Catharism.

'Foulque, tell him! Stop him! He mustn't!'

'I'll be all right, Mother. D'you expect to swaddle me for ever?' said Aigret irritably.

That was unfair. She had packed his saddlebags for him and sent him off to fight in the wars with the English. And even though she had seemed at the time to be packing her own heart and lights and brains in among the apples and leggings, she had said nothing, done nothing to stop them going to war. This was different.

'Foulque, speak to him. Don't let him go. It's wicked. It's a wicked Crusade.'

Since news of the Pope's new Crusade, Foulque had aged ten years. A permanent frown of bewilderment sat between his eyes, and his cheeks seemed to lack the strength to keep his mouth from sagging. The whole weight of his crumpled jawline hung heavy, drawing down the creases round his eyes. His hair was wild and unkempt. He had never believed it would happen.

Formerly, logic and cynicism would have told him it was bound to come, this righteous opportunity for northerners to seize the land of their southern cousins.

And yet he had not seen it coming - had never really believed it would come, this horror.

Recently Aigret had begun to read out Bertran de Born at mealtimes - declaiming it across the herb potage: ' "There is no such pleasure as when we see both mighty and humble falling in the grass by the moats, and the dead men with stalks of silk-pennoned lances thrust in their ribs!" '

'That isn't what it comes down to, son,' Foulque had said across his spoon, but nothing more. He could see the reproach in his wife's eyes that he had said nothing more. Now it was too late to say it.

'Foulquet of Marseilles - this zealot stirring things up - he was a southern troubadour, son,' he said. Just when Ouallada had given up all hope of him ever speaking again.

'I know that. I know that. So?' Aigret had worked himself into a frenzy of zeal. He was going to join the Crusade and nothing was going to stop him. He was just surprised his father was not more enthusiastic.

'Foulquet of Marseilles was turned down by the woman he loved, so he slunk off to a monastery to lick his wounds. Now he comes leaping forth to recruit for a religious war. Do you think that's honest? To use the Pope's wrath for an excuse to kill his old rivals in love?'

Aigret was taken aback. It seemed such a very *particular* quarrel to pick with a vast, noble enterprise. 'He's one man. There'll be hundreds of thousands.'

'All using the Crusade to their own ends!' wailed Ouallada.

'I wouldn't be.'

He said it with such ethereal integrity of soul, his eyes

closed, his long lashes curling out from his lids like the herls from an angel's wing, that Ouallada was rendered speechless.

Foulque wasn't. He gave the boy a clout and said, 'Don't be such a bloody prig, Aigret. And show your Mother some respect, will you? This isn't about pennoned lances and prancing steeds. This is about genocide, boy. It's about killing women if they won't recant. It's about killing their children so the canker can't spread. It's about riding your horse over the bodies of old men - old Frankish men - who look up at you and beg you for mercy in French.'

Ouallada went and took her son's face between her two hands. 'Aigret, Christ turned down water and vinegar on the Cross. Do you think He's changed so much that now He wants to drink the blood of the misguided?'

Aigret pursed his lips with the obstinacy of a prim virgin offered temptations by a wealthy lover. His cheeks flushed bright red. 'It's my duty. I know what I know.'

Confronted with such unmitigated bigotry, Foulque lost all his carefully cultivated reserve. 'I'll have you know I'm born of that stock, Aigret,' he said. 'Both your mother and I come from those parts. We know those people. We were . . . Listen to me, you *wet-eared pedant*! Your mother and I were both troubadours.'

Ouallada stepped round her son and laced her hands through Foulque's arm. She had been willing him to say it - would have said it herself had he delayed another minute, though it would have damaged their marriage irreparably. She was more grateful to Foulque than if he had dived into the Sablois and brought her son ashore safe from drowning. Now Aigret would have to reappraise his beliefs.

Aigret looked at them both. They thought that the admission - as shocking, surely, as a child's discovery that his father and mother cleave together in bed - would elicit a flood of questions. But Aigret assimilated the news like a man ridding himself of an overly large mouthful of bread, swallowing it down, his face contorting with discomfort. Then he said, 'Yes. But you were never *Cathars*. If you were, I'd hate you as much as I hate the rest. The Pope says we must wipe them off the face of the Earth, and I mean to do it. All Christianity's at stake - it's not me that says it: the Pope says so. And I for one mean to fight the Devil in his lair.' Weaving his head awkwardly on a neck rigid with haughty pride, Aigret negotiated the distance between his parents and the door, tangled his pannier buckle in the doorlatch, freed it again, and went out into the yard, leaving the door swinging. The rod of light entering through the hinge swung to and fro across the room like a blind man's cane.

'In that case I shall go with you!' called Foulque. 'Give me a half-hour to say goodbye to my wife.'

The city of Beziers was the very first target of the Crusade against the Cathars. (Albigensians, they were called after a while, rather than use the word *cathar* - 'purity' - to describe them.) On the ride south, as brothers, brotherhoods, villages, city levies, and free companies swelled the congestion on the roads, Aigret learned many interesting new facts about the Cathars from his fellow crusaders: how they sinned without compunction and gained 'absolution' from the next perfect they met; how they knelt and worshipped their perfects like graven images; how the priests fathered whole tribes of bastards on the virgins in their parishes - and just by blowing in their mouths, too! He found out that Cathar widowers fornicated with sheep and pigs, saying they were the reincarnation of their wives; how they never married, the better to sleep with every perfect, virgin and pig they met by starlight.

And Foulque could contradict none of it, for fear he demonstrate an inside knowledge or a sympathy for the Albigensians. They were the demons of the hour. All the resources of might and music, money and song had been levied in the cause of their destruction. On both sides troubadours were enlisted in a mutual lobbing of insults as crude and lethal as those terracotta grenades full of Greek fire.

Foulque was reduced to fuming like an old volcano, its bore blocked, its heat kept all underground, seething. There was no longer any mention of love in the songs, for the Great Lovers had turned their hands to the work of Christ (or Ahrimasdes, the Cathar Principle of Good). Their fellow countrymen became the dragons to be slain in pursuance of honour. The only lust these troubadours burned with was the lust to drive home a lance through their cousin's heart. *Sirventes* were the only fashion.

For Foulque it was like travelling backwards into the past. He recognised landmarks passed with Ouallada. He told himself that he recognised the very patches of ground where he had lain wrapped in his gabardine, contemplating the miracle of Ouallada's love for him, while she, an arm's length away, patiently craved his touch. So much time wasted. So many too many *sirventes*.

And too few lovesongs. None, in fact. None. He found he could no longer remember why they had banished music from their lives. Now he turned suddenly to his son, in the middle of a particularly rampant performance from a shaven-headed zealot, and said, 'I never wrote your mother a lovesong.' It seemed an appalling oversight, exaggerating the possibility of imminent death, of too little time remaining.

Aigret, reminded of his father's provenance, and finding it less reprehensible than usual, jumped to his feet. 'My father can give you verses! Foulque de Gloriole will give you a song, won't you, Pa? He was a troubadour-knight when he was young.'

'Foulque Nerra,' said Gloriole absently. 'I was Foulque Nerra-des-Etangs then.' There was a stir of acknowledgement. Some had dimly heard the name in connection with verses. Others remembered it only as the name of a Count of Anjou, founder of the Angevin Plantagenet line. 'But I'm Gloriole now. And Gloriole doesn't sing.' He tugged, the skirt of Aigret's short jacket, angry, put out. 'Not tonight, anyway.'

Aigret forgot all about the singing and the rhetoric and sat down abruptly. His father was full of untoward surprises these days, full of interesting news. 'Nerra? We're called Nerra? Why did you never tell me that? Does that mean we're related to .. .'

'Very distantly. Very. Cousins of cousins of cousins. A million miles removed. D'you think we'd be apple-pickers on the Loire if we owned tracts of Anjou and a conté or two? It's not a name I was sorry to lose. Gloriole's better. At least that was come by in battle.' He smiled in recollection. One day he might even describe that piece of Aigret's heritage to him - if the lines of communication remained open between him and his son.

'But Nerra! Related to the Plantagenet's!'

'What, does that raise us up somehow? A name? A word?' said Foulque hotly. 'What does a name matter? I'd as soon shed it. It was always a burden to me.' He was not prepared - had never been prepared to tell Aigret the legend of Fulk Nerra and his demon-wife Melusine - to burden him with the same nightmares. Sooner or later Aigret would hear it. But then nothing could - perhaps nothing should - be kept secret for ever. 'We're merchant stock, Aigret. Remember that if you ever think to give yourself airs over and above the diggers and delvers in the *salvetat*. Specifically, we're made out of salt - Camarguais salt like Lot's wife, for her silliness!'

Next night some of the crusaders recalled Aigret's claim that his father was a one-time troubadour, and pressed him for a song, a *sirventes*. 'Go on, Father! Did you never write *sirventes*?'

'Plenty. Plenty,' said Foulque recalcitrantly.

'Then give us one now! A *sirventes* in praise of the Albigensian Crusade!' He added in a pleading whisper, 'If you can't do it extempore, give them one from another war.' He was anxious not to be humiliated in front of the other men, afraid his father would let him down.

'Why? Do you think all wars are the same?' Foulque yelled into his face in a single paroxysm of rage. Then he got to his feet, so as not to disappoint. 'I'll give you a song. Not a *sirventes*. A lovesong. In praise of my mistress - that's to say my wife, since these are Christian days we live in.'

He did it, too.

She came to me upon a raft of stars,
Her waist a wand, her buttocks dunes of sand.
I fed from her breasts amid the bars
Of black hair, and to unlock I laid my hand
Upon a place already ope'd for me.
She swore there was no pain I could inflict,
Open the road, no toll, no tithe, no fee.
The wounds I bore away from where I licked
The tigress' milk are painless, singing scars:
She bore me off upon a raft of stars.

It was extempore, or at least came together from a day's unshaped thoughts, but he delivered it with the ferocity of a *sirventes* and the shameless gusto of an Arab sheik. Aigret was covered with embarrassment, did not know whether to protest or to slink away to a distance and dissociate himself from such a very ... very ... Aigret lacked the adjective.

The other crusaders felt no such squeamishness. They roared and stamped their approval, and took themselves earlier to their bed-rolls, to sleep with one hand between their legs and dream about women rather than heretics.

Next week they were singing psalms and litanies instead. Five thousand knights and twenty-five thousand foot soldiers advanced over fields full of produce, trampling the wheat, breaking the necks of sunflowers, treading windfall apples into the rich, soft ground. Bean-canes and twine snagged in their ugly accoutrements and dragged behind them, as Saladin trailed the True Cross through the dust after his victory. The gigantic wooden crucifix which went ahead of Pope Innocent's blessed army was a replica, of course, an imitation, but much bigger than the original. Better, really, in terms of symbolism. Absolution poured down from it over the heads of all those men - forty days' remission, a waiving of penance, the approbation and encouragement of God Himself to rob and rape and murder. The air was charged with strange emotions.

Like the unfamiliar Pyrenees standing sentinel over Beziers city, Aigret's mood soared and plunged. He was excitable to the point of flinching when his father touched him.

'What's the matter? Nervous?' said Foulque.

'No!'

Foulque himself felt no eve-of-battle forebodings. He had no doubt about what would happen next day. He had brought the horror of it with him, every inch of the way. To him the advancing Crusade was like a glacier, gouging up every foot of the journey, pushing ahead of it a murrain of rock-hard litter, doubling its size, doubling the aggregated misery. The glacier had only a little further to go to obliterate the living things in its path - here at Beziers and beyond, as far as foresight could see. Not a thing would be left standing, not a soul left alive. And yet Foulque's anathema for the Crusade in general - this genocide of Frank by Frank - barely troubled him in comparison with the figure of his son, standing in the path of the glacier, about to be swept to the icy extinction of all his peace, guiltlessness, innocence; about to be overrun by crimes for which he would never forgive himself, about to be gelded of humanity thanks to the zeal of his innocence. If he could, Foulque would have raced ahead of the army, through the berry hedges, across the meadows, and killed every man, woman and child with his own sword sooner than allow Aigret to enter Beziers city.

The boy bent over his equipage (such as it was) polishing the belt, pinning the surcoat flat with stones to take out its creases, spitting on his boots to shine them, except that he had no spit.

'Why clean them? They'll be dirty again soon enough,' said Foulque. 'Blood. Pieces of flesh. I was just over by Father Arnold's big tent.' He pointed in the direction of the Pope's pennon flying over his legate's siege pavilion. 'Someone came to ask him about the Christians in the city.' He waited until Aigret's brain allowed home the idea of Christians within Beziers city. Half and half, perhaps? One-third? Two-thirds?

'What about them? They'll come out, sure. Evacuate.'

'Or maybe they could put lamb's blood on their lintels, like the Children of Israel the night the Angel of Death passed over?'

Aigret looked defensively at his father. He did not trust that tone of bitter, agitated sarcasm, the excitable flicker of the mouth.

'Come with me,' said Foulque suddenly, grabbing him by the armhole of his sleeveless jerkin. 'Come with me. I know a place near here. Up yonder. On the treeline, see? Back there a way.' He was almost dragging Aigret along, his fist shaking, his arm rigid, the seam of the waistcoat clicking as threads broke under the strain.

'What are you doing, Father? Do you really think you going to take me off to some safe little bolthole to lie up while the fighting's done? Out of harm's way? To take home to Mother safe-and-sound?'

'What fighting? There'll be no fighting worth a mention. This isn't Harfleur, you jackass. No, no. I'm not taking you out of harm's way, boy. Not me. I'm taking you to a veritable den of Catharism. Tonight. Thought you might like to take first blood. Cut a historic figure in the annals of the war. The first hero for Christ!'

His father's strength was massive - those mace-bearer's arms - Aigret had never had cause to feel what strength there was in them. But this was not a father he recognised in any case: the man was half-mad with frenzy, and all that Aigret could attribute it to was the lust for battle, the lust Aigret had been trying to stir in himself, with no very great success, all day. Strange that he had never seen it before, in the wars with King John, this mania of his father's. He submitted, as much intrigued as bullied, and mounted up alongside Foulque.

They rode through the purple evening, when the sky and the rock path and the shadows and the grass and the cave-mouths and the soil verges were all a variant of the same imperial purple. Leaving the army below them, they were soon in a position to look down on it - the torches, the tapers, the fires, all casting a saintly brightness into the faces of the crusaders. Aigret was unwilling to step out of such a thrilling glow and climb into the stumbling darkness. He asked repeatedly where they were going - even after Foulque had told him already: Haut-Beziers. He kept on asking, as if there must be more to the answer.

'It's the fortified home of Aude d'Haut-Beziers, a Cathar and a sinner,' Foulque called over his shoulder at last. He drove his horse on up the path at such speed that Aigret wondered at his father's indifference to the precipitous drop alongside. He began to tire, too, when his father showed no sign of fatigue.

At around two in the morning, the so-called 'castle' of Haut-Beziers came into sight, haloed in moonlight, the constellation of Orion balanced on one turret.

'Are we to storm it single-handed?' panted Aigret with an air of desperate bewilderment.

'No need. My name's known here.' And sure enough he paused only to stuff his surcoat up inside his cloak and over one shoulder, to obliterate the Cross, before going directly up to the gate. '*Wake the Lady Aude and tell her Foulque Etangs-Nerra is returned,*' he shouted.

She sent word that she was coming, but kept them waiting a great while.

They waited for her in a chamber to the left of the entrance-hall: Foulque knew his way to it. A large book lay chained to a lectern, beside the purple windows. He knew that, too. There was no fire lit, the moon was too high to lend much light to the contents of the room. And yet Foulque went directly to the book and leafed through its valuable pages with a careless, gloved hand. Several of the sheets tore a little. Then he drew out his sword.

'Well? Draw, man. We're on Cathar ground here. In the Devil's lair.' It buckled his heart to breaking point to see how clumsily his son drew his weapon, the circumstances so different from those he had envisaged. 'What shall we talk about while we wait? Ah yes, I can finish telling you how Father Arnold means us to overcome the problem of the Christians in Beziers. Shall

I? Shall I tell you? 'Kill them all,' he said. 'The Lord knoweth them that are His.' His face was so white, so haggard that the moon seemed to be there, in the room with Aigret, its dark places and contusions, its hidden side and its icy cold. As for Foulque, he saw his son as if from the moon's hill - too far away to touch, too dear to look away. 'Is that what you came here for, Aigret? To kill Christians?'

'I –'

'No. That's why I've brought you here. No such anomalies here. No complications here. A staunch Cathar, the Lady Aude and all her household.'

'Aren't we ... a shade reckless, then? To come here?'

'Oh no. No very great danger, I think. I looked in the stables as we came in. There's only a handful of animals there. It seems most of "La Belle Aude's" following have run away. - Is that right?' He spoke across his son's shoulder, to the woman beyond, and Aigret turned suddenly, levelling his sword. Aude did not even seem to see it.

'I knew you'd come back to me,' she said.

A woman roused from her bed in the middle of the night is hard put, except when very young, to look her best. Aude had made every effort, however, to excite her hair once more into a cloud of gold, to smooth her face, cheer her mouth, and present large bright eyes to her lover. Her hair, rendered brittle and broken by colouring, stuck out behind her head like a deep-sea loofah. Her face shone with fard, like a plate of melted butter, and her eyes the black splashes of something dropped into the bowl. Her little jaw had not supported well the weight of Time, bearing down, bearing down, and a few dark hairs on her chin repelled the fard in tiny pendant droplets exaggerated by the candle she held close to her breast. She inclined her head forward, looking up through her top lashes in studied affectation. Altogether she conducted herself for all the world as if she were a girl of twenty. 'Who's this you've brought me?' she asked, crooningly, as she might have addressed a pet cat.

'This, Aigret, is the Lady Aude d'Haut-Beziers, target of our search.'

'You know her, do you, Father?'

'Oh yes, but don't let that cloud the issue.'

Aude gave a shrill pigeon coo. '"Father!" Now what surprise is this you've kept from me? This fine boy yours? There haven't been years enough ...'

'Why have you brought me here, Father? To see a mad woman?'

'Mad?' Foulque regarded Aude with his head on one side. 'Well, yes, I daresay there's fear enough built up here, knowing the Crusade's coming closer every day - waiting for it. Enough to drive a lonely woman to distraction. The end coming closer and closer. But what's that to do with anything? She's a Cathar. You have my word on it. Aren't you, lady?'

'A Cathar? Oh yes. I eat nothing that's come of sexual breeding. Not any more. Not for years and ...'

'Do you mean to make her recant?' Aigret's sword clattered inadvertently against a wash-bowl with enough noise to startle and confuse Aude.

'Come, come. That's not what you're here for, son. I told you what Father Arnold said. D'you think they're going to be asking for recantations down there? In Beziers?' He stepped behind Aude and closed the door of the troubadour chamber and bolted it fast. 'You see, Aude, my son here is come to kill Cathars.'

'Father?'

Foulque crossed to the window. It would be morning soon. The moon was setting. There was a distant noise - the river perhaps. Or the army moving against Beziers. 'Do you want to see this, Aigret?' he said, indicating the house book of verse. 'It's a song of mine. I remember it was received particularly well. The Cathar here asked me to set it down for posterity. Shall I read it out?'

Aigret went and peered at the book; he was breathing very fast. There was far too little light to make the words plain. 'I see you have ... sentimental attachments to the house, Father. From your singing days.'

'Oh yes,' said Foulque. 'I slept with this lady many a time.' He heard his son snatch in a breath. 'Before I was married, you understand. But you mustn't let that disconcert you. The attachment is quite broken I assure you. Besides, we mustn't particularise; I remember you telling me. They're all foul lepers, isn't that what the Pope said? So? Kill her.'

Aude's shapeless little jaw dropped, and she began to scream - not with any volume, but in the kind of doleful, birdlike cry of a hoopoe.

'Kill her?'

'Kill her.'

She ran towards Foulque for protection, still trusting to the sentimental dream she had nurtured for too long to be parted from. But he caught hold of her, spun her round and held her by her upper arms, letting go only to rip open her nightdress down its seam as far as the naval.

'In fact she's a considerable whore, this one. Not a

Good Cathar, as they say. Not much of a Cathar at all, the *perfecti* would say. But then again, much more than any of those Christians down there in Beziers. And we mustn't particularise; I remember you telling me. You'd best be quick, Aigret. I brought you here to give you first blood of the war. Best hurry if you don't want to be overtaken by men down there more zealous to do the work of the Lord.'

Aigret began to perceive something like ridicule, to resent his father's assumption that his belief in the Crusade was unthought-through, went only skin deep. He adjusted his grip on the hilt of the sword. Of course he found those drooping breasts, that sunken ball of a stomach within the fork of the rib cage repellent - piteous even. 'It would be the Devil within I was splitting!' he retaliated.

A torrent of urine splashed his father's boots and the woman hung suspended between his mace-bearer's hands, legless with terror.

'Do it, then. That's what they're doing down there. In the city. Old women, pregnant women, babies. For the sake of the Devil within, of course. Oh, you could rape her first, of course, if you like. To be sure of staining any purity in her. There'll be plenty of that down there, too ... But then it's so *rousing,* isn't it, doing the Lord's work. Go on! Pour a little brimstone on Gomorrah.' And he thrust his knee deep into Aude's back, arching her hips towards Aigret.

The younger man moved his boots as if he were treading water, swept his empty hand through the air as if battling against the current of his father's words. 'You know me better, Father! You won't fix that charge on me!

You know I bear a pure motive. You know I came here *because of my beliefs.*' He beat each word out of his chest with the side of his fist. 'If this woman's Cathar – yes - it is my duty to kill her. You're right. My Church charged me with it, and I'll carry it through. Step aside and I'll kill her, yes, I'll kill her. I'll do it mercifully, too - take no joy in it, if that's what you think!'

'What? Even though it purchases you a redemption of sins?' said Foulque, exaggeratedly incredulous, and let go his grip on Aude and stepped aside. She fell directly to the floor, like a puppet unstrung.

He could see his son's lips moving in prayer, his eyes staying closed longer with each blink. He was impelling himself to further movement, as a man might who stands on a mountain path, terrified of heights.

Outside the window, a lilac morning sky was filling up with birds. Flecks of black. Perhaps there were traces of smoke too - or perhaps just the low cloud that sits in valleys at dawn awaiting the sun's heat. They were city birds. And kites.

Foulque took off his cloak. The surcoat, bundled up over one shoulder came loose and he rent it at the shoulder seams to be rid of it. He went and crouched down beside Aude, wrapping the cloak around her, apologising in a soft voice, whispering. Aigret heard him say, ' ... a practical joke, call it. At your expense, this time.' Then he sat back on his heels.

'I shall bloody your cloak, Father,' said Aigret intractably. 'Move. If this is a test, you'll see...'

'Not a test. Call it an *assais*. Know the term? We troubadours know it well enough. An *assais*. A test of the real depth of a man's love.' Foulque uncinched his heavy leather belt.

'The True Religion's paramount!' said Aigret, his face an implacable mask, a little blue in the morning shadow.

'No, Aigret. The Truth's paramount. That's how I learned it. That's how it went in my youth. The Truth, son. The Truth.' He was wearing no mail, no plate. He reached inside his sheepskin and shirt and pulled out - almost as if he were disembowelling himself - a long, woollen cord. 'It's called a *kosti,* Aigret. The belt of perfection, we Cathars called it . . . But then the witch-hunters will've schooled you in that, won't they? One of those unspeakable objects of heresy. "*Kosti,*' Just a word. But one of the Devil's words, isn't that right?'

Aigret looked as if his gorge had risen beyond his power to swallow it down again. 'You? A Cathar?'

'And what will you do about it? Ah, yes. I remember you told us, back home. Hate me. As you hate all Cathars, isn't that right? Well, the Truth is, son, I'm making you choose. If you want to kill Cathars, you'll have to kill me first.'

Aftermath

The question is, whether Love or Hate is paramount. Sometimes a man can commit his life to a cause and waste all his best endeavour before finding it was not for the love of the thing he held most dear, but hatred, pure and simple. If hatred can be pure.

'Can hate be pure, Aigret? Can you kill me out of hate for the Cathars in general, and be a better man for it after? If you can, do it. All I ever wanted was your good - ever since you were born - your happiness. For you to do better than I did. Do better.'

'You're not a Cathar, Father. I'd know if you were a Cathar. Maybe once. Maybe you made a mistake once. Maybe this woman enticed you.'

'Oh, but are you sure? Only God knows a man's heart. How can you be sure of a man's religion? Arnold de Citeaux doesn't think you can. Kill them all, he'd say: "The Lord knoweth them that are His."'

'I'd know if you told me. Tell me you're a Cathar. On oath, tell me you're a heretic. Then I'll know.'

Foulque grinned. 'That's absurd, son. What do you want me to swear by? A principle you call false or a God I might not believe in? No, no. Swearing won't serve. Judgement's with you. Question is, how will you judge? The choice is between Love and Duty, you might say. Which do you prize: Mother Church and Fatherland? Or flesh and blood.'

Aigret's face was wet with sweat. He had run his hand so often through his hair that it stood out to either side of his head, that crisp, thick hair, like the hood of a crow. 'A knight would say that both...'

Don't tell me what a knight would say! You aren't a knight and I am. Don't presume to tell me what a knight would say!' He alternated between savagery and gentleness so unpredictably that his son swayed physically under the dual assault. His sword tip wavered. He rested it down on the floor, but Foulque only picked it up with his bare hands and placed it against his throat.

'Judge, then. And after you've judged me, judge the rest. All those others. Good Cathars. Bad Cathars. Doubting Cathars. Doubting Christians. Judge one and you'll spend the rest of your life in the judgement seat, meting out sentence of death to heathens and heretics; judging your neighbours against the perfection of Christ; judging your children ... But for sweet Jesu' sake, Aigret, don't ever look back over your shoulder at the carnage in your wake. Don't try to read the auspices like a Roman, in the lights of the child you just gutted, or the woman, or the old man. You won't like what you read. You won't find proof carved on their hearts, either. No "Good" inscription or "Bad". No "Cathar" or "Christian". Just a factor's stamp; Made in the image of God. By God. For

God's own purpose.' There was blood trickling down from his neck, matting the grey-flecked hairs of his chest as he pressed forward against the wavering uncertainty of the blade.

Suddenly Aigret withdrew a step before lunging forward again with a thrust of the sword which made Aude scream. He impaled the woollen *kosti* where it lay beside Foulque's hand, and held it up, like the viscera of a chicken, and dangled it over the candleflame. It burned with a fizzing, sheepy smell and a black serpent of smoke.

'Now you're a Christian,' said Aigret, and his mouth crumpled into tears, and he dropped the sword with a noise that seemed to go on and on and on echoing through the empty castle.

In their embrace they clung to one another: the son in search of comfort, the father given his child all over again. 'And now you're a collaborator. A shielder of the enemies of the Crusade.' He held Aigret off at arm's length. 'But a human being, all the same. A good, humane, man.'

Virgin intact. Innocence preserved. Foulque would have done almost anything to keep his son from participating in the wholesale butchery of Beziers: a wickedness which all the intuitions of his Nerra blood taught him would cling to a man for life, stain deeper than dirt, cling tighter than the soft red mud of the Languedoc.

Deprived of his shield of righteousness, Aigret watched later, with open, appalled eyes, the smoke rise off the rubble of Bezier church. All the old, infirm, women and children had packed together into the building's sanctuary, locking the doors behind them. And there they had been burned to death, on the instructions of the pious Arnold de Citeaux. But Aigret had been absent from the massacre. He had no need to legitimise the crime to himself (as his fellow crusaders did) in order to live with the memory of it. He knew it for the obscenity it was. He had no need to trust to the cleansing magic of the giant wooden crosses surmounting the siege towers 'at Carcassonne, for he had turned home before the city fell. He learned later how four hundred souls had been burned to death in a pious *auto da fé* - a show of spiritual wealth like Barral Etangs-Nerra extravagantly burning horses to death in a pit.

It was all Foulque had asked - that God should preserve his son from poisoning his life with sin through a surfeit of innocence. And God had granted his prayer. On his knees he prayed for the souls of the Cathars, but not in despair, knowing that Arnold de Citeaux was right in a way. God does know His own: Cathar and Christian and Saracen. God's grace was sufficient to enfold far more than just the holiday crusaders who rampaged now over the soil of the Languedoc turning it a deeper red. It was a heretical thought and not one he would have voiced aloud, but then Foulque had no intention of raising his voice any further in life - not to sing *sirventes* blasting his enemies, nor to noise his lady's fame abroad; not to debate the forbidden sciences, nor impersonate charismatic priests.

When the next year the Council of Paris forbad the reading of Aristotle, Foulque submitted meekly enough. Though it is true that when the Council of Avignon forbad bishops music at mealtimes, a certain motley assortment of instruments suddenly appeared on the walls of Foulque's dining-room, and he and Ouallada would take them down and play them after a meal had been cleared away.

Foulque had no expectations of preserving Aigret's innocence for long. (No great hope of it, either, since few fathers want a saint for a son.) The world was too wicked, the times too repellent for extraordinary goodness to swim long against the tide. But there again, in recompense, he was able to enjoy a degree more companionship with him in old age that came of their mutual acquaintance with failure and imperfection.

Ouallada said, when they came back from Beziers, that Aigret had only learned to forgive the human race, whereas Foulque had learned to forgive himself, which was the far greater miracle. She wrote in the front of the family Gospel the words of Saint Anselm:

God let me penetrate through love
    that which I taste through knowledge.

Foulque, watching her write them, realised that she had heard them first from him. What a quantity of years had passed since then. And all that time she had borne the words about, nursed them, lived by them, fought her way through his castle wall to take possession of him and teach him the meaning of the words.

It was said that a love existed in that flint house beside the river, worthy of recording among the annals of the troubadours - had the lovers been chaste or unmarried, or singers or poets - had the troubadours not died out with the Cathar wars, had songs and poetry been allowed to survive in a world given over to Order.

The *salvetat* of Gloriole-sur-Sablois was, in a way, a similar piece of innocence that could not last, a patch of Eden surrounded by forest and briar. It saw famines as well as feasts. Its housewives made grass pottage and baked bread out of acorns. But other years they ate venison, too, and salt bacon most winters. Contentment invited new arrivals, and Gloriole-sur-Sablois grew and changed.

The little flint house on the river's bend fell derelict as each successive generation built a home with more grandeur, more to say for itself. A hundred years later, when the incumbent lord demolished it to make way for a fortress, and quarried brown schist to pile three-storeys high, the sappers sinking the foundations attached no significance to the scraps of black robe they unearthed from beneath the caked floor. The Sablois had never seen a Cathar dressed in his black *sadère*; the signs and symbols of that outmoded cult had been forgotten along with the hundred thousand credents who had disappeared as completely as the children of Hamelin, led astray by magic.

'I knew you were never truly a Cathar,' said Aigret watching his father bury the *sadère* in the soft earth of his living-room by the light of a winter fire. The river moved by outside, like Time's continuum, only small races and eddies turning back on themselves now and again, and the fish biting back their bubbles.

'It's not the first time a lie was used in the interests of the Truth,' said Foulque, and his wife, helping to press the earth home, covered his hand and pressed that too, so that the prints of their fingers were left overlapping in the soil.

'Why not burn it?' Aigret asked. 'Why bury it here, right underneath us?'

'I've never liked fire for cleansing,' said Foulque.

'Since Beziers, you mean.'

'Oh, longer, longer. Since I heard how an ancestor of mine was burned to death by her husband and some fool put it about that her spirit winged it back to Hell whence she came.'

'Silly story,' said Aigret.

'Precisely. And besides,' said Foulque, 'a man should always build on his mistakes. And I mean to build greatly here.'

Glossary

ascesis self-denial, especially sexual, often in the face of self-inflicted temptation

assais a test assigned to a suitor by his mistress to prove the mettle of his love

court of petits amours a courtly diversion in which a lover was endicted for an abuse of romantic etiquette

domna ladylove (also **senhor**)

drut a loving friend

fegnador a would be suitor

fézélé a bright, dazzling song

jongleur singer, sometimes also skilled in juggling, acrobatics, fooling and acting

knight-trobar a 'knight discoverer', troubadour

kosti a knotted belt of strong mystical significance, worn by initiates of the Cathar religion

maouchah lit' embroidery': short lyric song full of rhymes,

per cuda dreamy absent-mindedness brought about by love

pied-poudre court 'Court of dusty feet': provincial, circuit-court; dealing summarily with petty offences

precador a suitor favoured above other suitors

pretz honour accruing to a chivalric man - a mixture of valour, courtesy and generosity

sadère plain black gown worn by Cathar perfects

salvetats new villages founded (often) by abbots, and not subject to market tolls or military levy; a social experiment intended to stimulate the rural economy

senhor 'lofty lord'; used to a lady by a suitor implying he is her lowly vassal and wholly at her command

tenson two troubadors 'contending' in a poetical duel or question-and- answer improvisation

winileodas song for-a-friend composed by a woman

WAR

baida an Arabian helmet

beffroi a wooden tower with drawbridge to enable the storming of battlements

byrnys a mail shirt; any landowner of over 300 acres was required to own one

casque de croisade a Norman-style helmet

coif linen 'balaclava' worn under a helmet

destriers battle horses, between hunters and shirehorses

Outremer Syria and Palestine at the time of the Crusades

parrein someone superior in rank to a competing knight acting as his second

razzia a fast, ferocious raiding excursion

saif a straight Arabian sword

tabar a double headed axe